Christmas in Coconut Creek

Edited by Makenna Albert at On The Same Page Editing

Cover Design by Sam Palencia—Ink and Laurel Design Studio

Christmas in COCONUT CREEK

KARISSA KINWORD

Playlist

Ceilings - Lizzy McAlpine
Feel Something Different - Bea Miller, Aminé
Santa Tell Me - Ariana Grande
Dog Days Are Over - Florence + The Machine
Bloom - The Paper Kites
Fever To The Form - Nick Mulvey
Don't Blame Me - Taylor Swift
Happy Xmas (War is Over) - John Lennon, Yoko Ono
Stay - RIZ LA VIE
Feels Right - Biig Piig
Elastic - Joey Purp
Rockin' Around The Christmas Tree - Brenda Lee
Watermelon Sugar - Harry Styles
White Christmas - Meghan Trainor
Movement - Hozier
Bad Intentions - Niykee Heaton
Wit It This Christmas - Ariana Grande
Cake By The Ocean - DNCE
Corona And Lime - Schwayze, Cisco Adler
Ophelia - The Lumineers
Nobody - Niia
Dirty Love - Mt. Joy
Stay - Post Malone
Slow Burn - Kacey Musgraves
A Little Bit Trouble - Brothers Osborne
Cold Little Heart - Michael Kiwanuka
Cardigan - Something For Kate

To everyone who loves a good Hallmark Christmas movie, but wishes they would just rip each other's clothes off already.

1

Ophelia

IT WAS SNOWING IN Colorado in December. Go figure.

I dragged the wheels of my hard-shelled suitcase out of the pile of slush the Uber driver had dropped it in carelessly, right before he left me in a puff of exhaust to fend for myself at the airline terminal.

I wouldn't miss this.

No, for three weeks I would be ice and shit-stained snow free—I couldn't wait to trade the insulated boots for strappy sandals. I'd even strategically layered my clothing for the change in climate: T-shirt, zip-up, baggy old Avalanche sweatshirt I'd *acquired* from an ex-boyfriend, a beanie that could be easily stuffed into the pocket of my carry-on, and my *least* thick pair of black leggings. All of it ready to be removed at the touchdown on a tarmac.

The main concourse of the airport was busy with travelers coming and going for the holiday, and although Christmas was still two weeks away, it seemed like everyone had the same idea. Either getting the fuck out of the torrential cold they'd grown sick of in their home state, or flying directly into it to spend the weekend drunk off their asses skiing black diamonds at Mount Sweet.

Mud-coated floors squeaked with the sound of wet shoes as I skirted through security, trying to fit my three weeks' worth of wires and technology in the same muted beige tray as my dirty shoes before walking awkwardly through the metal detectors. After struggling through security relatively unscathed, by ten a.m., I'd gussied up at the Gate 24B bar with a grapefruit mimosa just in time for my ten-thirty flight.

I was *always* early, or on time technically, because I thought that anyone arriving at the time expected was only one spilled cup of coffee or old lady at a crosswalk short of being late.

My life was organized, calculated, scheduled—down to the minute. Yoga on Tuesdays, coffee with mom on Thursdays, meal prep on Sunday afternoons. I left time for lesson plans after dinner and reading before bed, and I only washed my hair every third day if I didn't have any dry shampoo. Existing was a series of checking off boxes in a color-coded planner.

A vacation to Florida was exactly what I needed. To reset and reinvigorate before January so that I could start the new year with a new outlook on life. Between work and my personal life, the last several years had been like ripping wax off a labia—which I'd done two days prior, by the way—and Christmas in Colorado just wasn't the same as it used to be. Being the eldest, mostly forgotten, and more than a little chafed sibling had simmered my holiday cheer over time. I *loved* Christmas. Parts of me always would, and other parts were forever bitter with the way my childhood was torn metaphorically and literally in half.

My parents separated when I was a pre-teen. Mom got pregnant young, so it only made sense to get married young, both believing they were doing everything right for a newborn. Only for all that first-love sparkle to silently taper into a mutual agreement years later that Scott and Mae Brody weren't right for each other. That when their dark-haired, owl-eyed Ophelia was born, they hadn't even really grown up yet themselves.

They both remarried and had second families now, Mom and Josh in Banesboro with their two kids, and Dad and Amy in West Linn with my three other half-siblings. Holidays tinkered from a loving reconciliation of separated parents with their daughter, to trying to figure out who got "little Phee" for Christmas Eve/Day, and which Kings grocery store parking lot was the most convenient for the quick exchange of a child.

I loved my parents, I absolutely did. Although, maybe now I saw them more as the slightly older friends I grew up with. But at twenty-six I had a *real* job, a *real* apartment, *real* friends in Florida that invited me to stay with them for extended periods of time. There was no way in hell I was sharing a Christmas ham at the kiddie table with kids twelve years my junior. I did enough of that type of thing at my teaching job.

When I thought about it, I'd basically been a glorified babysitter for as long as I could remember.

Pulling my phone out of my sweatshirt pocket, I discreetly snapped a photo with the flute glass of champagne to my lips.

Ophelia: Ready to get my sunshine on, mimosa number one!!

Attaching the selfie to my text, I sent it to my contact *Nat babyyyy* accompanied by an embarrassing barrage of connecting emojis. I would change that eventually, but the silly wave of college nostalgia I felt every time Natalia's name came across my screen was something I couldn't bear to part with.

I met my best friend on our first day as freshman at Colorado State. Born and raised in Florida, she had never seen snow before, or mountains, or trees that sapped instead of swayed. She chose a school across the country despite her parents' adamant insistence she attend an Ivy League, and made sure to take advantage of *every* recreational activity Colorado had to offer. We moved into our tiny dorm together, spent the entire first weekend getting denied at bars with her older sisters' fake IDs that she swore always worked back home—and resorted to binge watching *Friday Night Lights* squeezed together on my twin-sized bed. Four years later we were still inseparable. Every memory I had of college started and ended in a doozy fog of Natalia Russo.

Nat babyyyy: Yes Phee! Starting early, love that for us

Ophelia: Technically I'm catching up because it's two hours from now in Florida and time is precious

Nat babyyyy: Truer words have never been spoken

Ophelia: I still have like half an hour before my flight. Are you sure you don't mind picking me up from the airport? I could grab an Uber no problem when I land

Nat babyyyy: Fuck that, I'll be there at 3:30, we're getting dinner and then going OUT. There's a huge party tonight at Jugg, wait until you see the outfits I bought us

Ophelia: I hate you and love you at the same time

Nat babyyyy: You're really gonna hate to love me later

Ophelia: Do I need to remind you that the holidays are a time for religious reflection and doing good deeds?

Nat babyyyy: Bacardi is my religion and I WILL be reflecting on it later

Ophelia: I haven't even left Pine Ridge and I'm already worried my soul will be lost somewhere on Pompano Beach

Nat babyyyy: Hopefully your panties too
Ophelia: K!! Love you!! See you in four hours!!

I bit my cheek, unable to keep a smirk from curling my lips at my ridiculous best friend and how excited I truly was for the next few weeks.

The gate was much busier since first sitting down, and I nursed another sip of my mimosa as I scrolled aimlessly through socials. All my friends from high school and college had started posting photos of their newborns and toddlers dressed in red and green. Smiling families visiting Great Value Santa Claus at the Pine Ridge Fire & Rescue, cutting down the perfect Douglas fir, hiding that fucking Elf on the Shelf and contorting his body to look like it was shitting Hershey's Kisses on the kitchen counter.

Festive.

As much as I could make fun of it by myself and with my other single coworkers, part of me couldn't help but long for that type of fulfillment too. To be the one to make my son or daughter light up with joy on December twenty-fifth when they came crashing down the stairs in candy-cane print pajamas. The excitement on their faces to find a brand-new bike or a Barbie Dreamhouse.

But for that I would need to have a *kid*, which means I would need to be *pregnant*, which means I would need to have *sex*, and to have sex there would need to be a *man* in my life. One that was not only willing to have sex with me—which wasn't the issue—but he would also have to be willing to have a *child*. That's a hell of a lot of steps and commitment for the twenty-four hours of joy a year that was pretending to be a fat guy in a red coat.

I opened the dating app on my phone anyway.

I had thought there would be slim pickings in an airport terminal, but it turned out quite a few men within a one-mile radius were looking to get their rocks off while they were in town for business meetings or heading to a ski resort.

Swipe left, swipe left. *Porn stache, not the good kind,* swipe left. *Broody looking, Carhartt beanie, hmm... Swipe right. Which one is he in this group picture?* Swipe left. *Handsome suit man,* swipe right. *Fish photo,* swipe left. *Fish photo,* swipe left. *Jesus fucking Christ, fish photo,* swipe left. Was there really nothing more to the thirty to forty-year-old men in Colorado? *This one is kinda cute in a "wears a baseball hat inside" kind of way,* swipe right. *I could forgive this one for being blond because he's holding a husky,* swipe right.

I followed a one-photo rule with dating apps. If the man in question didn't leave an impression in the first photo on his profile, then he was a dud. I was on the declining side of my twenties, agonizingly single, and ready to settle down. I wasn't interested in teaching a man how to present himself to the world, and that included on Hook(Up).

As I finished the dregs of my mimosa the gate steward came over the speaker to announce my flight to Fort Lauderdale was beginning to board first class passengers and active military personnel, of which I was neither. Instead of hurrying across the passageway to stand in line with my suitcase, I threw my usual punctual caution to the wind and ordered one more drink with my check. Then it was officially wheels up to Coconut Creek for three whole weeks.

THE WINDOW SEAT WASN'T the most ideal place to be on an already crowded coach flight, but at least I wasn't shoved into the middle. I'd celebrate life's little wins so long as the person inevitably sitting next to me didn't request to keep the shade down the entire three-and-a-half-hour trip. I could manage a few hours of headphone silence trapped inside two other people if I had a view, not so much if the view was a sticky beige wall and the ear of the person in front of me.

Luckily, the row was empty when I boarded, and I didn't have to press my entire pelvis against the head of a person in the aisle seat while loading my bag into the overhead bin. I could shed an overbearing layer of sweater off as well and, *fuck it*, take advantage of the extra space to trade my snow boots for the flip-flops in my backpack.

Sweating by the time the last shoe was shoved into storage, I plopped down aimlessly in a seat just as the *ping* of a notification sounded from the pocket of my zip-up. I expected a ridiculous photo from Nat of the outfits she mentioned we would be wearing later that night, or a "safe flight" text from my mom signed off, "Love, Mom & Josh" like she always did. What I was shocked to see was a banner across my home screen claiming, "It's A Match!"

Hmm.

I unlocked my phone and watched my own blue-eyed, brown-haired profile photo do a dance right alongside baseball-hat-inside man and a prompt to send a message. My timing was obviously impeccable; I was currently in a metal tube, about to be two thousand miles away for the next month, and this guy probably just caught a rideshare out of the airport.

Frankie, 35—*Guaranteed admittance to the Mile High Club.*

Charming. I was also now exceedingly less likely to venture into any airplane bathroom without seeing it was properly sanitized first.

I scrolled through the rest of his pictures. A candid shot taken on a beach somewhere, his hair in shaggy brown waves, eyes hidden behind a pair of Ray-Bans. The buttons of a Hawaiian half-open down his chest with a peek of the tan skin underneath. Another with him relaxed against a wooden trail fence, backpack strapped around his waist and chest, pulling his shirt taut to his body. He had a soft smirk on his face but was looking off to the right, like he was slightly embarrassed to be the subject of the camera. *Reserved.* Then a group shot with a bunch of guys, all arms wrapped around each other's shoulders, beers in hand. Thank God he didn't lead with that one. He wasn't even at the center of the photo, and the red eye made it look like someone had taken that shit on a Kodak disposable.

Actually...

I squinted a bit and realized that was exactly what it was. An old glossy photo he must have taken a picture of with his phone camera and uploaded to his profile.

"Christ." I giggled to myself, hiding a grin with the back of my hand. The decade of difference between us was showing, which I strangely found endearing.

Scrolling to the last picture, my nostrils flared and I groaned.

Frankie was standing in front of a helicopter wearing a tactical vest with a gun belt slung across his waist, cargo pants and shirt in muted shades of gray and beige. The stoic hard-jawed look on his face would have admittedly been ridiculously attractive if he wasn't—

"In the fucking military," I scoffed under my breath.

Angling my thumbs on the photo I dragged them outward to zoom in on his face—bringing the screen comically close to my eyes and squinting. A total shame, there was a lot of potential there. I could see the soft splatter of stubble, plush bottom lip. The tight sleeves of his shirt hugging all the right muscles on his arm. Even the cargo pants (which I wasn't a fan of in any circumstance besides job-related) were filled out exceedingly well. I shifted the focus until the zoom landed directly over the crotch of his pants and tilted my head.

A second later, someone cleared their throat from above me.

"Shit." I slammed my phone facedown in my lap and looked up at the person who undoubtedly just watched me analyze a dude's bulge. Only, it was much, *much* worse than that. "Oh—fuck."

"It's better in person." Frankie stood above me, smirking. There was a slanted, proud lilt to his lips that subsequently put me at ease and sent a flare of embarrassed heat to my cheeks at the same time. Of course this man wasn't catching a rideshare into Colorado Springs. Of course he was overhead carry-on tea-bagging me on the same flight.

"I—am sure that it is, that's..." I closed my eyes and squeezed them together hoping that when the television static that was the back of my eyelids subsided, I would open them and Frankie from fucking Hook(Up) would be gone.

Very wishful thinking.

"And what's the problem with the military?" He shoved his bag into the open storage and immediately dodged a snow boot cascading toward his head and into the aisle. "—the fuck?"

"Sorry." I reached down to pick up the boot off the carpet. "How long were you standing there?"

"Long enough to be both insulted and then eye-fucked—so approximately five seconds."

"I did not *eye-fuck* you," I argued weakly, holding the lone boot out to him and nodding up toward the storage container. His thick eyebrows knitted together but he took it anyway, stuffing it back in the compartment.

"What exactly would you call it then?"

"I don't know, the female gaze."

"Poetic." He looked unimpressed.

"Thank you."

"You could just say you were looking at my dick."

I rolled my eyes and pinched the bridge of my nose. Was there a way to retract inside one's own asshole?

"It's fine," he assured me. "I did it too."

"You looked at my dick?"

Frankie coughed out a laugh and looked around as a man shimmied behind him and further down the aisle. "I'm more of an ass man, to be honest."

"Poetic," I mimicked.

"It must be my male gaze acting up again."

I snorted, hiding a smile by staring at my lap.

The intercom crackled to life and a flight attendant introduced himself, asking everyone to be seated and buckled before the aircraft made its way to the runway. Another woman squeezed her way behind Frankie and gave him a less-than-impressed side-eye.

"Are you planning on standing for the duration of the flight? Are you one of those rule-breaking flyers that get up and use the bathroom when the seatbelt signs are on?"

"Oh yeah, it's just... You're sitting in my seat actually, so..."

I looked down and saw my ass was indeed incorrectly placed in the middle chair of the row, and it clicked to me that he *did*, in fact, put all of his belongings in the overhead right above the seats.

"Well, it's not likely a third person is coming to sit with us, so you don't have to sit *here*. You can take the aisle."

"Actually, as an avid rule-*following* flier, I'll have to stick with the assigned seat printed right here"—he pulled his ticket out of his back pocket and showed it to me—"on this ticket."

He was screwing with me. Bastard. I tried to call his bluff by staying put, but Frankie just raised an expectant eyebrow at me with a grin.

"Well played," I humored him as I scooted across the divide back to the window seat. He slid in next to me, stretching his back against the leather and pushing his legs out as far as he could in front of him. And goddamnit, he was huge. His left knee tipped across the invisible line between our two spaces with how wide he was spread.

"I should let you know, then, that I keep the reading light on the whole flight."

"Perfect." He nodded. "Because I play Candy Crush with the volume on. Helps keep me focused."

Well fuck—it was going to be a long three-and-a-half hours.

2

Ophelia

THE CABIN LIGHTS DIMMED as the plane cruised at altitude and attendants made their way slowly from front to back of the plane with refreshments. I wasn't sure how many passive aggressive elbow nudges over the shared armrest were too many before it was a lost cause, but either the man sitting next to me was enjoying getting under my skin a little too much, or he was in fact completely numb from the bicep down.

Just as I was about to surrender and stick my first earbud in, Frankie leaned over.

"You never answered my question."

"Pardon?"

"About the military. What's wrong with it?"

My hand stilled halfway to my ear and I shifted toward him. "No offense, but a guy in the military is kind of a walking red flag. Screams inability to commit."

"Being on Hook(Up) doesn't do that itself?"

"You know, you're making an amazing case for yourself."

Frankie lifted his faded black hat off his head and ran the fingers of his other hand through tousled hair. It curled in under his ears and flared out at the nape of his neck. "You had to have seen something you liked. You *did* swipe right," he added smugly.

"I have a one-photo rule on dating apps. If I don't like the first picture you get next-ed."

"What is this, MTV?" He snorted.

"How old were you when that aired? Forty?"

His tongue plunged into his cheek and he looked up at the ceiling. "You've got a smart little mouth."

Oh.

Something about *that* unfortunately and unexpectedly pinched me where it shouldn't have.

"Just saying." I quickly recentered the conversation. "If you led with the military photo, and that was the only one I saw..." I shrugged.

"No zoom job?"

I sighed, looking away from him out the window. "I'll never hear the end of that."

"Nope," he assured me. "And here I was, thinking women were looking for good humor and *commitment*. You just want me for my body."

"Says the man who's opening line is"—I unlocked my phone and made my way back to his dating profile to read it verbatim—"'*Guaranteed admittance to the Mile High Club*'. I mean, how much more forward could you be?"

"Okay, two things." Both palms lifted in surrender. "One: that was one hundred percent my friend's doing. He's much more crass than I am, and under any other circumstance, I would have vetoed it."

"And you didn't because...?" I hung the last syllable in the air.

"Because, two: I'm a pilot, and it's actually pretty witty when I'm in any other place besides an airport." He cringed. "Noted."

Damn it. That actually *was* funny.

"If it were up to me it would have said something more along the lines of, '*How do I tell my roommate's girlfriend that he and I are common law married and she's technically the other woman?*'"

"Is common law marriage even still a thing?"

"Not in Florida, but the *military*." He nodded. "Don't ask, don't tell."

"Jesus." I shook my head, pinching my tongue between my teeth. "So, let me get this straight—you're a thirty-five-year-old pilot with commitment issues, who's lived with his roommate so long you two could jointly file your taxes?"

"Sweetheart, if I'm your dream guy just say it." He jutted his thumb toward the back of the plane. "I think the bathroom door says vacant. We could make this thing official right now."

As if by divine intervention, the flight attendant stopped next to our seats and leaned over the cart. "Hi folks, any snacks or drinks?"

"How's it going?" Frankie smiled at her. "I'll do a Coke and"—he took a second to look at all his options—"the white cheddar popcorn. Please." Before I could tell the attendant my own choices Frankie spoke up again. "And the same for my fiancée."

"Not his fiancée," I quickly corrected, shooting him a glare with a playful shove to the shoulder.

"Just proposed," he added. "Still waiting on an answer."

Oh, game *absolutely* on.

"I recently found out that I'm the other, *other* woman," I explained to the confused and slightly horrified stewardess. "He has me, and then a boyfriend back home, and then his boyfriend has a girlfriend—I don't know if polyamory is for me."

Frankie offered a fake laugh, and put his *very* large, tan hand over my much smaller one on the armrest in a loving gesture. I couldn't even attempt to move my wrist; the weight of his palm kept me pinned underneath him.

"I love when you get territorial with me, honey." He turned his attention back to the attendant. "I always make sure she's well satisfied."

"I've never had an orgasm in my life," I announced, smiling at her and then mentally patting myself on the back when Frankie's eyes shuttered closed. "I'll have a Coke too, and the barbeque chips, thanks."

The stewardess shoved the cart forward as Frankie pulled down my tray table, cracking open my soda for me in an act of truce and pouring it into the tiny plastic cup of ice. "Thanks," I hummed around a chip.

"You've really never had an orgasm?"

This guy was unbelievable. Persistent, *overt*—if he really was the tamer of the two, I didn't even want to imagine the roommate. "Of course I *have*," I said. I wasn't about to have him thinking that I'd never been in a sexual situation in my life. "Not that a man's ever gotten the job done."

Frankie shifted in his seat, slouching lower, legs taking up more room in front of him, if that was even possible. He shoveled a handful of popcorn into his mouth and stared ahead, as if he was content to stew on that confession for the rest of the flight. Of all the comebacks he had for everything, he chose *that* to let linger in the silent space.

I cleared my throat when he tipped his head back and poured *another* handful of popcorn into his mouth, baring his neck and Adam's apple that I couldn't help but watch bob up and down.

"So, tell me about this throuple you're in. I'll need some more information about the company before I can make a decision."

"I don't share," he said matter-of-factly, gaze finding mine out of the corner of his eye. It would be much easier to pretend I didn't feel a heat at my neck over that declaration if he wasn't so easy to look at. "They're actually the *reason* I desperately need a girlfriend at this point. I don't know how much longer I can pretend we don't live in an echo chamber and the walls aren't made of looseleaf paper."

"Oof, that bad?"

Frankie ran a hand down his jaw. "Tally's got this *ghost moan*, like she's stuck in the in-between when she's getting fucked. I half think one night I'm gonna be dragged from my bed by the ankle to perform a seance."

"*Ghost* moan?" I arched my brow. "I can't even imagine what that sounds like."

"Well it's kind of like..." Frankie started cooing softly next to me.

"Oh, God, no." I giggled nervously as he continued growing louder and more animated. "Frankie—stop." He didn't, adding an extra octave instead and groaning like a spirit experiencing coitus. "*Frankie*," I whisper-shouted, slapping my hand over his lips. "You're going to get us ejected."

He finally stopped, moans giving way to raucous laughter that I attempted not to condone, but the way his eyes crinkled around the edges and his dimple stood out made me soften.

"Now you see why I don't want to be alone anymore," he joked. "This past week in Colorado Springs was my reprieve."

"What was in Colorado Springs? Don't tell me—an exorcist?"

"I wish." He took a sip of his drink. "A job, actually. An interview. I'm *retired* from the Army, by the way," he said pointedly. "But a flight school out there is looking for seasoned pilots to train their incoming classes. I know a guy who knows a guy."

"So this Hook(Up) thing—you were just trying to get lucky. No strings attached, hopping on a flight home the next day."

"Ugh, I know. And with my luck, she followed me right onto the plane."

I scrunched my nose playfully.

"I don't know." He sighed. "Doesn't everyone have that sort of forbidden fantasy? Go out on a business trip and get swept up. Fall in lust."

I turned to face him again, inflicted with surprise. "Um, hello? Are you the same dude that was moaning like the Grudge two minutes ago?"

"I'm full of surprises."

"I've noticed—and I'm a teacher in *Pine Ridge*, so going away on business isn't exactly a luxury I'm familiar with."

"So you have more of a teacher/bad student, 'smack him around with a yardstick for not doing his homework' fantasy."

"I actually have the opposite of that, because I'm pretty sure even thinking it would get me fired."

"That's true." He unsubtly ran his eyes down my neck, right to the curve of my neckline. "Well—now I have it, so thanks for that."

"It's been a long time since I've been ogled for simply existing."

"Do you hate it?"

I pressed my lips together and folded my half-eaten chip bag. "Not as much as I should." Frankie eyed the crinkling aluminum longingly. "Do you want the rest?"

"Thank God you offered. I'm so hungry."

I snorted and handed the bag over, then sat in silence while he finished the crumbs. "So why not try to find a job closer to home?" I eventually asked.

"The opportunity pretty much fell into my lap, so to get my roommate off my ass I figured, why not? Two of my buddies are a state over in Salt Lake City, so I could see them more often. A change of scenery might be good for me. Like you so rudely pointed out, the AARP has started contacting me about my retirement savings."

"And how *does* that look, out of curiosity?" I teased.

"Ah, there she is. It was never my body or a uniform you were after. The truth always comes out."

I shrugged.

"What about you?" he asked. "Running away from an ex?"

"Why do you say that?"

"You're on a plane, flying two thousand miles *away* from home just in time for Christmas. There's gotta be something chasing your tail. So, what is it?"

"Not an ex," I said. "I'm visiting a friend from college for a few weeks in Coconut Creek."

"No family?"

"Oh, I do, yeah. My parents are more like my friends at this point. They were married for a while after I was born but now they've been divorced a long time and have these perfect second families. My closest half-sibling is only fourteen, so I figured I would do something different this Christmas. Trade the pine trees for palm trees."

"It's nice to do something for yourself every now and then."

"I agree."

I stacked my empty plastic cup and soda can inside one another and shut the tray, unbuckling the flimsy seatbelt to stand. "I'm going to use the restroom now."

"Yeah?" He raised his eyebrows and unbuckled his own belt. "How long should I wait? Two—three minutes?"

"Alone." I patted his shoulder before squeezing through the tiny space between his squashed legs and the seat in front of him, ass first. "Nice try though."

"Tease," I heard him mumble from the aisle. I smiled to myself all the way down the row and into the miniscule bathroom.

The mirror wasn't much to look at, and the fluorescent lighting in the stall wasn't doing anything for me either. I still patted the undersides of my eyes to make sure my concealer wasn't creasing and fluffed my unwashed hair.

I was borderline catfishing the guy—the glamoured girl in my profile photos was not the same one staring back at me with barbeque chip dust on my chest. *Shit.* To be fair though, if I was on an *actual* date, I would have dressed the part. This was the steady relationship, comfortable not showering for three days Ophelia, and Frankie got her right out of the gate. Not that it deterred him in the slightest. I wasn't sure he even noticed.

I spent another few minutes checking for anything in my teeth and taming the halo of frizz over my forehead, and as I was about to leave, someone knocked on the door.

"Just a minute!"

Another knock.

Oh—*no way.*

He didn't actually think the two of us were gonna get each other off in the airplane bathroom? And why didn't that disgust me as much as it did an hour before?

I pulled the lock and swung the door outward. "I am *not* having sex with you!"

Expecting Frankie, a bucket of cold water was thrown in my face when the person standing outside was the flight attendant from the cart earlier.

"Are you okay, miss?" she asked skeptically.

"I'm so sorry, I'm fine. I thought—"

Before I could incriminate myself further, the freckle-faced attendant pointed at the blinking red seatbelt sign. "We're about to hit some mild turbulence. If you could just return to your seat."

"Of course." I ducked around her and beelined back to my row, not even caring about the dramatic way I flung myself over Frankie's lap and into the shadow between his shoulder and the window.

He studied me. "You okay? You look a little flushed."

"The flight attendant thinks I'm a voyeuristic, polyamorous whore."

His lips parted and a sliver of pink tongue poked out. "You were gone for like, two minutes, troublemaker."

"*You* were supposed to be the one who knocked on the door."

Dark brown eyes opened wide in surprise, and he pointed at his chest. "Me? You told me loud and clear." He mimicked my voice. "*Alone, Frankie.*"

"Wouldn't be the first time a guy didn't take no for an answer." I huffed.

He stared at me as the flush of my skin lessened from crimson to pink. "So should I..." He began unbuckling his seatbelt again, as if he was going to head to the bathroom himself.

"Sit!" I grabbed him by the bicep, feeling every hard ridge of muscle underneath the worn white button-down he had on. "Please, sit. We can't draw any more attention to ourselves. Let's just..." I tapped on the touch screen in front of me and started scrolling. "Watch a movie."

"I don't know," he tsked. "With your track record, how do I know you won't try to fondle me under the airline blanket?"

"Actually? You're not that funny anymore."

"But you *did* think I was funny?"

"No, I take it back. You were never funny."

"Too late." He pinched the skin above my elbow playfully, and the second I lifted it off the armrest, his own arm took its place.

"Perfect!" I found the same film title on Frankie's screen so we could hit play together. "*Top Gun.* Your favorite movie."

"Fuck Tom Cruise." He shook his head. "What an unattainable standard to have as a pilot. And introducing my bedroom to women as 'my personal cockpit' never got the reaction I hoped it would."

Frankie looked genuinely distraught and I tampered a laugh by sinking my teeth into my bottom lip.

"You're laughing at a man's pain."

"Oh come on, be my *wingman*," I joked, slapping my palm down right above his knee and shaking it. "Watch *Top Gun* with me."

His eyes were on my hand until I drew it back into my lap to untangle my earbuds. "*Fuck*, fine," he caved. "The things I do for a date."

I pumped my fist in celebration while Frankie pulled his own earbuds from his pocket and plugged the auxiliary edge into the armrest.

"My favorite movie is *Bridesmaids*, by the way," he said before sticking them in his ears and shimmying into the cushion.

———

IT WAS SEVENTY-EIGHT DEGREES and blindingly sunny when the plane landed in Fort Lauderdale. Frankie folded the sleeves of his shirt up to the elbows and undid a few buttons over his chest to acclimate, and suddenly it felt about ninety-five.

Of course the baggage claim, like in any other airport, was no less than three miles from the gate, and Frankie and I walked alongside each other with my snow boots hanging by their laces from the handle of my backpack while he guided us across the sparkling linoleum.

Very unfortunately, the man looked even better off the plane. Long legs and a cute ass that I kept sneaking looks at when his height carried him slightly further ahead of me. Up close he looked older, fine lines starting to crease his forehead, but when I saw him in this light, walking happily beside me, pointing out the different tourist attractions I might want to see and which ones he'd been kicked out of as a teenager—he was youthful still. Like a big kid in a very attractive older man's body.

When we finally hit baggage claim I took the time to check my phone and update my parents. Nat had texted me as soon as the flight landed.

Nat babyyyy: You're here!!!!! Waiting for you out in pickup. I have to keep circling, this bitch at the door is giving me the side-eye every time I try to park in the fire lane.
Ophelia: Grabbing my bag now. I had the craziest fucking thing happen to me on my flight.
Nat babyyyy: Tell me everything when you get in the car, hurry up!!!
Ophelia: Hurrying!!!

I shoved my phone in my pocket and watched the bags spin, spotting mine speckled in white polka dots coming toward me. I reached out to grab it, but Frankie pulled the handle and hauled it off the belt first.

"Thanks." I smiled as he stood next to me with his own suitcase. "Looks like the world's most insane Hook(Up) date has officially ended."

"It'd be hard to top that, I agree." He grinned back.

We still remained awkwardly idle as the crowd moved around us. If I could hear my nervous pulse thumping I'm sure he could too.

"Well, my ride's here waiting outside. So I probably shouldn't keep her." I sounded like I was asking for approval to leave more than telling him I was.

"Okay," he said softly, eyes roaming down my face like he was memorizing it.

"Okay..." I replied, slowly backing toward the rotating glass doors. "You've got my, uh..." He had my dating profile, which seemed appropriate. "You know," I finished sheepishly.

Frankie nodded, pulling his hat off to rake his fingers through his messy locks. "And you've got mine."

The humid Floridian air hit me square in the chest as soon as I stepped outside. It smelled like sand and salt, and the sun was just falling below the horizon, bathing the sky in vibrant purple and neon fire.

I spotted Nat in her car immediately, the nose of her yellow Jeep wedged between two waiting cabs and a barrage of horns beeping behind her. "The night awaits us!" she yelled, leaning over to push the passenger door open for me.

I shook my head, laughing as a smile dimpled my cheeks. Christmas in Coconut Creek wasn't looking too bad at all.

3

Frankie

I SHOVED THROUGH THE front door of the house with my shoulder, sweating as I pulled my luggage in one hand with the suit bag I'd borrowed from Mateo hanging from the other. It was a temperate enough night, but after spending a week in Colorado I quickly realized the humidity in this state couldn't be described as anything less than the underside of a ballbag.

The air out West was so fresh. I stood outside the hotel waiting for a cab to drive me to base every day just so I could breathe it in. I'd never known what *winter* felt like. That was abundantly clear when all I had for a jacket was a thinly-lined windbreaker that I'd only bought for getting caught in those late afternoon Florida thunderstorms.

My entire life had been spent in some sort of undying heat. My childhood in Southern Florida, and then when I joined the military, it was Georgia, North Carolina, Afghanistan, Guam. With Delta, it was Central American jungle.

I'd taught my body to adapt like a fucking lizard. A lizard was supposed to freeze in temperatures below forty-five degrees, but after a few days in Colorado Springs, I just wanted to play in it.

I threw my bags down right inside the foyer, tossing my keys on the entry table and shrugging away the sore shoulder I'd tell myself to ice now and completely forget about later. My back was like an ironing board. I'd gotten better at sitting for extended periods of time, but the flight wasn't particularly short, and coach seating was sure as hell not designed for comfort.

I hadn't even noticed though.

Three-and-a-half hours went by so fast I was cursing the palm trees on the coast when they started dotting into view.

It was my luck that some higher power would put a little spitfire brunette on the same flight as me. I'd seen her sipping a mimosa with her nose stuck to her phone screen all the way across the terminal. Partly because she was so gorgeous—long limbs and soft angles, the cutest fucking pout to her lips. But also because I happened to be looking directly at her photo on my own phone, scrolling one of those dating apps Mateo had made me download before I flew out for my interview. It was sheer boredom; it wasn't like I was going to find a girl to spend a night with at the airport, but fuck if it hadn't been something like fate.

The resemblance was unmistakable. Wavy hair, eyes like cornflower, a distinct little dimple in her right cheek when she smirked. I flipped back and forth through her photos ten times. Hiking through the mountains in an outfit that hugged every goddamn curve on the woman. Another standing under the stream of a waterfall. One with a glass of wine and a perfect sundress. Then more laid back, in jeans and a graphic T-shirt, a lanyard dangling from her neck and a gaggle of kids at her side.

Cliché as it was, one of my very first thoughts was, *Oh, Mom would love her.* All the others, however, were unseemly and entirely self-indulgent.

As the plane started boarding I hung back until the last minute, watching her impressively chug a second drink, and when she flung her bag over her shoulder and headed directly onto my same departing flight, I said fuck it, and swiped right.

I couldn't have even imagined the following chain of events. Catching her red-handed and blushing below me, a view I was already too eager to recreate. Then when she met me tit for tat, that sow-my-wild-oats mentality I'd brought with me to Colorado simmered to sow one oat—only, as soon as possible and sow it so good a garden bloomed beneath us.

At home, nothing had changed since I left. Mateo and I kept it neat and mostly barren. A few photographs from our unit above the mantel, a framed American flag on the wall. Call it male laziness or a blind eye for design, but he and I had become so used to structured routine and perfection in the military it only naturally carried over to civilian life.

When Delta cut us loose we were two guys that had been through Hell and back together for the better part of ten years, so we just kept the ball rolling. It felt ridiculous at the time *not* to go halves on the house. I wouldn't admit it three years ago, but I needed a lot more help than I let on after everything that went down on that last deployment. My pride was buried so far in the dirt there wouldn't be a shovel in the world strong enough to dig it back up.

The sliding glass door off the living room was cracked open, and I slipped outside onto the stone patio that opened into the backyard.

"Ay, look what the clouds dragged in."

Mateo was lounging in the hot tub with a dollop of sunblock on his angular nose, massage jets bubbling around his chest. He was right about the clouds too. In the minutes since I'd last been outside, the clear sunset had grayed and heat lightning flashed across the sky.

"Having yourself a night out here, Cap?" I dug into the mini fridge for a beer and popped it open. We all had call signs in our unit—Mateo's was Captain. And unfortunately it didn't matter if you loved it or hated it, nicknames always stuck.

"Relaxing before the night ahead, brother." He tipped his beer to me. "How was it? Got the job?"

I pulled a patio chair out and sank into it. "No, you know how this stuff works. It was preliminary shit. Touring the base, kissing ass, paperwork. Round one of a billion fucking interviews."

"Echo said you were a shoe-in; he has connections over there."

"I shot him a text on the first day. He said he was working some magic, but with Tyler that usually means he's gonna be getting his dick wet. Probably fucking the command's wife."

"You think that he'd have it any other way?"

"No, but I don't know if I can guiltlessly accept a job from a man I know is getting cucked on his days off."

"To each their own." Mateo shrugged. "But it went well though, you're excited?"

"You know I'm still on the fence, man. I told you before I went, I'm just putting out the feelers on it. I haven't flown in..." I trailed off, picking at the damp label on the sweating beer bottle. "Then there's Addy and my mom. That'll be a lot for them, not having me around. It's a lot to think about."

"Your sister and mom are fine," Mateo assured me. "They'll survive, you've done everything for them since you were fucking twelve years old, Pike. I don't know if you know this, but Florida is like Heaven for the sixty-five-plus crowd. They can walk around the clubhouse pool with their tits down to their ankles in a bikini top and no one is batting an eye."

I shuddered. "Don't put that picture in my head."

"Maria's still got it. She's gone on a couple dates."

"My mother? Has gone on a couple dates?"

"I call your mom. I'm her favorite son."

Mateo was the *definition* of momma's boy. Those Italian sons grow up too spoiled for their own good. My mother was fawning over him from the moment she met him. Instead of a friendly wave, my best friend had pulled her into a bear hug like you've never seen before, letting her hold his face and kiss his cheeks, giving her that dazzling Mateo smile with his sharp canines sparkling like a fucking Crest commercial.

Every time I talked to my mother, she asked about him. *How is my Mateo? He looks so handsome in his new pictures on The Facebook. You should really cut your hair more like his, Francesco, no one can see your eyes when you're in that hat all the time. Has he found a girlfriend yet? Adriana is still single, you know, and your sister needs to have babies soon.*

I wouldn't let my sister near any of the men I was in with, not with fucking riot gear on. Especially not Mateo. Besides that point, he'd been shacked up with Tally for almost a year now, and apart from the paranormal sex dungeon they seemed to be sleeping in, she was a good girl. I was happy for them.

My mother dating, on the other hand, made my skin itch. I knew the possibility was always there; my dad had been gone for over twenty years. There was no reason she shouldn't, but the idea of someone slipping into my well-earned shoes and assuming caretaker over my mother without even meeting me first didn't sit right.

"She said she's dating someone?"

"Don't get your panties in a bunch." Mateo chuckled, standing from the bubbling water and sloshing it over the edge. He dried off, grabbing another beer from the fridge before sitting down next to me. "Forget your mom, man. You can call her yourself, don't kill the messenger. I want to know about *you*."

I rolled my eyes. "You're going to be disappointed."

"Don't tell me that," Mateo complained. "Not one fuck? The whole week?"

"You say that like I can just go around collecting women to have sex with like fruit in the produce section."

"I set up the apps on your phone specifically designed for finding people to fuck. It's like fishing in a man-made pond. You're gonna fucking catch something. Close your eyes and cast a line, Pike. Jesus Christ."

I *did* cast a line. I spent basically *all* of my free time in Colorado, actually, scrolling through the thousands of pictures of women on those apps. My problem had never been finding a person, it'd been finding the right one, at the right time. I did the dance when I was in my twenties. Fuck, the first half a decade I was in the Army it was a revolving door. You get orders, you deploy, you make your fucking bed with the sheets so tight to the mattress you can bounce a quarter off of it, and then you get a girl naked in them. Rinse, repeat.

Then my buddies started getting married to the women they were sleeping with, and it felt like I was all of a sudden playing the game wrong. I wanted what they were having. Those sappy fucking military homecomings where wives came whipping down the airport terminal and jumping into their husband's arms. Showing up unexpectedly at a Little League game in my camo. A newborn baby meeting Dad for the first time.

I jumped into the first relationship to present itself, and seven years was a lot of time to spend with someone for it not to work out.

"Don't make me say it, Pike," Mateo mumbled.

"It's not about her."

"It's been three years, and Vanessa is a fucking bitch for what she did. I'm sorry, but that's the only way to say it. You gotta shove it to the side, get back on the field. It's time."

At first it was about Vanessa, but then it became a total disconnect with dating. The pool for women my age was thin. They were either married with kids, or divorced...with kids. All the rest were twenty-somethings, and all social interaction started and ended online. I'd had the same conversation so many times the answers all started to blur.

Until Ophelia.

"I did meet one girl," I said, nonchalantly.

"See, you're holding out on me!" Mateo shoved my shoulder. "What was that like? It's been a while. Did you at least give her more than a two-minute ride?"

"I didn't have sex with her, Cap."

But man did I think about it.

"What do you mean? You took her out?"

"I met her on the flight here, actually. We sat next to each other on the plane."

"So she lives here?"

"No, Colorado." I finished my beer, and the second I discarded it, I pulled my hat off and ran my fingers through my hair. "She's an elementary school teacher. Her parents are divorced, and she feels detached from the family. Absolute knockout. Smart, funny, confident, she's got a little feist in there if you push the right buttons. A ten. More than a ten."

"All right, I'm gonna stop you right there."

I glanced over at Mateo who was watching me with a crease in his brow.

"I love you, man, I really do. But you're supposed to be on a rebound tour, not learning the family dog's name. You have to stick your feet in first, Pike. Don't get attached. Especially not to a girl who lives in fucking Colorado."

"I'm not getting attached." My chest panged. Ophelia was a hundred percent the kind of woman I would want to pursue—not just have a one-night stand with. It wasn't my fault she was also the first woman since Vanessa that I actually liked enough to explore something physical.

"I just don't want to see you how you were when it went to shit with the ex again," Mateo said. "You're a hopeless romantic. You'll go on a few dates with this girl, sleep with her, fall head over heels, and she doesn't even live here, Frankie. You're setting yourself up for failure. You might not like my advice, but I say nip it in the bud before that happens."

I clicked my tongue against my bottom teeth. The last thing I wanted to do was stop something good before it started. When I left the airport, I'd already decided to reach out to Ophelia sooner than later. My finger hovered over the message button on her dating profile the entire Uber ride back to Pompano. I had to mentally castrate myself not to seem like such an eager teenager.

She'd be around the area at least through Christmas. But now with Mateo breathing down my neck about it, I was taking all the plausible disasters into consideration.

Ophelia wasn't the kind of girl you rebounded with. She was the kind you took out to the pier after dinner and kissed in the mid-day monsoon instead of running from it for cover. Cap may have been right that I got attached too easily, but even more than that, trying to justify seeing her any way as a rebound felt borderline disrespectful.

"Don't look so deflated." Mateo mussed my hair like a brother would. "We're meeting Tally out at Jugg tonight. We'll find you something to play with the old-fashioned way."

A lone drop of rain fell at our feet, followed by another, and several more after that. My roommate stood from his chair and collected the empty bottle out of my hand, walking toward the sliding door inside. "Grab a shower, wash your balls, and...find a Sharpie."

"A Sharpie?" I squinted.

"Don't worry about it. Have I ever steered you wrong?"

"I stopped counting."

The door closed behind him as a humored, "Yeah, yeah" snuck through the crack.

I scratched at the day-old stubble shadowing the underside of my jaw and stared out at the yard as the sprinkler system kicked on ironically in the onset of a storm.

I'd be better off leaving the girl on the plane. She was visiting friends anyway; it's not like she'd leave them to spend time with a stranger. The entire scenario screamed *Dateline*. It was unfortunate, I hated it—but it was what it was.

A crack of lightning turned the gray sky white as I stood for the door, my clothes covered in a thin sheet of rain. I pulled my phone from my pocket and opened Ophelia's profile again, swiping through the pictures one after the other. My thumb hovered over the message for a second too long before I sighed, and then deactivated my account altogether.

4

Ophelia

THE OBVIOUS FIRST STEP to a night out drinking was carb loading, which is why after driving through the stormy sunset, Nat and I ended up sitting on a splintered bench at the outdoor patio of Sand Saloon.

"I can't believe he caught you looking at his dick."

"A *picture*," I corrected my friend. "A picture of the crotch of his pants. It was, like, the absolute most humiliating thing you could ever think of."

"That would probably be if he caught you stalking his mom's sister's neighbor's Facebook profile where he was tagged in a picture from six years ago."

I squinted with a bite of juicy burger halfway to my mouth. "Yeah...that oddly specific scenario would have probably been worse."

"Anyway, he was a good sport about it. That shows *maturity* in a man. He's self-aware."

"Maybe it just means *he* was the one looking at my grandma's best friend's son-in-law's Facebook profile and figured that he shouldn't judge."

Natalia rolled her eyes and I peered over the side of the patio where it hung into the water. Two kids a few booths down were throwing French fries over the barrier to a famished shoal of largemouth bass while their parents argued quietly across the table.

Oddly, the kids reminded me of my own siblings back home. Or maybe they reminded me more of myself. At that age as an only child, I didn't realize what kind of problems lay right beneath my nose because I had no worry over "grown-up" things. My parents had many hushed arguments hidden behind the background noise of the television while I played in the living room. But ugly words always sounded sharp.

That's not to say they didn't have their better moments, too. I knew what *love* was, what it looked like—but it was never in my sphere, never really in my home, not in the years I could remember, anyway. But then as a teenager I began to notice it again. My mom with Josh, and my father with Amy. I saw it in my best friend's parents, and in my Aunt Shelly and Uncle Ray.

"But, you said he made you laugh. That's hard to find," Natalia pondered. "Most guys nowadays are so into themselves it's disgusting. It's like they expect you to be enamored by their existence alone. The bar is in Satan's asshole."

"If that's what you think in West Palm Beach, then the bar in Pine Ridge is in that little space between his asshole and his sack."

"The gooch."

I nearly spit the Bay Breeze I was drinking all over the table. Pineapple juice stung the inside of my nose and Nat giggled as she passed me a clean napkin across the bench.

"Exactly," I said, recouping. "I'm swimming in Satan's gooch pool, and you're out here telling me *your* bar is low."

"The tides are changing, Phee. Here I was, thinking I'd be spending my Christmas season helping you get laid, when it looks like you don't even need me. I'll be picking your ho-ho-ho ass up at a Publix tomorrow morning with your reindeer ears on backwards and Hook(Up) guy's dick print on your cheek."

"This is a family establishment, Natalia Russo."

She rolled her eyes. "Show me a picture. Is he *hot* hot? Or hot because he's got a fun personality? Because you're not hooking up with fun personality guys anymore. I'm putting my foot down."

"You are like a meninist's worst nightmare," I said, swiping my phone off the table to pull up Frankie's profile. "Do you ever just, like, *look* at a man's thighs and wonder what kind of horsepower they have?"

Nat pointed the soggy, limp end of her French fry at me. "See, *this* is why you're my people."

I opened the app and there was another match there. The blond holding a husky who I found myself much less physically attracted to than I did at the airport that morning.

"He's a little older, is that bad?" I asked. Frankie wasn't *old* by any means, but nine years would be a bit of an adjustment. "Should I be worried he's hiding a wife and kids or something?"

"I like older. They know what they want. Maybe he's divorced?"

"Well thank you, ex-wife, he's aged like fine wine."

I scrolled top to bottom and side to side on my phone, hitting the back button and refreshing the page once, *twice*. My stomach tensed uncomfortably when the face I was searching for had entirely vanished. "No *way*. That fucking *gooch*hole."

"What? What happened?"

"He unmatched me."

"Shut up."

Nat plucked the phone out of my hand and inspected the screen, scrolling just as frantically as I had been a minute ago, looking for the lost remnant of my flight-date's profile.

He had really lost my contact the minute we walked out of baggage claim.

I tried to act unbothered, but it was harder than expected. Fuck yes, I was embarrassed, and *a lot* insulted, but more so than I wanted to admit, I was *sad*. Sad, when I should have been relieved that the trash took itself out before my trip really started.

I *actually* thought Frankie was genuine. A rare man that was easy to talk to because we both felt the same platonic chemistry on that plane. I laughed while he told me dumb fucking pilot jokes for forty-five minutes and that geriatric unmatched me because I didn't give him head in the bathroom?

"Oh, hell no." Nat handed my phone back to me. "Fuck that guy, he probably *was* married and looking for a quick fuck in the airport. When you didn't put out he cut his losses and went home to Karen and the crotch-rockets."

Natalia was right. It made so much sense.

I shoved the leftover basket of fries to the edge of the table and chugged the last of my drink. "Where are we going tonight?" I asked, suddenly ready to get wasted in a dingy McDonald's parking lot if that was the only option.

"That's my girl." Nat flashed me a mischievous smile. "First things first, we're doing shots." She looked around my head and caught the eye of the waitress walking toward our table. "Then, Christmas in the motherfuckin' Caribbean, baby. We're getting you heavy-petted tonight."

"Cheers to *that*."

———

CHRISTMAS IN THE CARIBBEAN was exactly what it sounded like: a themed party at a club tucked into a local casino. Nat wasn't joking either when she said I was going to hate to love her once I got a gander at the outfits.

I walked into Jugg with my tits up to my chin in a red velvet corset, white snowball pom-poms dangling from my cinched waist. The same fluffy white material hemmed the neckline and the peplum style bottom, and Natalia and I both wore barely-there fishnet stockings that cut off mid-thigh. Santa's wet dream.

Nat pulled me by the hand across the crowded venue, floors already sticky with alcohol that I could feel on the heels of my knee-high boots. The place was decorated to the nines, neon palm trees dotted with Christmas ornaments and string lights, sparkling green and red garland wrapped around every column and molding that shone in the dim light.

Even the wait staff was all in; cocktail waitresses wore tiny bikini tops and hula skirts, reindeer ears with little bells on top of their heads. The bartenders working the busy wooden counter dressed as elves in candy-cane leggings and pointed top hats. Standing behind a booth made to look like a grand old sled, the DJ was head to toe in a red velvet suit and white beard.

"This is legit!" I shouted at Nat over the thumping bass of music.

She nodded, swinging her hips back and forth to the beat while we both waited at the side of the bar. Our drinks came served in coconut glasses with pretty little umbrellas sticking out of the top, and just for good measure Nat ordered them as doubles with a round of tequila shots to chase. The alcohol blanketed my body in a warm buzz the second it hit my stomach.

There was just something about being blissfully drunk. That first shed layer of inhibition when all that I cared about was the company and the music. I loved the way my eyes got soft and my smile got lazy, my words flowing more seamlessly. I was more *myself* when I wasn't perpetually stressed.

Nat leaned over and spoke close to my ear. "Don't make it obvious, but there's a guy right behind you checking out your ass."

My eyes darted to the mirror behind the bar to try to catch a glimpse of him without turning around. Strobe lights flashed off the reflection and kept me from seeing more than a cluster of bodies in red and green. "Is he hot or is he creepy? Do we need to move?"

"No, no, he's cute. I think. He's wearing a hat."

I scratched the side of my neck and slowly rotated so my torso was flush to the curved bar top. "Is he still looking?" I asked out of the corner of my mouth.

"Oh yeah."

Inhaling a deep breath, I cleared my throat, then tilted my head to the side flirtatiously as I turned toward the stranger and caught his eye for the first time.

"Love the outfit," he greeted me, tipping his lowball rocks glass toward my coconut in cheers.

Okay, he *was* cute.

Long blond hair fanned out from beneath a Santa hat. He had on dark red jeans that were tucked into all black high-tops, and was totally shirtless minus two suspenders lying across his lean chest. Pointed jawline, hazel eyes. His lips were a bit thin, but his teeth were straight and white when he smiled at me as I clinked the faux coconut against his glass.

"You look way heavier in photos," I joked, shouting at him over the music. His blank expression searched me for the explanation

I didn't think I'd have to give. "Because you're dressed like Santa." I pointed to his hat. "Like sexy, shirtless Santa."

It took another second before his shoulders relaxed and his head tipped back as he laughed. "Ah! I get it. Funny."

"Yeah, it's probably hard to hear me over the Christmas EDM. Imagine Santa listened to this while delivering presents? Just head-banging through the Northern Lights."

The dead-eyed, empty gaze returned like he was trying to decide if I was joking or not. As if a grown woman wearing a lingerie corset in public, on *purpose*, may actually still believe in Santa Claus. Behind me, Nat kicked the side of my calf.

"I don't believe in Santa," I said to revive the moment but quickly realized I was nursing a one-sided conversation with a cadaver.

He squinted. "Not even *sexy* Santa?"

Oh, thank fuck, a pulse.

I shrugged playfully. "I could possibly be swayed."

Nat physically relaxed at my back, probably relieved she wouldn't have to fake her period and whisk me away from my social autopsy.

"I'm Lucas," he shouted to me.

"We probably should have started with this," I shouted back. "Ophelia."

"What fruity mix of juice am I ordering for you, Ophelia?"

"I'd actually like to enjoy what I'm drinking, thank you very much. I know you don't walk around with a tumbler of Tullamore Dew because it tastes good."

"Tullamore Dew? That's insulting. This is Macallan."

"Every whiskey is just a different flavor of finger paint."

The corner of his mouth twitched upward, amused. "I think I need to refine your palate."

With a satisfied grin I gestured to the bartender for another drink. Nat was still stuck to my side, swaying back and forth. I swung my arm around my girlfriend's shoulder and pulled her toward me.

"I fucking love you, and Florida, and palm trees." I stared up at the flickering neon lights behind the bar. "Why do I live in Colorado where it's perpetually raining and my neighbor steals my *Times* right out of the mailbox every Sunday?"

"Who the actual fuck still gets a print copy of the newspaper? Christ, maybe you *do* belong in Fort Lauderdale."

I hummed, leaning on Nat's shoulder while the hazy rhythm of booze and bass vibrated my body to a steady level of intoxication.

Who *cared* about Frankie from Hook(Up)? This was going to be the most incredible three weeks with my best friend. Sipping and sunning on the beach, cooking our own Christmas ham with the little cherries and toothpick-stabbed pineapples. We would listen to Michael Bublé, and make thumbprint cookies, light a different holiday-scented Yankee Candle in every room of Natalia's apartment.

Coconut Creek could be a *new* Christmas tradition for me. Something that was entirely mine, untouched by familial expectation or faint reminders of the cheery childhood holiday that I lost somewhere along the way.

Nat shuffled my jelly-limbed body with hers as a familiar song started mixing into the previous. "Where's your drink?"

"Lucas is buying me drinks, right, Lucas?"

The blond to my right chuckled and handed over a refilled hollow coconut of alcohol. "Does sexy Santa get to disrobe Mrs. Claus later?"

"Let's see if you can keep up first."

I took a clumsy sip of my drink and spun around with Lucas's hands on my hips as Nat squealed excitedly beside me. She was staring at her phone screen, blue hues dancing across her glittery eyeshadow, and jumping up and down like she'd just won the lottery. "Ah! Come on, come on!"

"Where are we going!" I shouted as she pulled me by the elbow to the complete opposite side of the bar. "Natalia!"

"He's here!"

"Who?" We pressed through the crowd of partiers with Lucas trailing slowly behind.

Nat looked down at her phone again and then pushed up onto her tiptoes to case the rows of people standing against the bar. "Just...someone I want you to meet." She wiggled her eyebrows at me and then grinned as she finally found who she was looking for leaning against the counter.

She tapped on his shoulder twice before the handsome, sun-kissed man turned around to face the both of us with a disarming smile. His dark eyes roamed Nat's velvet-covered body hungrily, then he grabbed her face with two big hands and crushed their lips together.

What the fuck?

She melted as his tongue swiped against hers, seemingly in their own little world while I stood there stunned. Natalia had to clear her throat and shoot a glance in my direction before he even noticed they had company.

Biting her lip, Nat gestured to the mystery man she'd just Frenched as I looked back and forth between the two of them. "Phee, this is my boyfriend. Mateo Duran."

"Hi," I managed, pushing a hand out towards him. Mateo took it and placed a friendly kiss on my knuckles in lieu of the handshake as he slid his arm around Nat's waist.

I felt like I'd entered a different dimension. Nowhere in the last *year* had Natalia even *mentioned* a boyfriend. Sure, we both lived busy lives—I was often working or grading, planning new lessons for the classroom. But even then, I'd made time to fill my best friend in on the woes of my serial dating over several months.

Unless, somehow I'd spent so much time talking about myself and the never-ending cycle of failed dates that I was completely oblivious to the changes going on in her life.

"Nat, where on *earth* have you been hiding this one from me?" I asked teasingly, brushing off any tension.

Mateo was wearing neon orange swim trunks that only came down to his mid-thigh, and the buttons of his Tommy Bahama shirt were completely undone. Black-rimmed sunglasses pushed up into his coiffed, golden brown hair, and Nat twirled the lei he had around his neck between her fingers.

"I know, I *know.*" Nat winced. "I'm sorry, but I know you Phee. If you thought you would be a third wheel, you never would have agreed to come down here for the holidays and I *want* you here. I'm so happy you're here."

Ugh. She was right.

I was reluctant enough when I thought it'd only be the two of us celebrating together. On top of using all my saved-up time off in one hit for an extra week away, leaving the familiar comfort of the mountains for almost an entire month, and *then* having to break the news to both my parents that I wouldn't be house-hopping for the holiday, knowing my attention would be shared with Nat's boyfriend would have been the straw that broke the camel's back. Especially now seeing how Mateo kissed her in *public.* I couldn't compete.

"Tally's been talking you up for weeks," Mateo vouched. "She was so excited when you bought your plane tickets."

"Tally?" I raised an eyebrow at my friend's new-to-me nickname. A pang of familiarity made itself known in my chest.

Before the conversation could go any further, the guy standing next to Mateo with his back to our little crew turned from the bar with two beers, nudging Nat's boyfriend with his elbow.

"Here, Cap."

No.

"Oh fuck *off*," I blurted. My filter had apparently dissipated along with all the liquor in my cup.

As if Nat introducing me to her secret boyfriend wasn't enough adjustment for one night, the secret boyfriend's roommate happened to be the exact reason I was six Oriental Trading coconuts of vodka deep in my pity-feels.

Frankie looked up at Nat and me at the sound of my voice and his mouth dropped open. "Fuck *me*."

Mateo and Natalia exchanged a confused glance, just as Lucas caught up and shimmied his body next to mine.

"Easy there big guy, turn the creep down like a hundred." Mateo patted Frankie on the chest through his open button-down. The two of them were wearing similar outfits. "I'm sorry about that, sweetheart, this is my friend, Francesco. Despite whatever the fuck that was, he doesn't usually speak his thoughts out loud."

Frankie squeezed his eyes closed and shook his head.

"So nice to meet you, Francesco," I offered sarcastically, also noticing the handwritten sign hanging around his neck that read, *Trying to get lei'd* completely unironically in black Sharpie. Which only further reminded me that the man was a player, and I'd narrowly avoided becoming another unsuspecting notch on his bedpost. I made a point of hanging onto Lucas's bicep as I pointed at the sign and said, "You should try an airport."

Frankie stuck his tongue in his cheek and then let it sweep out across his teeth and top lip, eyes darting between me and the man on my arm. Despite the theme of the night, he still wore that same weathered black ball cap that he lifted as he ran a hand through his hair. A nervous tick I'd caught onto.

"Nat, bathroom?" I prompted my friend.

"Yup." Sensing the shift of energy, she grabbed me by the hand and whirled me away.

5

Frankie

I WATCHED TALLY DRAG my Hook(Up) date through the crowded club and disappear. The tiny pair of shorts Ophelia was wearing had apparently cut off circulation to my brain, because it wasn't until Cap shoved me and sent a cascade of cold beer onto my hand that I realized my jaw was still hanging open.

Holy shit.

The odds of meeting her on that plane were low, even more so when we ended up sharing leg room. But this? *This* was like hitting the lottery on your first try. It would be impossible to avoid her if she was visiting Tally, and a disproportionate amount of excitement shook through me at that.

"What the fuck is wrong with you, man?" Mateo shouted over the lifting crowd.

I rubbed the back of my sticky hand against my pants. "That's Tally's best friend who's visiting for Christmas."

"Yeah, and you just fucking terrified her. Forget what I said earlier about hooking up, you need to go back to square one and learn how to converse first. It's like you've never seen a pair of tits before."

"That's the girl I met on the plane."

Mateo's eyes widened. "You gotta be shitting me."

"No, I'm not. You didn't tell me Tally's fucking college roommate was from Colorado and coming in on the same flight as me."

"To be fair, I didn't even know what day you were coming home."

I believed that. Mateo and I were closer than brothers but we weren't keeping tabs on shit like schedules. I worked for him, technically. That was as far as we went with keeping routine.

Beside us, the scraggly Tony Hawk wannabe who was following Ophelia around was still idling.

That was about to be short-lived.

It'd been all of six hours since the plane landed and I was already fighting for a seat at Ophelia's table. It made me immediately territorial, a trait I thought I'd long since lost.

"You could have warned me that she looked like that," I said to Mateo. "Did you know she looked like that?"

"If you think I've noticed anyone except that girl in the bathroom for the last twelve months, you must not be paying attention."

"This changes things," I decided thoughtfully.

"This changes nothing," Mateo quickly added. "In fact, this makes her more off-limits, Pike. I can't have you fucking up so bad that Tally's best friend hates you. I'm trying to keep this one."

I felt for Cap in that moment about as much as an amputee felt a lost limb. I wasn't going to make her hate me, that was ridiculous. If anything, I'd do the opposite. Ophelia and I had an undeniable chemistry that, while grounded in sexual innuendo and competitive banter, was the most natural thing I'd felt with a woman in years.

"Your relationship is safe," I assured Mateo. "It's not like I can steer clear of her now. Unless you're telling me you're not gonna see Tally for three weeks?"

"Of course I'm not saying that."

Hope bloomed in my chest. "I'll behave."

Mateo rubbed his forehead. "She's going back to Colorado, Pike. The rules still apply. Attachment—*bad*."

"What else do you know about her?"

He threw his hands in the air. "It's like I'm talking to a fucking brick wall."

"You're talking to your best friend who hasn't gotten laid since Bush Sr. was in office. I promise I won't propose to the girl, Cap. Give me a little bit of slack."

Mateo glanced toward the bathrooms. "All I know, because I'm dating one, is that women in their twenties are talking about husbands and babies at all hours of the fucking day. You want to stick your dick in something wet first thing in the morning, she wants to open a HomeGoods credit card."

I squinted. "Did you open a HomeGoods credit card?"

"That's not the fucking point." Mateo took an aggressive gulp of his beer. "Ophelia and Natalia are best friends, which means their brains are full of the same twisted, nonsensical DIY projects and seasonal candle scents. Ophelia is looking for someone to settle down with, the same way Tally is 'accidentally' leaving her laptop open to all-inclusive honeymoon destinations."

"That doesn't mean she's ruled out having a little bit of fun." I shrugged. "She *was* on a dating app in an airport."

Around us the crowd grew louder and denser until I couldn't see past the bar anymore. I desperately wanted to know what the fuck the girls were talking about in the bathroom, and if the reaction Ophelia was having to this insane chain of events mirrored mine.

"I'm just looking out for you, Pike." Mateo said. "Do what you want, but don't make me say I told you so."

Not a problem.

The warning was written in glaring red letters and wrapped in Christmas lights. I, on the other hand, was blind—and felt an awful lot like being risky if it meant taking Ophelia Brody home as the reward.

6

Ophelia

"THAT'S FUCKING HIM!" I shouted as soon as the bathroom door closed, hushing the loud music beyond it to a hum. "Frankie—*Francesco*, whatever the fuck his name is—he's the Hook(Up) guy from the plane!"

"No." She gasped, clapping a palm over her mouth.

"*Yes*," I confirmed, pacing back and forth with my hands on my hips.

"Holy *shit*, what are the fucking odds of that?"

"I'm too drunk for this." I pinched the bridge of my nose and faced the mirror. The movement and my vision were delayed, and I was pretty sure I was staring at a slightly different human being in the reflection than the one in my body. Like an evil twin that thought the right next move was to pour a drink on the guy I'd met for a few hours that morning.

"Frankie is Matty's *best* friend. Oh my god, this is nuts." Natalia cackled and fixed her hair next to me.

"Your boyfriend has terrible taste in friends."

"Agreed." Her laughter stopped.

"He's a player."

"Totally."

"Misogynist."

"Definitely."

"He unmatched me because I was too much of a cock-tease."

"Were you though?"

"Natalia!"

"Sorry!" She sighed, reaching over to pat the creasing green eyeshadow on my eyelid.

"Fucking shit. Why does he look so hot in those shorts?" I groaned.

Nat pressed her lips together to keep from grinning. Obviously she knew Frankie to a different degree than I did, but it didn't change the fact that he played me for a quick ride on our shared flight, and I *nearly* fell for it. I didn't even want to think about what it meant for the next three weeks that my host's boyfriend was roommates *and* apparently best friends with the guy.

My mind raced with the hours-long conversation I'd had with Frankie. The comedic quips he gave about the military, his long-standing relationship with his roommate, the girlfriend who moaned like a ghost.

Oh my god.

"So, what are we gonna do?" Nat asked, tucking her long black hair behind her ear on one side and applying a new layer of red lipstick. I bit my tongue, recalling the way Frankie mockingly moaned next to me in the flight cabin.

"Right now?" I sighed, unwilling to let the night get away from us over a freak coincidence. "I'm going to go back out there and keep getting my drinks paid for until sexy Santa whose name I can't remember—Lewis?"

"Lucas."

"*Lucas* realizes I was never gonna let him take me home."

"If I'm the meninist's worst nightmare, you're the photo they use on their dartboards."

"As we should be." I kissed her cheek and entwined our fingers. "Let's go, *Tally*."

***

ALREADY, THE WICKED PINCH of a hangover brewed behind my eyes, but I was way past the point of no return and opted for another sweet cocktail despite it. I'd rather black out and face the consequences than sober up before the rest of the party did and still end up bent over a toilet.

The bar must have run out of the coconuts, because when my new drink arrived it was in a plastic cup with noticeably less ice, and therefore warm all the way down my throat. I scrunched my nose and shrugged, taking several long swigs anyway.

"You move on fast."

Fuck.

My eyes rolled involuntarily. I'd never forget the cocky drawl of that man's voice for as long as I lived.

"Is that your type? Skater boy?"

I scoffed and took another long gulp, watching the way Frankie's eyes roamed over my body head to toe as I did. *Fine,* let him look. It was satisfying to know he might lie awake at night kicking himself over the loss.

"He's a little young, though," Frankie commented, leaning his hip against the ledge of the bar. "Probably not a lot in his retirement fund."

"And what's your type, exactly?" I flicked the sign on his chest. "Walks and has a pussy?"

"There's that smart mouth." His gaze shifted down to my lips for a fraction of a second while he toyed with the string of yarn that held his booty-call sign. "Cap's idea."

"I'm starting to think you need 'Cap' to wipe your ass too," I jabbed. "Maybe you should stop taking his advice on finding a woman to fuck you, because holy shit are you zero for two in one day."

Frankie pouted as he checked the time on his watch. "All I'm hearing is that I still have an hour."

"Good luck, soldier." I saluted him and began to walk away, but he grabbed me tenderly under the arm and pulled me back.

"Hey—wait, wait, wait."

My brow lifted skeptically, but I fell back into place.

Blame it on the alcohol. Definitely not the tall, dark-haired man with his bare chest nearly pressed to mine in the crowded club. Our breaths synchronized as I waited for him to say something, thinking he would take the time to apologize or explain himself. Instead his expression turned from contemplative to curious.

"What are you wearing?" He reached out to massage one of the fluffy white pom-poms hanging from my waist between his fingers, his knuckles brushing lightly against the material just below my bust.

"I know your game Frankie, don't play cute." I batted his hand away half-heartedly.

"You look surreal."

"Oh, you like?" I played with the hem of my top. "This is my 'get over the asshole from the airplane that unmatched me' outfit."

He averted his eyes, scratching at the stubble on his jaw. "You noticed that?"

"Of course I fucking noticed that! I'm telling Nat about the guy I met on my flight, only to see you unmatched me thirty seconds after I walked out of the airport. I guess it wasn't too much of a loss though. You probably wouldn't even last that long in bed."

"We could test it?" He shrugged.

"You could go fuck yourself."

"I'm *really* trying to stop doing that so often. That's kind of how we got into this mess in the first place."

I blinked rapidly, nursing my expression from amused back to unimpressed. I wanted so badly to hate the man in front of me, but I was uncharacteristically smitten and unavoidably fucked.

"And what you said about *Natalia*," I whispered accusingly, pointing at Frankie and narrowing my eyes.

"How was I supposed to know that *Casper the Friendly Ghost* was your college girlfriend?"

"I'm walking away now." I grabbed my drink off the bar top for the second time in as many minutes and made my way back in the direction of the dance floor.

"I'm an asshole, okay?" Frankie admitted, catching up to me in one long stride.

"You don't say?"

"But not for the reasons you think."

Weaving in and out of the crowd, I spotted Nat and Mateo grinding like they were the only two in the room and swung back around, coming face-to-face with Frankie. "Are you married?"

"What?" He recoiled. "No, I'm not fucking married. I told you I live with Mateo."

"You could have a girlfriend."

"I can hardly handle you."

I snorted, pleased with that answer. "So I'm going to go find a guy who can."

"Suspenders Santa doesn't even know what a clit is."

"Maybe I should introduce you then and you guys can swap notes."

As if summoned, Lucas popped through the partygoers and appeared next to us, smiling with a drunken hood to his eyes. I didn't oppose the way he laid his palm a bit too comfortably across my lower back when I glanced up and saw how amusingly easy it was to make Frankie squirm. His jaw was clenched so hard I could almost hear his teeth grinding over the music.

"Come dance with me?" Lucas asked.

"It's rude to interrupt a conversation, man."

Surprise sparked through me at the hint of possession in Frankie's tone. He didn't like anyone else playing with his toys. *Good to know.*

But I also wasn't his to claim as much as my traitorous body didn't hate the idea. Too many drinks into a night out with two hot men playing tug o' war over my snowball tassels was the beginning of a bad idea.

Lucas redirected his attention. "I think she was having more fun before you got here."

"I think she can speak for herself." Frankie took a step forward.

"You know what?" I chimed in. "This is a party, isn't it? I actually would *love* to dance."

Leaving my two half-clothed suitors to stare at one another in a pile of tinsel, I took off toward Nat and her *also* half-clothed boyfriend in the middle of the dance floor. I'd been in Florida less than eight hours and I was already two grown men deep in drama when all the drunk and frisky part of my brain could think about was two grown men deep in me.

Mateo had enough rhythm on his own to bop back and forth without looking like he was inconspicuously trying to work out a wedgie, so I didn't feel so bad stealing his girlfriend away—or when he left the two of us alone twirling in the strobe lights.

"Are we burying bodies tonight or what, chick?" Nat shouted over the music as we swayed in tandem.

"I can't decide if I'm destructive drunk or DTF drunk."

"I know you." She grinned. "You're borderline fuck-my-ass drunk but Frankie is on your shit list."

"He's on my do-not-fuck-ever list."

"Make him grovel, it's good for your skin."

"He's too much of a proud asshole to grovel." I glanced back to where I'd left the boys to find Frankie and Mateo watching from the sidelines. Matty whispered something animatedly in his friend's ear, pointing at Nat and me, making Frankie smirk. "I want to wipe that smug look right off his face."

"We could make out?" Nat suggested.

"We're talking punishment, not reward."

"The outfit you're wearing alone owns real estate in every cognitive area of his brain."

"Rent free." I laughed, shooting a wink toward the man in question who stiffened at my attention, even as Mateo carried on their conversation.

Part of me wished the afternoon played out differently—so I could give in to the obvious temptation hanging like an ornament between Frankie and me. The other part was happy to play the game. If we were bound to cross paths at some point or another over the coming few weeks, I'd make sure the next time he saw me he was exhausted from sleepless wet dreams of my tits in this fucking corset.

"At least one of us is getting laid," I said.

"You don't even know the half of it," Nat swooned. "Why don't we have the boys take us home for a nightcap? Frankie ordered a ride already."

"Bad idea." My words slurred. "I'm perfectly capable of getting myself back to your apartment."

"You're not going home alone. The sun will be up in a few hours anyway."

"We both know you and Mateo aren't making it until the sun comes up."

"Can you blame me?"

"No," I admitted. "But I'm trying my *literal* hardest not to blow his hot roommate and you're putting me through a clinical trial with this."

"Just...don't look at his dick."

"Who's dick?" Mateo asked, pressing up behind Natalia with Frankie at his side.

"She's not great at that," Frankie said.

I turned to face him. "That's bold coming from the guy who hasn't stopped staring at my ass for two hours."

"Funny you would notice."

"All right, play nice, kids." Matty smirked. "Santa's watching."

Frankie peeled his eyes away from mine to look down at the moving map on his phone. "Uber's here."

"*Andiamo.*" Mateo patted his girlfriend on her ass to coax her toward the door.

"No fucking funny business," I warned Frankie with a pointed finger as Nat and I strutted ahead out of the venue.

It only took the world's most uncomfortable cab ride through Coconut Creek with the four of us smushed into the back seat of a Ford Focus to realize I couldn't have cared less where I ended up asleep, as long as I was out of my clothes and lying in a horizontal position.

The quaint residential neighborhood Frankie and Mateo lived in was a smattering of similar-style stucco houses with colorful terra roofs. The grass was cut short and little solar-powered night lights lit up the driveway outside the two-car garage. Inside of the house was just as clean as outside in the dim ambiance of table lamps. I only noticed a stray coffee cup in the sink while I lingered around in the kitchen waiting for a change of clothes. As guessed, Matty and Natalia never made it to the nightcap that was promised. She did, however, make sure to throw a package of half-empty makeup wipes down the hall at me from Mateo's bathroom before disappearing behind closed doors.

So I begrudgingly found myself on the living room couch with a lethal case of the spins and wearing a pair of Frankie's boxer briefs and an oversized *Go Army!* crewneck.

"Socks, as requested," Frankie offered as he appeared from down the hallway carrying a comforter in his elbow. He tossed the rolled-up bundle to me and crashed onto the opposite end of the sofa. "You could take my bed, it's much more comfortable."

"Thanks," I muttered, rolling them onto my feet. "And, *no*, thanks."

He smiled amusedly. "Only psychopaths sleep with socks on, just so you know. What, do you have ugly toes or something?"

I squealed, tucking my feet under my thighs when he leaned over to look. "Get out of here, you creep!"

"*What* is so scandalizing?" His laugh lit up the room as he tried to pull my ankle toward him. "Is it bunions? Oh, don't be embarrassed, it's very common."

"I don't have fucking bunions, dickhead." I swatted his fingers away. "If you must know, I always wear socks when I stay at strange men's houses so I don't wake up in the middle of the night with a dude taking pictures of my feet for his spank bank."

Frankie's lips parted as he stared at me, blinking slowly. "You're a lunatic, and you're drunk. And if I was a guy that had a thing for feet, you just *wearing* my socks would be doing it for me and I'd never wash them again."

I grimaced. "You're not doing a great job convincing me you aren't that guy."

"But you still didn't take the socks off," he replied with a wink.

"I would sooner rip my own cuticles than put my feet on a dick."

"It feels necessary that I point out no one is asking you to do either of those things."

I chuckled lazily, sinking further into the couch and pulling the comforter Frankie had brought out for me over my body. "Fuck, my head hurts already."

Without another joke he stood and disappeared behind the dividing wall to the kitchen. I could still vaguely see him milling about and opening cabinets behind the pass through window, so I snuggled in further while he was gone, stretching out and dipping my nose beneath the blankets. Which was the *worst* thing I could have done.

My eyes were heavy, and the soft fabric smelled like laundry detergent and *him*. A warm, deep musk, like well-worn flannel and bergamot sand. Frankie must have pulled it directly off his bed and brought it out to me.

I hummed indulgently and wrapped the comforter tighter around my shoulders as he came back, carrying a glass of water and something to take the edge off my migraine. I was exhausted from the longest day of my life and struggling to even stay cognizant, but that last uninhibited part of my body pressed to stay awake. Just to spend more time in the company of the man I was meant to be mad at.

The one who *still* hadn't given me a good enough reason not to be.

"Drink that whole glass, please," Frankie said, sitting down at the end of the couch again and fluffing the blanket out to cover my legs evenly. His tentativeness wasn't lost on me, which made the resentment I felt harder to stick. His heated gaze followed me as I gulped down the pills, making sure I finished the water. Even as I put the glass down on the coffee table he didn't look away.

I tilted my head against the cushion, watching him back with my bottom lip clamped between my teeth. If we were going to be forced together for the next few weeks, left alone in a room in the darkest hours of the night, I needed to know.

"Why did you unmatch me?" I asked quietly.

His hand explored, finding my ankle over the blanket. The gesture wasn't loaded or expectant, but it still lit up my nerves. I loved that touch, so I let him run his fingers back and forth over the bone silently, until he finally murmured, "I almost messaged you two minutes after you walked out of the airport, Trouble."

I smiled faintly, his gentle touch and my exhaustion taking over so quickly I almost didn't register what was said beyond the ridiculous nickname and the gravelly way he said it.

"I don't know about you, but I'm an all-in kind of guy. When I want something, I tend to get selfish. So, let's just say I felt myself getting a little too selfish this morning."

His fingers traveled absentmindedly up my calf. I was drunk, but not enough to misunderstand the implication he left floating there, and maybe he was hoping I would. Maybe he expected I'd forget by the morning, or that he could take it back if he needed to. Or maybe he hoped that I wouldn't at all.

Maybe he wanted every single word to sink into my skin, so I'd know that he meant he wanted me too much to let himself have me. My body was buzzing to know what Frankie felt like when he was being too selfish.

I opened my mouth with a reply, but in the same breath a ghoulish groan from down the hallway filled the silence. My eyes widened as I sat up, searching for an explanation in an entirely amused and unsurprised Frankie. The noise continued, this time flanked with several *yeses* and high-pitched *Mattys*.

I gasped. "Oh my god."

"I told you."

7

Ophelia

I'D NEVER BEEN SO comfortable.

Warm, soft velvet weighed me down. It curled around my torso and supported my neck, diving between my thighs as I swung my legs around it. I was near the ocean, the morning dawn still purple beneath the horizon, the ripple of waves kissing and lapping at lukewarm sand just a few feet away. No one was around, the only sounds a distant caw of a seagull, and the far-off rumble of morning commutes crowding the intercoastal. The breeze was comfortable and playful on my bare skin as I waited for the sun to wake and nip the last brisk breath of air from the night.

A raspy satisfied groan came out of me as I felt lips on my chest, searing the already hot skin. A soft mouth explored me carefully, traveling toward my exposed collarbones, then my neck, the sensitive spot below my ear at the hinge of my jaw.

God, what is happening?

I hummed at the teasing scratch of stubble down my skin and whimpered, ever so softly, at the feeling of hands, deft and large, pressing carefully at the insides of my thighs, spreading them.

My fingers threaded through feathery brown waves of hair. The short strands tickled my knuckles as the head they were attached to swayed rhythmically down my body, leaving a torrid trail of tongue and teeth, licking greedily at my hip bones.

"God yes." I sighed, shifting my body to open wider. Somehow the cushion at my back gave like a well-worn pillow as I sunk further into the sand. The softest sand. It smelled like home, like cedar and cotton and the manly tang of teakwood.

The sound of the waves faded into background noise as my breaths quickened and the apex of my thighs ached for use. My brain screamed, *Kiss me there, touch me there*, but suddenly reprieve felt farther away no matter the very tangible pulse in my core. I reached for it, grinding my hips in circles until the throb was sated by the bundle of fabric caught in the tangle of my legs. I could do it. I could reach my peak like this, with the image of the ocean and the palm trees and those perfectly tan hands and demanding brown eyes flickering up to meet my gaze as Frankie—

The shutter of a camera cracked my fantasy like a strike of lightning to pine. My eyelids flipped open, adjusting to the space through the tired, crusted slit of my eyelashes. *Fuck*, waterproof mascara was a fickle bitch.

The lights were low. I could see a peek of blue sky and sunshine trying with all their might to breach through the blinds in the Delacora windows. My neck was unsurprisingly stiff; I grumbled and rolled it on my shoulders twice, activating the headache that had been lying dormant.

I laid back down, only to be met with another much louder and apparent shutter of a camera.

I flung into an upright position, immediately coming face-to-iPhone with Frankie at the opposite end of the couch as he had been when I fell asleep. Except now he tauntingly held his camera over my sock-covered toes in his lap.

"Good morning, Colorado. Were you just having a wet dream on my couch?"

"Ugh, sicko!" I tried to kick the phone out of his hand but he snatched it away quicker, showing me the screen. The front-facing camera had been capturing photos of his curly mop of hair and shadowed forehead.

"I had to wake you up somehow. You were performing parts of the *Kama Sutra* on my bed spread. It felt like a thing I needed to give consent for."

Indeed, his comforter was twisted in a braid between my legs and up the length of my body. I was hugging it like a koala bear would a tree trunk and there was absolutely no way to coyly untangle my limbs without spreading my legs.

I cleared my throat. "Why didn't you just get up and sleep in your own bed then?"

"I didn't want to disturb you after you fell asleep. You looked cute as fuck drooling on my pillows."

"I did not drool on your—" I palmed the cream-colored throw under my head. *Fuck*, I definitely drooled on it.

He smirked and looked down at his lap. "You know, for a girl who swore up and down last night she'd never put her feet on a dick, you're looking extremely comfy right now."

I registered then that my legs were still extended clear across Frankie's thighs. I'd claimed the couch as my own in the middle of the night under the influence of drunken comfort seeking. To be fair, it could have been *much* worse—that little dream I just woke up from could have been real.

I rolled my eyes and pulled my feet back under the blankets, but my heel caught something stiff and sensitive tucked into the band of his sweatpants.

"Oof." Frankie winced through his teeth. "Careful where you're kicking those."

My cheeks flamed. "Do you have a fucking hard-on right now!?" I tried not to look, I really did. The sweats did nothing to sway my gaze though. It was difficult enough to know it was there; call it Mission Impossible not to selfishly want to see what he was working with.

He shrugged. "It's the morning, I don't control these things."

"Put it away," I demanded. "Make it go away."

"Should I pack it a bag and buy it a plane ticket?"

"Frankie." I ground my teeth together. I was still nursing a buzz like a parasite from the club and half my body obviously wanted something in, near, or around it enough to send me to beach-fuck dreamland. The respectable half of my brain reminded me that Frankie wasn't out of the dark yet despite the late-night couch-talk, and if he wanted to be back in my good graces, it would take more than making a dick joke and wearing a pair of gray sweatpants.

"You're overconfident," I told him.

"Am I, though?" He tilted his head and watched me like he could see the gears turning inside my head. The tennis match of pros and cons that would come with letting him bend me over the arm of the sofa right then...

"Don't call me Colorado," I deflected. "This isn't *Zombieland*."

Frankie smirked. "You might change your mind if you looked in a mirror."

I glared in his direction, well aware of the state I must have been in. I knew what a night out did to the undersides of my eyes—I wasn't twenty-one anymore. Not to mention Natalia's makeup wipes were fucking scented, and I could feel the dry layer of skin begging for the expensive serums I had back at her apartment.

"I can't keep track of names. I just call every woman I seduce into wearing my socks by the state I found her in."

"So you should be calling me drunk and desperate, obviously," I said, scoffing.

The corner of Frankie's mouth lifted. He was pushing willfully at every button I had, trying to wear me down. "I've yet to see desperate," he said with an edge. "I'm looking forward to seeing desperate."

I choked up a condescending laugh that died on my tongue too quickly. It sounded more like a breathless grunt, further fueling the heat in my cheeks and neck as I found a place that wasn't Frankie's eyes or the outline of his dick to focus on.

"Okay then...O." His grin turned toothy, fueling the tension. "Who were you riding in your dream?"

"No one. I was *not* having a fucking wet dream."

"Those little noises you make put Tally's to shame."

I dismissed him. "You're hearing things."

"Right." His snide smile dialed up to ten. "So..." He leaned over, the leather of the couch creaking beneath his shoulder in the otherwise quiet room. He ran a soft trail up the inside of my exposed calf with his fingers. "If I touched your pussy right now, would I find out that you're lying to me?"

It was futile to hide the shock in my face, or the hitch in my breath. I had never met a man so outright unashamed.

"Do you kiss your mother with that mouth?"

"I wouldn't dare." Frankie kept his hand on my leg, drawing little circles with his thumb that reignited the thrum I felt elsewhere. "You know, avoidance is akin to admission," he said. "Women that lied to me used to end up with their sweet little ass over my knee."

I tilted my head, snorting complaisantly. It seemed like every reaction was lost in the delivery though; he was getting under my skin well and thoroughly. It was irking me even more that he absolutely knew it, too. As if he wasn't chomping at the bit just as much. If he wanted to make a game out of fucking with me, it was only fair I played defense.

I sat up on my knees, discarding the comforter on the way and dropping onto all fours. Frankie's eyebrow quirked, his pink tongue peeking out between his parted lips at my new position. I crawled toward him across the short gap and puckered my lips to his ear. This close, I could feel the sharp intake of his breath.

"Too bad I'm not a little girl, Francesco," I whispered, licking a teasing trail up the shell of his ear.

Frankie adjusted himself with the heel of his palm, tugging his pants away from his crotch. He wasn't the nearest bit subtle about it, and if anything, I'd sabotaged myself—*that* gesture further stirring the pressure between my legs. I wanted him to ache, but the feeling was unsatisfyingly mutual.

"You're a sadist," Frankie groaned.

"I'm starting to think so, too," I agreed.

"I'm going to go shower then and take care of this." He vaguely gestured to his dick, creasing a line in the fabric of his pants as he stood. "I'll leave the door unlocked for you, O."

"Don't flatter yourself!"

I WAS HUNGOVER AND sticky in all places a person shouldn't, and wouldn't, ever *want* to be. I ached for a toothbrush and some hot water to wash away the night before. There was glitter stuck to my fingers when I rubbed my face, which could only mean there was glitter in several other unappetizing areas of my body that would take the remainder of the trip to remove. And now that I was *very much awake*—thanks to Frankie and the visions of what he was currently doing in his shower—I needed some fresh air at the very least.

I stumbled across the house on my tiptoes. Now lighter than at midnight, it was easier to familiarize myself with the rooms. The floorplan was open, with lots of closets for storage and neutral gray and beige paints with white trim. Simple, but well maintained. A laundry room with *several* types of detergent—impressive, and also unheard of. Shoe rack, durable end tables, a few framed photos on the mantle of the gas fireplace.

I picked up one that I recognized. A group of men, arms and beers slung over each other's shoulders, Frankie on one end next to the man I now knew as Mateo. Two others were on his right—dirty blonds, with a brotherly resemblance.

"I knew it." I laughed to myself at the glossy photo I'd seen on his dating profile.

There wasn't much down the hallway. Closed doors that I surmised were more storage closets. Further down there was another wider one I knew was Mateo and Nat's. Then Frankie's bedroom, and the bathroom next door where I could hear the soft stream of a shower head running.

In the living room a sliding glass door opened to a lush, green backyard, and I slipped out into the thick Floridian air.

It had to have been mid-morning, but my phone was dead and still stuffed between the couch cushions inside so I couldn't check. I hovered a hand over my eyes like a shade; the sun was high and bright enough to burn my poor, overused retinas on impact. It was already too warm for Frankie's sweater and socks I had on, even for December, and I had to laugh thinking about the people back home at that moment in Pine Ridge slogging through two feet of snow. It was like I was on a completely different planet, never mind just in a different state.

I took the socks off, walking around on the warm pavers that provided a significant patio space in the backyard. There was a stainless-steel grill to one end, right next to a beautiful six-seat wooden dining table with comfy cushioned chairs that I gave a squeeze as I walked by. Opposite that, a big, covered hot tub sat under an oversized turquoise blue hanging umbrella. The rest of the fenced-in backyard was landscaped in grass, so short and manicured it looked like it was rolled straight off a golfing green, and then a large shed in the far corner.

"Giving yourself a tour?"

I didn't hear the sliding glass close behind me, but Frankie was standing quietly outside holding two hot mugs of coffee. He was fresh out of the shower in board shorts and *no* shirt, the curling ends of his hair damp and dripping at the nape of his neck. His skin was beautifully tan. A soft trail of hair swirled his belly button and disappeared beneath the peak of his boxers that made my throat feel like a desert floor.

"It's really nice," I complimented, taking the second mug from him as he came closer. "Not bad for two men, I gotta give it to you. You even have a hot tub."

"We like nice things, too. It's not an inherently feminine trait."

"What do you do for work?"

"Cybersecurity."

My eyebrows knitted together. "Cybersecurity? Seriously?"

"It's actually Cap's gig; he runs it right from home most days. Installing secure access software for larger companies in the area, monitoring the activity across all their channels looking for threats. I'm just his donkey."

"Fitting."

"I set myself up for that one."

"You did." I smirked.

Frankie snorted and took a sip of his coffee. "Uncle Sam paid for college so we did everything online when we got out. Honestly, it's nothing spectacular, but most people are technologically illiterate and think Cap's some kind of computer hacking, dark web surfer."

"So then why were you looking for jobs in Colorado?"

"I make out well doing this, but it's not *mine*. You know? It's Mateo's. Sitting behind a computer all day isn't what I envisioned myself doing. I'm good at flying, and I miss it."

"I get it." I gave him a soft smile. "I couldn't imagine doing anything but teaching. Seeing the passion in those kids and knowing I'm making a positive impact is worth every late night grading the same multiplication table over and over again."

"I wish I had teachers that looked like you in school."

I shoved him with my shoulder. "We were having an adult conversation for once and you had to go ruin it."

Frankie took another sip of his coffee and scanned my body. "There's a lot of things I want to do with you, O. Having adult conversations isn't exactly on the top of the list."

He was unabashedly checking me out, from the unruly frizz of hair to my bare legs poking out of his borrowed boxer shorts. Suddenly, I felt self-conscious despite knowing he clearly found me attractive.

"What?" I asked.

"You look really good all disheveled in my clothes."

"God, what happened to, '*I felt myself getting too selfish*' from last night?"

"I took a shower and changed my mind."

I tilted my head, challenging him and taking a few steps closer. "Well, I didn't."

He smelled so infuriatingly good up close, clean like his soap, and I could count the freckles on his perfectly smooth chest. His skin practically begged for my fingers.

I liked Frankie.

It was hard to admit to myself, but I knew if the circumstances were different, and he'd done a little more groveling, I wouldn't be fighting it at all. It was extremely entertaining to take him down a few pegs, though.

Over Frankie's shoulder there was movement in the backyard next door. An older man was watering a crop of tomato plants and stealing glances at the two of us out of the corner of his eye. I waved tentatively, causing Frankie to turn and look as well.

"Shit." He sighed under his breath. "Come here."

"Huh?"

"Come here," Frankie whispered more aggressively at me, pulling me closer and wrapping a forearm around my lower waist. He dialed on a smile and waved over the fence at the graying man. "How are you this morning, Mr. Barry?"

"Oh, just fine Francesco," the man shouted back in an accent I couldn't place.

Frankie squeezed me harder, until I was tripping over my feet and steadying myself with a palm on his stomach. "What are you *doing*?" I complained.

"All right, you have a great day! Tomatoes look fantastic!" he yelled over me, and then steered the both of us back in the direction of the sliding glass door.

"What was that about?"

"Let's just say our neighbor thinks Cap and I are more than buddies. You're a good decoy. Gino's probably already on the phone with the rest of the geezers from clubhouse bingo telling them about the ten in my backyard."

"So, you owe me one."

"What's that saying? You touch my dick, I'll touch—"

"What is it with you and dicks?" I laughed. "Gino might be onto something."

NAT AND MATEO WERE sitting at the kitchen table nursing their own coffees when we got back inside.

"Good morning, good morning," Mateo said cheerily, glancing at me and then tilting his head at his roommate as Frankie took the seat next to him.

Nat pulled me down to her eye-level by my baggy sweatshirt sleeve. "Did you..." she whispered.

"No!" I swatted her hand away. "I did not, thank God."

Natalia smirked at her boyfriend, who was watching our exchange closely, and then put her hand out toward him, palm up.

"*Fuck me.*" Mateo sighed, pulling a leather wallet out of the back pocket of his shorts and sifting through it to slap a crisp fifty-dollar bill in his girlfriend's hand.

"HA!" Nat snapped the bill tauntingly.

"Woah, hey now," Frankie interjected. "What the fuck, guys?"

I gaped at my friend. "Did you make bets on us sleeping together?"

"I knew you wouldn't," Nat boasted. "I know my best friend."

"I know *my* best friend," Mateo added. "Pike, I was rooting for you."

"Not exactly up to me." Frankie scratched the back of his neck. "Where'd you two run off to just now?"

"I was giving myself a tour of the house," I said to Mateo. "The place is gorgeous, but it's seriously lacking in Christmas decor. It's the middle of December! Where's the tree?"

"We haven't taken it out yet." Mateo motioned toward the hallway.

"Taken it out?" I gasped. "What do you mean?"

"Oh, no." Nat sighed at her boyfriend. "You got her started now."

"I mean—it's in a box. In the closet."

Frankie hopped off the stool he was sitting on and padded the few feet down the hallway to a storage closet, reaching inside and pulling out a rectangular box that couldn't have been three feet tall—then a smaller plastic container filled with ornaments.

"Where's the rest of it?"

"What do you mean?" Frankie flipped the larger box upside down and shook it. A lame little tree fell anticlimactically to the floor in a heap of plastic pine needles.

"You're kidding? *That* is not a Christmas tree. That's a decoration at most."

"We put it in the window."

My jaw hit the floor. Florida would freeze over before I spent Christmas without a real, bark and needle tree. There were some things I was willing to compromise on, and this was sure as hell not one of them.

"Okay, I've heard enough." I stood. "I'm declaring Operation Christmas on this residence. First order of business is the tree farm."

Mateo and Frankie both snorted, sharing a glance at each other and then back at me. Even Natalia hid a beguiled smile behind pressed lips.

"Why is this so funny to you three?"

"Phee." Nat put her hand on my shoulder. "You're in Southern Florida. There's no such thing as a tree farm."

"But hey," Frankie intervened. "We can go to a tree *lot*, okay? There's plenty of already cut ones to choose from."

"We have a tree already," Mateo argued.

"*Cap.*" Frankie's eye twitched at his friend. "Don't be a scrooge. Maybe O is right. We could use a little holiday *sprucing.*" He nudged me with a shoulder and winked at the pun.

Natalia and Mateo groaned as I high-fived Frankie. I could afford him one geeky tree pun if he was the only one on my side. I wasn't sure he was *on my side*, so much as he was trying to get in my pants—but he was on a mission for the latter anyway, and I could use his sway with this.

"So, yes?" I steepled my fingers together and stuck out my bottom lip.

The three of them shared a few hesitant looks before Frankie tilted his head and shrugged at his best friend.

"Fuck, fine." Mateo sighed, pinching the bridge of his nose between two fingers. "Get in the car."

8

Ophelia

THERE WAS A TEN-MINUTE ride across Coconut Creek with Nat and I tucked into the backseat of Mateo's truck while the boys argued over the height of their living room ceiling from the front.

If it were up to Frankie, I would have gone gallivanting in his clothes all day, completely unshowered, but even Mateo had the mind to make a pitstop for us back at the apartment.

I hadn't exactly had a chance to settle in the night before—going from the airport, to dinner, and then chaotically unpacking every item of clothing from my luggage while playing mix 'n match with Natalia's closet. The guest room had turned from pleasantly primped and welcoming to "department store on Black Friday" in a matter of minutes, and my pre-game brain never slowed down long enough to fix it. It was a sight for already sore eyes as I dashed in and out of the room with no time to clean despite the way I itched to organize.

My shower was much quicker than I preferred given the company lurking around, and I couldn't exactly leave the bathroom nude like I would have if it were just Nat and me. So, I skipped across the hallway into my bedroom wearing Frankie's clothes again with my hair wrapped in a towel.

"It looks like a bomb went off in here."

"Jesus *Christ*," I gasped with a hand over my chest. I turned to find Frankie lying on the bed with his hands under his head, surrounded by the disarray of my belongings and half-opened suitcase.

"I appreciate the sentiment, beautiful. But you can just call me Frankie."

"Get out." I pointed a finger toward the door.

"You know, there are perfectly good drawers for all of this?" He began rooting around in the pile next to him until something caught his eye.

"Yeah, well I didn't exactly expect to have a man in my bed this morning."

"Surprise," he replied, half to me and half to the lacy red pair of panties he lifted off the bed and dangled from his fingers. "Wear these for me?"

"Get fucked."

"I'm trying."

I grunted and flipped the towel off my head, ignoring him and the twinge in my lower stomach. I sorted around the floor and the mattress for shorts, a tee, and the light zip-up sweater I'd worn on the plane—actively ignoring my pair of panties and how tiny and...*shreddable* they looked in Frankie's hands.

"Fine, I'll just imagine it for myself." He stretched the cherry red elastic from ear to ear over his face, the crotch lying perfectly over his sharp nose.

"*Give* me those," I scolded him, hopping onto the bed to snatch them away. Frankie chuckled when I finally wrestled them out of his grasp. "Don't you have anywhere else to be besides up my ass?"

He quirked an eyebrow.

"Don't *fucking* say anything," I rebuked, kicking myself.

"We'll call it even, then." He smirked. "And no, Cap and Tally are summoning spirits so I figured I'd take a page out of your book and give myself a tour."

"Go and tour the kitchen."

"Sure. Right after I get my clothes back."

I looked down at the outfit I was wearing over my freshly showered body. I might have tried to steal the sweater all together in true one-night-stand fashion if I thought I'd never see him again. It fit like an oversized glove.

"Right now?"

"Take 'em off."

"I'm not wearing anything under it."

"I'll close my eyes."

"Oh, okay, in that case..." I shoved an arm up the inside of the sweater, letting my hand disappear. Frankie sat up off the pillows in anticipation as I brought the same hand back out a few seconds later sporting a middle finger.

"You're a cold woman." He frowned, standing from the bed and walking toward the door. "I think you're enjoying this as much as me, though."

"Out." I crossed my arms over my chest when he got close enough that we were sharing air.

"I'll take that as a yes." Frankie said, then snagged the red panties out of my hand, tucking them into the pocket of his shorts before walking out the door.

"WHAT ARE WE EVEN looking for?" Mateo lifted his sunglasses off his face, squinting at the rows of trees lined up under string lights in the supermarket parking lot.

The makeshift tree lot left much to be desired. It was run by a dirty looking man living in a trailer parked along the fence, still donning a fanny pack around his waist and a mullet unironically from the eighties and sucking on a wooden toothpick.

"Whatever one speaks to you," I told Mateo as the group of us walked alongside the first row of fluffy Fraser firs.

He snorted. "Honey, I don't know much about the verbal communication of trees in Colorado, but in Florida they don't whisper sweet nothings."

"Don't be a scrooge, Mateo." Nat came to my rescue, running her fingers across the needles of a tree. Frankie followed behind at my heels as I sized up a shorter, thicker one.

In all the winters growing up, the one thing I always looked forward to was picking out a tree. Mom, Dad, and I would squeeze together in the bench seat of the old Ford pickup and hold on for dear life as it rattled down the road toward Quail Creek Ranch. My father insisted the best trees were the furthest up the hill, so far that no one in their right minds would ever want to haul a tree that distance, but Mom and I would laugh and hook arms, following anyways and giving the thumbs-up when he finally declared he'd found the "best looking Christmas tree in all of Colorado". Neither of us had the heart to tell him we'd passed twenty trees that looked exactly the same on the hike, but that was part of the tradition. One I held onto for as many years as I could before the magic ran out.

"What about this one?" Frankie suggested, standing a tree up on its stump and giving it a twirl so everyone could see.

"It's too tall," Mateo pointed out.

"You're just short." Frankie put his elbow on his best friend's head like an armrest and got a playful punch to the ribs.

"I think it's beautiful, Francesco," Nat told him, sticking her tongue out at Mateo.

"What do you think, O?" Frankie only cared for my approval as I walked a circle around the fir and eyed it up and down. The branches were healthy and thick, no gaping holes where pine needles should have been. I was sure the ornaments back at the house were few and far between, but what little the boys did have would fit nicely.

"I like it," I admitted, giving him an impressed nod of approval.

"As good as they come back home?"

I patted him on the shoulder. "Now you're pushing it."

We stood back a few feet as Frankie bent at the knees and hoisted the tree and all its bristles to rest over his shoulder. The movement pulled his T-shirt up his torso and gave me a *damning* view of the lower half of his stomach and that teasing V of muscle below his belly button again.

He and Mateo started toward the sketchy tree park owner down the lane who was watching Frankie's show of strength with a little too much excitement.

"Put your tongue back in your mouth," Nat whispered.

I clamped my mouth closed.

"I need another drink, I think. The sun is getting to me."

"Sure, Phee. And Frankie hasn't been following you around like a puppy since you woke up this morning."

"He's pestering."

"You're loving it."

I rolled my eyes. "He told me he unmatched me because he was *too* into me. That's a cop-out, isn't it? It's a line to save his ass. I can't just *give in*; he's gotta earn it."

"Maybe. He might be serious. I've known Frankie for a while now, and he's not really the type to hit it and quit it."

"He obviously is if he was trying to get lucky in Colorado Springs on a stayover."

The two of us steered toward the front doors of the store and waited outside while the boys loaded the Christmas tree into the bed of Mateo's truck.

"He's in his mid-thirties. He's basically the other woman at his own house."

I giggled. "That's funny, he thinks the same about you."

"What?"

"Nothing—and besides the point. He could have been honest and just said I wasn't what he was looking for, and I would have told him it's fine."

"And then you both would have been lying." Natalia eyed me knowingly. "What's the worst thing that could happen? You spend your holiday vacation getting eaten out by an attractive older guy who lends you his socks and makes you coffee in the morning?"

"So—what?" I threw my hands out. "The four of us just shack up with our Christmas tree and our festive decorations and hot cocoa until New Year's and fuck like rabbits? Pretend I don't have a career and a life in Colorado that my round-trip ticket is waiting to bring me back to like we're in some big orgy snow globe?"

"I heard orgy snow globe?" Mateo chimed, tucking the car keys Frankie had just tossed to him into his pocket.

"They sell those in Walmart?" Frankie added.

"You're all on the naughty list," I scoffed, leaving them to catch up as I stalked inside.

9

Frankie

ALLOWING OPHELIA TO ROAM freely in the holiday section of a store was sort of like letting a kid have free reign in a candy shop. Anything that sparkled or sang caught her attention and ended up in the cart that I pushed along beside her, and I instantly regretted that I'd said to "go crazy" after she added a pair of novelty Christmas dish towels that read *Making Spirits Bright* with whiskey glasses embroidered beneath it.

"Dish towels?" I protested. "Who needs decorative dish towels? I can't even wipe my hands on them."

"It's about the ambiance," Ophelia explained, eyeing the next shelf over full of coffee mugs. "Where did the other two go?"

"Not sure." I played with the bells on a stocking as she chucked it, and three others, over my shoulder into the basket. "Something about needing rope and batteries, I think?"

"Oh yes, we're definitely going to need batteries."

I cruised along quietly, watching her and that tempting little tongue she flicked out when she was focused. Following her around a store felt entirely too domestic and comfortable for the reality of the situation. Anyone walking by would think Ophelia and I were together, holiday shopping for our home, running errands on a lazy Saturday. I secretly reveled in that idea, might have even played into it—reaching over her to grab something on a higher shelf, steering the edge of the cart with her, staring down any wandering eyes in her direction.

If she was thinking the same thing she didn't show it. Zoning in on the task at hand, which was apparently turning our house into Santa's fucking workshop while I made commentary hoping she might laugh. I enjoyed that girlish little sound so much I thought it should be bottled and sold. While O might still have been mad at me over the night before, I was creeping under her skin. Warming her slowly.

And despite Mateo's initial disapproval, he'd made bets on us falling into bed together, and I wasn't a man who didn't follow through.

Ophelia added a set of seasonal buffalo plaid throw pillows to the haul with a matching blanket, a multi-use garland, red and gold ribbon in various patterns and sizes, and two boxes of candy canes. When I finally thought she was done, the woman arrived at the wall of string lights and compared a few before sweeping an entire shelf full into the cart with her forearm.

"Woah! What's with all the lights? I'm no expert, but a box or two of those should do the trick for one tree."

"You need lights for the *tree*, and then you need lights for the *house*," she explained as another outdoor decoration nearby grabbed her attention and got added to the growing pile.

"The house?" I complained. "I have a bad back."

"Aw, old man has no mobility?" She teased me with a pouty lip and a rub between my shoulders. "That's okay. Mateo seems *very* nimble."

I scoffed and threw an extra box of lights in the cart. If my physical therapist knew I was offering to climb ladders he'd put me on the bad kind of stretcher, but I was always more competitive than cautious. "Oh I'm plenty nimble, sweetheart. You're trying to instigate me into climbing a ladder so you can check out my ass all day."

"What ass?"

Something inside me twitched. *This fucking girl.*

Right when I felt ten steps ahead of her in whatever game we were playing, she always knew how to give it right back. I let out a menacing laugh. "You're asking for it, Trouble."

She tried to hide her smirk. "I would love to continue talking about this, but I need to go sniff every candle in aisle eight."

"We don't need any candles," I argued. "I can tell that you like the smell of me just fine by the way I caught you sniffing my blanket like blow last night."

Ophelia left me behind with the cart as she pranced away. "Now I know you're hearing *and* seeing things!"

IT SHOULDN'T HAVE TAKEN as many hours as it did to decorate the house. The smaller stuff was easy; Ophelia and Tally had the living room and bathroom done up to the nines with ornamental snowmen and festive hand soaps before Mateo and I even got the tree over the threshold.

Of course he complained the entire time about the mess the needles were making as we shoved the branches through the front door jamb. I was the only one keeping my cool until I tripped over the coffee table attempting to maneuver the damn thing to the perfect spot under the girls' opposing directions. I might have toned it down over the past few years, but I could still let a string of colorful words fly like you've never heard before.

It turned out that Mateo was right, which he flaunted, and the tree was just a *tad* too tall for the ceiling. That set in motion a much longer chain of events, including finding a suitable hand-saw, *which we didn't own*, to hack off the tip of the tree after I tried and failed to strong man the stump with my bare hands.

Mr. Barry came in clutch, lending his own to Cap over the back-yard fence and also offering us a word of advice about keeping a live tree healthy and how often we should water it. I thought a tree was more of a decoration and less of a fucking hassle. Like a spiky green toddler that Mateo informed me, I, alone, would be feeding and cleaning up after, because it wasn't his brilliant idea.

When all was said and done, we still hadn't cut enough off the top of the fir to more than *clear* the ceiling by an inch, thus leaving absolutely no room for the expensive star Ophelia had picked out to top it. She stood there for a moment, tapping her chin before she climbed on the arm of the couch, stretching those long, tan legs, and improvising by tying the sparkler to the point with tinsel.

Thankfully we *did* own a staple gun. And a few long orange extension cords that came in handy as I reluctantly climbed a ladder to the tallest point of the house while Mateo coached me across the gutters from below.

The women made a show of pulling a couple lawn chairs out of the garage and setting up camp in the driveway, watching the shitshow unfold. Me, sweating like a greased pig and focusing on not putting a staple through my fingers, and Mateo, getting more frustrated by the minute trying to un-fuck the tangled lights and feed them up to me.

By some godly entity they were in place by the time the day-light decided to start creeping below the horizon—leaving just enough time for Ophelia to add some finishing touches while Cap and I sulked inside to clean up for dinner.

———

"WE'RE THE ONLY HOUSE on the block with this many lights up. We're running more electricity than the casino," Mateo mused around a slice of pizza as he ate it over the box.

"But it looks amazing," Tally complimented. "It's so homey and warm in here now. Doesn't it make you so much more excited for Christmas?"

Music played idly and a cranberry-orange candle burned in the middle of the coffee table.

It did look amazing.

Our house was nice on its own, but with these classy touches of festive decor it really felt like a place where we could relax and enjoy the season. The sun had long set on the day, and from outside, the hue of bright lights poured in through the windows and circled the wreath on the door.

"Let's see how the lights look in the dark," Ophelia suggested. "I have a surprise for you guys."

Tally pulled Mateo by his arm out the front door while Cap's grumbling voice complained the entire way. I hung out in the little arch between the kitchen and the foyer waiting for Ophelia to dry the last of the sink water from her hands on the *usable* kitchen towels before she joined me.

"The house looks great, O."

Her cheeks flushed. She had to know it looked good, because I wasn't being facetious at all. I'd genuinely forgotten the magic of the holidays until that very moment, staring out at my candle-lit living room under the golden blanket of light. It wasn't like Mateo and I didn't celebrate, but we weren't the types to decorate on our own. Up until a few years ago most of our Christmases were spent on a deployment somewhere, and it had always been secondary on account of it. But this... This was nice.

"Thank you." She smiled up at me. Her eyes were crystal blue, but that close I found yellow in them. Sunshine in the sky.

There was a singular part of me that knew I was fucked at that very moment. Comparing a woman's eyes to the goddamn sky. Most of me, though, was in complete denial. All I knew was that I wanted to kiss her. Which was a very normal, healthy, biological reaction to a beautiful girl looking up at you like an innocent little doe. Wasn't it?

Fuck, I was going to kiss her.

I had to know if I was reading things wrong.

Just a kiss. If she rejected me, then that was that. We could have a very friendly, PG Christmas, and I could move on to the next dead-end dating app that Mateo found to haggle me about.

It was like the fat man himself was rooting for me when I glanced up and to find a mistletoe hanging from the archway. Surely Ophelia didn't intentionally meet me underneath it.

"How'd that get there?" I pointed toward the hanging leaves.

Her attention flitted upward, eyes narrowing. Another creeping flood of blush pinkened her fair skin, but she didn't react negatively. In fact, that bright gaze drifted down to my mouth after a moment before leveling with me again. I still saw the ample curiosity in it, no matter how fleeting the moment.

I wanted to know exactly what Ophelia tasted like so badly, it almost fucking hurt. Was she tender? Would she wind her arms around my neck, or hold my face? Would she tease with her tongue or leave the pace up to me? I wanted to know these things the same way I wanted to know why, despite all, I was harboring this grade-school crush on a woman so inconveniently unavailable to me.

"You're always up to something," she murmured.

That mistletoe had nothing to do with me, but I'd let her believe it. "And you're always just out of my reach." She darted her eyes away. Self-conscious, embarrassed, nervous—who cared. I wanted her to look at me again, and I didn't want to wait. "Ophelia."

The second her chin lifted I leaned down and cut whatever string of words she was about to say in half with a sweet press of my lips to hers. It blindsided her. Our eyes were slow to shut, but when they did, the rest of her opened up. It was like the warm buzz of a first sip of whiskey, the kind that tempted you into drinking a whole lot more. Her body pressed to mine. My hand tangled in her hair. With little coaxing, Ophelia tilted her head to better reach me, dragging a curious palm up my neck that settled on my jaw as she slid her tongue against the seam of my lips, asking to be let in.

Gotcha, baby.

I was on the verge of giving her exactly what she was asking for. I'd have gladly swept that sweet ass right up and made a night out of getting her naked down the hallway behind closed doors. But that was too much, too fast, and this was just testing the waters. I wanted her, but I wanted her to want *me* more. If not because that kind of shit made me hot—because then I wasn't the only one in danger of getting too involved. As selfish as it was.

Instead I pulled away, eyes remaining closed for a prolonged second with our foreheads connected. "*Easy.*" I smirked. "Don't let me catch you slipping, O. Wouldn't want me getting any ideas now."

She hummed in response, recognizing she'd let those ice-cold walls down at my first touch, but hardly caring in the moment. "Definitely not."

"Let's get outside, Trouble." I pulled her along behind me and whisked us out the door.

"All right, what's this big surprise?" Mateo asked impatiently as we congregated in the driveway. I stood skeptically beside my roommate and his girlfriend, analyzing O's expressions under the glowing Christmas lights.

A breeze had blown in when the sun disappeared and everyone but her was wearing a sweatshirt, as if it weren't seventy degrees. Ophelia and I were different in that very trivial way. I felt things too hot, she was used to the unending cold.

"I figured since we're doing things a little bit differently this year, and you guys graciously opened your home to me to decorate all day long, I'd also add a little bit of a tropical feel to match the weather."

"The house is surrounded by palm trees," Mateo pointed out.

"Technicality." She waved it off. "Anyways, without further ado..." Bending down to the extension cord on the ground, Ophelia plugged a smaller wire in her hand into the butt end of it, sending a low thrumming spark through the cable.

I winced on impact. "Oh, *fuck*."

Above the garage, a neon yellow and green pineapple glowed to life where she'd anchored it secretly. It was ten times brighter than the rest of the colorful Christmas lights Cap and I had spent all afternoon hanging, and Tally snorted out a laugh as her boyfriend looked on horrified.

"Phee, I don't think you understand." Tally tugged her lip between her teeth.

"That's great." Mateo threw his hands up. "Now the neighbors think we're swingers, too."

10

Ophelia

It HAD BEEN TWO days since Frankie kissed me.

Nat and I decided on a recovery day after the first few in Florida felt more like a never-ending hangover than a relaxing vacation.

We were both young and shapely, sure, but somewhere along the way we'd also stopped being able to do three rounds of shots without suffering the consequences for up to forty-eight hours following.

Thank God for the highs and lows of Floridian weather, because for the vast majority of the following day it rained like a typhoon was passing through, so both of us were content to drink coconut water in the apartment while we reorganized the Renaissance painting that was the guest bedroom.

Regardless of the distance though, I couldn't spend more than half an hour without wondering what the man from under the mistletoe was doing or when I would inevitably be graced with his cocksure presence again.

Nat slipped away a few times to talk on the phone or close herself into her bedroom where I could still hear the breathy giggles of flirtation filtering through the thin wood. She and Mateo were so whipped over one another it made me grin just as much as it made me cringe.

I wanted something like they had. The inability to leave another person alone due to sheer adoration. I wanted to wake up to a text from a guy that turned over on his pillow in the morning and the first thing he thought of was me. Go grocery shopping together for no other reason than spending time in the same space. Have a little drawer in a dresser to put some of my socks and panties and a few extra shirts even though we both knew I'd just be wearing his anyway.

Every boyfriend in my life had been a crisis of convenience at best. Someone to accompany me at parties in college, a few months with a coworker to suppress my mother breathing down my throat. A blue-collar guy that brought me to his family's Sunday dinner—who turned out to also be seeing three other girls on different nights of the week.

I dated a school district administrator, a bartender, a fucking juggler. I figured out the younger they were, the more I was wasting my time, so I started shooting higher. Then I ended up dating married men that conveniently forgot to mention it.

At that point, I'd exhausted every option in Pine Ridge—and wasn't holding out on finding a forever kind of love anywhere in the city either. But what I really *didn't* expect was the hopeful buzz of whatever the fuck Frankie Casado had been injecting me with over the past four whirlwind days.

DOLED IN TANNING OIL and the stringiest suits we could find to take advantage of the sun and sand, Nat and I made the drive out to Hollywood Beach.

For mid-December it was unseasonably warm. The beach was littered with families crashing along the shore with each wave, groups of people throwing Frisbee and bumping volleyballs to one another. There were pinwheels of blue umbrellas and nautical chairs dotted asymmetrically down the sand, and the heat of the day beat down so hard on the landscape that the skin under our feet burned with each step to an open plot.

We laid out on towels next to one another, listening to the tiny speaker Nat had packed and sipping vodka lemonade behind the discretion of our travel mugs. There may not have been many rules in Florida but apparently open containers were where lawmakers drew the line.

"That's it, I'm spending every December for the rest of time in Florida," I said as I flipped over onto my back. "A white Christmas is so overrated."

Nat giggled, clinking the metallic edge of her cup against mine. "The invitation is indefinite. I say you stay forever, actually."

"I wish." My mind wandered to what my classroom of kids back home might be doing. It was hard to leave them just as the semester was ending, but I was seriously enjoying the break. "How can you take so much time off work?" I asked. "The bank doesn't mind?"

"What?"

"The bank doesn't care that you're taking a vacation?"

Natalia's confused eyebrow evened out under the thick frame of her sunglasses. "Oh, right. No, I basically make my own hours. I'm at the top of every performance report."

"Huh," I mused. "I don't remember you ever being that great at math in college." I closed my eyes and nestled my shoulders into the sand, digging my heels into two little divots for support.

"Sometimes it pays to step outside your comfort zone," Nat suggested. "You never know what you might be missing."

"Okay, I know we're not talking about you being an accountant anymore, Natalia."

"Would it really be so bad to let him in? You fucking kissed him already. You invited the need."

"Put the phone down, Patti Stanger." She'd been attached to her cellphone for the better part of two hours at the beach. "If you and Mateo are plotting some 90-Day Fiancé bullshit via text, I'm putting my foot down right now. Yes, okay, he's hot," I admitted. "Yes, there's some sexual attraction there. That isn't *unordinary* by the way. There's like twelve guys within eyeshot right now that I'd let Baywatch me in the lifeguard tower."

"Stop pop-culture-splaining me," Natalia groaned.

"All I'm saying is that hooking up with my best friend's boyfriend's best friend is an inevitable disaster waiting to happen. I'm not interested in long distance, and do you understand how awkward that'll be when we're forced to plan a Jack and Jill for your wedding?"

"I have three sisters."

"And we both know group sex in a college baseball house outranks blood by a considerable margin."

"Channel your inner sorority girl," Natalia declared. "Twenty-year-old you would have already smashed and dashed him. The only difference now is that you're both *adults*. Casual sex is like grocery shopping—sometimes you take the indulgent cookies off the end cap even when you know you shouldn't."

"Are you trying to say men are marketing ploys? Because I agree. They're functional art at best. We have evolved past the need for penis."

"No. I'm reminding you that you don't have to clear your life schedule to sneak a little dick into your Christmas vacation."

"Jesus forgive us."

"And neither you or Frankie have any expectations past getting piss drunk with your friends on New Year's. He's trying to get back out there, you've been trying too hard to find a husband. You both need to relax."

I sighed, snuggling back into the sand and looking into the blinding sun. Something inside me welcomed the idea of a time capsule relationship with the retired pilot. A funny, you had to be there type of nonchalance for the future if Nat and Mateo happened to stick it out for the long run.

She was partially right; there was no contract to be signed where Frankie and I were concerned. No fine print defining what each of us would have to give and take. And wasn't that the whole reason for my spontaneous deviation to Florida? Doing something outside the realm of expectation?

I was *expected* to spend my holiday in Colorado. I was *expected* to celebrate Christmas day split between two households pretending like I wasn't more like an estranged aunt than a doting older sister. I was *expected* to keep doing the balancing act of obligation and honesty to appease the people in my life, even if it meant putting myself dead fucking last.

Flying to Coconut Creek for three weeks was finally breaking the chain tethering me to the expectations.

"Can't I just enjoy some much-needed relaxation on a beautiful beach with my best friend?" I closed my eyes and shifted again on the towel. "Is that too much to ask for?"

On cue the sun fell into shade and the hot breath of the day was wiped away by a sea breeze. "Apparently so," I huffed.

I sprung to my elbows intent on using the lull to mix another drink from the liquor stash, and instead damn near caught a knee to the forehead. Straining to look up, I found the epitome of a beach babe eclipsing my sunshine and staring down at me on the towel.

"That bikini belongs in the Louvre, O." Frankie whistled.

I shot a look at Natalia, who shrugged as Mateo dropped a backpack in the sand and leaned down to kiss her.

"You're like a fucking caricature." I poked Frankie's ribs as he fluffed out an oversized towel next to me and sat. The few buttons on the shirt he'd managed to clasp came undone effortlessly with a tug of his fingers.

"Whose idea was this?" Mateo complained as he unpacked a hat, a bottle of sunscreen, and two flasks from his bag, tossing one to Frankie. "We have a perfectly good beach five minutes from the house."

"The shopping is better here," Nat replied, sounding bored. "Frankie probably drove anyway. Didn't you, Frankie?"

"I love this beach." He nodded, his eyes laser focused on my chest in the stringy red top. I pushed his jaw away playfully.

"I want it to be known that I had no idea the two of you were playing tagalong today. *Natalia and I,*" I said pointedly, "thought we'd get some sun and some dinner, do a little Christmas shopping, and then see the tree lighting on the boardwalk tonight."

Mateo grimaced before taking a sip from the flask of what I could only assume was Everclear based on his reaction, and coughed it back up.

Next to me Frankie got comfortable and tugged his hat lower over his forehead. Even after several shirtless run-ins, I still couldn't keep my throat from drying over the flex of his triceps or the broad stretch of his golden brown shoulders in the hard sunlight.

Nat stood up to cover Mateo's hard-to-reach places in sunscreen, her petite frame complimenting his thicker build and defined lines like lock and key. Mateo wasn't a tall man but he made up for it in looks and allure, and next to Nat, you wouldn't even blink.

"Still mad at me?" Frankie asked, his honey gaze piercing me. "The unmatch thing is so last weekend."

"I'm not mad, I was annoyed. There's a difference."

"I apologized. I sold myself out."

"Right. Selfish man with his heart on his sleeve."

"I meant what I said." Frankie shrugged. "I wouldn't have said it if I didn't."

"You didn't even think I would remember it at the time."

Nat and Mateo sauntered past hand in hand and Cap dropped the Banana Boat in Frankie's lap. "Going for a swim. Coming?"

"Catch up in a few," Frankie told him, popping the top open and squeezing a glob into his palm as they walked away. He massaged the lotion into his arms and neck, then down the planes of his chest. I watched, mesmerized, until he started flailing like a fish to reach the place between his shoulders.

"Need some help?"

"If you're offering." He flashed me a sideways smile, squinting one eye closed to shield it from the sun.

I knelt behind him, taking the bottle as he handed it over his shoulder, then got to work lathering the lotion down his spine.

Frankie was all soft skin and lean muscle, perfectly placed beauty marks that I counted as I touched them. He was an attractive man, that was undeniable. Every unsheathed part of him only heightened my curiosity. And maybe his forward confidence might have looked bad on another person, but he plucked at every beguiled string of mine with practiced fingers. Never crossing a line he didn't first make sure I drew myself.

I was enjoying the flirtation a bit too much, if I was being honest. It felt good to feel *wanted*. Transparently. Too many times I'd entertained a guy that spoke to me in riddles. Unanswered messages, two a.m. texts, fire-emoji replies to my stories. Was that modern day chivalry? Frankie showed his hand the very second it was dealt—it was always my move.

"Any suitors answer the Bat-Signal?" I asked, referring to the neon pineapple stapled to the garage.

Frankie dipped his head and chuckled, the sweet sound of it twisting my lips into a grin. "Gino was out back grilling naked last night, now that you mention it."

"That old dog." I swiped my palms across his lower back, tripping the tips of my fingers across a faint scar above his waistband as I evened the sunscreen out. "There, all done."

Out past the surf break, Nat and Mateo were attached to each other and wading in the water. Just the sight made it clear that I would rather scrub sand out of my vulva than awkwardly tread next to them. I brushed my hands off on my thighs and then returned to lying stomach down on the towel next to Frankie's.

As if he'd had the same revelation, Frankie cleared his throat and turned to me. "Need a reapply?"

Handing him the sunscreen without even bothering to look up, I snorted. "You don't want to swim with the honeymooners either?"

"Fuck no."

WHEN THE SUN FINALLY fell below the blue line of the ocean Frankie and I had shared enough sips from his flask to be booked on public intoxication. We all showered off under the outdoor faucets, myself rubbing grains of beach from my cleavage and backside that Frankie so helpfully pointed out, before finding a spot for dinner on the boardwalk.

"So why are you called Pike?" I addressed the table but looked at Frankie as I dabbed melted butter off my lip with a napkin. He had one arm resting against the wooden deck railing and the other slung over the back of my seat.

He sucked his teeth and groaned, peering over at Mateo who sat up in his chair, a shit-eating grin on his face.

"Which version do you want?" Matty laughed.

"The truth."

"Because a pike is a long spear and he had the biggest dick in Delta."

"Mateo!" Nat swatted his chest, rattling something off under her breath that made Frankie wheeze into his elbow.

"Do you all just swap genital trading cards in the military?"

"It's the Army's Pokémon," Frankie cajoled.

After Nat had given him his earful, Mateo kissed her hairline and turned back to us. "The PG reason is that when Pike first joined our unit out in the Pacific, he was coming into an already tight-knit group of guys and needed the proper welcome."

"Assholes," Frankie mumbled, playing with his food. I could make out the touch of blush under the brim of his ball cap.

"So we took him out on an inaugural fishing trip," Mateo continued. "A rite of passage into Delta with the whole crew. Not even an hour in, this guy catches the biggest fucking Northern pike fish any of us had ever seen."

I looked over at Frankie, impressed, only to find him with his arms crossed and staring at his friend with his tongue in his cheek.

"I mean, we measured this thing and all, broke out the tape, had him hold it up for a few pictures, he was so excited." Mateo was all hand gestures and facial expressions when he talked. "I told him, this is a rare species. No one ever gets the catch on these out here because they're, like, basically a myth, right? I had a couple buddies on the Coast Guard and even radioed in for them to take a trip out and see it for themselves."

Frankie sighed beside me.

"How have I never heard this story before?" Nat chimed in.

"Frankie was holding that fucker up for them to see before the anchor even went down. We were all chanting, 'Pike! Pike! Pike!' behind him, making out like he was gonna be a local legend back at base."

"So?" I asked.

"It was all bullshit." Mateo's shoulders rattled as he unleashed a choked laugh into his fist. "We were busting his balls. Anyone who'd been out there longer than a week would have known the fish he caught was the most common spawning salmon in the South Pacific. A Northern pike wouldn't be found dead in Guam."

Natalia and I shared a gasp at Frankie's expense that quickly trickled into muffled giggling.

"Thank you for that." Frankie tipped his cap to his friend. "I felt very welcomed."

"Just some good-natured hazing." He winked. "But, we've called him Pike ever since."

Frankie lifted his hat and pushed his hair back with his fingers, laughing along at his own expense. As humiliating as the whole thing must have been, the relationship between Frankie and Mateo obviously weathered the highs and lows of what came with the military. I wasn't sure I'd ever seen two men so close without being siblings.

"Now tell them why everyone calls you Captain," Frankie suggested, sending a knowing smirk in his best friend's direction.

"Nah, now's not the time."

"I'd like to know!" I piped up, leaning back into my chair, right into the warmth of Frankie's forearm against the back of my neck. It felt nice. This whole dinner, the whole day—it felt *right*.

"Story time!" Nat clapped her hands together.

"It's because I call the shots, sweet girl."

"Get calling then, brother," Frankie agreed. "I'll do tequila, next round's on you."

AFTER DINNER, IT WAS still warm enough for just the cover-up dress I wore over my bathing suit, and the beach had long been cleared in exchange for the dinner and shopping crowd on the boardwalk. Store windows were decorated in faux snow and sparkling ornaments, and a soft hum of classic Christmas music filtered out of open doorways as people walked about the pavement dressed in festive reds and greens.

Nat tugged Mateo by his hand toward another boutique after browsing several stores with nothing to show for it, but Frankie's callused palm on my elbow pulled me back before I could follow them.

"Walk with me?"

I looked back at my friend and her boyfriend who hadn't all but stalled in the store's open doorway. Natalia was conniving, but it was because she loved me and wanted me to take a fucking breath and enjoy myself. I hadn't stopped pushing go since we graduated, and I didn't plan on it. Obviously to her, the best way for me to relax was spending some time alone with the man offering.

I raised my eyebrow at Frankie. "Why?"

"Because you want to."

With a petulant sigh that didn't at all mirror my actions I started walking. It was becoming harder and harder to play the mind game when Frankie was so obviously controlling the board between us. After that kiss, pretending I wasn't interested in him would only directly fuel his ego, because he could obviously call the bluff.

"There are a lot of Christmas gifts I'm expected to bring home and you're keeping me from getting them," I stressed. "Angry pre-teens will be looking for answers."

"They'll survive," he assured me. "They know you're busy."

Frankie led me off the well-lit boardwalk and back into the sand toward the water, the light breeze dancing through the hair sticking out from under his hat.

"I doubt it. I've been here four days and the last text I got from anyone was when I landed. Well, and Cindy my substitute who lost the fucking thumb drive with all my lesson plans on it. I had to log in to the school network from Nat's hardwired computer. Mateo has so many security walls on that thing that Snowden couldn't crack it."

"Fucking Cindy," he humored me.

"I'm old enough I shouldn't care, but it's still a reminder I'm no one's center of the world anymore. Not like a kid is supposed to be for their parents." I frowned. "I guess a phone works both ways, huh?"

Frankie worried his bottom lip with his teeth for a second as we walked. "I'll text you then," he decided. "I'll text you every day. You should have my number."

"Oh, should I?" I laughed. "I don't know how many more unsolicited dick pics I can handle."

"How many do you get?"

"That's none of your business."

"So...zero. Smooth way to admit you'd want mine though."

"I don't."

"Phone, please."

Hesitating briefly, I gave in and handed it over to him. The dim blue light illuminated his mischievous grin as he tapped away eagerly before handing it back.

I looked down at the screen. There was a text to my new contact labeled *Frankie <3*.

God damn, you know your way around a woman.

"Perfect." I snorted sarcastically. "And I was worried about a dick pic."

"Just keeping it for my records."

"Are you this forward with all the women you date?"

A smirk tugged at the corner of his lip. "I haven't *dated* anyone in ten years. I was with my ex for seven of them."

Ten years. He'd been out of the game longer than I'd been in it. Curiosity flagged me. His ex was with him through his years in the military, then. Mateo *definitely* knew her.

"That's a long time," I commented.

Frankie adjusted his hat on his head. "It was. And to answer your question with another question, are the guys you date *not* this forward with you?"

Obviously whatever had happened with his ex-girlfriend wasn't a topic Frankie loved revisiting. He was a confident exterior, but every now and again the cracks did show.

I shook my head. "I can hardly tell if the men I date actually even like me."

"You're making my stomach hurt, Ophelia," Frankie groaned. "I'm all about a woman exploring her sexuality, but please, *God*, please tell me you don't sleep with these fucking idiots."

"Not *all* of them," I admitted, wincing.

"What am I doing wrong?" Frankie joked. Then, more seriously said, "That makes me crazy. Hearing you're not getting what you deserve."

I was thankful for the veil of night at that moment. If I could, I would have made like a sand crab and buried myself in the ground to hide. Instead I stared down at my feet, wondering how I was going to keep my own promises. With Frankie, nothing felt disingenuous. He always said exactly what he was thinking and that made him all the more attractive.

"I guess you're forgiven," I mumbled.

He stopped in his tracks. "What was that?"

"Never mind," I decided, continuing a few steps until I felt the familiar hold of his fingers around my bicep.

"Not *never mind*." Frankie blinked down at me with a sweet grin. "Say it again."

"You're loving this, aren't you?"

"It's important to me."

In all the relationships I'd been in, I didn't think one man had ever told me my approval was important to them. Of course the first man that did was thousands of miles beyond my wildest reach, and an unbelievably bad idea. The latter reason was becoming less and less convincing by the minute.

"You're forgiven," I repeated.

"Good," he said. "Now I won't think about it before I kiss you again."

I paused in the sand, but Frankie continued on as if he'd just said the most normal thing in the world. Like my heart hadn't stuttered and my feet hadn't stumbled over one another before I built up the courage to follow.

"You coming, slowpoke?" He asked over his shoulder.

There was something so simultaneously comforting and terrifying about the ocean at night. The way I couldn't see ten feet in front of me but still knew exactly what lay ahead. The milky light of the moon was the only thing keeping us from being completely shrouded in darkness, and while I could still make out Frankie beside me, there wasn't another soul around to bear witness to us.

"I've never gone swimming in the ocean at night," I said, taking a few steps into the water.

"There are sharks in there." Frankie bristled next to me, apparently hoping I wasn't about to do what it looked like I was about to do.

"They're all sleeping." I laughed.

"No—nope, I don't think they are."

Throwing every caution to wind, I gave him a teasing wink and pulled the hem of my cover-up over my head, unveiling my bathing suit. The cool breeze sent a wake of goosebumps over my skin.

"What are you doing?"

Ignoring him, I tiptoed into the surf until the foam tickled my knees, and then sunk in even further, submerging the entire bottom half of my torso.

Frankie stood with his hands on his hips at the shore, worry wrinkling the gap in his brows that I could see all the way from Alaska. "C'mon, O," he complained. "Stop playing around."

"Join me, Francesco. The water's fine."

"I won't be doing that." He swiped his hat off his head and scratched nervously at his scalp. "I'll actually be standing here with the Hollywood Beach EMS on speed dial while you get your ass cheek ripped off by a great white."

I snorted, his unease enticing me to take it a leap further with the incentives. Giving the shoreline another quick onceover I hooked my thumbs into my bikini bottoms and shuffled the stringy material down my legs, bunching them into a ball then chucking them to land at his feet. "Better give them something good, then."

Frankie registered what was soaking on the ground in front of him in slow-motion. His eyes rounded and his pacing stopped. "Oh, you little cocktease," he groaned.

If there was anything more beautiful than the soon-gone look on Frankie Casado's face right then I'd yet to see it. Suddenly all I could think about was that sweet, heated kiss under the mistletoe and what I wouldn't give to taste it again.

"Me?" I pouted.

"You," he confirmed, unironically at the same time that I pulled the flimsy tie at the back of my neck loose and let my whole top fall.

Frankie's first instinct was to shoot a protective glance at the beach behind us to shield me from prying eyes. *Such a gentleman.* When he knew we were alone his eyes fluttered closed and I glanced down to appreciate the effect I had on him in his tightening swim trunks.

He turned his face to the stars and mumbled something incoherent to me over the crashing waves.

"Still waiting," I taunted, dipping down into the water.

Less than thrilled, Frankie tossed his hat and pulled his collar over his head, then tread warily into the dark water to join me with his head on a swivel as he reached my depth.

We circled one another timidly in the shallow, cool water. Frankie's gaze kept dipping down to my bare chest, where the tight tips of my nipples were becoming exposed every so often with the change in tide.

"Is this the type of show and tell where you pass it around the class, Ms. Brody?"

"It's more like the kind I leave on the table, if you want to come see for yourself."

"Hmm," he hummed, getting another searing look at my chest and then using his size to his advantage—catching my wrist in his hand in one calculated reach.

He pulled my body to his, arms winding around my lower back until my toes left the sand beneath the water and my entire upper half was pressed tight against his chest. His skin was warm, fever touched, and I could feel just how hard he was tucked into his waistband against my stomach.

"You should lose the shorts," I breathed. "It's only fair."

"I don't think you're the authority on playing fair right now."

Still he released me just long enough to slide his trunks off and throw them the impressive distance to shore.

"If my balls get stung by a jellyfish, you're pissing on them for the rest of the week."

"That's fucking disgusting." I laughed. "And it's not even true."

"Yeah it is." His hands trailed down my naked ribs mindlessly as I clasped my arms around his neck. The feeling of being held went straight to my center. "I got stung in Guam and Cap insisted on being the one who peed on it for days."

I pinched my lips together to stifle a grin, watching helplessly as Frankie went ghost white and pieced another one of his best friend's rouses together.

"Fucking asshole!"

"I'm sorry." I winced, rubbing a comforting thumb over the back of his neck. Our gazes met through watery eyelashes and I offered a sympathetic head tilt, one that seemed to take the breath clear out of his lungs. His eyes danced from mine down to my mouth and back several times.

I couldn't think of a place I would have rather been: caressed by a beautiful man in the shallow, lapping ocean, stars above twinkling around the full moon. And he was naked, so gloriously naked and looking at me like the world may pause just to let us live in the blinking cursor of it a little bit longer.

Maybe Natalia was right—there could be something so indulgent about giving myself to Frankie, be it only for three weeks. We could figure that all out when the time came, but for now the only pressure I felt was the one in between my legs. A pulsing ache that amplified every second Frankie spent looking down at me like he might lose himself trying not to tear me apart.

"You're very beautiful, you know that?" he said.

I bit my lip. "This is a bad idea and we both know it."

"I've never seen a bad idea that looked this damn good."

My legs wrapped around his hips as his hands instinctively dropped to cup my ass, holding my pelvis against him. I sighed in unabashed approval. To hell with it.

"Are you gonna kiss me now? Or are you still thinking too hard about it?"

"Yeah." He licked the seam of his lips in preparation. "Yeah, I'm gonna fucking kiss you now."

And he did with so much need that my eyes drooped closed on impact.

Frankie held me tight against the first sweep of his tongue through my mouth. There was no coy warm-up; kissing him was like being consumed, drowning under a wave and not even caring to come up for air. He tasted like sea salt, and I licked it off his lips greedily as I wound my fingers through the damp locks of his hair.

Every part of my body was screaming to be touched, and predictably, I couldn't help but rut my hips in tiny swivels against him, searching for the sweet relief of friction. He grunted from deep in his chest and swallowed the sound with my mouth as his hands began to explore.

"I am so fucking hard for you right now, O. You're making me lose my mind."

I tugged his bottom lip with my teeth and then grazed his chin, the patch of stubbly hair on his jaw, again on the lobe of his ear. I was completely in control of the situation, and hearing him react, unashamed to groan in that husky baritone of a voice, I was slowly becoming enraptured. I felt *sexy*. Frankie was *making* me feel that way.

"This smart mouth of yours." He prodded my lower lip with his thumb. "I just want to stick my dick in it. You have no idea how many times I've thought about you on your knees since I sat down on that plane."

I felt the impact of his every word in my lower half like a tidal wave. I reached down between our bodies and grasped him under the water, and I could tell from touch alone his size would stretch me to my limit. Just thinking about it sent my neck rolling back.

Frankie righted me immediately, his fingers tightening in my scalp to the point of pain. "You can play with it all you want, sweetheart, but I'm not fucking you until I can get you spread out on a hard surface. I'm not one of your little boyfriends."

Christ, he really was *not*. Frankie had outdone every man I'd seen in the last eight years in about eight fucking seconds.

"I'll play with you, too, though." He snagged my lips between his for a balancing kiss. "You want me to play with you, Ophelia?"

"Mm-hmm," I managed, feeling the first brush of his fingers between my legs, before he abruptly pulled them away.

"Use those words for me. I know how much you love to talk."

I hurdled past the point where my brain turned off and left my vagina to rationalize. Embarrassingly, I would have sang him a fucking song if he asked. The best thing about it, though, was that he wasn't asking me—he was *telling* me. He held my stare with parted lips like an atom bomb was about to drop if I pushed the right button.

"Play with my pussy, Frankie."

His eyes darkened as my words landed, pulling an appreciative grunt from deep in his throat. Frankie could dominate my senses, but I unraveled him with one sentence and a sultry bat of my eyelashes.

"God *damn*," he gritted out, then crushed his lips to mine.

It was like his fingers and tongue were battling for my attention. Inside my mouth he swept that devious muscle in perfect circles, flicking it against my own, claiming me desperately. His hand that wasn't wrapped in hair at the nape of my neck was cupping my sex, stroking eagerly at that throbbing bundle of nerves that had my thighs tightening around his hips.

He unwound one of my legs from his waist and pushed it open, giving himself the access he craved, and I clung to his side.

"I want to feel you from the inside so badly my cock is fucking aching, baby."

I gasped and stroked him faster, giving back to his mouth the desperate tongue fucking he'd taught me he liked. I wanted to learn so much more of his body, the things that made his breathing stunt and his muscles flex. What special twist of my wrist or motion of my hips would have those gorgeous brown eyes glazing over.

Frankie released my lips to bite at my neck the same moment he slid a finger down my core and pushed it into me. As if he wanted to hear what sounds I would make the first time he penetrated me completely uninhibited.

"Jesus *fucking* Christ," I swore. The thick slide of his finger touched every screaming pleasure point it needed to. I bucked into his hand, nails digging tiny slants into the skin of his shoulder. He pressed the pad of his thumb down against my clit and let me leverage myself on his hand.

"Use my fingers." He licked a searing line over my breast, then caught my nipple between his teeth and tugged on it. "Show me how your pussy likes to get fucked."

How this man was single was a mystery. No one had ever spoken to me like that. Unhinged filth, filtering like a bottomless colander. I was completely at the mercy of it.

I dragged his lips back up to mine, moaning into the open cup of his mouth when his fingertips curled inside me. I rode the horse but he pulled the reins, brushing me methodically inside and out, making sure I had everything I needed, but could still take so much more.

The high of his pulsing fingers, the soft breeze biting at my nipples with each passing wave, the danger of the open sea around us—it all heightened the pleasure already amplified with every sting of his lips to mine. If I knew this was how it would feel to touch him, to be touched by him... Fuck, it bruised me to even think it, but maybe the mile-high-club thing wasn't so far-fetched.

Frankie quickened his circles and I *moaned.* I moaned like a fucking pornstar, still pistoning my hips onto his fingers inside of me. A familiar feeling built rapidly underneath the pressure.

Oh God. Is he...?

"I-I think you're gonna make me—"

"Yeah, Ophelia. I fucking know I am."

I focused harder on his pleasure in my palm, stroking it with a tight grasp from base to head. The need to make him feel as good as I did momentarily tore my focus away from the orgasm queueing restlessly, but I still felt like I needed an anchor to keep me from floating completely out to sea.

"No," Frankie protested, batting my hand away. "I'll get mine, troublemaker. This isn't for me."

I groaned insolently, obeying despite the nagging demand of my body to satiate him along with me. Instead, he held me stiff to his chest, taking my ability to move away and replacing it with the devastating rhythm of his fingers.

He had learned the pace I wanted, the map of my hips, the touch-starved places inside of me that had me whimpering every time he brushed them. Up to that point I'd been showing him what I needed, and now he was showing me what I'd been missing.

"There she is," he teased, watching my lips shape into a soft circle. "I can feel you shaking, sweetheart. You're gonna give me what I want, right? So close."

I dropped my cheek to his shoulder, that familiar feeling tightening deep in my core, my last stunted breaths finding purchase on his neck before getting stuck in my throat.

I managed a half-lidded glance back at the shoreline, in time to see a trail of approaching headlights that gave me immediate pause. "F-frankie, *fuck*," I gasped. "Th-there's someone coming."

Without stopping for a beat, he assessed the obviously patrolling Jeep and turned back with an irritated grunt.

"Not happening." He shook his head. "No, no, no, you focus on me. You're gonna show me how this tight pussy gives right now, O." He kissed me again, stealing every worrying crease from my brow, any thought that wasn't the grip of my tight walls around his fingers, buried under the heat of his assaulting tongue. "Tell me yes."

I nodded in reply, just as my legs locked up around him and that first shattering wave of release flooded from inside of me. The breath that was caught in my throat relinquished into his mouth on a whimper, one that he swallowed and replaced with a growl of his own.

"Ohhhhh, *God*." My body trembled, then fell entirely slack.

Still pulsing with aftershocks and unraveling from my vice hold on his hips, I hung on with enough self-preservation to find cover under the waves as those bright truck lights found us both in the wake.

Frankie tilted my chin up, looking deep into my eyes before he dipped down to kiss me delicately, once. "That's what it feels like when a man makes you come. Don't ever fucking forget it."

As if I ever could after that.

The echo of a hand speaker sparking to life was all that kept me from jumping him again.

"You can't be in the ocean after dark," a crackling voice called over the crash of the surf. "Please exit the water."

I could faintly make out two men standing in the topless Jeep and looking down at Frankie and me. The probe of the lights blinding as I hugged a forearm over my chest while my other came up to shade my eyes.

"Yeah, all right," Frankie shouted back, both of us realizing there was no way around climbing stark naked out of the ocean for an audience. "Stay put," he ordered me.

I giggled behind him as the bright lights silhouetted that slim figure and bubbly little ass while he emerged from the water with his hands cupped over his modesty.

I felt like a teenager again, getting caught fooling around by my parents. Except this time it was much more humiliating, because Frankie was pushing forty and the men in the car had every reason to have us both arrested for public indecency. That would have been a humbling phone call.

"We were just leaving anyway," Frankie added, pulling his shorts back up his legs while trying his fucking hardest not to flash the chub I knew he had to be sporting. I pinched my lips together as he picked up my clothes and kept me in the shadow behind him. "And, Merry fucking Christmas."

11

Ophelia

I DIDN'T KNOW HOW early it was when a crescendo of incessant buzzing stirred me awake the next morning. The blackout curtains in Natalia's guest bedroom were worth their weight in gold.

I groaned with my eyes still closed, blowing weak gusts of air through my lips in an attempt to fan away the strands of knotted hair in my face. Instead of tending to the phone on the nightstand, I flipped around and dug even deeper under the covers, pulling the floral duvet up to my ears.

Whoever it was could wait. As far as I was concerned it was the middle of the night and I was on vacation.

Another minute passed peacefully before the vibration started again, somehow louder and more insistent than it had been the first time. I grumbled into the pillow and then pulled it over my head, willing myself to ignore the annoying wake-up call.

"Answer it or throw it into the ocean," a voice rumbled beside me. I peeked one eye open at the intruding body in my bed to find my raven-haired best friend splayed out under the covers. We'd taken two bottles of pinot grigio into the room when we got home and never resurfaced. Every sordid, saltwater detail was confessed and relived in vivid, colorful detail.

I began to protest but Nat darted a hand out, pushing my pillow onto the floor and making it impossible to get comfortable again without getting up. With a sigh I rolled back over to the nightstand and answered the buzzing call without so much as looking at the lock screen.

"Hello?"

"Oh, thank goodness, Ms. Brody, I've been trying to reach you for an hour."

I squeezed my eyes closed and tampered my voracious need to growl into the speaker. "Cindy, you know you can just call me Ophelia, right? And I only had one missed call, two minutes ago."

"I could have sworn it was more than that."

"Is there something you need?" I asked. "I sent the slides for the full week's worth of lessons directly to your district email."

"The children are losing it, Ms. Brody. Little Brandon has told Emily that Santa Claus"—she lowered her voice to a whisper, and I could imagine the plump old woman attached to the wall phone with a hand cupping the receiver—"isn't real."

I sat up straighter in bed, pressing my back against the wooden headboard.

"And now the entire class is either in tears or in shock, and they're looking to me for answers. I think Emily is two steps away from shoving a sparkly pinecone up—"

"Cindy," I interrupted. "They're eight years old. I understand the stress, but please don't let a kid derail the entire day over Santa Claus."

"What do I do?"

I hopped out of bed and trekked across the hallway into the bathroom. Teaching was never simple, especially at that formative age where opinions were being developed and solidified. Sometimes the solutions were obvious, other times they required a bit more mental gymnastics. Of course I didn't have any kids of my own, but I grew up surrounded by siblings over a decade younger than me and watched the way my parents handled the hard questions firsthand. Santa Claus, the Easter Bunny, the Tooth Fairy—God the world was so magical when you were a kid.

I wedged the cell phone between my ear and my shoulder as I dolloped toothpaste onto a brush. "My best advice is to give them another activity to do, and then assign homework tonight on the mystery of St. Nick. This is something that we shouldn't touch with a ten-foot pole. Send out an email to all the parents while the kids are at lunch explaining what happened and the reason for the homework. That's really all you can do. Like I said, they're eight; it's only a matter of time before the veil comes down, but it's not up to us."

"Right, right, okay. I can do that," Cindy said breathily on the other line. "Kids, can we all clean up our colored pencils and get into our reading circles?"

"See? Problem solved. If everything else is fine, I was actually still in bed when you called."

"It's eleven in the morning there, Miss Brody."

I stuck the toothbrush into my cheek and pulled the phone away from my head to check the time. "I don't tell you how to live your life, Cindy," I quipped, and then hung up the phone.

Despite the headache, the wine hangover was mild and when I looked at myself in the mirror I almost felt—pretty? There was a dewy glow to my freckled cheeks, and my eyes looked brighter and bluer than usual.

I touched two fingers to my bottom lip to explore the still tender, swollen skin there. Then, traced those same fingers down my jaw to my neck, to the hint of a blush pink love bite just beneath my ear.

Even in the hour I'd spent rehashing the night swim to Natalia my lower belly hadn't swirled like it did staring at the evidence of what Frankie and I did in the reflection of the mirror. It brought everything whirring back like a tornado.

The peaks of my nipples pressed against my thin tank top, and I let my fingers drop to trace them. The stimulation was delightful but the memory of Frankie's tongue against the hard buds was more than enough to stir the throb between my thighs to life. I wasn't sure the aftershocks of my orgasm the night before had even entirely dissipated, or if I would just truly never forget the way Frankie had demanded me not to.

But God, if I didn't want more.

My cellphone on the bathroom counter vibrated again and broke the trance I'd fallen into. I snatched it up with an annoyed grunt, assuming Cindy was having another meltdown, but the name on the screen gave me pause.

Ophelia: God damn, you know your way around a woman.
Frankie <3: I appreciate that Ophelia, you know my door is open anytime

I snorted at the exchange, trying and failing to tamper the fluttering feeling of wings in my stomach. He was witty, I'd give him that, and he'd earned his bragging rights fair and square. There was a growing ache already rearing inside me again at the promise of more.

Ophelia: Not sure I could fit through with your head already stuck in it

Frankie <3: Which head?

Ophelia: Point made

Frankie <3: How's my O after her first O?

He was really never going to let me forget it. And something about Frankie calling me *his* had me biting my lip and rereading the line of text several times.

Ophelia: Way to be humble about it

Frankie <3: I was shouting it so loud off our rooftop last night, Gino threatened to call the cops

Ophelia: The neighborhood is petitioning to have you and Mateo removed by New Year's

Frankie <3: First the pineapple, now this. What are you doing to me, Trouble?

Ophelia: Don't blame me, bingo club already had their eyes on you boys and your perfectly manicured lawn way before I showed up

Frankie <3: I told you, there's nothing wrong with two men shacking up together and taking meticulous care of their personal belongings and outdoor landscaping

Ophelia: Are you trying to convince me or yourself?

Frankie <3: Do I need to convince you, Ophelia? I thought I was pretty convincing yesterday

Frankie <3: I could convince you again though, if you ask me real nicely with those bedroom eyes

Ophelia: I knew giving you my number was a bad idea

Frankie <3: I doubt any of your other conversations are as entertaining

I had a stupid smile plastered across my face as I walked back into the guest bedroom, pausing in the doorframe to lean against it and type out another message.

Ophelia: That's where you're wrong. I just got off the phone with my sub back in Colorado who was having a conniption over a rumor taking over the classroom that Santa isn't real

Frankie <3: Fucking Cindy

I giggled out loud, staring down at my phone like a teenager with a crush. I dug my polish-chipped toes into the plush carpet and thought to suggest to Nat that we do a spa day at a place I saw online. The only obligations I let myself have when I planned the trip were rest, relaxation, and whatever local fare Natalia suggested was worth experiencing.

The men slightly complicated those plans.

Nat could barely go two days without seeing Mateo. A week prior that would have put a damper on my mood, but now I found myself looking forward to the additional company.

I finally glanced up from the phone to find my friend awake and regarding me with a cheeky smirk. Nat had fluffed up the pillows and was scrolling on her own screen.

"Let me take a wild guess and say that's not Cindy making your titties tight."

I blanched and looked down at my chest. "Jesus, is it cold in here?" With a forearm across my overzealous nipples I dove back under the cover of blankets beside Natalia, scooching up the headboard next to her. "You should turn your heat up a little bit," I suggested.

"It's seventy-five and you literally live in Colorado; you can't bullshit a bullshitter. What's he saying?"

"Why do you assume it's a he?"

Nat gave me a knowing glare. "I don't assume it's a he, I assume it's *him*, and because you once told me the texture of a vagina reminded you of a Hot Pocket."

"Sounds...delicious," I grimaced.

She reached over and tried to snatch the cell phone out of my hand.

"Okay! Okay, Christ. He just wanted to say good morning."

Natalia rolled her eyes and righted herself on the bed. "I'll drop it for now, but the second you start sexting I demand input. Don't even fucking think about sending a nude without my review."

"First of all, I would never."

"Never say never."

"I would *never* send a nude to a guy I barely know, and he's already seen me without my clothes on."

"He's seen the *top* half."

"A pussy pic, Natalia? I'm an elementary school teacher, not kickstarting an OnlyFans. The confidence a woman would need to send a crotch shot is not within my pay grade."

She shouldered me playfully. "I wasn't suggesting full frontal, Phee. Not that I think Frankie would protest whatsoever. He'd probably print it and keep a copy in his wallet."

I looked down at my phone as it buzzed again.

Frankie <3: What are you girls up to today?

"See? Double texter. He's obsessed," Nat pointed out.

I shielded my phone screen as she read over my shoulder. "Don't you have a boyfriend to be sending butthole snaps to?"

Natalia flipped her shiny hair off her shoulder, slapping me with the ends as she stood from the bed. She cleared the side tables of the empty wine glasses and bottles and swayed out the door. "Remember! No nudes without approval!"

When I heard the click of a door being closed down the hall, followed by the soft rain of the shower, I focused back on my phone.

Ophelia: Thinking about making it a spa day. I could use a good massage

Frankie <3: Something making you tense?

Ophelia: Fighting off tireless men

Frankie <3: I wouldn't call what you did to me "fighting me off" exactly

Ophelia: Can't a girl have a moment of weakness?

Frankie <3: You can have as many moments of weakness as you want O. I encourage it. Actually I implore it

Ophelia: Big words there from a military brat

Frankie <3: I had to adjust my game for the hot teacher I'm trying to impress

Ophelia: She's impressed

Frankie <3: How impressed? Like, meet me on my lunch break for another go impressed?

Ophelia: Like, continue texting you despite your frat-level insistence impressed

Frankie <3: Ouch

Ophelia: You're right, that was a little harsh

Frankie <3: No quarrel, Ms. Brody. It was grossly incompetent of me to assume something so outrageously promiscuous. I'll see to it that I keep my egregious masculine urges to myself henceforth.

I snorted and played with the drawstring on my shorts.

Ophelia: Are you on thesaurus.com?

Frankie <3: Would it make you wet if I said yes?

Ophelia: No comment

Frankie <3: I'll make a dirty girl out of you yet, O

I swung my legs off the bed and padded down the hall into the kitchen. I couldn't remember the last time I felt this impending infatuation toward a man. Which was as exhilarating as it was terrifying given the circumstances. I wasn't even sure at that point if a glaring red flag tagged "will end badly" would deter the path toward Frankie. It felt as though every second I tried to stave off any involvement, the pull toward him just became more magnetic.

I flipped on the coffee machine and leaned against the counter as the grinds began to drip.

Ophelia: Does Mateo pay you to text on the job?

Frankie <3: I'm not texting, I'm testing the internet speeds

Ophelia: Slowest internet ever

Frankie <3: Part of the reason this install is gonna take the next two days

Ophelia: Ah, that must be why Nat and Mateo are having a sleepover on Friday. Two days without sex probably feels like a prison verdict

Frankie <3: First I'm hearing about it. What does that mean you're doing?

Ophelia: Making cookies, wrapping gifts, singing Christmas music at the top of my lungs in an empty apartment

Frankie <3: Fuck that, come over with Tally

Ophelia: You don't think that's infringing?

Frankie <3: Last time I checked I paid half the mortgage and utilities, so whatever raw cookie dough I do or do not put in my oven is no one else's business

The coffee came to a sputtering stop in the pot and brought my attention back to the room. Nat was idling around the kitchen with a towel around her chest, pulling two mugs from the cabinet above the sink and cream from the fridge.

"Would you care if I tagged along on Friday?"

She raised an eyebrow and then fitted me with an knowing expression as she put two and two together.

"Why, oh why would you ever want to do that, Ophelia?" she teased.

"Can we save the I *told you* so's for when they're necessary? We're just hanging out. You and Mateo are hanging out, Frankie invited *me* to hang out. It's friendly."

"What Mateo and I are doing is *far* from friendly."

"We're just baking cookies."

"Is that what the kids are calling it nowadays?"

I took the two mugs from my friend and poured the steaming coffee, attempting to hide a smirk. There was no telling exactly what would come of spending time alone with Frankie, but I also wasn't naive enough to believe some salacious activity was completely off the table.

"So, you're cool with it?" I asked, handing the mug back to Nat.

"Of course, Phee. I'm glad actually. I felt like shit leaving you for the night as it was. Now at least I know you're in capable, strong, *veiny* hands."

I swatted Natalia's ass as she turned away, laughing and heading back toward her bedroom.

Ophelia: Sending you a list of ingredients, don't forget anything

Frankie <3: Atta girl

12

Frankie

THE DIGITAL MARKETING AGENCY I was working in for the next couple days was right next to a grocery store, so it'd be easy to hop over on my lunch break and find the list of things Ophelia texted me.

I was in over my head already, but for some reason I couldn't bring myself to stop.

It might have been the season. Didn't everyone get all sentimental and clingy during the holidays? No one wanted to spend Christmas alone, surrounded by people in happy relationships while they got blasted on eggnog alone at a family gathering.

It was entirely likely I was just sick of feeling excluded in my own home, and jealous of the attention that Mateo was giving Tally all the time.

I was bored. So unbelievably fucking bored with the mundane in and out of everyday life. Shit used to be so exciting for me. Five years prior I was hiking in Colombia with my ops team, gunslinging, kicking down doors. I hadn't felt an adrenaline rush like that since...

Well, since the night before, actually.

Since I had Ophelia Brody riding my fingers in the pitch-black waves on Hollywood Beach.

Fuck, that was so dumb. We could have been swept up in a tide and gone without a trace, not to mention whatever could have been lurking beneath the water.

She was making me stupid. That was the best way to describe it. I was forgetting how easy it was to make the wrong decisions when it came to women. It'd not even been a full twenty-four hours and I couldn't stop thinking about the next time I would be able to get Ophelia alone. So when she mentioned Tally and Mateo's date night, I jumped, despite never baking a cookie in my goddamn life.

Behind me on the desk the computer made a sad beeping noise for the fourth time already that morning as the screen went black. "Fucker," I growled.

I tapped aggressively at the keys until the desktop lit back up and the coding window opened for me to work in. Then starting from scratch, entering several lines of letters and symbols, I worked until my phone vibrated with Ophelia's name and I abandoned everything to pick it up again.

About ten seconds later Mateo pushed through the front door of the storefront with a tray of coffees and caught me leaning against the table staring at my phone.

I was supposed to be downloading software onto the main server in the lobby, but every few minutes I would get distracted by my cell going off and get timed out by the airtight system Mateo insisted we install for our clients.

He was meticulous about his business, and I hated that I didn't care more. I did my job well, that wasn't the problem. But tending to computer viruses and monitoring firewalls was the single most fucking tedious day job I could have ever agreed to. Up until recently though, I didn't have much of a choice.

When shit changed for me and I couldn't fly anymore, I was lucky to make it out of bed in the old apartment before three p.m., let alone make it to a job. I was living in a den of self-pity, cashing disability checks and spending it all on booze, shutting everyone important to me out of my life—then watching all those relationships crumble. The last straw for Mateo was when he found me surrounded by a case of empty cans of Bud Heavy, passed out on the living room couch on my fucking birthday after I'd missed my own surprise party.

The next day, he was in my bedroom with a dustpan and a spray bottle of Windex, rattling off something about starting a company and getting my shit together before he called my mother and made her drive out to kick my ass herself.

The last thing I needed was my mom finding out the pathetic state her only son was in. My entire life I'd been the rock for our family, always showing up when they needed me, paying the bills, fixing the problems. I vetted every Tom, Dick, and Harry that Adriana befriended in high school, haggled with car salesmen when the Corolla shit the bed and Mom needed a new ride. The whole reason I joined the military in the first place was to secure benefits and start getting paid *good* money. Not that grocery store minimum wage I was making before I turned eighteen. The Army was going to pay me while I served, pay for me to go to college, pay me to fucking live somewhere—and every extra cent got wired to my mom's account back home.

That was taking care of them. That's what my father would have done.

So Mateo mentioning my mother got me out of bed.

Within a week, the two of us had put an offer in on the house, filed for a business permit, and started looking for clients for TechOps.

"What did I tell you, Pike?"

I shrugged and grabbed my drink out of the cardboard carrier. "Not to shave my balls with your razor?"

"Very funny," he said sarcastically. "Yes. But no."

"I don't know what you're talking about."

"Want to guess what my girlfriend just called to tell me?"

I had an idea. If Tally and O were as close as I thought they were, my best friend's girlfriend probably had exact measurements on my dick by then.

"That they're going to the spa today?"

He made a lewd gesture with his right hand. "That you finger fucked her best friend in the middle of the Atlantic Ocean."

I coughed. "Fuck, man, you are dramatic." There were very few people working in the cubicles along the wall, but Mateo's voice carried. I looked around and smiled at the turning heads. "What's the issue here?"

"The issue is that you even know where the girls are gonna be today without me having to tell you. There's casual hooking up, and then the type of shit you do where you're texting good morning and running her errands."

"It's just a few things to make cookies," I rationalized.

Mateo paused with his coffee halfway to his mouth. "See? This is what I'm talking about. That was a joke, and you just fucking proved it."

"The only thing you said to me was not to get attached. If buying some flour and chocolate chips means getting attached to you, you're just as much of a pussy as you think I am."

"Hey, watch your mouth," he reprimanded me. "There's people working here."

The truth was—yes. Obviously I was feeling something *more* for Ophelia, but it wasn't anything I couldn't handle. What she was giving me was the missing piece of all the other women I'd tried to get to know lately. An actual fucking pulse. I was being reactive to that. A beautiful, intelligent woman with a good head on her shoulders and a mutual attraction—of course I wanted to hop into bed with her.

I understood that our situation was complicated. Vanessa was the only woman I'd been with in the last ten years, and Ophelia had made it clear she was dating to settle down. But we were both stuck in a pocket of time where happenstance overran circumstance.

She wasn't going to find a forever guy in Coconut Creek, and I wasn't ready for anything to get serious. So why not make the most of one another while we could?

"We're just having a little bit of fun," I assured Mateo. "You're the one constantly preaching to me about getting back out there. Now the minute I do you're giving me shit about it."

"No, I *want* this for you, Pike. I want you to find someone." He put a hand on my shoulder. "If she lived here, man, I would be poking holes in the condoms."

"You're a sick fuck." I shook my head. Knowing him, he probably wasn't even joking.

"Listen, if you really think you can keep it casual"—he shrugged—"then I fucking hope you prove me wrong. My girl-friend seems to think Ophelia needs the release, too."

After the previous night, I didn't think you could pry me away from that girl with a crowbar.

I wanted her. Plain and simple.

I wanted to feel her again, and *hear* her again. The way Ophelia's entire body reacted to me was one of the sexiest things I'd ever fucking seen. And we'd barely even scratched the surface.

It could have been the years' long dry spell, but just touching her between those thick, perfect thighs gave my dick ideas. Ideas I needed to see through before the next two-and-a-half weeks were up. I'd always been a vocal lay, but even some of the shit I was saying to her in the heat of the moment shocked me. It was like a primal flip had switched.

From the minute I stepped foot on that plane I was down for Ophelia, and I was damn near positive that she felt the way I did. It was a perfect opportunity to help each other out. As long as we didn't let it get too far and mutually agreed to put it behind us after the new year, nobody was getting their feelings involved.

"I appreciate how much you care about me, Cap." I smirked at him. "I think we both realize it's gotta be casual. I promise you, if things go south, I'll be the first to admit that you told me so." Just then the computer behind me timed out again, making that beeping sound of agony. "You gotta be fucking kidding me."

Mateo sighed, reaching over to turn off the monitor. "Come on, take a ride with me. You can finish this later."

I raised an eyebrow. "Slacking off today?"

"I need your opinion on something for Tally."

The only time Mateo needed my opinion on something was figuring out what takeout we were going to order for dinner. He was always entirely sure of himself and overly stubborn—a decision maker, through and through. Which is why he earned that Captain nickname in Delta. Our whole unit knew he was the leader without having to be told. So Mateo needing my opinion on something, especially involving Tally, had to be important.

"Are you doing it?" My mouth widened into a grin.

He wrapped his arm around my shoulder and pulled me toward the front door. "Yeah, brother. I think I am."

I patted him on the back, laughing. "Well if I'm losing you, we're going out with a fucking bang."

"Vegas?" he suggested.

"Over Tally's dead body," I joked.

"We'll all just have to go together."

God, shit was about to get so much crazier.

13

Ophelia

"THIS PLACE IS REALLY nice." My voice carried over the sloshing of water at my feet.

The boutique spa we ended up at was bright and airy, desert-toned walls warming the space as the natural light of the day basked through the floor-to-ceiling windows. Lush greenery hung from macrame baskets and overflowed from oversized potted ceramic in every corner of the room. Soft whispers of instrumental strings played as we soaked our feet under warm jets tinted in aromatic lavender incense.

"I got a massage and facial here once as a surprise from Mateo. Best three hundred dollars he's ever spent. That man didn't walk ten feet in the house without me dropping to my knees for a week."

"I'm surprised he'd even have to spend the money."

Nat swatted my arm across the leather chair and popped a complimentary chocolate-covered acai berry into her mouth. "Some people say your twenties are your prime, but I feel like the older we get the more unrelentingly horny we become."

I hid a laugh behind my fist and looked down at the two women working at our feet. One thing I'd always loved about Natalia was her unhinged transparency. Nothing seemed to make her blush or cringe. Growing up surrounded by three other hard-headed, outspoken sisters seemed to have done that to her. At home she constantly battled for attention, but in the real world that brazen confidence got her everything and anything she wanted.

My phone vibrated and I slid it open to read a new text from Frankie.

> **Frankie <3:** What's your favorite color?
> **Ophelia:** Like an aqua blue, turquoise-ish
> **Frankie <3:** ish?
> **Ophelia:** Why does it matter?
> **Frankie <3:** Curiosity
> **Ophelia:** What's yours?
> **Frankie <3:** Green-ish

I made a humored noise that earned a flashing glance from the woman painting my nails.

> **Frankie <3:** How many siblings do you have?
> **Ophelia:** Aren't you a little old for Twenty Questions?
> **Frankie <3:** I didn't peg you as an ageist, O. Is it not fun to do things that make you happy before you inevitably die?
> **Ophelia:** An ageist and a cynic playing Twenty Questions sounds like the start to a terrible joke
> **Frankie <3:** Are you done, smartass?

Ophelia: For now. I have five younger half-siblings. My dad and his wife
have Leo, and the twins Stella and Daisy, and then my mom and her
husband have Gavin and Laila

Frankie <3: Nice names. Leo is the oldest?

Ophelia: Yup, just turned fourteen. What about you?

Frankie <3: I have a younger sister, Addy

Ophelia: Does she live in Coconut Creek too?

Frankie <3: She's down near Miami with my mom

I felt an irking need to ask him more about his family, about the
father he didn't mention, but decided against prying too deeply.
Nat reached over and put a bubbling champagne glass down next
to me on the table with a wink and then reclined backwards.

Ophelia: Do you visit a lot?

Frankie <3: I try to when I can. The last couple months have been kind
of hectic

Ophelia: Too busy trying to get laid in the airport

Frankie <3: I'm playing the long game

The tension of home and work unfurled from my body and
relaxation settled in with every minute as Nat and I glided across
the spa from comfy chair to cushioned table.

The rough hands of a massage therapist pressed into my back
like leaded weights, and I groaned involuntarily. Modesty was not
the policy where beauty care was concerned, especially not in
this high-end spa where it almost felt rude *not* to get naked. I
was entirely too exposed with my tits squished underneath me
against the linen-sheeted table and more than a healthy helping
of my ass crack on display.

I'd gone to the same waxer for ten years back home in Pine
Ridge, and a level of trust had to be built and nurtured over that

full decade before I even felt comfortable showing that much hole to a fluorescent light.

Ophelia: What's your sign?

Frankie <3: Aries

Ophelia: I knew you were a drama queen

Frankie <3: Do you really buy into all that shit?

Ophelia: Of course I do. I'm a textbook Libra—social, perfectionist, and I'm hilarious

Frankie <3: And vain, so very vain

Ophelia: Confident

Frankie <3: What else does the star thing say about me?

Ophelia: You're passionate, stubborn, don't mind putting work into your relationships

Frankie <3: I'm not stubborn

Ophelia: You enjoy a challenge

Frankie <3: Accurate. What does it say about how I am in bed?

Ophelia: Disappointing, quick on the trigger, selfish

I snorted to myself as I sent the message. My face was becoming numb against the half-moon pillow it was cradled in, and my arms under the massage table tingled like television static.

Frankie <3: I'm gonna make you eat those words, sweetheart

I began to reply but another text came through first.

Frankie <3: And maybe those pretty red panties I stole too so your friend doesn't have to hear it all the way down the hall

My phone slipped through my fingers and clattered to the hardwood beneath the table.

"Shit," I swore, attempting to reach it without moving too much as the hands on my lower back stilled.

"You good, Phee?" Natalia asked from somewhere to my left.

I stretched my fingers as far as they would go to no avail. The text screen lit up and mocked me from a distance.

"I'm good," I lied, then attempted to sit up so I could grab the phone myself before the masseuse did. In doing so, the very small towel covering my modesty pooled behind my knees and left me entirely, embarrassingly exposed in the small room.

"I've got it, ma'am," the woman said, lifting the towel again to cover me.

"No, no, no. Don't worry, don't touch—thanks. Just leave it." I chuckled nervously as I lay back down. "Distracting thing anyways. Don't need it in the slightest."

OUR CONVERSATION CONTINUED WELL past the hours spent at the spa and bled into the next day. Frankie texted me from a Piggly Wiggly as Natalia and I sorted through racks of vintage clothes at a consignment shop across town.

Frankie <3: Who knew there was a difference between baking soda and baking powder?
Ophelia: Most people
Frankie <3: No fucking way

"Did you even get any sleep last night?" Natalia stole my attention as she held two shirts up against one another in the mirror.

The real answer was no, because even after Frankie and I mutually decided on calling it a night, I scrolled like a psycho through the full day's conversation with a dumb grin under the covers in the dark.

"Did you know Frankie actually speaks three languages?" I asked Nat.

"English, Spanish, and desperate. Did you sext him after I went to bed?"

"No, Jesus Christ. I told you we're just chatting."

"Nobody 'chats' that much." She flung one of the shirts back onto the clothing rack. "Just let me know when I have to plan the shotgun wedding. What are you giggling at over there?"

My lip quivered. "He doesn't know the difference between baking powder and baking soda."

Natalia looked at me like I'd grown an extra head and a confused wrinkle formed between her brows. "Holy fuck, Phee. You've got it bad."

After a full day of browsing without the *physical* distraction that was Frankie, I had thankfully returned to the apartment with all my Christmas shopping done. The hardest part would then be figuring out a way to fit all the extra baggage in my suitcase in two weeks—but that was a hurdle to jump when I got there.

Nat had long since retired with her phone to her ear and a sultry lilt to her voice as her bedroom door clicked closed. I couldn't help but feel like an intruder on her and Mateo's relationship no matter how adamantly she shot it down. Maybe I'd never felt the way those two did about each other with someone before, but if it was even a hiccup of the warmth I felt simmering with Frankie, I couldn't blame Nat as far as I could throw her.

Frankie <3: Tell me something good

When I chanced a look at the time glowing in the corner of my phone I realized it was nearing one in the morning.

Ophelia: Like what?

Frankie <3: When did you lose your virginity?

The metronome of my pulse picked up inside my ears.

Ophelia: Not until college actually

Frankie <3: Who was he?

Ophelia: Don't laugh at me

Frankie <3: No promises

Ophelia: My childhood best friend's older brother

Frankie <3: I thought that only existed in porn

Ophelia: How cliché right? Friend's older brother/sister

Frankie <3: I never had a crush on anyone's sister

Ophelia: What was Frankie Casado's first sordid fantasy?

Frankie <3: Michelle Pfeiffer, Catwoman

Ophelia: I was secretly hoping it would be embarrassing but that's a pretty good one

Frankie <3: You want to know what my most recent one was?

I worried my lips together, desperate to find out what he was going to say but not sure I could keep true to my word with Natalia once I slipped down that rabbit hole. My thighs slid against one another softly beneath the covers and I felt an embarrassing amount of relief.

Ophelia: I promised Nat I wouldn't sext you

Frankie <3: I didn't promise the same, so you can just listen then

I flipped from my side onto my back in bed as I stared down the text bubble idling on the screen.

Frankie <3: Because I haven't been able to go twelve hours without fucking my hand over the way your pussy felt coming around my fingers

Fuck me. I knew Frankie wouldn't take it easy, but that one sentence sent me barreling back to the middle of the ocean with his hands all over my body like a brand.

Frankie <3: I have never been so desperate to have somebody underneath me in my life, Ophelia
Frankie <3: and I'm laying here in bed right now, hard as a fucking rock over you again, but I won't touch myself if you don't tell me to

I turned my head into the pillow, willing my resolve to hold out. The ache between my legs begged for attention my fingers were too eager to give.

Ophelia: Tempting...no
Frankie <3: No?
Ophelia: I'll see you tomorrow night
Frankie <3: Ophelia
Ophelia: Goodnight, Frankie

I was torturing myself just as much as I was torturing him. It must have been a whole minute of watching the screen flash with three angry dots over and over again before a final text came through.

Frankie <3: Sweet dreams, Trouble

14

Ophelia

WHEN I WAS TWELVE years old, Robby Clancy invited me over to his house for a birthday party. My teeth were train-tracked with bright pink braces, and I still hadn't grown into the freckles on my face. I used my mother's drugstore concealer that was a shade too pale for my skin to cover them up, and then *pat, pat, patted* a thick powder over the top. My hair was twisted into pigtail braids, and my wide-leg jeans were shoved haughtily into a pair of cream-colored, fleece-lined boots. Not ideal at all for a winter in Pine Ridge when the snow would undoubtedly seep through the toes and permanently leave dirty water stains on the material.

I'd had a crush on Robby since the moment I saw him in class the first day of seventh grade. He had spiky brown hair and a Broncos jersey on. He sat straight across from me and asked me if I had an extra pencil. I had thought that was so funny of him. Who didn't have a pencil on the first day of school?

The days Robby forgot his homework, I would let him copy mine, which was most days. When he had football games, I would draw his number on my cheeks in paint and chant his name across the field. When Robby sprained his ankle, I offered to lug his backpack *and* mine across school from class to class.

Eventually the crush turned into somewhat of an infatuation. I'd expected us to be doing what everyone else was doing in our grade—holding hands, or *kissing*, or something. But Robby seemed content to keep me in the friend zone.

I spent two hours at the mall finding a gift for his birthday that year while my parents followed distractedly behind. They were arguing about something, I remembered, their voices getting more cutting and definitive with each word. Too busy with their impending divorce to even give it a second look as I picked something out and swiped the credit card out of my father's hand without a thought.

I expected Robby to finally take the hint when he opened the hand-wrapped box in front of everyone at the party, unveiling matching bracelets, one for him and one for me. The hanging charm was one half of a heart that fit together with the other bracelet. Instead, Robby had turned a brilliant shade of tomato red, quickly laughed it away, and messed the hair on the top of my hair like an older brother would.

A month or so later Robby Clancy was dating one of the cheerleaders who walked around school wearing his oversized jersey on game days, and *that* was the first time I had ever gotten my heart broken.

That experience had unknowingly set a precedent for every relationship to come for me, and if I thought hard enough, it might have even been the reason I was still single at twenty-six. I was *cautious* of men, to say the least. There was a staggering pattern of miscommunication, infidelity, and all-around inability to commit in my rearview.

And *mommy issues*, for some reason, which might have actually been the worst of it. Nothing parched the pussy quite like a grown man with an Oedipus complex.

All of this fed into my hesitation with Frankie, or what *was* my hesitation with Frankie. I wasn't an idiot; I knew what we were doing was pure, lust-filled philandering with a clear end in the not-so-distant future. Maybe that's why I couldn't make myself hit the brakes. I'd never have to worry about Frankie showing up to my sister's seventh birthday with a bottle of vodka and a funnel.

Anyways.

Any reticence was tossed out Natalia's car window as we whizzed beneath the sunset to the house. I was wearing my bawdiest bra and panty set beneath an otherwise conservative outfit. My legs looked spit-shined and my hair smelled like vanilla and cardamom. I'd taken a razor to places I'd never even seen before with my own two eyes. The shampoo bottles in the shower got a free show.

In a way, it was kind of like what had happened that fateful day at Robby Clancy's birthday party all those years ago. Except instead of matching bracelets, I was gifting matching lingerie, still hoping the man it was meant for wouldn't balk at it and give me a playful noogie in return.

At least I knew Frankie wouldn't be breaking my heart.

That was the deciding force when I slipped into the black lace set I thought I'd only packed as a precaution. The line in the sand with the pilot was drawn, and it made whatever debauched fling we had going on feel safer than starting a relationship on cloud nine and then realizing I didn't have a parachute.

Their living room still looked as perfect as we'd left it. The candle on the center of the coffee table was lit, and the tree was sparkling in strands of green and gold tinsel. Four perfectly matched stockings hung from the mantle of the fireplace that was mimicking fire and softening the room in a warm dim.

Mateo and Natalia had disappeared, leaving me staring at the ceiling—until I noticed the spread of baking ingredients I'd requested perfectly organized across the island waiting to be made into cookies.

I smiled to myself, running a hand over the unopened bags of flour and chocolate morsels. Chopped walnuts, *not whole*—he'd gotten it right. Several different brands of condensed milk, coconut flakes, graham cracker crumbs, steel cut oats, baking powder, bright red and green M&M's. Stacked beside them were way too many mixing bowls, and inside the one on top was a whisk, three wooden spoons, a spatula, and a scraper with the tags still attached. I picked one up and twirled it under the kitchen light.

"Hey."

A deep voice rang out from across the room and I dropped the new scraper back into the metal bowl with a clatter. Frankie was leaning against the wall, the strands of dark hair around his ears still damp from the shower he must have just been in, and the shirt he had yet to put on bunched in his fists.

He stretched the neckline of the white tee between his fingers and then pulled it over his head, his eyes only leaving mine for a brief second. That tiny disconnect was all that kept me from begging him to drag me down the hall and show me what he would have done to me the night before.

"Hi."

His gaze swept down my legs and back up again. The frilly cutoff Daisy Dukes I had on obviously doing the job I hired them for as I watched his tongue traverse his bottom lip.

"You got everything, it looks like." I gestured to the table and tore my eyes away from the man across the room. His blatant appraisal scorched the back of my neck and the tips of my ears. I felt completely naked under it.

"Looks like I did." Frankie inched into the kitchen behind me, his feet shuffling against the tiles. I didn't turn to face him; instead, I busied myself with the counter, starting to aimlessly move the ingredients into piles. My nervous energy materialized into obsessive organization.

"So I think we should start with the cookie bars because they take the—" I couldn't finish the sentence before a warm, hard body settled at my back. Frankie's impressive, sinewed hands came down right outside my own on the marble, and the tops of his thighs pressed my hips against the cold ledge.

We both heard my breath catch.

"You wore these shorts to torture me," he whispered against my ear, nudging his nose through my hair. "Because you want me to look at you and forget how to keep my hands to myself."

His grainy, hushed voice was like a kindling to my core. I should have expected he'd cut directly to it. Why dance around the inevitable? Frankie had never done that, and I didn't think he intended to start then. Naively, I'd assumed I would have at least a batch of snickerdoodles in the oven before my panties were around my knees—but, then again, I wasn't exactly complaining. We had all night.

I closed my eyes and rubbed my lips together, basking in every inch of his chest as it flattened against me. I was both fearful and intoxicatingly powerful in that moment, but instead of inching away I returned the pressure, rocking my hips back and forth slightly.

"Don't start something you don't intend to finish, O," he warned me. "If you're gonna rub your sweet little ass against me like that, I'm gonna do something about it."

"They could walk in and see us."

His lips went to my neck, warm and wet, kissing my pulse point. "I don't give a fuck."

I wasn't sure I did either. The last thing on my mind was self-preservation, and at that point I imagined Natalia and Mateo were well occupied beyond closed doors. My hips ground more overtly and Frankie dropped his face into the juncture of my shoulder, groaning.

"I've been strung out all day thinking about this," he confessed. "You're a devious little thing, leaving me throbbing like that last night."

"I don't break my promises."

Frankie ran his hand up my arm softly and then threaded his fingers around the base of my neck like a collar. My heart boomed rapidly against the heat of his palm.

"Promise me something, then?" He twisted me carefully so that his lips were inches from mine and when he spoke next, I could feel the silhouette of the words against my trembling mouth. "The first time I make you come tonight, you'll look me right in my eyes and say, 'Thank you, Frankie.'"

I pressed up onto my toes and closed the gap between us immediately, diving tongue first through his parted lips. Frankie reacted with a smug smile that I could feel as he kissed me back. Our teeth clashed, and his fingers around my throat tightened like a pressure band.

I had kissed plenty of men before, but not one compared to the tender intensity of this one. Frankie claimed without even trying to. We mimicked each other perfectly; when I went high, he went low. I gasped and he swallowed. He licked and I moaned around the taste of his tongue.

Frankie's hand not holding me flush to his chest dipped down to the apex of my shorts, rubbing languidly against the zipper, toying with the brass button. I could feel him hard and ready, so little material between the satisfaction we both wanted.

"We have to talk," he murmured.

"Right now?" I asked breathlessly. What the fuck did he want to talk about so badly it couldn't wait past an orgasm or two?

"Right now." He nibbled on the lobe of my ear, and a warm current buzzed beneath my skin like lights on a Christmas tree. "Because it's the difference between what I'm doing to you at the moment and what I'm going to be doing to you next."

"How about a little incentive?"

Jesus Christ, who am I? My body had apparently been abandoned and occupied by the Ghost of Horny Holidays Past.

A short, amused scoff left his throat. "Why don't we play teacher, Ms. Brody? Where I pull these shorts down and give you a *very* extensive lesson in anatomy." His fingers found their way between my legs.

"What warrants extensive?"

"Touch." He squeezed me there. "Taste." Then licked my lips.

"Start talking, Casado."

He looked like he would kiss me again, just as a door clamored shut down the hallway.

"Cookie time!" Mateo's burly voice announced.

I instinctively pulled away from Frankie and curled into myself, swiping my bottom lip with the back of my hand just as both our friends bounded down the hall together. Frankie glared at his roommate as Mateo weaseled to the island with the baking supplies and started opening bags of chocolate morsels.

"I thought you guys were having a date night." I cleared my throat to hide the octave of arousal. Putting several steps of distance between myself and Frankie, I joined Nat at the oven where she was setting it to preheat.

"You don't get this ass from eating grass all day, honey," Mateo answered, pointing to his rear and shoveling a handful of holiday candy into his mouth.

"Give me that." Frankie aggressively swiped the bag from his best friend's hand and tossed it back on the table. Annoyance was not only apparent but prevalent as he sulked to the cupboard and pulled out a cookie sheet.

Mateo glanced between us with a grin curling his lip. "Are we interrupting something?"

"No," I said at the same time Frankie answered, "Yes."

Nat hid a smirk behind a pair of oven mitts.

"The more the merrier," I quickly continued. "Now it'll only take half as long." I grabbed the pan from Frankie, pleading with him with my eyes to behave.

His knuckles brushed over mine as I stared at him. "You're killing me, woman."

"Yeah," I agreed. "I'm killing me, too."

15

Frankie

THE GIRLS SHOULD HAVE taken over the baking from the start. Mateo and I had never cooked a dessert from scratch a day in our lives and despite being amply skilled in assembling weapons, measuring sugar and melting butter without burning it was proving slightly more difficult.

An hour later the dough for the first batch of cookies was only finally being whisked together, I'd watched Mateo eat more chocolate chips than had even gone into the batter, and my shorts were covered in flour. It was all over my hands and undoubtedly my hair where I had a habit of running my fingers through it. But I was determined to bake those cookies if it was the last fucking thing I did that night. All while hoping eagerly that it wasn't.

I couldn't keep my eyes off Ophelia across the table. Cracking eggs into a bowl, measuring vanilla extract, swiping her finger through the mixture to taste it on her tongue. There was really nothing quite like a beautiful woman making eye contact while she sucked her fingers clean.

She knew exactly what she was doing.

I was pretty sure my balls had solidified over the span of three days, waiting to see her before doing anything about the ache there.

I'd almost lost it the night before though. Completely unable to help myself in those early hours of the morning when all I could think about was the way her body looked in those waves, and the salty taste of her nipples in my mouth.

She had every right to shut me down, but it only made the need more colossal. We were adults, there was no use denying palpable attraction, and neither of us had tried to. But I also figured that Ophelia was keeping herself guarded from me for a different reason, one that I had yet to cross the line and question.

All I knew was that I wanted her. And she wanted me. We could have casual, unhinged sex for a couple weeks like single people do, and then part amicably if that was what the situation called for. I'd forgotten how to be a hook-up guy, but maybe that needed to change. Maybe if I stopped looking for a permanent staple I could eventually find the woman that wouldn't love me and leave me.

Despite all of that though, something about Ophelia felt inconceivably *right*. Like flame to a wick. She was getting under my skin in all the best ways.

And what did I expect today? That she wouldn't show up in those little cutoff shorts with the fringe hanging down her thighs? That her tits wouldn't be pushed up just enough that I saw nothing and imagined everything at the same time?

Tease, I mouthed to her across the island. Ophelia popped her finger out of her mouth with a grin and pushed the bowl of cookie batter toward me.

"Try it."

"Oh, I'm gonna try it. Just you wait."

Whether willfully oblivious or ignoring the rising temperature in the room, Tally and Mateo worked dutifully next to each other shaping round balls of dough and putting them on a tray. There were several times Natalia scolded her boyfriend for making his too big or with not enough of the "good stuff" inside.

"How was work this week, boys?" she eventually asked.

"It was work. A bunch of dinosaurs behind desks treating us like IT guys when they're struggling to open a spreadsheet," Mateo complained. "I don't know how to tell them we're there for security installation, not tech support, without sounding like an asshole."

"Try teaching them the program when they can't even open a spreadsheet, Cap."

"That's why I pay you to do it." Mateo took a bite out of a ball of cookie dough Natalia had just put on the tray. She quickly smacked it out of his hand with a glare.

"Have you heard anything from the base in Colorado, Frankie?" Tally asked.

I glanced toward Ophelia as she turned toward the refrigerator and opened it, rummaging inside for a carton of milk.

"Not yet. It's still pretty soon. They probably had a bunch of candidates to sort through and interview."

"Yeah but Echo has a buddy on the interview panel," Mateo said. "That's a shoe-in, brother. There's not much Tyler Swan likes to do more than talk about the glory days in Delta. They probably knew more about you before the interview than you even told them."

Ophelia joined us back at the island and started whisking milk into a new bowl of loose ingredients.

"Who even says I'm ready to get back out there? You know?" I wasn't in the mood to rehash the details of my discharge from the military, nor was I looking for any more pity. But sometimes those intrusive thoughts spilled in and I forgot that it was okay to be vulnerable.

"Pike, you're the best pilot I've ever flown with. They'd be shitting in their soup not to hire a salty fucking Ops guy with impeccable character references."

"Are Sam and Tyler still coming down for New Year's?" Natalia chimed in.

Mateo nodded. "Confirmed."

My attention slid to Ophelia again, checking for a flicker of interest at the mention that two of our unit buddies would be paying us a visit. Sam and Tyler were good looking guys, the type that didn't ever have to try to get laid, and when they came in a brotherly package and turned on the charm—it was open season. I'd seen it firsthand.

She just continued on listening and stirring melted peanut butter.

"I'll talk to him when they get down here," I relented. "But I don't want to seem like a kiss-ass either. You know that's not my style."

I was still coming to terms with making that kind of life-altering relocation anyway. The part of me that wanted that job more than anything was completely overshadowed by the part of me that wanted everything to remain safe and the same. If I stayed in Florida I would tolerate my job for the rest of my life, but at least I'd have my best friend, my sister, my mother. Comfort and stability.

God forbid they ever needed me—I would be entirely too far away in Colorado to do anything about it, and that was something I couldn't think about without getting anxious.

"You're not being a kiss-ass, you're being persistent," Mateo said. "Another one of your long list of qualities."

"You could say that again," Ophelia agreed.

"See?" Mateo shrugged, licking the flat end of a scraper clean.

The entire kitchen looked like a bomb had gone off in a bakery, and I was certain we'd used pots and pans I'd never seen before in my life.

When we first moved in, Mateo's mother bombarded us with appliances. Air fryer, coffee pot, dehydrator that I wouldn't even know what to do with if someone gave me a step-by-step instruction. If it wasn't odd enough that two men in their thirties were moving into a house together, add in gifting us things you'd only find on a fucking wedding registry and it all started to feel like we should just take it to the courthouse.

That ridiculous line I'd fed to Ophelia about being common law married might have made that flirty little dimple on her cheek shine, but I was hardly joking.

The oven door closed and Tally turned around, wiping her hands on her shorts. "All right, first batch in, second batch chilling." She set a timer on her cell phone and slid it in her pocket.

Silence swelled between us. This entire night was built on the understanding that Mateo and his girlfriend would be occupied with one another, therefore leaving Ophelia and me to our own devices. I stood there with my hands in my pockets, waiting for one of the two of them to hold up their end of the agreement so that I could get back to negotiating mine.

Mateo made a clicking noise with his tongue to get my attention and vaguely nodded his head in the direction of the hallway.

Yes, *dumbass*, I insisted with my eyes.

"We'll be back." He grabbed Tally by the hand and pulled her toward the bedroom, mumbling something that made her laugh.

Ophelia had started busying herself at the sink, touching and cleaning things, running the dirty mixing spoon under the tap and soaping up a sponge.

"Leave it," I instructed her. I didn't want her thinking she had to make a fuss over the mess, and I absolutely didn't want to give off the impression I expected a woman to clean up anything in *my* kitchen.

"It's the least I could do," she said with a soft smile. "Thank you for setting this up. I can't remember the last time I made Christmas cookies for fun. I used to do it with my parents all the time before the divorce." Her little smile evened out.

I could never identify with the toll it must take on a kid to feel like an outsider in their own home. When my dad passed away, my mother made sure we never went a day without saying "I love you." Things like that were so vital to the unit we built in the absence of a father figure. It was strange to understand a family dynamic with a lack of communication, or lack of undoubted love.

While my mind raced with the prospect of continuing that hot and heavy segment with Ophelia, I cared more about making her laugh again at that moment than anything. I cared more about making sure she knew I *cared*, rather than getting under her.

And this way, we could talk without the raw temptation of sleeping together being the focal point. Friends with benefits didn't mean anything without the *friends* part first.

"What's in the bags, Trouble?" I motioned to the tote the size of Santa's sack on the couch. "Hiding a body?"

She lightened up again and my chest unclenched.

"My weight in presents to wrap." She giggled. Then she said, "I thought you wanted to talk...?"

I walked over and dropped onto the couch cushion next to the bag of gifts, waving her over. "I can talk and tie bows at the same time."

16

Ophelia

I ALREADY THOUGHT FRANKIE was attractive. Now he was somehow even more so while I watched him try with fumbling fingers to crease and fold a sheet of Mylar. His eyebrows knitted together in the center of his forehead, and his tongue stuck out of the corner of his mouth in concentration. Those deep brown eyes focused like he was trying to thread a needle. He'd measured and cut an entire piece of sparkling red and silver paper, centered the box of saltwater taffy on top of it, and then growled—*growled*—when he realized the sides were two inches too short.

I reached over and rotated the box diagonally, then handed him the roll of tape. "Have you never wrapped a gift before in your entire heckin' life?"

"You're sitting across from someone that made a career in the military. Please refrain from using the term *heckin'*, Ophelia." His voice was terse and distracted. I curled my lips into my teeth, amused.

Tasking Frankie with the smallest, squarest items was my first mistake. Especially after seeing that every cut of paper he managed came out an unnamed oblong shape that would better suit a circle. As I was busy wrapping more intricate gifts with tissue paper and burlap bows, Mr. Smooth was accidentally ripping the decorative side of the wrapping off with Scotch tape.

"Need some help?" I teased.

"My fingers are much more useful for other things," he grunted, tearing the tape and snapping his digits together until the clear plastic flung across the living room. "Who's the poor kid that gets this sad wrap job?"

"My stepdad." I giggled. Josh was a simple man. Where my mom was a busy bee bred for social interaction and planning, her husband was a laid-back stoner. He kept her grounded and filled her cup, and she fed his artistic soul with endless projects. They yin and yanged.

"What about all these other ones?" Frankie gestured to the floor.

I went on to explain how my two oldest half-brothers were near impossible to shop for nowadays, so they were getting sweatshirts and gift cards, because they'd probably hate anything I tried to pick out anyway. *Teenagers.*

But Gavin was always barricaded in his room playing video games, so I bought a few of them despite knowing absolutely nothing about it, or if he even played those ones in particular.

Leo loved fishing with my dad on the weekends, and Florida had some amazing bait and tackle accessories in a little shop I found walking around downtown. I bought those with some stickers to add to his tackle box because he was always collecting.

The twins were obsessing over makeup, so I splurged on the good stuff that I usually bought for myself so they weren't stuck with my stepmom's used drugstore palettes to play with anymore. Then I went a little crazy at the thrift shop because for some reason every twelve-year-old was dressing like Fran Drescher in the goddamn nineties.

Finally Laila, who was only seven but already over her head in books in the second grade, was getting the full collection of Junie B. Jones that I'd already secured back home, and one of those collectable name keychains that said LAILA in all capital letters across a Florida license plate.

Frankie listened with rapt attention the entire time, leaning back on both palms on the carpet with a smile on his face. "They're very lucky to have you as a sister."

I waved it off, blushing.

"No, seriously," he continued. "It's obvious how much you care about them, your attention to the little things. They're young, and maybe they don't understand now, but one day they will. You're making them feel seen and special, which is something kids really fucking need."

I, too, was feeling very seen and special at the moment. Frankie brought on that weird tingly feeling in my stomach far more in the last week than I'd felt in twenty-six years.

The truth was, I *did* crave that validation from my younger siblings. I wanted them to know how much they meant to me, regardless of the intense age gap, and I wanted them to return that love. I'd never be as close to Leo as he was with his twin sisters, or be able to share a bedroom wall and chat through the floor vents like Gavin and Laila. But I still wanted to *be there*.

"I think gift giving is just my love language," I joked. "It makes me happy."

"Your *love language*?"

"Yeah, everyone has one, or a couple." I tossed Frankie the scissors and instructed him to start cutting again. "Gift giving, acts of service, physical touch, words of affirmation, quality time."

He didn't look like he believed me.

"It's how you show love to others and want love shown back to you. It's a real thing, look it up."

"I'll take your word for it," he murmured. "I guess mine is...acts of service. No wait—physical touch."

"I think you just like to touch," I quipped.

Frankie's eyes dimmed a shade darker, and that smirk was accompanied by the swipe of his tongue across his bottom lip.

I liked looking at him way too much for my own good. With a hat on, he was brooding and boyish, but in this perfect orange lighting with his thick, shaggy, finger-combed hair—Frankie was *fuckable*. There was no better word.

"I agree with acts of service." I nodded. "I noticed it even when we were on the plane."

"Sitting next to you is considered an act of service?"

"No." I snorted, twisting a piece of burlap into a bow. "Filling my soda cup for me, pulling my bag off the carousel, little things. But things a stranger wouldn't normally do. Then that night when I was drunk you *totally* babied me."

The oven sheet panged from the kitchen and the entire house smelled like mouth-watering chocolate chip cookies as Frankie sat there contemplating. "I didn't baby you, I..."

"Serviced me."

He grinned. "No, that wasn't until a few days later."

I ignored him and organized a new present into the middle of the silver foil fray. "You're distracting me." Quickly, I measured the paper, cut it, folded it neatly over the rectangular box, and cinched it with tape.

"Now you're just showing off," he commented. "Whatever happened to a good old-fashioned gift bag?"

The eyeshadow palette he was wrestling with looked like it'd been wrapped by a blind elf with no thumbs, but he did it without complaining. It would be an interesting day answering for the state of the gifts to my family, and I had half a mind to blame the entire thing on Natalia instead of explaining who Frankie was to me.

I wasn't even sure who Frankie was to me.

A casual hook-up? A one-time fling? A friend? Friends didn't go back and forth the way the two of us had for the last week. As much as I loved my friends back home, I most definitely wasn't looking at them like I was looking at the man across from me.

I wasn't letting them talk to me or touch me like he did either.

With Frankie it was like zero to sixty with no breaks, and that was terrifying and exhilarating because I knew we were destined to hit a wall. A very large, hard, unmoving wall.

But I'd rather take my chances on the airbags than not experience the ride.

"All right." I stopped wrapping. "What did you want to talk about?"

Frankie stopped fidgeting and took a deep breath. I could tell his tongue was perusing the roof of his mouth and his mind was moving a mile a minute, which was about as long as it took for him to say anything.

He straightened his back with a weak grunt, and clasped his hands together on his lap. "Have sex with me."

I blinked rapidly, and my pulse stuttered.

That was the most blatant way a man had ever tried to coerce me into doing him. It was also comical that this was what Frankie needed so desperately to talk to me about that he *stopped* doing the string of things that would have led directly to me having sex with him.

I was so taken aback that the only real response I gave was a confused, nervous laugh.

"Yes, Ophelia. Have a lot of mind-blowing, filthy sex with me."

"What's the catch here?" I asked. "You're saying a lot of things that I'm liking, but I know there's something else rattling around in that head."

"It's obvious that we're in dangerous waters with each other," he said. "I can't look at you for more than ten seconds in those fucking shorts without thinking about what they'd look like on my bedroom floor."

Now I couldn't either.

"There's no hiding that I have my shit with my ex. I'm just looking for someone to get me back on track, and I know you're a hundred Olympic snowboarders deep in Colorado."

I snorted. "I fucking wish."

"The point is, both of us are in a situation where we can have some fun right now."

"Like, friends with benefits?" I raised my eyebrow.

"Like friends with benefits."

I must have fallen asleep and started dreaming. The only reason I was even *moderately* hesitant with Frankie was for fear of forming an attachment when we lived so far away from one another. Him being the one to bring the title to the table was not only incredibly assertive, but also made parts of me weep that weren't my eyes.

It would be like signing a contract. Transactional pleasure for the both of us, no emotion down, and then my hot-pilot-fuck-buddy lease was up in two weeks—satisfaction guaranteed.

My head swam with the possibility. There was only one hiccup.

"What's in it for me?" I asked.

"What?"

"I'm here to visit Florida and spend time with my Nat. What happens when we're done hooking up or she's holed up with Mateo for the night?"

"You know you're welcome in my bed as long as you'd like, O."

An idea formed like a storm cloud in my head. I snapped my fingers and pointed at him. "No, if we're gonna do this, let's do it right. You want to start dating again, you need some help, some gentle nudges back onto the lady scene—let me be your crash test dummy."

Frankie narrowed his eyes. "You want me to *practice* how to date with you?"

"The last time you dated casually cell phones didn't even have internet. There's been an entire revival of women since then, and not all of them are falling for your broody pilot act."

"Act?" He scoffed. "I'm a fucking retired fighter pilot. I've seen shit, Ophelia."

"You haven't seen anything until you've seen a millennial on Bath and Body Works Candle Day."

"You are chock full of weird little analogies, you know that?"

"Think about it," I prompted him. "Treat me like you would any other date you picked up on Hook(Up), and I'll be like a live critique partner."

Teaching was literally my *thing*. I didn't get a master's in education and spend six years peer reviewing others in my field for nothing. I was the perfect guinea pig, and I got to *have sex with him* as an added bonus? My highlighters were itching.

"You're on to something," he agreed. "And on my end, I'll show you what you *should* be expecting from any guy that takes you out when you go back home. No more fucking the bottom of the barrel because they bought you a Frosty."

"That was literally one time."

Frankie pinched the bridge of his nose in embarrassment.

"Kidding." I reached over and slapped his thigh and he grabbed my hand and kept it there.

"I'm serious about this. You took this trip to do something for yourself for once. So have some fun, make the most out of me for the next couple weeks. Drive me crazy, which I already know you love to do." He pulled me toward him and my knees dragged across the crinkling wrapping paper until I was sitting awkwardly in his lap.

Without any warning he leaned forward and kissed me, but not in the all-consuming, heart-sputtering kind of way we'd done before. This one felt oddly akin to the adult version of a pinky promise. Where Frankie was agreeing to act like a perfect gentleman for the next two weeks while he let me use him like a well-endowed dildo.

"Kiss me back," he said.

"Is this us shaking on it?"

"Consensual, mind-blowing, no-strings-attached sex. New year, we call it."

I nodded, in utter wonderment over the whole thing. "You touch my dick..."

"I touch yours." He smiled.

My fingers weaved through his hair as I tugged his lips back to mine.

Holy fuck we're doing this.

I couldn't sink my tongue into his mouth fast enough, and Frankie answered more aggressively than ever, hiking my knees up close to his hips and settling my center down over his.

The only time I'd held onto him was in the ocean where we both swayed back and forth in the waves. I could tell he was a solid wall then, but now with his back pressed against the couch and his hard chest to fully lean on, it was so easy to get lost in the feeling of his body against mine.

Frankie wound an arm around my waist, corded his fingers through the hair at the back of my head with the other hand, and held me. "God, you're fucking fun to kiss."

Answering, I tugged his lip between my teeth and sucked on it, which he *really* seemed to enjoy, because a low groan slipped out of his mouth that stirred me further awake between my legs.

I didn't know what it was about men moaning, but the sheer knowledge of being the cause of unbridled pleasure turned sex into a competition for me. How strung out could I get him? What could I do to make him grunt the loudest? How could I make him so uncontrollably horny he flipped me on my back and pulled my pants down to my knees just to slip inside?

"Back atcha," I breathed, diving back in. Frankie tasted rich and sweet like the chocolate morsels we'd baked with. His teasing fingers slipped beneath the material of my tank, just above the waistband of my shorts, and mapped sensuous circles. My skin pebbled, my core ached, my nipples hardened to needy little buds. All my senses were in overload.

"Tell me what you like," he said. "I'll make it feel good."

I ground my hips onto his lap for some friction and earned another one of those grunting sighs that made my eyelids flutter. "This feels good."

"This is fucking child's play," he huffed. "Tell me where to touch you. It turns me on."

Further turning him on might have put a hole through his shorts. I could feel exactly how ready Frankie was poking at my inner thigh. I shifted and lined my hips up over it.

"I like getting kissed here," I murmured, leaning down and demonstrating on his neck just under his jaw. His skin was hot and pulsing beneath my lips.

Following my instructions beautifully, he tilted my head back and licked my throat. My entire body shuddered as I moved back and forth on his lap.

"Fuck, do that again," he told me. "You want it there so bad, don't you?"

"Do you always say exactly what you're thinking?" I sighed as his teeth sunk into my neck, followed by a kiss.

"Only when I know you're thinking it too."

Fuck it. If we were going to go all in on this, we might as well be vocal. "I want it here," I said, guiding his hands to my chest.

His eyes gleamed at my forwardness. Leaning in, Frankie closed his teeth around my breast and bit into it, leaving wet circles over the thin material of my shirt. He wasn't even touching skin and my body reacted as though I was completely naked. His hands kneaded my tits together, putting my cleavage on display, and he ran his tongue right through the middle.

"You want me to fuck you there?"

I wanted him to fuck me everywhere. "Yes."

"Jesus *fucking* Christ, Ophelia," he groaned. "Pull these down."

He tugged at the button on my shorts and freed the zipper, then lifted me with no effort whatsoever so I could shimmy the tight denim to my knees. Instead of taking them all the way off, he flipped me around, so my back was against his chest and my bare ass was in his lap with nothing but a black thong between us.

"Tell me where else you want me to touch you," he murmured against my ear. "Right here?" His fingers slid between my legs briefly, teasing the damp material. "Fucking hell, O. I wouldn't even have to lick my fingers, would I? They would just slip right in."

My chest heaved as my hips found a slow, circling rhythm. His hands moved to my lower back and I recognized the telltale sound of his zipper being unleashed. Then his ass lifted and his shorts came down just enough.

"I want to feel skin," he said. "Keep riding me like that, Trouble. I'm about to fucking blow in my pants like a rookie."

Instinctually I reached back to touch, curling my fingers around his shaft and pumping it. His briefs were sticky with precum where the tip tented and I pinched and played with it. A tortured noise slipped through Frankie's teeth.

"Look at that," he whispered. "You made me a mess."

Everything felt hazy and hot. The room was darker, the flickering candle barely touching us. We were too attuned to one another to care about anything going on outside our little dry-humping bubble. Frankie kissed my neck until my back arched and my entire spine tingled.

"I want to taste it," I said. "Put it on my tongue." He stilled for a second, understanding what I was asking for. The way we were sitting, I turned my head and our foreheads touched. "Do it."

Frankie's attention remained on my parted lips as he reached a hand down into his boxers and tugged at himself. Our harsh breaths mingled in anticipation and I let out a soft, involuntary whimper.

I don't know what in the world possessed me to ask that of him. I'd never done it before, but every part of my body was screaming with need and my senses begged for something more.

A moment later his hand returned, where we could both see the tips of his fingers coated and glistening with exactly what I wanted evidence of. My mouth watered, and my thighs clenched together so hard I could hear the friction.

"Open your mouth," Frankie said. I did as I was told and stuck my tongue out for good measure. Those two fingers pressed down on the muscle and my eyes did nothing short of roll back in my head.

Who did I think I was? Rubbing my ass on a man on his living room floor with my pants around my knees, begging to taste his fucking precum. Was this the kind of thing I would be into if I could actually find a guy I wanted to screw as much as the one I was sitting on? Foreplay with Frankie felt better than all the sex I'd ever had.

"Show me how good you can suck," he instructed me. My lips clamped down around his fingers and I took them all the way to the back of my throat. "That's fucking right, so perfect, O."

Before I could blink he had me off his lap and on my stomach, my hips lifted, and my entire ass on full display. He tugged at the G-string and snapped it against my pussy. "Oh my god," I whined.

"That piece of scrap isn't hiding anything from me. You should see how juicy this cunt looks." He spread me open and hummed. "Can I have a taste, too?"

If he didn't, I was going to lose my mind. We were both too far gone to rationalize anything. So when the room started to fill with a sheen of thin black smoke, and a simmering sound became more violent in the kitchen, it didn't distract us in the slightest.

A second later, with Frankie's mouth inches from that happy place between my legs, the fire alarm started shrieking above us.

"What the fuck?" He jumped up off the floor holding his ears.

"The cookies!" My eyes rounded. "Frankie, the fucking cookies are burning!"

We sprung up in a whirl of half-naked limbs. I hobbled across the living room and into the kitchen, pulling my shorts back up my legs just as Frankie swung open the oven door, waving a towel at it. A barrage of smoke came first, followed shortly by a dozen hockey pucks as he reached in and snatched the burning tray from its fiery confines, ditching it all in the sink and pulling the faucet.

"Fuck!" He winced, sucking his burnt fingers into his mouth.

I climbed the barstool and stood inches away from the ceiling, fanning another towel at the screeching fire alarm as Frankie dashed around flinging all the windows open.

By the time the noise stopped, we were surrounded by an oily fog and the mood of minutes prior was as burnt as the fucking snickerdoodles. Frankie's zipper still hung wide open on his shorts as he stood across from me with a crease in his brow and his hands on his hips.

Our entire relationship thus far had been a series of unbelievable events: the plane, the club, the beach, these fucking cookies. Maybe it was the universe trying to ward us off one another, but instead of heeding that advice, I just started to laugh.

A maniacal, uninhibited, holding-my-gut laugh.

"Is something funny about this, Ophelia?" Frankie attempted not to smirk. "You almost burned my house down."

I laughed harder, tears pricking the corners of my eyes.

"You keep this up, you won't make it back to Colorado in one piece." He finally chuckled and kicked the dish towel at his feet across the floor. "Who was in charge of the timer?"

"Natalia has it on her phone," I said. "Where did they go?"

We made our way down the hallway toward the bedrooms where the hum of music seeped through the walls.

"I don't hear a summoning." Frankie shrugged.

I glanced at him hesitantly. "Maybe they fell asleep."

"Playing throwback jams?"

"It's like...nineties ASMR."

Frankie rolled his eyes. "Come on, the cookies are already burnt anyway. We don't need them."

A pesky intrusive thought hammered me in the head. "What if they're dead?" I asked. "What if they're dead and we're standing out here making jokes about them?"

"Ophelia, that's fucking insane."

"You're right," I agreed. He was much more rational and I needed someone to talk me down off the anxiety ledge. "There's no way."

We didn't make it three steps in the direction of the living room before Frankie groaned and turned back around, mumbling under his breath. His fists connected with the bedroom door. "Cap, you good?"

After a few seconds without an answer, I joined him in knocking. "Nat! The cookies burned!"

The longer we stood there waiting for a reply the greater the pit of despair opened in my stomach. My worried expression must have gotten to Frankie because a second later he announced his entering and shouldered his way through the door.

Our collective jaws dropped like the fucking ball on New Year's Eve.

Across the room Natalia's phone buzzed incessantly in her tangled shorts on the floor, completely drowned out by the sound of music playing from a speaker on the dresser. All the lights were dimmed, save for some red and green mood setters that illuminated the walls behind the bed. Mateo's impressive desktop setup was on and streaming, tiny icons hopping up and down where a video window was open. At the foot of the king-sized mattress sat a tripod with a giant circular light pointed down at the bed.

It was what was happening on the bed that left Frankie and I speechless.

"Oh, shit." Mateo looked up and caught us standing in the door, shocked we'd actually pushed our way inside.

Nat was on all fours in front of him, that skin tight Mrs. Claus corset unbuttoned and her fishnet stockings ripped open as she offered her ass to her boyfriend who was dressed as the fat man himself. Red jacket, red pants, a fluffy white beard fastened around his head with elastic.

"What the fuck are you doing, Mateo?" Frankie spoke first. His voice roused Nat, who until that moment was none the wiser, still performing for the jumping icons on the computer screen. "Jesus." He smacked his palm over his eyes and turned back toward the open door.

She screamed, flinging her body off the bed and shielding herself. "Phee! Oh my god!"

"Fuck, guys." Mateo hurriedly tucked himself into his pants, clambering over to the camera to end whatever sexy live stream they were hosting.

A wave of shock washed over me, and when I thought it would subside, I took another look around the room and got hit with it again. "Lady Marmalade" unironically sifted through the speaker in otherwise silence like a sick joke.

"It's not *exactly* what it looks like!" Nat crooned.

I couldn't have cared less if my best friend was having sex on camera. I just needed more than thirty seconds of adjustment. We almost lit the house on fire and then I watched Natalia's boyfriend mount her like a reindeer for an audience. Another one of those what-the-fuck waves crashed into me again.

"Nobody's judging," Frankie assured her, pointing to his roommate. "But, why the fuck are you dressed like that?"

"It's an act." Mateo ran his fingers through his fake white beard. "Mrs. Claus and Old Saint Dick."

17

Ophelia

NOTHING WAS TOO SCANDALOUS to say at brunch. I'd sat through many PTA meetings over bagels and coffee and listened to parents show their true colors over school district politics.

You'd be shocked to hear the kind of gossip that gets spewed when someone's kid isn't getting first class attention in a classroom of thirty to one. Which PE teacher is sleeping with the new divorcee, whose English teacher is writing naughty romance novels on the side. I'll be the first to agree that we're not paid *nearly* enough money to deal with parents. The kids are fucking cake in comparison.

So—brunch was good for open conversation, first and foremost. A few bellinis, some eggs benedict, avocado toast on house-made everything bagels. And Natalia and I playing a game of *who can keep their mouth the fullest the longest* to put off the inevitable discussion about the events of the night before.

It didn't take long before Natalia's fork clattered onto the plate in front of her. "Frankie saw my whole rack, didn't he?"

"Likely," I admitted. Leave it up to her to break the ice. "And what a rack it is."

She shook her head, smiling. "I'm sorry I didn't tell you."

"No, don't you dare," I said. "You don't need to apologize to me, or to anyone. It's no one else's business. *I'm* sorry, we just—when you didn't hear the fire alarm—"

"Mateo pulled that shit out of his ceiling when the battery started dying."

"Completely valid."

The corner of her mouth twitched upward. "We've been keeping the whole cam thing between us for *obvious* reasons. I just don't want you to think I was afraid of your reaction, because I totally wasn't, Phee. I knew you'd be a rockstar about it."

"It was just—*shocking*," I told her. "Old Saint Dick's...dick was all up in my face."

She cackled. "Was it as big as Frankie's?"

"Isn't it a conflict of interest to talk about your boyfriend's best friend's dick?"

"You've seen my guy's, your guy has seen mine. We should all just stand naked in a room together and get it over with."

"That sounds like an orgy."

Nat took a sip of her drink and pondered something. "How comfortable are you in front of a camera?"

"I love you, but absolutely not." I snorted. "With my luck, my vagina would get plastered all over Pine Ridge by the parent-teacher association and they'd protest outside my house with pitchforks. My siblings already pretend I don't exist. Imagine if that became my legacy."

She frowned. "Worth a shot."

"You guys look like you have it all in the bag without us," I joked. "I'm sorry we found out the way we did, but I'm selfishly glad I know."

"I am too." She let out a deep breath. "Having no one to talk to about it is exhausting. I feel like I'm tiptoeing around constantly."

Nat was one of four in a strict, traditional family. Every sister had their father wrapped around their finger, but there wasn't a doubt in my mind that neither Nat, Camilla, Isabella or Mia would want to deal with the cardiac arrest Mr. Russo would experience knowing one of his daughters was selling sex.

"What is it like?" I asked around a spoon of yogurt. "Since when?"

"I was so sick of working in that bank every day. I just wanted to be in control of my own money and time. I needed *freedom*. This ass is too perfect to be sitting on it all day."

"Understandable."

"I was doing it on my own for a little while before I met Matty. Just some solo stuff, live camming, photos. When we started dating I didn't tell him, and I stopped performing because I was head over heels and I didn't want to jeopardize it. But then I was back to the same shit job, and I wasn't *happy* anymore. Mateo noticed."

"As any good man would." I refilled both our empty drink flutes with the pitcher.

"So I just fucking told him." She shrugged. "I said, I love you but I hate my job, and before you I was making a lot of money doing the cam thing. I knew it wasn't for everyone but it was for *me*—and I wanted him to love all of me."

"Obviously I know the ending of this fairy tale."

"He made me quit the bank the next day," she said. "Everything has always been so easy with Mateo. I knew right then it was him or nothing. That's my lifer."

My heart swelled. "Now you're gonna make me cry." I sighed, swiping under my eyes. "You and your money-making titties are making me cry."

We used to lay in bed and manifest having the kind of relationship Nat was in now. Through hook-ups, break-ups, dating a different guy every semester of college, planning our weddings on corkboards when we got snowed into our dorms that one freak October at CSU.

I was so happy for her.

Guilt twinged in my gut, however. Because no matter how elated and excited I was, a piece of me still burned with jealousy. Wondering if I would ever feel that all-encompassing, ride-or-die kind of love.

"Mateo was just the cameraman at first, but then he got a little possessive." She laughed. "People really responded to the two of us together, and that little bit of wild in our relationship keeps it fun. Plus, now we're swimming in it."

"So the boys don't actually do cyber security?"

"Oh, no, that's legit. Matty has our network so wired that if anyone tried to find us they'd be looking in a rainforest in Southeast Asia."

"You two are like the dream team."

Natalia winked. "God, I would kill to be a fly on the wall for his conversation with Frankie."

There was no coming back from walking in on our friends engaged in Christmas-themed coitus. We might have been able to recover after the cookie debacle, but I was fairly positive Frankie's blue balls had turned to snowballs, and I couldn't stop thinking about the type of person who would pay to watch the Clauses do it doggy style.

"What I can tell you for sure is that seeing his roommate half-naked in a Santa suit sucked every last ounce of libido from his body."

"Were you fucking?" Her eyes widened.

"Not *yet*."

"You fucking slut."

"Hey!" I tossed a polenta fry at her. "You know what he asked me? To be *friends with benefits* while I'm here."

"You're saying this like it was Frankie's bright idea, when, *hello!*" She pointed at her face. "I was the first person to tell you to take advantage of the hassle-free dick."

Natalia was about the furthest thing from coy, and her voice carried through the dining area like an echo. I glanced around and met the shocked glances in our direction with a shy, apologetic smile.

"I was worried it would get too messy," I reminded her. "I don't have the emotional bandwidth to be let down in both Colorado and Coconut Creek. This is a vacation."

"But you're gonna do it."

I hid my embarrassment. "Yeah."

"You *fucking* slut," she repeated with a jovial smile.

How Frankie managed to convince me so quickly probably had something to do with the fact that I couldn't look him in the eyes without wanting to melt into them. I was crazy to think I'd make it three weeks without crumbling.

Less than one.

I was *not* the face of unwavering stances. Trying to convince myself not to sleep with him after he got me off in the Atlantic was like convincing myself not to color code all my lesson plans. AKA, not happening.

I wanted Frankie to make me come again. Kill me for it.

"We laid some ground rules. No confusion, no questions, and *no* attachment."

Natalia bit down on the edge of her straw and regarded me across the table. I'd seen that look before. Her "sounds like trouble" look. One I didn't entirely disagree with, but was choosing to ignore for purely selfish reasons.

"Listen, I don't know too many details," Nat said somberly. "But I know his ex screwed him up, and he hasn't dated anyone since. I don't think the guy's so much as gotten a *blowjob* since."

"Well that's part of the whole agreement."

"Blowjobs?"

The older woman at the booth behind us turned and glared at Natalia.

"I can't take you anywhere." I snorted. "No, not blowies—helping him get over his ex. I'll be like...his test run before he gets back on track."

"In exchange for...?"

A blush crept its way up my neck that had nothing to do with the alcohol buzz. "Directly out of Frankie's mouth, *mind-blowing, filthy sex*."

She sighed wistfully. "Ugh, God. Now I'm horny."

"You're welcome." I clinked our glasses together. "Now you don't have to feel bad about leaving me alone all night while you and Mateo...film."

"You'd be shocked at how busy the holidays are for us. People are lonely this time of year. I mean, think about it. Everything is so cheery and festive and then there's people who are just alone in their house with no family, no significant other. It's depressing."

I tilted my head and raised an eyebrow.

"That didn't come out right." She paled. "Not *you*, you're not the same at all. You're like, young and hot, and you could go to the grocery store and pick a DILF out of the butcher section buying a ham and take him home with you."

"Relax, I know you didn't mean it." I chuckled, considering her thoughtfully. A rush of warmth overcame me. "I'm so proud of you, Nat. I want you to know that, seriously. You're the coolest person I know, and you're authentic, and brave, and passionate—and I'll always be cheering you on."

Her eyes glistened and she reached over the table to squeeze my hand. "Now you and your big teacher titties are making *me* cry." Her full bottom lip jutted out and trembled with unshed emotion. "Love you more."

"Love you more," I answered, then cleared my throat. "Just out of curiosity though, if I did want to find a certain webcam couple for those lonely nights..."

She laughed. "Phee, you just ask, and we'll give you your own private show."

18

Frankie

I HADN'T TAKEN A woman out on a date in a decade. Flirting merci-lessly with Ophelia was one thing, it was as natural as breath-ing—but a proper pick her up, open the car door, impress her with my charm and intelligence outing? That was something else entirely.

Why the fuck was I so nervous?

Mateo was taking Tally to her parents' house for the day in Fort Lauderdale, which was like pulling teeth because she didn't want to leave Ophelia for the few hours they'd be gone. Natalia didn't know the random lunch with her family wasn't random at all, and that Mateo had a string of things he needed to check off a list before Christmas—a private conversation with her father being one of them. Cap promised the girl that her best friend would be perfectly occupied, protected, and taken care of, as if I was a paid bodyguard and not a retired, disabled veteran.

She would be all of the above, of course, but tasking me with the inevitable seemed a little dramatic.

It wasn't even technically a real date. It was day one of my What Women Want course taught by the one woman I was ironically not allowed to want. Not in a way that breached the bedroom, at least.

Vanessa used to love when I'd get dressed up on a weekend and surprise her with a night out. We'd take the truck and drive seventy-five down the highway with all the windows open, singing at the top of our lungs on our way to Lola's in Jacksonville. We had a table that was *our* table, unofficially. And if that table was taken when we got there, we'd get loose at the bar for as long as it took to open up.

She always ordered a tex-mex wrap and drank too many margaritas, and by the end of dinner I was piggybacking her across the parking lot and letting her fall asleep with her head in my lap on the ride home. Those dates were few and far between after I joined Delta, and sometimes I'd be gone months at a time in a different country with no service and no way to talk to her. But in the middle of the desert I'd still be thinking about Saturdays at Lola's and my girl in a sundress.

That turned out to be a very one-sided daydream.

I put on my least wrinkled button-down and a pair of shorts, combed my hair for the first time since the Army, and realized I needed a haircut worse than I needed to get laid.

Fifteen minutes later I was still staring at myself in the bathroom mirror, wearing the same clothes from ten years ago, trying to recreate the man I was when I took women on dates but hating every perfectly coiffed strand of hair on my head. Because that guy wasn't *me* anymore.

I flipped off the boyish version of myself in the reflection before changing my entire outfit, shaking my head like a dog and slapping on my hat.

Frankie Casado in his twenties was a cocky, reckless, unchecked son of a bitch. In my thirties I was one misstep away from another spinal surgery. That dramatic change was at the heart of my insecurities, along with my ex and, most recently, the inability to keep a girl interested past a dating-app-mediated text conversation.

Getting this day right with Ophelia was more important to me than I initially realized. Sure, it was showing her how a man should be treating her, but it was also proving to myself that I was still the kind of man who knew how to do that. No matter how many times Mateo fanned my ego and reassured me of my self-effacing bullshit, I couldn't shake that I was the issue. That I was the reason I couldn't find the right person to settle down with.

I parked outside the duplex apartment Tally lived in and shot a quick text to the girl inside. We'd gone back and forth a few times that morning, mostly O complaining that I wouldn't tell her where we were headed because apparently it was imperative to her outfit choice, and me telling her that shoes were required but panties were not—which earned one of those eye roll emojis and a middle finger.

Before the phone was back in my pocket it started ringing. I checked the screen expecting it to be Ophelia calling to stall—or worse, cancel the whole thing, which would have really put a wrench in my day. Then I'd have to collect her from upstairs using a fireman's carry out to my car in ninety percent humidity. My back ached just thinking about it.

It wasn't her, thankfully, but it wasn't any less stress-inducing.

I picked up the phone. "Hi, Ma."

"What's the matter, Francesco, you don't call your mother anymore?" Her lighthearted voice caressed me through the receiver.

It'd been too damn long since I saw my mom. Somehow the fall season came and went while I was on my ass with new clients for Cap and buried in job applications for the air base. The trip to Colorado itself took a week out of me, and now I was sitting on the phone with my mother as I waited to take a woman I couldn't mention on a date.

Explaining whatever the fuck Justin and Mila shit Ophelia and I were up to was not on my to-do list.

"Take it easy on me, I'm getting old," I deflected.

"Don't talk about old to me. I'm more than halfway to my grave with no grandkids."

"You might have grandkids somewhere."

Her disapproval burned me from forty miles away. "You're lucky I'm not there to smack you."

My sister and I were used to being berated about our love lives, or lack thereof. Adriana hadn't ever seriously dated anyone, and I was sure at that point my mother wasn't above posting her photo on telephone poles like a missing animal looking for a mate.

She liked when I was with Vanessa—because the girl gave her something to look forward to. Engagements, weddings, babies. When she and I broke up my mother was more hurt to lose *those* things than she was to lose the future daughter-in-law, which should have said all it needed to. And I never even told her the whole story.

I changed the subject. "That reminds me, why is Mateo telling me about you seeing someone?"

"Mateo calls me, so he gets to know things."

"I'm your only son," I pressed. "So I should know *all* things. Always."

A curtain in the upstairs apartment window rustled and I squinted at it.

"Well that's why I'm calling you, to make sure you're still coming to dinner this week. Your sister has to work Christmas Eve, so I'll cook on the twenty-third. We want to know all about the job and the trip. Adriana forgot she has a brother."

"No she didn't. She just sent me one of those chain messages from two thousand seven with a picture of Rudolph boinking Clarice the other day."

"I don't know where I went wrong with you two." She sighed. "Thursday, Francesco, you're coming?"

The way her voice hitched at the question made my chest tighten. I needed to fucking show up more. As if over a decade in the military wasn't enough time away, now I was flirting with taking off to Colorado permanently. Not once since the idea was first planted had I been as hesitant as I was hearing my mom pleading for me to simply *have dinner with her*, over the phone.

"Of course I'll be there, Ma. I wouldn't miss it." My phone vibrated and I pulled it away from my ear to a text from Ophelia that she was on her way down. "You need anything?" I quickly asked. "Cash? Everything at the house is working?"

"The only thing I need is my handsome son at the kitchen table."

"Can do," I promised. "I gotta go, I have some stuff today, but I'll see you in a couple days, all right? I love you, Ma."

"Love you. Tell Mateo Mama Casado said hi."

The call disconnected and I watched out the passenger side window as the door to Tally's apartment opened. Ophelia stepped outside and I couldn't help but notice how well the Florida sun suited her.

Gone was that creamy shade of skin from the flight down. A few days on the boardwalks had replaced it with a perfect golden bronze. Her long hair was up in a messy mop of a bun, curly tendrils of it curtaining her face and tickling her neck, and the yellow dress she wore made her glow like a daylily. My pulse quickened as she turned to lock up and I realized the hem barely covered her ass.

I didn't know what it was about women in flowy little dresses, but my hands started to sweat knowing it was all right there to take.

I met Ophelia on the sidewalk, smirking at her adorable half walk, half skip toward me. I instinctively pulled her in by the waist for a hug but she put her hand to my chest and kept me at arm's length.

"Ah, ah," she tsked, stepping back and giving me her tiny palm to shake. "It's nice to meet you, Frankie."

I furrowed my eyebrows. "Oh, so we're really doing this?"

She reached down and pulled a pocket-sized notepad and a gel pen out of her purse, scribbling something on the first sheet aggressively. I didn't have to look to know that every "I" on that page was dotted with a heart.

"She's taking notes, too."

"So that we can go back and assess your strengths and weaknesses."

The woman was an enigma. Every interaction was like a new room at a fun house. I thought I had her figured out, and then all of a sudden, I was surrounded by mirrors and walking directly into double-sided glass. You open one door and you get a smart and organized Type C teacher; the door directly next to it swings like the entry to a wild west saloon and the woman inside has a mouth like a sailor and is throwing back beers to match.

"You're the boss," I conceded, dragging her in a second time until her cheek was flush to my chest. "But even if I were meeting you for the first time I'd lead like this."

"That's a bit forward," she mumbled into my T-shirt.

"You seem to have forgotten what meeting me for the first time was *actually* like."

"Trust me, I didn't."

"So I'm being tested and graded"—we walked toward the truck and I opened the passenger door—"and you just get to enjoy the best fucking date of your life?"

"Let's not get too cocky, Maverick."

"Again with the *Top Gun*," I complained, helping her hop into the seat. I gave her a playful smack on her ass on the way up and she yelped. "Just get in, Trouble."

"You're getting points deducted for that." Her silly notepad got a fresh lashing.

I was as competitive as the sun was hot, and knowing Ophelia was probably putting my name in a column on a spreadsheet next to a hundred other guys made impressing my fake date like a special operation. I was going to be this woman's new standard whether she liked it or not.

I closed the car door and leaned in through the window. "Somehow, I think I'll survive."

19

Frankie

BUTTERFLIES ARE COLD-BLOODED CREATURES. Most of them can't even fly in temperatures below sixty degrees—their little bodies can't handle it. The hotter the better, so there was no better place to have an entire museum and gardens dedicated to watching butterflies than Florida.

We lucked out, because while Decembers are fairly stable as far as temperature, the little buggers won't come out on a cloudy or rainy day either. They like to rest and their wings are too delicate for raindrops.

There wasn't a cloud in the sky or a breeze to be felt when I turned at the sign for Butterflyland and watched Ophelia's lips twitch into a smile out of the corner of my eye.

"Your big bad walls are coming down, Frankie," she quipped. "I didn't know men who elected to spend their day at botanical gardens existed."

"That line is going on my dating profile like an editorial." I laughed. "In quotes and everything, next to 'Ophelia, 26, *stunned and satisfied*.'"

"*Mile High Club* was such a winner though." She scrunched her nose playfully, and for the first time I noticed that she had a perfect constellation of freckles right over the bridge.

Comparatively, Ophelia was the easiest woman to look at that I'd ever met. She was soft in all the right places, perfect lips, pools for eyes, hair so silken I wanted to run my fingers through it constantly. Whatever shampoo or lotion or perfume she wore smelled like it was literally designed for me to enjoy. Her pheromones triggered a primal response in several key places in my body.

The sexual chemistry was overwhelming—and I hadn't even been inside the girl yet. She had me wrapped around a dainty little finger, strung up so tight it was cutting off circulation and I was just begging to be let loose.

You know how those commercials tell you to call your doctor if you have a hard-on for more than four hours? Well, I was going on seven days and I hadn't fucking taken anything.

After I parked, Ophelia walked the entryway semi-circle for ten minutes, fawning over the bottlebrush, and it crossed my mind I could have just let the tailgate down right there for a few hours and it would have satisfied her.

But that was nothing compared to the kid-at-an-amusement-park excitement in her entire body when we finally got inside.

"Look at how gorgeous this is." She gasped. All around us were flowering green plants and tropical leaves, waterfalls, colorful birds, hundreds of butterflies circling, and greenhouse glass overhead like we had entered our own little fairy-tale terrarium.

Then right there in the middle, the sylph herself putting all the spirits to shame. Bright yellow and unbelievably distracting.

"There's over twenty thousand butterflies floating around in here," I told her as we walked along the guided path through the aviary. "Sometimes more, it depends on the time of the year." As I said it, black and cobalt blue wings fluttered between the two of us. "Swallowtail."

Ophelia assessed me suspiciously. "Did you study the brochure for some extra brownie points?"

"I would never mislead you like that."

She leaned over the barrier to stick her nose in some pink petals. "How does the fighter pilot know so much about butterflies?"

"What, do you think all my brain can comprehend is camouflage and gunfights?"

She bit her lip. "No. I just can't seem to figure you out."

"Well good, we're on the same page then." I said. "When Cap and I started the business, one of our first clients was right across the street from here. I kept passing the sign every morning on my drive and curiosity got the best of me."

"Solo butterfly date?"

"Kind of." Ophelia looked up in awe as several wings circled our heads. "I spent a lot of time alone back then. I was here for three hours by myself just trying to see how many of them I could find."

"And how'd you do?" She tried to catch one fluttering by on her finger, but it landed on my shoulder instead. Her blue eyes widened and she clung to the arm of my shirt to get a better look.

"Monarch." I nodded at it, the sound of my voice sending the orange bug away. "I counted forty-seven before Mateo was blowing up my phone wondering where I was."

"You guys are really close," she said, continuing our slow walk. I liked the height difference between the two of us, because I got to watch her little legs work double time to keep an even pace. "I never got to ask how the whole cam sex convo went."

It went exactly how you would expect two grown men to act around each other after something like that. We sat outside on our back patio under the bulb lights, beers in hand, and stared silently into space as we drank them. Mateo picked at the label on his bottle and made a face that looked like he was either contemplating or constipated, and I pulled the brim of my hat down low enough he couldn't see my eyes.

I didn't care if my buddy was fucking on camera. That was between him and his girl, and they both seemed pretty on board with it given the Broadway-level production complete with lighting, music, and costumes.

My only wish was that I didn't have to see it to believe it. The full-frontal view of Tally burned into my mind made me feel like a permanent pervert. She was like a fucking sister to me. I wasn't sure if Mateo was sitting there waiting for an apology, or waiting for me to address the fact that I now knew what his girlfriend looked like on all fours.

The girls had long been scattered when I broke the tension and asked, "Old Saint Dick?" to which he replied with a shrug, "Paid for the chair you're sitting on."

And that was the end of that.

"I've seen Mateo naked more times than I care to remember," I said, amused. "So walking in on that was like any other Friday."

Ophelia paused next to the rail to look at a Cabbage White perched on a leaf. "Nat suggested we film an orgy," she announced nonchalantly.

My steps faltered as that image materialized. "Is that what you consider proper first date etiquette? Laying all your kinks right out in the open?"

"You were just thinking about it, weren't you?" She grinned, pointing a teasing finger at me.

I grabbed that little palm and brought it to my chest. "You wouldn't have an orgy with our best friends."

She tried to make herself bigger—rolling her shoulders back, tilting her head, licking her lips a bit to entice me. Maybe she liked some kinky shit in the bedroom, but I was calling that group activity bluff.

"Wouldn't I?" She shrugged.

"No, because you're selfish, just like me." I leaned in so I could whisper. "You need a man on his knees for you, and only you. I've told you this before, O, I don't fucking share."

We were in our own little bubble under the hanging plants for a moment. Our hands still clasped together at my chest, focus wavering between mouths and eyes, the soft panting of a thousand wings overhead. Ophelia swallowed and I watched her throat contract with rapt attention.

"You're right, this isn't first date material," she said softly. "You should focus more on getting to know my personal thoughts and opinions on the current political climate."

I huffed out a laugh and dragged her along the path by her hand. "For some reason I don't think we have nearly enough time for that."

AT THE RATE WE moved through the exhibits, our trip to the museum would outlive the butterflies themselves. We lingered in the tropical rainforest, reading the park map, identifying what was flying above us as I bent over the informational brochure with my hand on the small of Ophelia's back.

Natural.

Everything was natural. Spending time with her was kind of like slipping beneath the covers into freshly washed sheets. You just laid there for a while with a dopey smile on your face, kicking your feet around because it felt so damn good.

"Look at this one, Frankie." Ophelia called me over to stand in front of the running waterfall, pointing to a butterfly with brown wings and bright yellow edges perched on a leaf. "What is it?"

I assessed it. "Mourning Cloak." There were very few butterflies with colors that dark.

"You could be totally making this up, and I wouldn't know either way."

I flipped through our little pamphlet and found the page with common butterflies listed and pointed it out. "Don't insult me, Trouble."

She snorted, reaching over to try and touch the little guy. "Their wings are so cool up close like this."

"They're actually translucent, believe it or not." I examined it as closely as she was. "There are scales covering the actual wing that reflect light to make them different colors."

"Fun fact." She smiled. "My sisters would love this place. I should send them a picture."

"I'll take one," I offered.

"Oh no, I don't need to be in it." She chuckled nervously.

"You look like you belong in this garden, Ophelia. Now get your cute, sunshine ass up on that bridge so I can take a fucking picture."

"So bossy," she commented. Her hesitation only lasted a moment before she was positioning herself at the center of the tiny walking bridge that crossed over the stream. "Is this good?"

I pulled my phone out of my pocket and opened the camera. "Move a little bit to the left." There were people walking around in the background ruining the shot. "Now lean against the post—no, not like that, that looks like you're a department store mannequin."

As she readjusted herself I snapped photos, catching those candid moments where I could tell she didn't know whether to kill me or kiss me.

"Add 'Instagram boyfriend' to your dating profile," she suggested.

"I don't know what that is." I squinted. "Can you move that one piece of hair behind your ear?"

"You're unbelievable." She laughed, swiping the pesky strand away from her face. "Better?"

"It was never bad; you know you're killing me in that dress." Her forearms settled on a spot on the railing where the sun found its way through the thick leaves. "Now smile like you're enjoying leisurely butterfly watching with the man who's going to blow your back out later."

Her eyes widened and a broad, amused grin lit up her face. *Perfect.*

When my camera roll could easily incriminate me as Ophelia's stalker, I waved her back over. "Got some good ones," I said. "Just had to loosen you up a bit."

"I think you still get some points off for vulgarity."

"But I get some points added for photography, so we can call it even." I reached down and nudged her hand with mine, pleased when she grabbed it without question. "Is this okay?"

She nodded shyly.

Holding hands felt like a foreign gesture. The little things about being in a relationship were what I'd forgotten: opening doors, sharing meals, offloading about our shitty days. A partner was like an extension of yourself and being able to open those previously locked doors with Ophelia when it came to dating felt like reintroducing myself to, well...*me*. The version I shoved in a closet and turned the key on.

I didn't talk to Mateo about butterflies. I didn't talk to anyone about anything most of the time, because I viewed my vulnerability as weakness, and being weak was never an option for me.

My father died and I had to be strong because my mother and sister needed it. I went into the Army and I had to be strong because my country needed it. I joined Delta and my only choice was to be strong because I needed it.

The truth was, the only reason I ever walked into that butterfly museum the first time was because I felt that sick, pressing weakness trying to carve me open and I needed to shut it down. My mother used to tell me that my father was with her all the time, and whenever she was having a rough day, she'd see him in the butterflies. So I went alone, looking for my dad, embarrassingly enough, because there was no one else to talk to—and I kept going back. I went back all the time.

But that wasn't the kind of deep life shit you opened up about to a girl you barely knew.

"Women like it when men take the lead. First dates are supposed to feel like the beginning of a good book."

"Interesting," I mused. "And when you get to the end of the chapter you want to keep flipping the page to see what'll happen next."

"Exactly." She said. "If you couldn't tell, I got my degree in English lit."

"I can get down with some Jay Gatsby. Specifically the version of him that got to make out with Carey Mulligan."

"You know what happened to Jay Gatsby, right?"

"Didn't he move to New Jersey or something?"

She started to pull her report card notepad out of her bag and I plucked it out of her hand.

"I know you're not teaching English lit to eight-year-olds." I paused to point out a grazing Spring Azure that Ophelia marveled at before it flew away.

"No, but I'm *introducing* them to greater works of fiction," she explained. "We do more reading in my classroom than district standard requires, but I find it's at the heart of creativity. The more the kids are reading, the more they're talking and sharing. It becomes less of a tedious requirement and more of a stimulating activity."

"High school was hard enough." I said. "I worked too much to be a good student."

"When I was in high school my parents were having newborns, so I was like a pseudo-caregiver. Maybe I would have enjoyed teaching at the secondary level, but with my siblings, watching them grow up, I felt like that was the age group I wanted to focus on. It was important to me that they knew they always had a friend. It's kind of stupid but I think that's what all kids that age really need."

"That's not stupid, Ophelia." I shook my head. "You have a habit of doing that, you know?"

"Doing what?"

"Dulling all these admirable things about yourself. Stop being meek."

"I'm not being meek," she argued. "Talking about second graders is never an interesting topic on a date. Men want to know things like where I've traveled, what the craziest thing I've ever done is, my body count—"

"No one should ever be asking you how many other people you've slept with," I interrupted. "And any guy that's even re-motely worth your time is going to think *everything* about you is interesting. Because it is."

Her glossy lips parted slightly.

Fuck. I hadn't processed how desperate that sounded before it came tumbling out of my mouth. I was coming on way too strong for a first date and way too emotional for a fuck buddy. My north and south brain were doing a juggling act with no handler.

As if she could tell I was kicking myself over it, Ophelia pulled me back along our path and pointed out another cluster of colorful wings by the ceiling. "I've never seen anything like this," she murmured.

"No butterflies in Pine Ridge?"

"Nowhere to go and appreciate them all."

"So far Colorado has a rainy season, a snowy season, and a critical lack of butterfly museums. I'm not totally impressed."

"You never even got to *see* Colorado," she insisted. "It's one of the most beautiful states in the country. The mountains, the lakes, there's everything you can geographically think of from deserts to waterfalls. The Springs are a metropolis, but you can still take a day trip to visit a national park."

This girl was so animated when she was passionate about something. Her dimples deepened, her eyebrows jumped up and down. Everything Ophelia did could be categorized as cute in one way or another. And even if I was just teasing her about her home state, it made me want to instigate further for the selfish pleasure of watching her react.

"Have you ever skied?" She asked.

"I grew up in Southern Florida, got deployed to the Middle East, then spent the rest of my career island hopping in the Pacific and hiking in Central America. So no, Trouble. I've never skied."

"When I was a kid we would do an annual weekend trip to the mountain to ski." She smiled to herself. "Mom was a natural. She could do all the hard slopes, but I was more interested in the hot chocolate at the lodge. Dad and I used to sit there for hours and watch her come down the mountain like a badass, cheering and waving at her from the window."

"Sounds like you and your dad had the right idea."

"I learned how to ski eventually," she said. "When my legs were long enough to keep up. I love it now, but you know what my favorite thing about the mountain actually is?"

"Tell me." I absentmindedly rubbed the soft spot above her thumb with mine.

Her baby blues sparkled and she took a long, hesitant breath. "The sky."

My attention piqued.

"You can see every single star in what looks like the entire galaxy on a clear night. I used to do this really silly thing"—she looked down coyly—"where I would go out at night outside the cabin, lay on my back in the snow, and just stare up at the sky. There's a moment where it's deadly quiet and snowing and the flakes look like they're stars falling toward you. It's endless and mesmerizing, and even though your face is chilled to the bone, the cold is really the only thing tethering you to reality. You almost feel like you don't exist."

Somehow I could imagine exactly what she was describing on that mountain. We weren't standing in a tropical greenhouse anymore—we were stargazing at the peak together. Merging our two separate and contrasting lives into a shared moment.

I was worried about giving too much of myself away too soon, but I realized that might be what Ophelia needed out of me. Good conversation, unlike what she was probably getting with the other men she entertained. Someone who would sit and talk to her about existential crises and conspiracy theories and space. Stimulation in more ways than sexually.

I'd never been caught in a snowstorm, or skied down a mountain, or swam beneath a waterfall. But we could pretend for a little while.

"You're such a romantic," I teased her. "I also love the sky. That's why I spent ten years up there."

"You and Mateo were in that top secret soldier crew together."

"The Army."

She rolled her eyes. "Delta Force."

A memory of Cap and I bunked together in a tent the size of the cab of my truck crossed my mind. It was fuck all strange that Delta was what we considered the good old days now. The two of us and the Swan boys were either at each other's throats or on each other's backs twenty-four seven.

"Ah yes, otherwise known as 'top secret soldier crew'. How could I forget that?" I winked.

"Did you always want to be in the Army?"

"No," I told her truthfully. "I wanted to take care of my mom and help out my sister and the Army was the quickest way to make a lot of cash right out of high school."

We sat on a bench while I went back and forth with myself, deciding how to broach the subject of my father, who I didn't usually talk about. Rip the fucking bandage off, I guess.

"When my father passed, we really struggled for a while. The heart attack was sudden, and he was so young. I took on being the man in the house, but there was only so much I could do as a teenager. I worked at grocery stores to get discounts on our food and at the car wash on weekends until I saved enough money to buy us a used car. With the Army, I was doing what I knew my dad would have done—but I ended up loving it and making a career out of it."

Ophelia didn't pity me; she listened as if absorbing every word and breath in between. Talking about my dad didn't make me emotional anymore like it did when I was a kid. In fact I hadn't even had a moment of dejection over it since my last birthday, when I realized I was as old as my father had ever been.

"Sounds like you're the world's best son." She nudged me with her shoulder. "I don't know them, but your mom and sister have to appreciate you more than you realize. You basically gave your life to them."

"No." I laughed, having never thought of it in that way. "We're family, we take care of each other. They *are* my life."

"Look at us, pseudo-mom and pseudo-dad before we hit puberty."

"Do you want kids?"

Her eyes flashed to mine. "Yes." Then, she continued more seriously, "But I don't want to fuck them up. I'm terrified to settle and get married and have kids with the wrong guy, and then repeat the same cycle as my parents. I can't do that."

"That makes a lot of sense," I agreed. "You shouldn't get on yourself for being picky or deciding not to date someone because you're expected to. I'm nearly forty. I'm not married, I don't have kids, but it's not because I don't want those things. It's because it hasn't felt right to do that yet."

"Nat mentioned something about your ex."

Discomfort panged in my chest.

Did I want to rehash the disaster that was the end of my military career, paired with the crumbling of a near decade-long relationship right then? Not exactly. We were having a thoughtful, insightful conversation that was going surprisingly well without dipping below depression level. I wanted to tell her, but I wanted to keep her smiling way more. I wasn't going to let Vanessa creep in and overcast the sunshine sitting beside me with her fucking storm cloud.

"Rule number one is don't talk about your exes on a first date." I stood and pulled her along through the final bend of the aviary. "Nothing is going to dampen my mood. We're surrounded by a thousand butterflies, and I'm currently courting the most interesting girl in the world."

"That's not true." Her cheeks turned a dusty shade of rose. "I've lived in the same town my entire life, the craziest thing I've ever done is a keg stand, I have lunch with my mom every week at the same place and time, and I date endless, unsatisfying men."

"I was in the military," I reminded her. "Where interests are limited to drinking, fucking, and blowing shit up."

"Bet that uniform got you anything your pretty face wanted," she teased.

"Maybe, but it wouldn't have gotten me you."

I stilled, holding a palm out cautiously toward Ophelia and making a shushing gesture with a finger to my lips. She stopped walking, and I could tell she was tamping down a rush of unjustified panic. A giant Blue Morpho had landed right on the crown of her head and was sitting there like it'd found a new home.

"That's incredible," I whispered, slowly inching my phone out of my pocket to take a picture and show her.

"Holy shit," she gasped. "What do I do?"

"They like when you sing to them," I told her.

"Really? Like, what kind of song?"

"Like a slow jazz number."

"Are you fucking with me?"

My mouth turned up on one side. "Give us your best Etta James."

Ophelia rolled her eyes, and even more spectacularly, the butterfly started crawling onto her forehead.

"Oh, fuck. Oh god, I can feel its little feet on me."

"Fun fact," I started.

"No, fuck off with your fun facts."

"Butterflies use their feet to taste," I continued. "It's probably sampling your skin juice to find a suitable place to lay its eggs."

She curled in on herself. "Get it off me, respectfully."

I reached out to shoo it away, but the bug fluttered and landed on my forearm. "Hey, little guy."

"There, now it can slurp on your juices."

I grimaced. "God, O."

"I know, okay? I knew the second I said it."

"Can't take you anywhere."

We walked toward the exit and the butterfly remained, stuck to my arm hair, legs tangled in the brush. If it stayed, I would stay there all day, too. But at the door, as if it knew it couldn't keep us company anymore, it took off.

"It was attached to you." Ophelia smiled. "You should have snuck him out in your pocket."

"That's theft, you little klepto." I pinched her side. "Fun fact—"

"Can't be worse than the last one."

We pushed through the doors of the exhibit. "A butterfly's life expectancy is only two to four weeks. So by the time you leave Florida, most of them will be dead."

O paused in the walkway with a scowl. "Give me that." She ripped her notepad out of my back pocket, swatting me in the ass with it before jotting down an aggressive note.

I cackled all the way through the rose garden.

20

Frankie

HOURS LATER WE HOPPED back in the truck and I cranked the air
conditioner to full blast. Both of us stuck our faces to the vents,
letting out long, satisfied sighs to be out of the heat. Ophelia's
skin was flushed red, her cheeks like apples. A bead of sweat
trickled down her neck behind her ear and I didn't care how hot
it was anymore after that.

I found myself imagining what kind of assholes were passing
this woman by as we drove through town. She was the definition
of a girl you took home to meet the family. So attractive it kept
you awake at night, thinking about the way it'd feel to have her
underneath you, at the same time so charming you wanted to
protect and take care of her just as much as the physical stuff.

If that wasn't enough, she was *challenging*. Smart, funny, effortlessly unhinged. Coy, but never shy. She gave my shit right

back to me, which maybe some insecure little boy might find intimidating, but I ate it up.

She wasn't a *girl*, though. Maybe that was the problem. Ophelia was dating men that wanted tame and behaved. They wanted low aspiration, stay at home with the kids, have dinner ready when they got home, and missionary sex lasting long enough to get her going but never enough to get her off.

Knowing she'd likely settle for that had me squeezing the steering wheel a little too tight.

In the passenger seat she was studying her notepad with the pen between her teeth. Her dress had ridden up a dangerous amount, tan legs sticking to the leather seats. She had to know how much skin she was showing—she always knew exactly what she was doing.

"You're certified gold at random butterfly trivia." She smiled around the end of the pen. "Great location choice, interesting conversation, good humor"—she rolled her eyes—"but could be better."

"Boo," I protested.

"Extra points for opening doors, holding hands, not sweating on said hands. Appropriate and well-fitting outfit." Her eyes roamed over me. "A haircut wouldn't hurt."

I shrugged as we passed beneath a traffic light. "More to hold onto."

She laughed. "God, do you ever turn it off?"

"Why would I when you're sitting in my passenger seat with your dress around your hips like that practically daring me to pull over?"

That perfect bottom lip got a fresh bite, and she flipped her notepad closed. "Negatives: frisky touching, suggestive commentary—"

"Flirting," I corrected her.

"Complete misunderstanding of *The Great Gatsby*."

"The eyes are watching, the weather is hot, the green light blinks."

"If flight training doesn't work out I'm sure they'll hire you at CliffsNotes." She shifted in her seat to face me, and that dress slid up even higher. *Fuck, please be wearing panties or I'm gonna drive off the goddamn road.*

"Anything else, smartass? I might not be too dusty after all."

"Yeah, your truck."

"My truck?" I scoffed. "This truck is a machine. What's wrong with my truck?"

"No bench seat."

I lifted the large center console to reveal a middle seat between us. "Try again."

Ophelia tossed her notebook onto the dash and unbuckled her seatbelt.

"What are you doing?" My attention waned between her and the highway. She stretched her top half across the bench, lying on her stomach. Her head was so close to my crotch that my palms started to sweat.

"Date's over," she noted mischievously.

I blew out an unsteady breath and my dick picked up a pulse as she reached out and unfastened my belt buckle, little fingers working at the bulge of my zipper. My entire stomach tensed in anticipation.

"Tell me you're wearing your panties."

She stopped briefly to smirk up at me. *Fuck, that view.* Then, she pulled her dress up past her perfect, tan-lined ass to show me there wasn't even a goddamn string of fabric between my fingers and that sweet pussy. "You're fucking trouble," I mumbled. "But you know that already, huh?"

"I want to even the playing field." She continued working on my shorts until my fly was completely loose. "So far I'm the only one that's gotten any benefits out of this friendship."

"I've gotten plenty," I rasped, right hand abandoning the steering wheel to slide down her back and take a handful of bare skin. "This is breaking a whole list of laws, O."

I checked the rearview and the side mirrors to see how alone we were. My chest pounded and every ounce of blood in my body did a deep dive to my crotch the second she reached beneath the band of my briefs to pull me out.

Another room at the fun house. This was roadhead Ophelia, and I hoped I never figured her out.

"Oh," she mumbled. Seemingly to herself, but I heard every soft note of it.

"You don't have to," I told her, all the while using my free hand to massage the tense muscles at the back of her neck. She wrapped her fingers around me and I groaned like a fucking virgin. "It's been a while."

"Just drive, Frankie." My focus shifted entirely to my lap as that first sampling lick of her tongue swept across the head of my cock. "Sweet," she whispered.

Sweet. She called the taste of me sweet, and my legs tensed so hard I probably pulled a muscle. Then she licked me again, and again, and the knot in my stomach unfurled with pleasure and spread its way down to my toes.

"That's real fucking good." Flyaway hairs started falling in front of her eyes and I pushed them to the side. "Get me all wet."

O took that literally, reeling her head back the tiniest bit and spitting on it.

"*Jesus Christ.*" My knuckles turned white on the wheel and I slowed to barely fucking sixty in the right lane. Nearly four years of pent-up sexual frustration felt close to spilling out of me already.

She worked her palm up and down, keeping her lips around the tip like a lollipop, and my hips lifted looking for more.

"I needed this." My head fell back on the headrest and my eyes lidded. "Needed you so bad."

I could feel her smile around me, the sharp edges of her teeth grazing everywhere I was sensitive. I was so hard it was starting to fucking hurt and her mouth was the perfect answer. How could I ever forget how good this felt? Did it ever feel *this* good?

"You have a really nice dick," Ophelia murmured.

I was going to blow my load all over her face if she started telling me things like that.

She dipped and closed her mouth over the first few inches, finally putting an end to the tongue tease. I let out a long, low groan that would have been embarrassing if I gave a fuck anymore. "You're good at this," I bit out. "Look at you."

Her eyes flickered up and I knew the image of that pretty freckled face getting fucked would be what I got off thinking about for a long, long time.

My fingers were itching to touch but I was tied up driving. I just kept scratching her back, soothing the skin across her shoulders, and squeezing her ass when the pleasure got so good I needed an outlet.

Her messy bun bobbed up and down and started to come loose, so I fisted a hand in her hair and held it back. She moaned at the gesture, the vibration of her noises and her tongue tightening my groin. This was about to be over.

"You like rough," I noticed. "You like when I hold your throat down on my cock."

She nodded as her hand stroked all the way down to my base and held there, lips following. I lifted my fist and bit down on the knuckle.

Then she choked.

"The whole thing, huh?" I could hardly breathe, let alone focus on the exit I was supposed to be taking as I turned off the highway. "That's a lot of fucking dick in your mouth, Ophelia."

She continued to take it all, up and down without stopping for a sip of air. My lower back started to sweat and my balls tightened.

"Goddamnit, O," I groaned. She flicked her tongue around it. "I'm gonna come down your throat."

She didn't stop, only moaning more, sucking harder, working faster. Her fist and her mouth in perfect, lethal tandem. It felt so fucking good my heart was thundering against my rib cage. I wanted the feeling of reaching that peak to last forever.

It was over. God, it was so fucking over for me.

We reached a stoplight and I could finally give her all my attention. I guided her up and down with both hands, racing my own release to see how much longer I could keep her going.

"You want it?" I asked, voice stilted.

"Yes," she breathed, briefly pausing before taking me right down to the back of her throat.

That did it. I slammed both hands into the steering wheel and rode out the ropes of my orgasm, grunting through clenched teeth. Years' worth of pent-up release emptied itself, filling her mouth. My pulse didn't even out, though; it remained in my ears like a hammer all the way to the very last drop.

Thirty-five years old and I had never come so hard in my life.

Ophelia finally lifted, dragging her bottom lip along the underside of me on the way, sending shivers down my spine. She planted a kiss on the sensitive head and made sure I watched as she swiped her thumb across her lips, then sucked the excess off of it.

I forgot where I was when the car behind us laid on the horn and Ophelia startled, smacking the back of her head on the steering wheel.

"Shit," I panicked, hitting the gas and rubbing her head at the same time. In the rearview a woman in a minivan was flipping me off and I gave her one back. "Are you okay?"

O started giggling, crawling backward out of my lap and shimmying her dress down her legs as I tucked myself away. Her laugh made me laugh, and we were both hysterical when I pulled back into Tally's complex.

"You talk a lot when you're about to come," she said. "You get real filthy."

My cheeks heated. What I wasn't going to say was that I had never spoken to a sexual partner the way I was letting every salacious thought fly with her. Ophelia was getting a different, hungry edge of me that we were both meeting at the same time.

"I'll tone it down," I assured her.

"No," she objected. "It's hot."

Tally's car was in the driveway, so Mateo must have been at home waiting for me to fill him in on all the dirty details. Which I wasn't going to do, because the last ten minutes of my life were reserved for me and only me—and the girl I shared them with.

"Are you hungry?" I asked, attempting to keep her with me longer.

"I have dinner plans with Nat."

I wanted to know what was going through her head. She'd just gotten me off; she must have been at least a little bit turned on. I walked my fingers across the bench seat and tugged at the hem of her dress. "Give me a couple minutes with her?"

"Did you just refer to my vagina as *her*?

"Them?"

"Goodnight, Frankie." Taking her bag, she pushed out of the passenger side door.

"What are you doing?" I shouted.

"I'm taking your advice." She walked backward toward the door. "Not sleeping with a guy on the first date."

That was suddenly the worst advice I'd ever given.

I sighed, watched her wave and disappear through the threshold, and then dropped my head to the steering wheel as I turned the ignition to drive back home.

21

Ophelia

"ARE WE SPENDING THE night?"

Steam billowed toward the light above the shower and an indie rock playlist filtered out of Natalia's phone on the bathroom sink. I aggressively filed my nails from my perch on the lid of the toilet seat as the room turned into a sauna.

"It's not like we both don't have a bed to sleep in," she answered.

She couldn't see me roll my eyes, but I did. "Staying the night kind of crosses the friends-with-benefits line, don't you think?"

"Your situation is crooked as fuck. The lines are already blurred."

My situation was both the most convenient and inconvenient thing I'd ever experienced at the same time. Frankie scratched an itch I didn't know I had when it came to men. Which was exactly what was so inconvenient about the whole thing. I already knew I would be struggling to find a guy back in Pine Ridge that fit his mold. He was somehow the perfect gentleman and the perfect scoundrel.

Attractive, smart, vulnerable, begrudgingly funny.

The convenience was that thing he was working with below the belt. *Christ.* I wasn't a girl easily impressed after having had my fair share of hook-ups. A dick is a dick, right?

Wrong. So very, very wrong.

So what I first categorized as a convenience was actually the number one glaring inconvenience, really. I thought it'd be hard to find a man to match his first date habits, but in reality, I was putting myself on the fast track to being completely unsatisfied sexually for the remainder of my life.

And he hadn't even been inside me yet.

"Do you think I'm being stupid?" I groaned.

"I think you're being a single twenty-six-year-old woman on vacation with a vetted, clean, unattached, attractive man."

I tapped my cheek with the nail file. "You're right. I'm just paranoid."

There was the click of a bottle top opening and closing behind the curtain. "You're both in the same situation, Phee. I'm sure Frankie has the same concerns as you do about it. Which is *good*, because it's been addressed already."

I nodded to myself. A question I'd thought about briefly but hadn't entertained crossed my mind. "Do you think he'll take that job in Colorado?"

After a short pause the shower curtain whipped back and a soapy Natalia peeked her shampooed head out. "What an interesting question."

"Is it?" I stood and turned toward the mirror, avoiding her eyes but finding them anyway in the reflection.

"One might ask that if they were interested in someone beyond a physical relationship. Which is definitely not the case with you." She raised a dark eyebrow. "Right?"

"No, right, exactly," I rushed out. "Just curious, in general. He seemed on the fence about it."

She closed the curtain and I let out a trapped breath.

"It'd be a miracle to get that man to move that far away from his family."

"But he was gone for years," I argued.

"Temporarily," she countered. "Florida was still his home."

Add family man to Frankie's disarming list of generous qualities.

"Think about it though, he's barely had a chance to sit down since he was a teenager. Now he's deciding whether or not he wants to settle in a place he's the most comfortable, with the people he loves, versus a completely new state on the other side of the country with nothing familiar."

"It's a big decision," I agreed. "I would never leave the Springs. As much as I love this sunshine, my family is there, my job, my mailman."

"How would you ever survive without your mailman?" she asked sarcastically.

"Doug knows not to leave the packages on my front porch because they are *constantly* stolen. He walks them around the back. We have a system."

"Of course you do."

"The point is that I couldn't abandon my routine either. And if I ever find a man on this sordid fucking plane of existence, I'd want him to get to know my family, and take my brothers out to go fishing, and feel comfortable spending time with my mom if I wasn't around. So relocating my life away from them would never be an option."

The water stopped and Nat's hand jutted out to pull a towel off the wall. A minute later she stepped out of the shower with her hair spun up in it.

"You really do have the perfect tits for porn," I commented.

She looked down at her chest with a smirk. "Have you talked to your parents by the way?"

I sighed. "I sent a group text with that picture of me that Frankie took at the butterfly museum."

"And?"

"My mom asked if the dress I was wearing was hers, because she could have sworn she had the same one. My dad sent a Bitmoji of himself wearing a butterfly costume, and Stella was my only sibling to answer and she asked if I could sneak one of them home in my luggage as a Christmas present."

"God, I'm sorry, Phee." She rubbed a dab of lotion into her cheeks. "Forget that I asked."

"Everyone's busy," I justified. "It's not like that."

It was definitely like that. But deep down it felt selfish and immature to demand attention from adults when I was an adult, and my siblings didn't know any better.

"Push it to the back of your mind anyway. We're gonna have fun tonight. Without cooking, baking, or indecent exposure."

"*Unsolicited* indecent exposure."

She pulled the towel off her head and whipped me in the ass with it on her way toward the door. "Shower, trim your bikini line, spray some perfume on your panties."

"Can't I just wear my pjs?"

She snapped her fingers and pointed at me, wide-eyed. "You beautiful genius. Christmas pajama party."

I RUMMAGED THROUGH THE spare closet in the hallway searching for the board games Mateo swore were on the second shelf from the top. As far as I could see there were some dumbbells, a box of old DVDs, and a stack of paper that looked like a terms and conditions agreement.

At my feet, I was stepping on two camouflage duffle bags full of God knows what, trying to see as far back as my height would allow. I tested the durability of one with my toes. *Sturdy enough.* If I lost my balance and fell, at least it was only a foot to the ground and the worst thing that could happen was a small set of free weights crashing down on top of me.

I stepped off the bag and bent over, fluffing it with my hands to double check.

Sliding everything out of the way, I hoisted myself up and got a better look into the closet. Behind were two old shoe boxes kept together by layers of silver electrical tape, one unmarked, the other labeled PIKE in black Sharpie.

I chewed my lip.

Down the hallway I could hear Nat's soft laughter, and Frankie had yet to come out of his bedroom after we arrived and told him to get his pjs on for our Hallmark special occasion.

Was I above a total invasion of privacy? *Yes.* Was I still curious enough about the man I was finagling with? *Also yes.* I'd probably just be looking at some souvenirs from overseas, or pins and medals or whatever it was they gave you in the military that didn't really rank as home decor but you definitely shouldn't throw in the garbage.

The box was much lighter than I expected when I pulled it down, balancing the edge against my ribs as I flipped the lid open and peeked inside.

"Cute."

I picked up a photo of a much more youthful, much less scruffy Frankie with a buzzcut. He was stone-faced, staring into the camera in his Army uniform. He had to have been twenty pounds lighter and over a decade younger.

The same piercing brown eyes, but somehow the ones I had been introduced to were a shade darker. Like a cloud hung over them where there used to be sunshine. Beautiful, in a more devastating way.

There were dozens more photos behind it, several stages of his career, in different places with different people. I stopped on one with the same familiar faces from the picture Frankie and Mateo kept on their mantle.

Four friends, sitting in thick mud and rain together in all their gear. Frankie had one eye open as he laid back against a tree trunk, Mateo sat beside him making a ridiculous face and a "hang loose" hand gesture. The two others sat on either side of them looking wet and uncomfortable.

I flipped the photo over and saw written in pen, *Swan boys, Colombia.*

Mateo mentioned something about the brothers that were coming to visit for the new year. Somehow every single man added to this insane equation was ridiculously attractive and looked great in muted greens.

Maybe I wasn't as immune to a uniform as I initially thought I was. Or maybe a certain insistent, salacious soldier was getting to me a little too much.

I continued fanning through, wondering where Frankie kept all the film rolls it must have taken to develop that many pictures. In the corners of most were faded numerical dates from the years before a camera and a phone were one and the same. I spent those same years out at recess striking out in fucking kickball while the two men in the other room were risking their lives every day halfway across the world.

My perspective shifted substantially, realizing that what Frankie did to take care of his mother and his sister was literally gambling his life. That even if anything happened to him at war, they would be taken care of by the government that sent him out to die.

And it didn't end with the Army. He reenlisted, and then joined Delta.

I gnawed on the inside of my cheek and shuffled the photos around in the box, but in doing so a different one caught my eye.

I couldn't know for sure, of course, but the hollow feeling in my gut as I looked down at the woman in the picture with her arms snug around Frankie's waist told me it was the infamous ex. She had parts of him I never would, and that made me inappropriately envious. Friends don't get jealous of their friends having ex-girlfriends. Unless there were feelings involved, and that was something I couldn't afford to let happen.

"She would look like that," I whispered to myself. The woman was like a *Sports Illustrated* cover model. Long curly brown hair, thin nose, upper lip just as big as her lower. I mean, who was actually blessed with that?

She could have been Sofia Vergara's younger, hotter sister. Same fucking boobs.

They fit each other like two pieces of a puzzle, and he looked down at her smiling into the camera like she hung the goddamn moon, too.

I knew it ended badly, but it was hard to imagine what would have separated them after seven years and all that they had gone through to keep a relationship alive deployment after deployment.

How did you give up on a love like that?

I put the photo back in the box and rooted around for more to confirm that the girl in the picture was who I thought she was. At the bottom of the box was something else though—dozens of something else's—tri-folded on looseleaf paper.

"Phee! Need some help?" Natalia's voice rang from the living room.

"Be right there!" I shouted back. I knew I should have stopped while I was ahead, but my stubborn, shrouded brain insisted I push my lapse in character further. I snagged a letter off the top of the bunch and opened it.

No sooner than I read the first line, *Dear Vanessa*, was it snatched out of my hand and dropped back in the box.

"That's not a board game." Frankie's sharp voice met the shell of my ear.

I lost my balance on the bag beneath me in an instant, yelping as my feet and head threatened to switch places.

A strong arm wrapped around my waist and righted me before I could hit the ground, depositing me back on the hardwood floor beside him.

"You scared the shit out of me." I held a palm to my chest.

"Boo," he teased, trading me a glass of chilled white wine for the shoe box I miraculously still held onto.

I stood there studying my socks like a kid that just got caught stealing money from their mother's purse as Frankie reorganized the mess I'd made. He reached up and slid the box back to where I'd found it, then reached up one more shelf and grabbed two board games that were absolutely unmissable from his height and pulled them down for me.

"I'm so sorry," I murmured. "I should *not* have been so nosy. That was totally fucked up."

"You're using my uniforms as a stepladder and reading my Dear John letters in the dark now, Ophelia?"

I stuttered out a string of vowels. "Y–you're right. I'm so embarrassed. What a creep."

His lips flattened into a line and a crease formed between his brows for a moment. If he was going to be angry at me, at least let him keep it between us. It was mortifying to explain myself once; I didn't need to be making excuses to leave the party early to save some face with Mateo, too.

"Sorry," I muttered again. My lower lip trembled.

"I'm fucking messing with you, Trouble." Frankie reached out and pinched it. "O, I'm not mad. Relax."

The balloon of air that had accumulated in my chest released in a deep sigh. "God, you suck." I punched his arm. "But I guess I fucking deserved that."

Frankie looked back at the open closet door before kicking it closed behind him. "You want to know anything about me, all you need to do is ask."

"Snooping through your supply closet was so much easier."

"You should have checked my underwear drawer. All the good stuff is in there."

My embarrassment eased. Had I caught a guy I barely knew helping himself to my shoe box of intimate memories, it would have disqualified him immediately. Now, however, I was even more curious about the past Frankie was clearly avoiding confronting.

Vanessa. The supermodel. The woman he sent letters to while he was at war like he was headlining a romance novel. The ex that screwed him up so good he swore off dating for years.

I was *not* his ex. In fact, we probably couldn't have been more different. If I had to pass judgment, Vanessa would be the type that carried a different designer bag around every day and drove an Audi. She was the woman who survived on a strictly liquid diet and had one of those fifteen percent, first name discount codes on a sportswear website that paid her to take a photo in their clothes.

I wore mom jeans and I wasn't even a mom.

In the living room the coffee table was cleared of my carefully curated festive decorations to make space for a few bowls of snacks and coasters for our glasses. The whole house smelled like caramel popcorn and melted chocolate, soft murmurs of Bing Crosby drifted from the radio, and the Christmas lights outside shone through the cracks in the blinds casting a warm glow onto the carpet. Frankie walked over to the fireplace and lit the tiny flame, adding even more cozy ambiance to the room.

Four days until Christmas and it finally, actually felt like a holiday again to me. The bells had stopped jingling the year my parents separated, which was also the year I stopped believing in the myth, uncoincidentally. Things started to make sense when I realized the Santa that visited my dad's apartment wrapped gifts the same way Frankie did, and also hid the wrapping paper in the closet of the spare bedroom (my bedroom) instead of at the North Pole.

"What kind of Christmas pajamas are those, Pike?" Mateo laughed.

Frankie glanced down at his worn, faded, flannel bottoms. The drawstring was completely uneven and there was a very obvious hole in the inseam of his right thigh.

"They're fucking plaid, man." Frankie huffed. "Sorry, I'm not like you with your matching set of candy canes." Nat and Mateo made the same mildly insulted face as they sat there wearing the his and hers version of the same outfit.

I laughed and my sauvignon went directly up my nose.

"Just sit down and help us pick a movie," Mateo suggested. "Don't do it too fast though, or you'll tear that hole all the way to your ass."

Frankie took a seat next to me on the floor in front of the coffee table and I nudged him playfully.

"I like your pjs," I said. "Classic. Timeless."

"Can I tell you a secret?" He leaned over, whispering. His fingers walked a trail from my knee to the hem of my cotton shorts. "I actually sleep naked."

My skin lit up where he touched it. Like candle wax searing into me. Blaming it on the wine was a cop-out—I barely had a buzz yet. The implications of the night weren't lost on either of us. I could feel it like a layer of dust in the air. This was all fun, wine, popcorn, and games until bedtime. When Mateo and Nat waddled off to their sound studio and Frankie and I were left to fill in each other's blanks. My nerves were on edge, despite how casual the hooking up was meant to be. It hadn't been as long for me as it was for Frankie, but I was still out of practice and the pressure to satisfy him loomed.

What happened in the truck was just as much for me as it was for him. A way to test the waters and boost my confidence. Judging by his reaction, we were both just as dazzled by each other's sexual prowess. Maybe I could be the girl who demanded what she deserved and never let a man know my next move. More spontaneity, less domesticity.

I fingered the button on my pajama shirt. "Even with a stranger in your bed?"

"Especially with her in my bed."

I pushed Frankie's tumbler of amber alcohol toward him, and with unspoken understanding, we clinked our drinks together and downed the remaining liquid.

22

Frankie

TWO-AND-A-HALF GLASSES OF WINE. That's how much alcohol it took to get Ophelia Brody so tipsy she started cheating at Scatter-gories.

She leaned into my shoulder more when she laughed, and her lips lingered on the rim of her glass when she smiled. Her words came out slower and in a deeper, sexier baritone that for whatever reason crept up my spine and vibrated like live wire.

That's a good voice, I thought. One I wouldn't mind hearing on a late-night phone call, long distance. One I'd never delete out of my voicemail just so I could go back and rehear it.

But those weren't things I was supposed to be thinking while I sat next to her on the carpet, sneaking as many secret looks as I could at the way the fireplace brought out the hidden auburn in her hair. I wasn't supposed to be committing her favorite wine to memory, or remembering her siblings' names, or spending my entire lunch break researching the best hiking trails in Colorado so I could save them in the notes on my phone, just in case.

None of these things were supposed to be happening, but I was in too deep to swim back to shore. Parts of me knew Ophelia was right there with me, but neither of us had the guts to fight the tide and save ourselves from fucking drowning.

For the first time in over three years, I didn't even get a knot in my stomach when someone alluded to Vanessa.

Hell, Ophelia had uncovered a box of the pathetic fucking love letters I'd sent to her from overseas that I should have taken fire to the minute we ended things. As soon as I found out everything I was too naive and in love to see coming.

I should have been angry when I caught her snooping. That was the justified emotion. But, in actuality, I felt *relief*. Relief because it meant the girl I couldn't stop thinking about was thinking about me, and my life, and my past, and my tours, and the shit that made me a thirty-five-year-old bachelor with a roommate and a season pass to Butterflyland.

I wanted her to ask me. Because for some reason, I wanted to tell her everything. Unload all the things I'd been holding onto for so long like she was a time capsule and it didn't matter what I said, or how ridiculous it sounded. In two weeks it would be buried and anyone else that found it wouldn't fucking understand anyway.

At the end of the day, that's what we were doing, right? Using each other. I just had to keep reminding myself of that.

Three glasses of wine in, and Ophelia was going at it with Mateo like they'd known each other all their lives, throwing popcorn across the table at him, deducting points for his spelling mistakes, quizzing him on all facts about Tally as a distraction.

But then that *became* the game. I would ask a question, and Ophelia and Mateo would write their answer down with a mini pencil on their sheet of paper. Tally would shout the answer, and her boyfriend and best friend would reveal theirs. We were all laughing, the drinks were flowing, and by the end of it, Ophelia had stamped Mateo with her personal seal of approval—which meant more to him than she'd ever know.

No one knew where the hours had gone when the credits rolled on the third movie. The wine opener sat next to a pile of discarded corks on the table and the four of us lay happily drunk on the couch in our pajamas.

I felt satiated. As weird as that sounded. There was nothing else I could have wanted out of my night. The beast of lust that always rumbled and growled around Ophelia had settled to a contented purr. Still easily awoken, but much less aggressive.

She folded herself into my side like it was the most natural thing in the world, and I could tell that sleep wasn't too far off. On the other side of us Tally was already out cold, slung across her boyfriend's lap.

"I'm gonna take her to bed, guys," Mateo whispered. "Few too many for my girl."

Ophelia smiled softly as he stood with Tally in his arms bridal style and blew the hair falling over her forehead out of her eyes.

"She's totally in love with you," she murmured. "Head over heels."

Mateo's answering smile was enough. He nodded at the both of us and took his girlfriend down the hall to bed.

Ophelia and I didn't move a muscle, but the energy between us shifted so abruptly it was like the room turned a completely different hue. Her fingernails tightened on my T-shirt, and my hand that was resting behind her on the couch drifted to play with a few wild strands of her hair.

I liked touching her so much it made me feel like a lunatic.

My fingertips brushed her shoulder and her whole arm erupted in goosebumps.

"Cold?" I asked, concerned. We never kept any throw blankets around the house. Neither Mateo or I spent a lot of time lounging in our living room. Most things in the house lacked a much-needed woman's touch, which I'd come to realize since O showed up.

"Not cold at all, actually," she said. "You're like a space heater."

I huffed out a laugh. "You have chills."

A second passed before she sat up and started tidying the empty bottles and bowls on the coffee table. "Do you guys recycle?"

I furrowed my eyebrows. "Stop cleaning, I'll take care of it later."

"I don't mind," she stammered, standing and gathering the glasses. "Are you still hungry? I could make you something."

"What's going on with you?" I grinned. "I don't want anything, except for you to sit back down and tell me how you got so good at cheating at board games."

Her lips twitched into a smile. "I don't know what you're talking about."

"For some reason I don't think the word 'moulage' is one you use too often."

"Psh." She snorted. "I'm just...extremely well read."

"And versed in military jargon."

"Exactly." She said, still attempting to fit as many things into her hands off the table as possible.

Her avoidance was adorable. Being alone together had its insinuations. After all, we'd decided to have sex days ago and had yet to cross that threshold—but there was no expectation, like she probably thought there was. I was still reeling over the fact that she wanted me in that way in the first place.

I reached out and wrapped my forearm around her waist, pulling her directly down into my lap. Her soft gasp did all it needed to wake that lust back up again. I carefully settled every-thing back down in front of us.

"You're just as stubborn and competitive as I am," I teased.

"I've been competing for my family's attention for almost two decades now, so I've gotten pretty good at it."

Her words were lighthearted, but her expression didn't match. There was so much more going on in that pretty little head than she let on.

But she was starting to let me see through the cracks, though. In the same way that I was saying things I hadn't even said out loud to myself in years.

"Come here." I twisted her in my lap until I was being straddled. Her hands went to my chest and those eyes lingered at my mouth before finding glossy focus. I could read her mind in that moment; we were speaking our own language. So I tucked her hair behind both ears and pulled her lips to mine.

Immediately, Ophelia's eyes fluttered closed and her fingers swept through my hair, holding on like an anchor. She kissed me *good*. With a more confident determination than she ever had before. Her mouth set the pace, gliding over mine, teeth sinking into my lip every so often as our breaths mingled. She tasted like honeyed white wine and *candy*. Like I'd never get her sweetness off my tongue.

My hands explored her chest, down her ribs, settling in the perfect dips at her hips, and rocked her gently. Even that slow, barely-there movement made my breath catch in my throat. The accompanying grunt got her attention.

"You didn't kiss me the other day," she mumbled, moving herself back and forth against me without my timid guidance. "On our date."

I slowed her down, sliding my hands underneath her button-up pajama shirt and squeezing gently. She needed to take it easy on me. "I'm kissing you now."

"Were you trying to be a gentleman?"

My touch traveled upward, taking an aggressive handful of her breast over her bra. I didn't want to feel fucking lace, I wanted to feel skin, so I pulled the fabric down and pinched her tightened nipple between two fingers. "No."

Her back arched.

"Do you not like to kiss women after you come in their mouths?"

My God.

I laughed, my head tilting to rest on the back of the couch and exposing my neck that she then leaned down and started sucking on. Everything in my body was rigid and buzzing, getting needier by the second. "Are you a little tipsy, Trouble?"

She bit my pulse and then my jaw. "Answer my question."

"We can answer it together later."

Her lips crashed back into mine and the thin soft cotton between her legs started rolling against me again. It felt incredible, but all I could think about was getting her naked, splayed out on my sheets for a whole night, and making her come so many times she lost count.

Grabbing her hair in a ponytail in my fist, I jerked her head back and kissed a line from her chin to her ear. "Do you want more than this?"

My grip was tight, but she nodded against it.

"You don't have to say yes," I told her, pressing my lips to her jaw. "You can sit in my lap and kiss me all night. I won't mind."

"I want you to kiss me in other places."

"Thank fucking God." I lifted us both and started down the hall with her limbs wrapped around me like a koala. "I gotta put my dick in something wet before I lose my mind."

She giggled into the crook of my neck as I swept her faster than I'd moved since Delta into my bedroom. The door hadn't even closed before we started peeling each other's clothes off. Scrap by scrap, my shirt over my head, her little white shorts down her thighs. Ophelia's body would never not surprise me; I found something new and lovely and perfect every time I saw it.

Tonight was no different. The soft light from the bedside lamp made it look like there was a golden halo around her entire silhouette, her frizzy hair like an untamed crown.

I kissed her again and again, moving us slowly toward the mattress as she kicked her shorts off her ankles and hopped on one foot and then the other, pulling off her fuzzy socks.

"Don't get any ideas," she joked. Her knees connected with the edge of the mattress and I caught her by her elbows before she fell back.

"You have no idea how offended I am that you still think I'm one of those guys."

Contrary to my words I pulled her back to my mouth eagerly, sliding our tongues together in a desperate rhythm. I didn't know what it was with this girl but I never knew what to do with my hands. They were in her hair, cupping her jaw, holding her hips. Roaming like I'd discovered a brand-new texture and I wanted to fucking memorize it. Commit the shape of her to my muscle memory.

We were wearing entirely too many clothes for me to properly do that.

As if she had the same thought, she ran those sharp red fingernails down my chest to my stomach, my entire torso tightening like a bungee cord ready to snap. I was swollen to a point in my pants, not hiding in the slightest behind the fabric. Her gaze lingered there as her bottom lip disappeared between her teeth.

"Touch it." The deepness of my voice demanded her attention. "Take it out for me, O."

A wicked smile stretched across her pretty face. She curled her fingers into my waistband, wiggling them against the hair that disappeared beneath. "Space heater," she commented.

I felt like I was dangling off the edge of a cliff, stomach in knots of anticipation, and she was cracking jokes about my body temperature. So I did what any sane man would have done and grabbed the little tease's wrist and shoved it down my boxers. I kept it there, too. Folding my fingers over the back of hers and showing her exactly how I liked my dick to be held.

"Nice and slow, sweetheart." Together we gripped me at the base and stroked. I squeezed her fingers harder as they reached the tip and let out a needy, brutish grunt.

She answered with a whimper that sounded so sweet I needed to hear it again immediately. Her little desperate voice shattered my already cracked filter, so I leaned down and whispered against the shell of her ear, "I'm going to put all this cock inside you."

"Frankie..."

"Tell me you've never had one this big." I helped her stroke me again.

Her silence was all the confirmation I needed. I pulled our hands off my shaft and met her glazed blue eyes with the fire I could feel in mine, then hoisted her up and dropped her on her back on the bed.

"Pull your panties down," I directed as I helped myself out of my worn, plaid bottoms. I sprung free of my briefs and her attention followed. She did as I asked, as perfect as ever. I wanted to make her feel so good for that. Keeping me guessing outside the bedroom, but letting me own her in every possible way when it was just the two of us alone.

She tossed her lacy thong off the bed and spread her legs wide open for me. And *God strike me dead*, if that wasn't the prettiest fucking pussy I'd ever seen. Plush, wet, perfect. The sexiest patch of curly hair pointing me right where I wanted to be.

"Should I lick you before I fuck you?" I pushed her knees down to the mattress and lined my shoulders up between them.

"You should get a condom," she hummed, trailing her fingers down her body, undoing every last button of her top on the way to her clit.

I should get a condom.

My blood chilled.

Fuck.

Ophelia watched my demeanor change and sat up on her elbows. "What?"

"I don't have a fucking condom." What kind of idiot that planned on having sex didn't have a condom? The kind whose last sexual encounter was over three years ago with a woman that had an IUD for the entire seven that he was with her.

O dropped her head back on the pillows in anguish, but her hand lingered between her legs, fingers circling her blushing, swollen peak.

I gnawed on my knuckle. "Jesus fuck, you're driving me crazy."

She arched her back, sliding her sparkly red fingernail all the way down to her opening, and dipping it inside.

"Shit," she gasped.

"Ophelia," I growled in warning.

"I'm on the pill."

Ninety-nine percent of my brain was shouting at me to push her knees back to her fucking ears and shove my cock inside her bare.

But that other persistent one percent banged on my skull, reminding me that it was completely stupid and irresponsible to risk it with someone I barely knew. Not only that, but her chances of me blowing my load too soon—which, judging by the way my dick was spasming watching her finger herself—was very likely to happen. She might be on the pill, but that wasn't foolproof.

"You gotta give me five minutes," I begged.

She sat up, removing her top and unclasping her bra, tossing it hastily to the floor. My eyes fluttered shut at the sight.

I jumped her, pushing up between her legs, grabbing her wrists and pinning them to the mattress on either side of her head. The box spring creaked under the weight of us.

Nose to nose, I mumbled against her lips, "Five minutes, Trouble. You can touch yourself, but don't you dare come without my tongue or cock somewhere inside you." I kissed her hard, dragging it on for longer than I intended to, and then shoved myself off the bed and pulled my briefs back up my legs.

"Where are you going?"

I pulled open the door. "To find a way to fuck you so hard you think you hear reindeer on the goddamn roof."

My first thought was Mateo. I jogged down the hallway toward his bedroom and hesitated outside. He was either awake or he wasn't, there was no use pussyfooting around. I rapped on the door. "Cap, help me out."

I paced in a short circle, scratching the back of my neck, willing my erection to calm the fuck down before I offered Mateo more ammo to give me shit for the rest of my life. It was only a minute but it felt like thirty when the door opened and my best friend peeked a squinty eye out.

"What the fuck do you want?"

"Condom. Now."

His squinty eye opened all the way and his grumpy expression lifted. "You getting laid, brother?"

"Listen, I don't have time for fucking tea and biscuits. There's a naked bombshell of a woman sprawled out in my bed right now, and I need a rubber before I nut in my fucking pants."

"I don't have one, man." He crossed his arms over his bare chest, laughing. "I'm sorry."

"What do you mean you don't have one?" I flung my arms around. "You're a fucking pornstar."

"I prefer sex worker," he corrected me. "But when's the last time you saw one of those wearing a fucking condom, Pike?"

My fingers flexed at my sides, frustration seeping out of me. I took another short, despairing lap up and down the hall. "This can't be happening."

Mateo checked the time on his watch. "Ron's still open for another half hour." He shrugged.

I clasped my hands together on top of my head and stared at the dim lights on the ceiling. If I drove out to the gas station it would be at least twenty fucking minutes there and back, but what choice did I really have?

"Nothing in the bathroom?"

"Dude, be my guest." Mateo pushed the bedroom door open and waved me inside. "Don't wake my fucking girlfriend up, she'll kill you."

I sprinted past a snoozing Tally into the bathroom and pulled open every goddamn drawer underneath the sink, sorting through the contents like there was a delivery boy at the door and I couldn't find any cash to tip him.

"You're cleaning all this shit up." Mateo leaned against the door frame and blocked the light from completely seeping into the bedroom.

There were tampons and cotton swabs falling to the floor. I rearranged a perfectly organized accessory box and flung about a dozen ponytail holders onto the tile. Mateo's travel bag of mini shampoos and grooming tools got unzipped and dumped out into the sink for me to root through more efficiently.

"I'll clean your fucking toilets if I find a condom in here." I pushed one drawer shut and flung open the mirrored cabinet over the sink. Band-Aids, ibuprofen, nasal spray, three different fucking flavors of lube.

"Fuck!" I slammed the cabinet closed.

Mateo shook his head. "I told you. Now you just wasted time." He checked his watch again. "You can still make it to Ron's."

This was not how the night was supposed to go. I fumbled royally forgetting the most basic rule of casual hook-ups. Ophelia was in there wondering where I was, probably getting herself off because I was too busy sifting through my roommate's bathroom for a Trojan like we were back in the fucking barracks.

"All right, I'm going." I opened a drawer and swept everything I'd thrown on the counter back into it with my arm.

"Pike!"

"No time, brother. You said it yourself."

"You're lucky I want you to get some fucking ass more than I want to kill you right now." He dodged me as I hurried out of the bathroom and back into the hall.

Still in my underwear, I needed to get dressed, grab my wallet, and promise the girl in my bed that if she gave me ten more minutes I'd be on my knees for the rest of the night if that's where she wanted me.

My buzz had completely worn off and I was laser focused on the task in front of me. Turn off my south brain, turn on my tactical one.

She wants you, Frankie. She said it herself.

When I pushed open my bedroom door all that went directly out the window.

Ophelia's naked body was curled up on one side of the bed, cuddling the blanket to her chest. Eyes closed, rose pink lips slightly parted.

"O?" I whispered. I leaned back on the door and let it click shut, slowing my sprint to a sedentary crawl. Her chest rose and fell rhythmically.

She was out cold on my pillow and all that lust and energy from seconds prior warmed to something soft and tame inside me. I wanted to play with that sexy, vixen side of Ophelia, but the way she looked asleep in my space, right at home in my bed, filled that need with something different...better.

All my life it'd been my nature to be a provider, protector, a sure thing. An undeniably safe bet. You needed me, I was going to be there. Situationally, but also in my relationships. The need to feel indispensable might have been an issue I needed to work out; it sure as hell cost me a lot of fucking sleep after Delta and a lot of mind games with Vanessa. Some might even call it a flaw, but I thought it was the only thing keeping me human half the time.

Ophelia—feeling *safe* with me, trusting me, confiding in me—was tuning that long-forgotten string again.

I walked over and sat on the mattress beside her, lightly pushing a fallen strand of hair away from her face. Her eyelashes fluttered, but she didn't move beyond that.

You forget that warm, soft buzzing in your chest when you're watching a woman sleep in your bed. It makes you want to do everything for her. Keep her warm, keep her happy. Keep her...keep her. Period.

But that was the night talking, and the circumstance, and the adrenaline, and every other loose thread we needed to tighten as soon as fucking possible before my brain started tricking me into thinking there were ways this couldn't end in a disaster.

Because nothing like this could end in any way but disaster.

Despite all that though, I still leaned down and softened that wrinkle between her brow with my lips.

23

Ophelia

THERE WAS NO BED quite like my bed back in Pine Ridge. We're talking luxury bamboo bed sheets; silk pillow cases that never wrinkled; chemical-free, temperature-regulated fabrics; weighted blankets. The whole nine. Night-time routines were also a ritual: red light therapy at least twice a week, HydroStem serums, jade rollers.

I didn't fold easily on any of those things. In fact, there were many nights back home that I told a little white lie to get out of a dinner with a guy or an invite from my colleagues for happy hour just so I didn't sacrifice any "me" time. I needed to apply that eighty-dollar night cream that promised to keep the bags under my eyes from turning into raisins before I hit thirty.

Then I touched down in Florida, and suddenly I was sleeping in men's boxer shorts on canvas couches with uncovered throw pillows. *Willingly*, I might add. And waking up with my daily contacts still stuck to my dried-out eyes.

No bed was like my bed.

It wasn't possible.

But Frankie Casado's came pretty damn close.

One sleep-crusted lid lifted and I peered out into the bedroom as I woke up, collecting my bearings. The clock beside the lamp on the oak nightstand said it was nine in the morning.

I yawned and stretched my legs as far down the bed as I could, sinking further into the soft mattress. Instead of getting up, I curled the blankets closer to my chest and inhaled them, breathing in the familiar scent of Frankie, who, at that moment, was probably thinking of a million and one polite ways to get me out of his sheets.

I fell asleep. Horny, wine-influenced Ophelia made a grand show of herself, and then exited the stage before the final act. We were so close. So fucking close. My skin still remembered his lingering touch. My lips twinged at the echo of us clashing. There were parts of me that ached for him, and only him now.

I sat up, comforter falling to my waist, my arms instinctually crossing over my bare chest. Only—that wasn't the case at all.

I knew I'd fallen asleep naked. I knew that. The last recollection I had was convincing myself I could rest my eyes for the five minutes it took Frankie to find a condom. A quick power nap to refresh for a night of bliss with the handsome, hung pilot.

But as I looked down, Frankie's white T-shirt from the night before was draped over my body, hanging nearly to the knees of his torn plaid pajama bottoms that sat on my hips.

He dressed me.

In his clothes.

I stared in disbelief. Where the fuck did this guy come from, and why on earth couldn't it have been Pine Ridge, Colorado?

Heavy steps sounded outside the doorway a moment before it popped open, and a freshly showered Frankie traipsed inside, toweling off his long, wet hair. The cloth around his waist was hanging on by a thread. I could blow a gust of air as hard as I'd blow out some birthday candles and the thing would be cascading to the floor.

"Morning, sleepyhead." He was carrying a mug of coffee in one hand, steam swelling from the top as he set it down on the bedside table.

"Is this for me?" I pointed to the mug, trying not to gape at his body.

"Of course." He shrugged. "Sleep okay?"

"Great, actually."

I felt like an idiot sitting there in his clothes, drinking the perfectly prepared cup of coffee he'd made me, gazing longingly at his happy trail that dipped beneath the towel, and not apologizing for attributing nothing to our mutual sexual agreement.

This was why my dating life was such a mess. I couldn't even pretend to play the part.

"Did you sleep in this bed?" I asked. "With me?"

Frankie chuckled, opening and rooting through his closet across the room. "It's my fucking bed, Ophelia. Of course I did."

Heat flooded my cheeks. "About last night..."

"You snore," he cut me off. "Like a grizzly bear."

My jaw dropped open, simultaneously at his words and his toned, dimpled ass as he let go of the towel and replaced it with a pair of black boxer briefs.

"Heard a lot of grizzly bears snoring, have you?" I crossed my arms. "When I drink I get...nasally."

Frankie mimicked what I perceived as the sound of a chainsaw revving to life.

"Fuck off." I laughed, ripping the pillow from behind me and launching it toward him, pegging him right between the shoulder blades.

He turned to me with a grin, fluffing out a gray T-shirt before pulling it over his head.

All right, maybe he wasn't as disappointed as I thought he'd be with how the night turned out. My nerves took a back seat as I sipped from my mug and he joined me on the bed.

"About last night," he repeated. "I had a lot of fun." A heated look crossed his face briefly. His gaze drifted over his clothes on my body, no doubt reimagining what was hidden beneath them. "I don't have any expectations, O. You don't owe me anything. Just know if you want it, I'm ready to give it."

He somehow always knew exactly what to say. We never had an awkward moment, our personalities meshed, we finished each other's sentences. Two cogs on the same wheel.

And had a man ever looked so good in his underwear?

His competency turned me on more than anything as pressure flared between my legs.

"Right." I swallowed. "I do—want to be given it."

My chance to make up for the night before presented itself. Miraculously the wine hangover was minimal, but the same willingness was still filtering through my bloodstream. I danced my fingers across the cap of his knee.

The corner of his mouth lifted, smugly. "In that case we'll have to make a pitstop while we're out shopping."

He stood and crossed the floor to the window, jerking open the curtains and hitting me in the face with a burning beam of morning sunlight. I fell back onto the bed, groaning, and pulled the covers over my head.

"Oh no you don't," he chided. A second later my ankles were being gripped and dragged from beneath the blankets, my entire tired body following.

"It's so early," I complained as I came face to face with him at the edge of the bed. "I'm on vacation."

"Cap and Tally won't be out of their dungeon for hours, and I need your help."

"With what?" The soft stubble on his face had grown a bit longer since we first met on the plane. The shadow of a beard made him look older and more angular; his jaw was so sharp already it could cut glass. I reached out and brushed my finger down his chin. Call me easily distracted.

"Should I shave?"

"No, I like."

"Good."

I dragged the same finger down his throat to a maroon, Rorschach looking blot next to his Adam's apple. My eyes flickered up. Frankie's hooded gaze was already pinned to my lips like he was identifying the culprit.

"I wouldn't have pegged you as a biter," he said in that gritty, not remotely suitable for nine a.m. on a Wednesday, bedroom voice.

My skin pebbled, and a twist of lust made itself known between my legs again. "I never was," I admitted quietly.

A tortured, unmissable grunt filtered from his throat. He pinched my bottom lip between two fingers and tugged on it. "*This mouth* is gonna get me in trouble. Because if you don't get out of my bed right now, I'm gonna fuck it. And if that happens, we won't be leaving this room until the sun sets again. Then my poor mother and sister will have to wonder why they didn't get a gift from me for Christmas...and that will be all your fault, Ophelia."

I closed my teeth around his thumb and bit down, shrugging innocently.

Frankie watched me intently before blinking out of his daze and unhinging my jaw with the pressure of his finger. "Where the fuck did you come from?"

"The North Pole," I joked, finally hopping out of his bed. "And we take gift giving very seriously there."

MY BARE FEET RESTED on the dash of the truck as it idled in the gas station parking lot. The passenger seat was tilted back like I owned it, and I'd not only convinced Frankie to let me play DJ, but my phone was now saved directly to his Bluetooth—which gave me a juvenile satisfaction thinking about another woman in this same seat eventually finding my name there.

Chalk it up as one of those silly, honest mistakes we make, like leaving scrunchies in cup holders or planting hairs in the bathroom. A modern version of *Ophelia wuz here*, but instead of in black marker on a frat house wall, I was leaving my very obvious digital footprint on the man's very expensive, financed vehicle.

Growth.

My phone pinged with a text I'd been expecting from Natalia.

Nat babyyyy: Matty said I shouldn't be worried, but I'm still worried
Ophelia: Last-minute shopping

It was just like a man to wait until three days before Christmas to buy presents. I was relieved that Frankie was at least normal in that respect. Every other way was surprisingly too good to be true and he desperately needed a humbling for my sake.

There was definitely such a thing as too much of a good thing. And I knew that, because if I let him bring me a coffee in bed one more morning, I was going to go back to Colorado with expectations not even my regular barista at Starbucks could deliver on.

The driver's side door swung open and Frankie hopped inside, casting a plastic bag full of things onto my lap.

"I guessed," he told me, draping his arm over the back of my seat as he backed out of the parking lot and drove away.

I opened the bag to sift through and my eyes widened. A slow, embarrassing heat licked from the base of my spine to the nape of my neck.

He checked the rearview mirror nonchalantly. "I thought Snickers were a safe bet, but I guess you can have the KitKat if you really want it."

"Are we running a marathon?" I gaped at him as I lifted the variety box of condoms out of the bag.

He sniffed out a laugh. "Am I being scolded for being *too* prepared now? After last night I'm never making that mistake again."

"You said you weren't upset about that," I reminded him.

"I'm not at all, I just..." He paused, looking over at me and glancing at my legs stretched out across the cab. "I feel like I can say this to you, so I'm going to."

"Say it." I tethered myself in preparation.

"If I fuck you once, O, I'm fucking you ten more times."

"Oh." I stared blankly out of the windshield. "Thanks for your honesty."

"Too much?" He reached over and grabbed my thigh, resting his heavy hand there like it was the most natural thing in the world and not blazing me from the inside out. "I figure we're past the point of beating around the bush."

"I think that's...exactly what we're doing." I laughed.

His eyebrow arched and then flattened, the innuendo catching up like watching a car crash in real time. "You're a sick, twisted

CHRISTMAS IN COCONUT CREEK   235

person and I don't know if it's because you're worse than me, or if it's because it's like looking in a mirror."

Frankie hooked a left and turned into a garden center parking lot. The displays outside housed several colorful hanging and potted plants. We would absolutely find something in there for his mom, and I needed out of the car like I needed air to breath. Between the mega box of condoms, his hand on my leg, and the way I could smell every note in the soap that he used like it was directly under my nose, I couldn't think straight.

"So your parents used to garden together?"

The blunt tips of his fingers tightened behind my knee. "They always had a big flower garden, nice landscaping, perfectly trimmed hedges, but she hasn't done it in years."

"This'll make her so happy." I said. "You can help her plant."

"I hope so." He sighed. "I'm still clueless about Addy."

I tapped my finger on my chin. "What is she like?"

"Pain in my ass."

"I'm sure she thinks you hang the moon," I volleyed. "What *does* she like?"

He lifted his hat and swiped his fingers through his hair. "Art."

"That's a start." I inclined my head toward him.

"She paints. Everything. I mean, when we were kids she was painting our bedroom walls like her own personal mural, and it wasn't even as bad as you're imagining. Eclectic as shit, sure, but it was like Pablo Picasso level of abstract."

"Family trait?"

"I don't have an artistic bone in my body," he admitted. "I was always too busy to have hobbies. I was jealous of Addy in that way. She would tell me that she wished she could see half the shit I've seen, but if she knew what that meant I know she'd take it back."

I studied his profile, the hard, straight line of his nose, his naturally full bottom lip. "You don't talk about the service that much."

"Government secrets," he rebuffed.

"I'm excellent at keeping secrets."

"Delta was both the best and the worst thing that ever happened to me," he replied thoughtfully.

"How's that contradiction?"

"I was free for once, which is ironic because I was technically considered property of the United States." He smiled to himself. "Like I said, I wasn't a creative kid. I played football in high school because I was big and it was something to do, but I never did it because I wanted to be in the NFL or anything."

"You could be making millions."

"That would soften the blow of permanent brain damage."

"Sometimes you have to make sacrifices," I said.

"I wasn't free, as in I could do whatever I wanted—I was free from making decisions." He inhaled and cleared his throat. "I didn't have to be the point guy like I was at home, I just got told what to do and I fucking did it. I boozed on government money, messed around, made friends—Mom was good, Addy was in college, so she was good."

"You got to be Frankie for you, and not for everyone else."

"Something like that, Trouble." He scratched his chin. "What are you doing? Turning me into some sentimental asshole?"

Another message came in from Nat, and this time instead of answering it from the privacy of my phone, Frankie hit the play button on the touch screen in the console and let voice to text do the job for me.

The clipped, robotic voice read out loud, "'Did you finally take his born-again virginity?'"

I shot up and punched the A/V button so hard my thumb bent backward. Marking your territory via Bluetooth came with its own unique set of consequences unfortunately. I slid my feet off the dash and shoved them back into my sandals, hitching the sling bag I'd brought with me over my shoulder in preparation to dash out of the truck.

"Nat is so colorful, isn't she?" I coughed.

Frankie drummed his thumb against the steering wheel and shook his head, barely hiding a smirk. God, he looked sexy and self-satisfied, and now he knew that my texts were a petri dish of unsavory conversations about him. Heat blossomed on the apples of my cheeks.

"My born-again virginity, huh?"

"Three years is a long dry spell." I tried to drown the flame but instead doused it. "For your age."

"My age hasn't bothered you yet. You like to make jokes but I think it turns you on, Ophelia."

I started to laugh, but it tapered into a little deceiving gasp of a thing when he locked the doors with a click. His seatbelt unwound and he turned to face me, the air thickening with my shallow breaths until it felt claustrophobic.

"Am I the oldest guy you've ever fucked around with?"

"No," I answered quickly. Then I thought harder, with my tongue in my cheek. "Maybe."

"Which is it?" he pressed. "Am I your type, or do you have some extremely unaddressed daddy issues you need me to work out of you?"

That was a *great* question. My lips parted to reply, but before I could, Frankie reached across again and pulled my chin toward him.

"Because, I think," he murmured, the soft skate of his breath against my lips, "I'm the first man that's ever gotten you there, and no matter who you take to bed after me, you never forget your first."

A single, pathetic sound escaped me defiantly, and Frankie's mouth twitched.

"Yeah." He nodded triumphantly. "Just like when I told you to get up this morning and get in my truck, if I wanted you to call me daddy, sweetheart, you fucking would. And something also tells me..." He looked down as I squirmed. "If I told you to get in the back seat so I could eat that desperate little pussy I know is begging for some relief right now—you might react the same."

A lump formed in my throat as any protest got caught there. Usually I didn't fold over and put my ass in the air like that, but he hit it like checking off items on a grocery list. We were in no place to be working each other up so intensely, and the outside of the garden center at Levi's Homestore was a shadeless, privateless place. There wasn't a chance in the world we would get away with it.

But *hell* if I wasn't considering it.

Frankie and I were like an hourglass being turned over and over again without ever letting the sand completely siphon out. When he turned away, hopping out of the car, it was like flipping it back over again.

He rounded to the passenger side, slowly, seemingly battling something in his mind, before he pulled open my door. A soft crease split his brows, and his pupils were dilated. Hidden behind the door where only I could see it, he reached down and adjusted himself in his shorts.

"Let's try to cool down," he suggested, but his hands asked for the opposite. I shifted in his direction and calloused palms slid up my outer thighs and he leaned in, running his nose across the dip of my neckline. "I know I like to mess around," he said, his voice vulnerable, "but don't let me convince you that you're not affecting me the same fucking way, O."

"That's why you're preying on my weaknesses?" I briefly wound my fingers through the sweat-damp locks at the nape of his neck.

"I am, aren't I?" He retracted a step, giving me his hand to help me hop onto the ground.

"Now my therapist has to hear about how the underlying trauma from my parents' failed marriage has inadvertently fed into my sexual deviancy as an adult."

I hadn't really thought about it until that moment, and there wasn't a handbook for teens whose parents got divorced and started new lives. I was so far removed from that chapter anyway that I couldn't tell if I displayed a behavior in certain situations as a response to it, or if it was just an easy excuse.

Everyone preferred honesty, nobody liked to be deceived, people expected open communication in relationships, and commitment, and connection, and that had nothing to do with the things I'd experienced, or the lack thereof, in my youth. I, now, as a result, knew what I wanted and what I didn't, but if that also had something to do with being manhandled in the bedroom then so fucking be it.

"You think I'm onto something?" Frankie guided me into the large greenhouse and we were immediately hit with the earthy, humid scent of herbs and terracotta. The walls were wet with condensation, and my skin took it on like a sticky film.

"I know that most of the things I feel inadequate about in my life directly correlate to either abandonment, or overcompensation," I explained. "I'm competitive as a reflex, I'm impulsive because I don't want to miss opportunities, and I'm, embarrassingly enough, an attention seeker, so I do things that are memorable and over the top as a response."

"You're saying all of those things as if they're negative." Frankie grabbed a cart and started loading topsoil into it while I held it still for him. "Why don't you turn it around and think about all the good things that come out of those in-your-face, psycho-analytical buzzwords?"

"Do you go to therapy?"

"Physical." He grunted as he hauled a giant ceramic pot into the cart. "It doesn't take a professional to see that you think there's something wrong with you that needs to be fixed—when maybe you just need to rewire the system."

"How computer-techy of you."

"Seriously," Frankie said. "Competition is healthy. Impulsivity is your way of trusting your gut. There's nothing wrong with being a little fucking cocky either." He picked up two pairs of gardening gloves off a rack and held them next to each other for me to choose.

"You're right." I pointed to the yellow and orange ones. "But we're talking about major life decisions. Like, who I'm going to potentially marry and have children with. That needs a considerable amount of calculation."

Frankie turned his back to me and started filing through the display of seed packets. "I don't think you really know how a guy is gonna be with kids until you give him kids. Or what he's going to be like as a husband until he becomes a husband. It's all educated guesses up to that point. You can't *make* someone be the right person for you—they just are."

I sighed. "This is why dating apps are fucked. In a perfect world I'm not flipping through pictures of men all day with blind hope."

He snorted, looking at me over his shoulder. "You don't think Prince Charming is in Pine Ridge?"

"If he is, he's already married with kids."

"Or he's just not in Pine Ridge." Frankie shrugged, pulling the cart along without another word.

I walked beside our growing pile of potted plants and gardening tools playing botanist, picking out the brightest petals and biggest flowers. Frankie paid less and less attention to my choices and more to the sheen of sweat on my collarbones every time I asked him to load another into the cart.

I was no better, because Frankie pushing me aside to do the heavy lifting was like watching softcore porn. His shirt was stuck to his body with sweat, and the hair on his neck was curling in damp waves. Every muscle from his broad shoulders to his calves flexed for my personal enjoyment.

His gray T-shirt was darker down his spine and under his arms, and his grunts of exertion, while completely innocent, registered oppositely in the little neutral headspace I had left. My mouth went completely dry thinking about getting that man home and treating him to a long, soapy shower.

"Don't hurt yourself," I murmured.

Frankie straightened and lifted his hat, wiping the moisture from his forehead with his sleeve. He huffed, catching his breath, and before I could stop myself I was reaching out and wiping away a bead of sweat that threatened to get lost in his facial hair.

Such a shameless gesture, and yet it stole the air between us. Frankie's eyes flared.

I'd slowly become obsessed with touching him. In small insignificant ways: a pinch, a pull, fixing the tag sticking out of his collar, tapping the face of his watch to see the time despite my phone sitting in my pocket. I knew this showed attachment, and disregarded it.

As soon as the holidays were over it would be like turning out the lights at the end of the night.

Frankie took my hand, inspecting it as if it'd burned him, and then dried my thumb by running it down the center of his chest. Too slowly to be harmless, too quickly for someone shopping around us to notice. The rhythmic thump of his heartbeat picked up beneath my touch, and the muscles in his abdomen twitched the lower my fingers dropped.

"I think we have everything we need," Frankie muttered. He looked around the room and shuffled closer to me. My stomach flipped as he guided my hand lower, to his belt, then lower again. "All day like this," he whispered. "All day for you."

I gasped, feeling him hard against my hand. Our eyes met, and that same dark, glazed look from the parking lot was back—and with fervor.

"I'm ready to go home," he said.

"We didn't find anything for your sister."

"I'll take care of it," he assured me, nodding his head toward checkout. "You did good, O. Thank you."

"I don't know if you're talking about the flowers or the hard-on," I remarked.

"Yes you do." A playful smile danced on his lips. "You know me better than most people by now."

My heart and my brain were playing a game of tug of war with the need I felt between my legs. One second Frankie was irritatingly sweet and playful, and the next making me wish we could be cloaked in darkness and going at it against a wall.

He was like a patchwork quilt of all the qualities I'd ever found attractive in a man sewn together. Nothing matched, the thread was different colors in places, there were parts I'd forgotten existed somewhere down a tunnel between adolescence and adulthood. But if I waved it out and held it far enough in front of me, everything looked pretty fucking on theme, and soft as butter to boot.

I liked him. I wanted to spend time with him, get to know him, *sleep* with him. And I could have every last one of those things if I wanted it—so goddamnit, I was going to be selfish for once in my life and deal with the consequences later.

"I can hear you thinking," he said curiously.

We stopped against the checkout counter and Frankie pulled his wallet out of his back pocket, handing over a card to the store clerk.

"It's mostly elevator music," I lied.

He wrapped his forearm around my lower back, and slipped what he could fit of his fingers into the back pocket of my shorts. There was the faintest of squeezes, a secret, cheeky gesture between the two of us. "Can I listen, too?"

That dragged an embarrassing smile out of me and I bit my tongue to suppress it. "Get me back to the house and I'll give you every little depraved detail," I promised.

Twenty minutes later the bed of Frankie's truck was packed and we were taking each and every road home so gingerly you would think there was a sleeping baby strapped in the back seat.

The radio blared as he sang out of tune to a country song sifting through the speakers. His voice hopped, skipped and jumped over the notes, cutting in and out, sometimes throwing a bluesy twang on the end of a line. Every time I laughed, Frankie got a little louder, finding some type of satisfaction in bringing the high-pitched sound out of me.

The cool, December air filtered through all four windows as we drove, the breeze knocking every untamed hair out of my loose bun until it was dancing freely, whipping me in the face, sticking to the headrest. I tried and failed to tie it back up until my arms were aching above my head. With a disgruntled sigh I let it all fall gracelessly down my shoulders, ready to give up entirely until I felt the plop of a hat on my head.

My attention jolted to Frankie, his wild brown locks being thrown this way and that, a cute, barely-there crease right above his ear that wrapped around the back of his head.

"Better?" he asked, assessing me softly.

I adjusted his hat on my head, tucking the flyaways under the bill so I could see clearly out the window again. His scent fell over me, masculine and inviting, comforting in a way I wanted poured into candle wax so I could have it all the time. On every cold, winter night back in Colorado and also every wet, rainy afternoon. I wanted it for the evenings while I was grading papers, and in the autumn when the leaves started crisping and falling to the dry, grassy floor.

I smiled appreciatively. "Better."

The highway turned into suburbs, and the truck slowed to a crawl through the development leading up to the house. Then, instead of a right turn onto his road, Frankie forked and took a left, driving us in a different direction.

I opened my mouth and then shut it, deciding to give myself freely to spontaneity, trusting I wouldn't regret my impulse to let him take me wherever he wanted to.

Apparently though, it wasn't anywhere specific. We zig-zagged down streets in the neighborhood, making a right turn and then two more. My forehead creased in confusion. But nothing about circling the same pond three times was as odd as Frankie's quiet reverence and I started to wonder if our elevator music sounded the same. The fourth time we paused at the same stop sign, beside the beige barn mailbox with the rooster on the roof, I got suspicious.

Was he...prolonging the drive?

"Lost your way?" I joked.

"I'm thinking about something."

"Yeah?"

Another left turn and the houses started looking familiar. I realized we were just approaching their well-decorated driveway from a different direction.

"About how I'm going to get you into my house, and then into my very well-pressurized shower, and back into my bed without your best friend noticing first."

My pulse picked up. Part of me wanted him just as he was, sitting beside me in the car. Ripe from the day, tense with longing, more than a little aggressive if I was reading the situation right. But then, just as before, I started imagining the flow of water sliding down the planes of his chest, his long hair slicked back, the muscles in our bodies relaxing in the heat against each other.

"Well," I drawled, "that would take skill and training that I'm not sure anyone has."

"I'm overly willing to test that."

"We could pull over somewhere," I proposed.

Frankie rounded a curve and turned into the driveway a moment later. The ignition idled over our silence for an extended second before he rolled the windows up and cut it. "When we finally do this, I'm not getting you quick and dirty in the back seat. Do you understand that?"

Heat spread at my center like running water. I understood nothing but what my body was telling me to, and that was to spread my legs at the simple sound of the voice speaking to me. Being around Frankie was like having a fever. One minute I was comfortable, the next I was burning up. Everything ached in one way or another, my head swam, my focus wavered, and things stopped making complete sense.

I must not have answered his question, because he continued on, slithering his hand across the back of my neck and holding it. "I'm going to take my time, and use my tongue, and you're going to come apart all pretty for me like I know you do."

I leaned over the console, daring him confidently while a nervous knot tightened in my stomach. "You promise?" The previous vow to behave earlier had been all but forgotten. I brought my elbows together, pushing until my breasts started to spill over the top of my shirt.

His eyes dropped slowly, and a long sharp breath pulled through his teeth. I didn't need his words then, telling me something I already knew the answer to. I just needed his mouth.

"Come here," I whispered.

Frankie's grip on me tightened as we crashed together frantically. A day's worth of tension coming to life through the hungry motion of our lips sparring one another. He dragged his tongue across mine, tasting every unexpressed moan of desperation as I let them go freely. My fingers latched onto the wind-swept locks of his hair, and he knocked his hat off my head to the floor and dragged me even closer to him.

Everything that wasn't Frankie and I disappeared into the background of our kiss. Roaming hands and soft sighs fueled that feeling of complete intoxication the longer we remained attached.

He pulled at my lips with his teeth, our mingling breaths igniting pleasure down my body. My skin hummed for touch, and the tighter his fingers dug into my hair, the more ravenous my need became.

I reached out and palmed his shorts and he groaned into my open mouth before throwing his head back against the seat.

"I want this," I breathed.

"God, you're fucking hot when you're desperate." Frankie's hips shifted and more of him pressed into my hold.

His mouth claimed me again, both his hands wandering to my ribs, and then my chest, circling my breasts and kneading them. The car was stifling, fog starting to cloud the windows, enclosing us into a perfect storm.

Frankie wrapped his arms around my back and pulled me, intent to bring me completely onto his lap. And I would have gone—if a wild head of black hair, attached to an amused, entirely too excited face hadn't materialized just outside the driver's side window.

"Time's up, horndogs!" Nat knocked on the pane behind Frankie and he jolted, instinctively shielding me in his shadow.

"Jesus Christ," I mumbled, straightening my shirt and slinking back to the passenger seat.

Frankie exhaled shakily, composing himself before entertaining my short spritely best friend hoisting herself up on the running boards to peer inside at us.

"Tally." He rolled down the window reluctantly. "You're killing me, babe."

"You've had her all morning. I won't let you steal any more of my precious quality time."

"Ten minutes wouldn't make a difference."

"Ten minutes is amateur work, Francesco." She scrunched her nose. "What are you gonna do in ten minutes?"

"I'm sure O would have filled you in," he said pointedly.

"You think Gino wants to come outside to water his hydrangeas and see you humping in the driveway?"

I snorted, shouldering my bag and letting myself out of the car. Natalia circled to join me, her hazel eyes flaring with excitement and more than a little bit of mischief as she tried to comb through my hair with her fingers. The evidence of the last five minutes was clear as day on my complexion, and secretly left me lukewarm and sticky between my legs.

Frankie joined us slowly, with his hat on his head again and a defeated expression.

"If Santa doesn't put coal in your stocking, Tally, I fucking will."

"Tell Ms. Casado I said hello tomorrow." She patted him on the shoulder and turned to me. "Ready?"

"Mm-hmm," I hummed, walking slowly backward down the driveway toward the car. Frankie's eyes pierced me longingly, holding a layer of emotion I wasn't neutral enough to pick apart, but made me hesitate with the need to kiss him goodbye. "Text me," I settled on.

"Sext her!" Nat shouted from the driver's side.

That beat of amusement cut the tethered line of tension stretching like a rubber band between us. I shrugged suggestively, and Frankie stuck his hands in the pockets of his shorts and followed me to the passenger door.

"Good luck with the garden."

He nodded, pausing for a moment before he said, "I'll see you Friday," and then shut me safely inside.

24

Frankie

THE HOUSE I GREW up in was a modest, one-level, single-family home on a corner lot in Coral Grove. The siding was steel blue, the shutters were eggshell white, and the oversized bay window off the front-facing living room never had any curtains; my mother loved the natural, brandishing sunlight and apparently hated privacy.

You could always see the Marlins game playing clear as day from the driveway, or the street, or even *down* the fucking street, because our house was one that every car drove by, every family walked past with their stroller after dinner, and every kid in the neighborhood stopped at to whistle me and my sister out the front door.

My father spent any time that he wasn't at work outside in the yard, talking to neighbors, holding the sprinkling spout of our hose over his azalea bushes, and nitpicking the way I mowed the lawn that week. He said it was an outward representation of how people viewed us as a family, and nobody would want to invite the *Lumpy-lawn Casados* to potluck.

He was kidding, but my father inadvertently prepared me for bootcamp by regularly instilling me with the fear of missing out on pigs in blankets and seven-layer bean dip.

After he died, I mowed the lawn once a week, religiously, exactly the way he would have wanted it done, and I kept the bushes trimmed and watered, and tried to make small talk with Mr. Santana across the street.

When I joined the Army I wasn't home to do the work myself anymore, but I hired a guy and paid him every week from wherever I was, sometimes months in advance, to cut the grass for my mom so she never had to do it herself. Part of me thought she would take it upon herself to keep up the landscaping because by then it had been almost six years since we'd lost Dad, but I knew deep down that much like the garden that she'd let perish, it was the same stitched wound.

Now, reminding her not only of my father, but of me being gone, too.

So my heart dropped like lead into my stomach as I pulled into the familiar, white stone driveway of the home I was raised in to see the front yard perfectly dressed. Black mulch, trimmed hedges, the flowering plants bright and dappled in moisture as if they'd just been watered.

I stood outside the dark wooden door on the front step, assessing the home like I'd somehow accidentally ended up at the wrong one.

The gutters were different, replaced from the rusted, splintered metal I'd last seen hanging over the windows to a brand new, sturdy white finish. My eyebrow furrowed and I scratched at my short beard.

There was no way my mother replaced the gutters herself. Or even thought to do such a thing.

Mantled just below the roof at the corner of the house, something else caught my eye. A...security camera?

"Are you just going to stand outside all afternoon?" My sister's voice crackled to life, but she was nowhere in sight. I stepped back, nearly falling off the top step onto my ass. The doorbell started blinking with a blue light as Adriana's laughter drifted out of it.

"I had to make sure I was at the right house," I grumbled, putting my eye as close to the little camera on the console as possible.

"Ugh. Creepy. Get inside, Ma told me I couldn't eat until you got here."

"Is that any way to treat your brother?" I pouted. "No loyalty."

The door sprang open and Addy stood there with her arms crossed over her cream-colored sweater. A scowl looked adorable on her long, thin face, especially as her pink cheeks lifted defiantly.

"Give me a hug." I grinned, stepping over the foyer and pulling her into my open arms.

I was a full foot taller than my sister, so I rested my chin on the crown of her head as I looked around the living room. All my military headshots were propped up in a line on the old oak bookcase next to the television, a very proud, ominous shrine that made it seem like I was more a figment of my family's past than a living, breathing piece of it that just happened to live half an hour down the interstate. Mom didn't drive, she never had, and Addy was as busy as I was. I didn't blame them for the distance any more than I blamed myself.

"I like this." I pulled at a few strands of Addy's hair that were cobalt blue against her naturally dark roots. "Trying something new?"

"Malia did it. She's experimenting with stuff at the salon, and I'm her guinea pig."

"How's Malia?" I asked, making my way down the hallway toward the smell of garlic and lemon. I stopped short, my fingers drawing a line down the wall curiously as I noticed the burnt orange shade of paint I'd always known was now a cool, neutral gray. "Did you paint?"

"She's good." Addy pushed me along, skirting over my question. "She's having dinner with us, actually. She'll be here soon."

I pinned my sister with a knowing, enthusiastic expression. "Christmas Eve dinner? That's pretty serious."

The heel of her palm dug into the place between my shoulder blades and pushed me forward into the kitchen with more force than necessary. "It's not even Christmas Eve."

"One day off," I argued. "I can't believe the boss is making you work tomorrow."

"EMTs are necessary, *especially* on holidays."

I knew my sister better than anyone. We spent years attached at the hip, doing our homework across from one another at the kitchen table, sharing a bathroom as teenagers, hanging out with the same groups of friends throughout high school.

After Dad passed it was like pulling the threads of an already tight knot tighter. The bond was so strong you'd never be able to loosen it.

When all the girls in her grade started dating and going to the school dances with the boys in her class while Addy wanted nothing to do with it, I knew something was different. She wasn't interested in dressing up, or doing her hair every day, and couldn't care less about the boy band taking over every other girl's bedroom walls. By the time we were seniors I was sending warning glares down the hallway at any guy that dared to look at her twice, but my sister was more interested in who I was bringing home.

Mom, on the other hand, couldn't be more oblivious. She'd hounded Mateo for months before he met Tally to take Adriana out to dinner, never realizing *Mateo* wasn't the one opposed to it.

In the kitchen my mother had covered every flat surface in some sort of plastic wrap or tinfoil, and pots and pans were piled on top of one another like Jenga. The pungent aroma of fish in the oven assaulted my senses, and I was hit with the nostalgia I'd missed all those years I'd spent deployed.

It happened like this every time I came home. My mind turned into a highlight reel of the childhood I spent in Coral Grove and what I wouldn't give to have another morning around the dinner table, just the four of us again.

"Francesco!" The delicate, relieved sound of my mother's voice welcomed me from across the room. She floated toward my sister and I with a soft smile and a streak of flour across her cheek.

"Mama." I kissed her clammy forehead, squeezing her way too tightly for comfort.

"Look at this face." She rubbed her thumbs through my thick brush of facial hair and then over the mustache on my upper lip. "You look homeless."

"I think I look rugged and sexy."

"You look like a hipster."

Addy cackled behind us, tugging at the ends of my hair like she did when we were kids. "You go to Colorado for a week and now you're turning into a mountain man."

"So you're saying I'd fit in?" A foreign feeling tightened my chest at the mention of Colorado. Subsequently Ophelia found her way to the forefront of my thoughts, like she'd been doing all day. I'd made it halfway to Miami on the car ride down before I realized I hadn't even turned on the radio, too busy replaying the several times I'd almost had her and lost out to a technicality.

That was never going to happen again.

"Have you heard any news?" my mom asked excitedly.

"Nothing yet. But if I left Florida, who would make me clam sauce on Christmas Eve?" I walked over to the kitchen table and tried to dig my fingers into the uncovered bowl of calamari my mother was filling and got a swat on the hand instead.

"You worked so hard, Francesco. Your back is better. The doctor said you're brand new, didn't he?" She rubbed her dainty fingers down my spine and gave me a good pat right above my tailbone where there was a small, faded pink scar.

"Something like that," I deflected. "Like I said, I haven't heard anything yet, and I might not be the right fit for the program anyway. I haven't flown since..."

"You're the best fucking pilot," Addy cut me off.

"Adriana!" My mother swatted her then as well and I stuck my tongue out.

"You two will be the first to know," I promised them, squeezing each woman into my side and kissing them on the top of the head. "Now, put this down for a minute and come outside." I helped my mother out of her dusty apron, throwing it haphazardly onto the counter. "I have gifts."

THE TAILGATE OF MY truck dropped open with a creak and I was pleased to see my jigsaw puzzle of potted plants and bags of soil weren't scattered across the bed. Some petals were a little worse for wear but what was nature if not a little wonky?

Addy whistled lowly, the corners of her lips tugging into an impressed smile as my mother followed her down the driveway. Not many things in life stuck so solidly in my memory as my mother's happiness. Especially in the years since I joined the service. Every time the soft wrinkles around her eyes creased, and the honeyed hazel of her irises brightened, I cataloged it like a scrapbook page.

"I figured we could get the garden planted again." I gestured to the truck. "I'll do the dirty work, of course. We still have some shovels in the shed, right?"

"Yes," Mom murmured, wrapping an arm around my waist. "You picked all the best ones. The pentas are my favorite; they attract the butterflies." She dipped her head and stuck her nose into the star-shaped pink and red flowers, smelling the nectar. "I love it so much, honey."

Her glossy gaze penetrated a locked chamber of sentiment inside me, stinging my nose with unshed emotion. I cleared my throat, trying hard not to give in to the weaker, hidden side of my grief before it reared its head.

"I'll get started after dinner. Should only take a few hours. I brought some old newspaper and cardboard boxes I'm finally getting rid of from back when we bought the house."

"You should keep those handy," Addy suggested. "To pack away all five of your shirts and the one hat you own for Colorado."

"I'll just wear them all on the flight. Problem solved." I hooked my sister's elbow and deposited her in front of the truck's rear door. "I didn't have time to wrap anything," I said. "Save the fucking turtles or some shit though, right?"

She pushed up on her tiptoes, trying to see over my shoulder into the cab.

I turned back around with an arm full of oil paints and a rolled palette of expensive hog bristle brushes. Then went back for the several different-sized canvases that had done all they could to prevent me from using my back window on the ride to Coral Grove.

"It's nothing crazy," I said. "I figured you were probably due for some new stuff."

My mother and sister stared at one another with the same owlish commiseration. Their eyes held a secret conversation that I was lost to. Eventually, Addy turned her attention back to me and grinned. "What's her name, Frankie?"

"What?" I choked on a laugh, looking away.

"Why didn't you tell me you're seeing someone, Frankie?" my mother added.

"I'm not." I shrugged, bumping the door closed with my hip and walking toward the hatchback of Adriana's SUV. "What's going on with the two of you?"

"Bullshit!" Addy followed hot on my heels, inserting her petite frame between me and the trunk. "When did you meet her?"

I easily lifted my sister under the arms, dropping her back down with our wide-eyed mother so I could start loading the canvases for her to take to her own apartment. "Meet who?" I played stupid, schooling my face into a brick of indifference.

"The girl that told you exactly what to get us for Christmas." She poked my arm.

I was apparently as transparent as a glass vase.

"Why didn't you bring her here?" My mother was at my other side, caging me in like I was a misbehaving dog and they were both trying to figure out what I had in my mouth.

"Is it so hard to believe that I would buy the perfect presents for my family, whom I love and know better than anyone else on this planet?"

"Candles, Francesco." My sister huffed. "Every single year I expect a candle and a card, sometimes a coffee mug. One year you got real crazy with a T-shirt."

I pouted. "You loved that T-shirt."

"I did," she agreed. "Now spill it."

"This is ridiculous."

"She's not from here," Adriana guessed.

"Still don't know what you're talking about." I lifted my hat, running my fingers through the thick waves. Damn, I needed a haircut. "You think I need a haircut?" I asked no one in particular. Anything that would get me out of the current conversation.

"She's not like that last one, is she?" Ma scowled, crossing her arms over her chest. I frowned.

"Nothing like her—"

"Ha!" They both pointed at me in unison.

Mom and Adriana had never looked so much alike, the wide-lipped beam and heralding posture. Same height, same eyes, same haughty expression.

I was prepared to pay for that verbal hiccup for the remainder of the day, probably the rest of my life, really. Now that they knew Ophelia existed it'd be a miracle if my sister didn't find her on Instagram within the hour, no name necessary.

"I promise it's not what you guys think it is," I said. "I'm *not* dating anyone."

"Okay..." Addy slammed the trunk closed and stuck to my side as we raced each other up the driveway. "You're not dating her, but you're fucking her."

"Adriana!" Mom looked near ready to faint.

"Nope, not doing that either," I confessed, speeding through the side gate that led into the backyard, suddenly wanting to see exactly how much elbow grease would be necessary to get the buckets planted. Hopefully a fuck ton so I had an excuse to skip dinner, because I was no longer hungry or in the mood to talk about my love life and Ophelia any more than I already had. You don't bring your friend with benefits to Christmas dinner for the same reason you don't talk about them at Christmas dinner.

Because it's like metaphorically sitting with your dick out at Christmas fucking dinner.

"Mom." Adriana paused, eyes widening to saucers. "This one is serious."

I laughed. "You're reading so far into this, it's hilarious."

"So if it's nothing, why are you hiding it?"

"It's not nothing." I shook that sentiment away. "But it's not *something*—never mind, can we drop it? She's not from here, she's too young for me..."

"How old is she?"

"Not old enough."

"Just tell us her name!" Addy fired back.

"Why—" My heels stuck into the grass at the center of the backyard, a spark of something between shock and discontent straightening my spine.

The plot of land where the garden was gnarled and dead three months ago was now sowed and replenished, fresh grass growing in bright green patches, a little sprinkler system waving back and forth over new seeds.

"The garden..." I pointed at it. "You cleaned it up."

"I had some help." My mother's shoulder lifted, too small a gesture to be a shrug.

"Not me." My sister shook her head as I turned to her. Judging by her apprehensive expression I could see I was about to be introduced to a situation I wasn't prepared for. My skin prickled in anticipation, the heart-in-my-gut feeling returning tenfold.

"Who?" I asked sternly. The tables had turned quicker than the weather on a Florida afternoon.

"It was me." A foreign voice ripped my attention to the sliding door off the back porch as it closed. To a man I'd never seen in my entire fucking life, standing on the outside of it, as if he just let himself in and out of my mother's house like he owned the place.

My pulse drummed in my ears. Who the *fuck* was this guy? On my porch in his tailored chinos and Christmas sweater? With a dorky looking combover like a regular Clark Griswold?

My gaze narrowed. "Who's me?"

The stranger stepped off the deck and joined us in the center of the yard. My instinct to protect had me sliding in front of Addy and Mom like a barrier.

"Charlie Wright." Clark Griswold extended a palm. "Excuse the cliche, Frankie, but I've heard so much about you."

"Charlie." My mother stepped between us. She reached for him, but tellingly decided against it. "Frankie."

"Yes, we've established that," I mumbled.

"This is Mom's new boyfriend," Addy inserted herself. "They met at the clubhouse. He's been helping her do a lot of updates around here. You noticed, Frankie. The paint, the camera..."

"I noticed." My blatant assessment must have been making Clark uncomfortable, because he laughed. I suddenly couldn't wait to tell Ophelia how funny I was. I couldn't wait to see Ophelia, actually. I wished like hell she was standing right next to me at that very moment.

"The food is ready inside, Mar." Clark put an arm around her lower back, and up until that point, I'd never before thought about how easily I might be able to snap an arm if given the appropriate reason.

"Perfect!" My mother clapped, waving us in the direction of the back door. "We can talk more over pasta and smelts. Charlie, Frankie bought me the most incredible flowers. You can help him plant them after we eat. Yes?"

"Of course." He nodded enthusiastically, following her lead toward the house.

Addy nudged me onto the deck behind them, warning me to behave with a tight squeeze of my wrist. "Come on."

I brushed her off, hurt I'd been kept in the dark for so long. Long enough for this guy to stick his claws in and claim something that clearly didn't belong to him. Long enough for a stranger to slide into the place at the table I comfortably occupied for the entirety of my adult life, and before me, the father that raised us and loved the woman he married with all of himself. Long enough for the gutters to be replaced, and the walls to be painted, and the garden to be fucking replanted.

Mateo knew something before I did. It was one thing for her to be dating around. A dinner here, an afternoon coffee there. Casual companionship—that's what I was expecting to be briefed on. But a place setting at Christmas dinner, playing fixer upper, *nicknames*? What kind of bullshit was that?

This was my home, that was my sister, my mother. My family.

I wasn't an asshole for feeling disrespected.

Loyalty. One thing I would never falter on, and one thing I'd been so sorely stripped of by the people I never expected it from in my life. First Vanessa, now this.

The muscle in my jaw clenched and my teeth ground together as I tried not to let my emotions get the best of me. But the little voice in my head decided that sewing my mouth shut would only make the outburst worse later on.

I passed my mother on the way to the table, then cold as ice and loud enough for the room to hear, I said, "*That* is my father's garden."

25

Frankie

IT'S USUALLY A GREAT sign when everyone is silent during a meal. Only the occasional comment about the sauce or seasoning, a beckon to pass the pitcher of water across the table. It means mouths are full and the food is delicious.

The sounds of metal utensils clinking against the decorative Christmas dinner plates my mother only brought out once a year were not that of content, though. The air was so thick in the small, crowded dining room I could taste Addy's wine as she swirled it around in the glass next to me.

I shoveled food into my mouth from the head of the table, keeping my back hunched and my head down, unwilling to field any type of small talk. It was a bit late for that. Poor Malia caught the ass-end of everything when she skipped through the front door with three bottles of wine, ready to celebrate, and was immediately muzzled by the deafening silence.

A stabbing pain erupted in my shin, and I dropped my fork, slowly realizing it was Addy kicking me underneath the table. Visibly she remained indifferent, sipping her wine and acting impressed with the notes of fruit and herbs to satiate her partner. Her eyes flickered across the table toward Mom and then back toward Malia.

My mother ate quietly over her dish, shoulders slumped like the branches of a willow tree, a tired, disappointed shadow over her usual bubbly body.

I hated that. It made my stomach roll like an unruly tide.

It was two days before Christmas, and I hadn't seen my family in months. I wanted this to be a perfect, relaxing day where we could reminisce and laugh and enjoy one another's long-awaited company, and now it felt so unbelievably fucking ruined.

I didn't regret what I said. It could have been worse—fucking hell of a lot worse if I decided to put the master's degree in colorful vocabulary I'd gotten in the military to work. The only thing I felt apologetic about was the fallout.

I cleared my throat. "This fish is delicious, Ma, you outdid yourself." My voice cut like nails on a chalkboard through the room. Everyone stiffened instinctively.

"Really, really great, Mama," Addy agreed, and Malia hummed her appreciation around a forkful of seafood salad.

"She's been prepping for days," Charlie added.

Fucking Charlie.

My mother smiled modestly, dusting her hands off on the napkin in her lap. "It's always been your favorite, Frankie."

"I'm spoiled." I put my larger palm over the back of her hand on the table and squeezed it appreciatively.

"So, Charlie was in the Marines." Adriana addressed me when she said it, obviously moderating a less awkward, more informational dinner conversation.

"Oh yeah?" I leaned back in my wooden chair until it started creaking.

"Infantry," he added. "Couple of gunslingers, you and I."

A muscle in my cheek jumped. "You ever killed anybody?"

"Frankie." My mother laughed nervously.

"It's just a question." I shrugged.

"Frankie's a pilot," Adriana said quickly. "He's thinking about making a move to Colorado to teach flight school."

Charlie crossed his utensils on the plate. "Of course, I know. Your mother told me about the accident."

I winced, pulling at the collar of my T-shirt, the fabric suddenly making my skin itch. "Did she?"

"You look great," he offered. "Strong."

"You got a crush on me, Charlie?"

Malia sputtered into her glass of water and everyone's attention landed on her. "Sorry," she choked. "Is it hot in here?"

"So hot in here, right?" Addy stood, bounding to the sliding door and pulling it open. "Must be the oven."

A loud thump shook the table, rattling the utensils and glassware. My mother was up from her chair, still barely taller than me in my seated position, but with a scowl that made the hair on the back of my neck stand up.

"I'm sorry, Francesco." She sighed. "I'm sorry I haven't been honest about my new relationship. I know how you are, and I was worried you would react this way. I didn't want to bring another person into our lives until I knew for certain it was serious." She tucked her hair anxiously behind her ears. "Maybe this was a mistake, thinking we could all be adults—"

"Ma." I shook my head, feeling embarrassingly reprimanded.

"No, you listen to me for a minute. No one will replace your father in my heart. Charlie knows that, Adriana knows that, the neighbors know that. Everyone—" She paused. "Everyone knows that."

Malia quietly slunk out of her seat at the table and joined Addy where she'd disappeared onto the deck, leaving me to have the long-awaited, candid conversation with my mother.

"He's been gone for over twenty years."

"I know." I frowned. "But I still feel like the door might swing open and he'll walk right back through it."

Her tired eyes glossed over. "I used to think that too," she murmured. "But we can't live that way, right? I don't want to spend the next twenty years looking at the front door."

My chest tightened painfully.

I did want her to live comfortably. To be taken care of, and enjoy every second of every day because she deserved nothing less than everything my sister and I could give to her. I wanted her to go out to the beach, and join clubs, and read books, and plant flowers in the backyard so she could drink her coffee on the deck in the morning and look out at them. I needed that for my own well-being, clarity, consciousness. Leaving Florida was never going to happen if that didn't happen first.

"I only want you to be happy." I swallowed my pride.

She reached back and held hands with a silent, reverential Charlie. "I am happy, Frankie. I am very happy. More so than I have been in years, and I will never take your sacrifices for our family for granted."

"It was never a sacrifice." I stood, pulling her into a long, tight embrace. "Just love."

My body relaxed, remembering to inhale and exhale again, the emotions of the day rolling once more in an ever-changing tide. I felt seasick. The hurt still lingered, but it was bandaged enough for the time being.

Charlie stood with us, waiting patiently behind my mother. With gratitude and a subtle apology, I offered him my hand.

"How many people do you think I've killed, Charlie?" I asked.

His lips curled into an appreciative smile. "Let's hope I never find out."

"All right, then." I kissed Mom on the head. "Now help my mother clean this up. I have some flowers to plant."

"Is the nameless girl following you out West?"

I smeared the dirt off my hands and onto my jeans. Black dust had weaseled all the way under my fingernails and into the pores of my skin. I'd need a shower for the first layer and a Brillo pad for the residual mess.

Adriana climbed the short hill to the garden with two beers in hand, the lights from the house and the hazy coral backdrop of evening the only two things still illuminating my workspace. It had dropped down to a temperature that penetrated my thin T-shirt and made the sweat cool against my skin.

"I'd be following her," I confessed, grabbing the bottle and taking a long swig. "She's from Colorado."

"No shit." Addy said. "You're going, then."

"I didn't say that."

She plopped down on the grassy area beside the holes I'd dug out and started primping flower petals. "Why not?"

"What, are you sick of me? You see me once in three months and you're already trying to send me across the country."

"What's the difference between here and Colorado Springs if we already see you so little?" She tilted her head and snatched the small shovel out of my hand as I tried to start digging again.

"I can't take care of the things I need to when I'm two thousand miles away."

"What are you even talking about?" She threw her head back and lay in the lawn, wild blue tendrils of hair splaying out over the green. "Look around, brother dearest, everything is better than ever. The garden is taken care of, the house is painted, the gutters are replaced, the toilet in the fucking basement doesn't gurgle when you flush it anymore. That envelope of money you mail over here every month? In a little safe in Mom's room, untouched."

"That's her money to do whatever she wants with." I pierced a shearing knife into the dirt and rolled over next to Addy, both of us staring up at the pockets of constellations brightening with the looming sunset.

"Charlie had the cameras installed so she would feel safer alone in the house all the time. He's *good* for her, Frankie."

I closed my eyes and inhaled the sweet scent of flowers. Each deep breath felt more and more like a release of tension I'd been storing for longer than I thought possible. Years' worth of worry and resentment, blame I'd placed on myself for the shit luck I'd had in my life until recently. Until I let myself start feeling worthy of something more again.

Until Ophelia.

"Why didn't anyone tell me?" I complained. "Now I look like a fucking loose cannon."

"I don't think that was avoidable; it's part of the reason we put it off for so long. It was gonna be a shitshow one way or another."

"I need fucking honesty, Adriana." I released another aggravated breath.

Her hand looped with mine in the grass. "We know."

"Too much change is happening right now. I'm trying to catch up but it feels like..." I paused. "You know what running feels like in your dreams?"

"Yeah." She giggled.

"That's it. I'm trying to keep up with everyone going in a hundred different directions, but my legs won't move. They want to, I'm kicking, but some weird outside force I can't fight is keeping me in the same place."

"It's the protector instinct." She squeezed my hand. "You've been the man of the house for longer than Dad was at this point. That's not an easy torch to pass, especially to someone you don't know." A beat passed. "Look at me."

We both turned our heads in unison.

"Would I ever let someone I didn't think was worthy of Mom into our lives?"

I sighed. "No."

"Exactly. I don't know if you know this, but you are one scary motherfucker when you want to be."

I cracked a reluctant smile. "Shut up."

"Literally no one could fill your shoes, Frankie, you are too good. You're the best person I've ever met. Selfless, loyal, humble, hardworking—funny." That last word came out under her breath. "But you need to be all of those things for *you*, not for us anymore."

"What does that mean?" I snorted.

"Go to Colorado."

I swallowed the challenge bubbling in my throat. "What if it's the wrong choice?"

"You would have never even gone out there for an interview in the first place if you thought that."

We both sat up again, staring down the hill at the silhouettes of Mom and Charlie moving about in the kitchen through the windows. Malia stood close by laughing at something animated he was describing with his hands as Mom smiled into the sudsy sink.

"They have to know." I gestured to Malia before turning back toward my sister.

"I think Mom is just waiting for me to say it first," Addy admitted. "She hasn't given a random guy at the deli counter my number since Malia started coming around."

"Quite the matchmaker."

"Apparently not." She grinned, her teeth bright against the darkening curtain of night. "I have friends with teenage children, Frankie." Her eyes widened and she shook me playfully. "Teenagers!"

"Well, I'm happy for you anyway." I threw an arm around her shoulder. "Everyone's paired up, huh? Just in time for Christmas."

My sister leaned her head on my shoulder. I knew her curiosity still ran rampant, the questions ping-ponging through her head so loud I could hear them. I wanted her to pry a little more. Which was bewildering, given that until that moment I'd wanted exactly the opposite.

Maybe it was knowing that everyone I cared about had it all figured out and I was still stuck in a limbo, waiting for something to happen. Mateo and Tally, Adriana and Malia, Mom and Charlie. Even if they didn't have it figured out, they still had each other.

I was far from settled, and I definitely didn't have my shit together. But I did have one thing that was quickly becoming the best part of my tangled, inexplicable chaos.

"Are you gonna tell me her name now?" Addy asked expectantly.

The corner of my mouth twitched upward. "Ophelia."

26

Ophelia

THE DOOR TO FRANKIE'S bedroom clicked shut, just in time for me to casually throw myself on the bed and answer the video call coming in before it turned to voicemail.

I made myself at home amongst the pillows, answering it with my brightest smile as a pixelated image of my mother filled the screen. She was sitting in the sun room, dusk not quite reaching that side of the country yet, whereas I was shrouded in night and lamplight.

"Are you in a man's bed?"

So perceptive.

"Hello to you too, Mother."

"Hi honey," she backtracked, her lips twisting into a grin. "I feel like I haven't seen your face in months. It's lonely here without you."

"Is it?" I blushed, tugging at a loose strand of my ponytail. It was comforting to hear her say that.

"Like a piece is missing," she told me. "We have to figure something different out next year, something better for all of us."

"Has it been hell getting everything ready for Christmas?" I picked absentmindedly at the dark thread of Frankie's comforter.

"You know Gavin, doesn't want to wait another minute for the gifts. But Laila's still on the Santa train, so it's been a nightmare keeping him out of the basement storage for the last week."

"You should have left everything at my place." I laughed. "That's what Dad does."

"Smart man. Why didn't I think of that?"

"I'm sure it was Amy who thought of it, but she would never ask me herself."

"She's a shy one." My mom giggled. "Anyway, tell me what's happening in Florida. It's been snowing for a week here."

"Natalia is practically engaged, can you believe it?"

"Naturally." She shrugged. "A good guy?"

"Yeah, he's pretty great. Perfect for her. They're so in love it's disgusting." I said. "We're at his house now, and I'm hiding out in his roommate's bedroom."

My mom's eyebrows danced provocatively. "Nice of him to let you get so comfortable."

"You're prying without prying."

"I just think it's nice. You're practically snuggling with his pillows. Must be an accommodating host."

"Maybe he is." I stuck my tongue out.

"Fine, I won't pry."

I bit my lip, but it was useless pretending I didn't want to talk about Frankie. The praise was nearly dripping off my tongue. "He's ex-military." I covered my mouth. "A pilot."

Her face lit up and she got closer to the camera, trying to inhale the details through the screen. "Handsome?"

"Irritatingly."

"Caring?"

"Emotionally and physically."

She gasped. "Don't fall in love in Florida, Ophelia. I need my daughter back."

"That's ridiculous." I hid my face in the pillow and inhaled the subject of discussion's galvanizing scent. "We're just having fun. God knows I need a break from husband hunting."

"Make him crazy then," she said. "Throw out the sails, have a tête-à-tête. Everyone deserves a torrid love affair at least once and there's no aphrodisiac like a ticking clock."

"Mom!" My body vibrated with laughter. "If Josh could hear you now," I teased. "His wife, the harlot."

She shifted the camera and I caught a glimpse of my stepfather sitting on the leather recliner to her side reading a book. His attention hardly waned from the page, but he wore an amused smirk.

"Hi, Josh," I chirped.

"Hiya, Phee." He looked over the rim of his glasses resting on his nose and into the camera briefly. "Missing you here."

"I miss everyone, too." My heart warmed inside my chest and I sank further into the mattress, my phone outstretched above me. I missed them in a different way than I did a week ago, though. I missed them like you miss a lifelong friend. One that you know will always be there waiting for you no matter how much time goes by. You miss them, you love them, you want to see them—but if something else gets in the way, that's okay too.

Not how I knew I'd be missing Frankie. He was a slow growing addiction that scared me as much as it made me feel on top of the world. Even if I didn't want to, my body would still be seeking out that fix of him. Wishing we existed in the same place at the same time.

"Another week or so and I'll be back. It'll go quick," I said reassuringly.

"We'll be counting down the minutes," Mom promised. "I'll call you on Christmas, honey. Go enjoy your night, I don't want to keep you."

I sat up in bed and blew a kiss toward my phone. "I love you, talk soon."

"Love you," she repeated.

The call cut out and I threw myself back into the mattress, a delighted, weightless groan following. I was maybe the easiest woman to make happy, or just thrived on mutual emotion, but a conversation as short and simple as that with my mother was like a mood elixir.

I caught a sideways glimpse of myself in the standing mirror and was amazed at the satisfaction in my expression. Things were so fucking good, I couldn't believe the person looking back at me was the same woman in the throes of self-deprecation two weeks before.

My confidence materialized into something brash as I lay there, heels digging into the soft give of Frankie's sheets. Alone in the quiet, dark, sensual atmosphere of everything that was him, without consequence.

I tapped my fingernails against my bottom lip and unlocked my phone again.

Ophelia: Hi

A few seconds later three dots appeared on the screen.

Frankie <3: Hi, Trouble

Ophelia: How's Miami?
Frankie <3: You'll get an earful tomorrow

I stood and paced a slow circle around the wood floor in his bedroom.

Ophelia: That bad?
Frankie <3: Mom's got a new boyfriend
Ophelia: Fuck
Ophelia: Are you okay?
Frankie <3: I've been lying in the grass outside for two hours. Addy abandoned me for her girlfriend after beer number three
Ophelia: Are you drunk?
Frankie <3: And so, so horny

My finger dusted across the top of his dresser as I stopped in front of the mirror.

Ophelia: Need a distraction?
Frankie <3: Don't tease me, Ophelia

I snapped a flirty picture of myself in the reflection and sent it.

Frankie <3: Are you in my bedroom?
Ophelia: Seems that way
Frankie <3: Fucking Christ, why?
Ophelia: I'm supposed to be making gingerbread houses with Nat and Mateo

I opened the camera again, this time pulling the hem of my T-shirt up above my chest so my bra and a peek of cleavage stood out before taking the picture.

Frankie <3: Damn it, O

Ophelia: My mother told me to drive you crazy

I hatched an idea suddenly, wriggling out of my clothes and rooting through the drawers in the dresser for something of his to wear.

Frankie <3: You told your mother about me?

Busted.

Ophelia: She asked

Frankie <3: You're lying, and for some reason that makes this hotter

I opened and closed a few drawers one-handed, nudging them back into place with my hip and moving onto the next set.

Frankie <3: I'm tipsy enough to tell you I need more and not be embarrassed about it

I smirked, sticking my hand in the dark confines of what looked like his underwear drawer. Half of it was empty save for a scrap of red fabric that would have been looked over entirely if not for a sweeping sense of familiarity.

"What...?"

I lifted my own lacy red thong out of the drawer, the one he'd pocketed the very first morning in Coconut Creek. Hair rose from my neck all the way down to my tailbone. I sent another photo with the fabric dangling from my fingertips.

Ophelia: Explain

Frankie <3: Figured if you're my girl you need a drawer

My eyes shifted in and out of focus twice as I read his message, knees weakening to cheap rubber.

If you're my girl.

Ophelia: Taking this practice dating thing pretty seriously
Frankie <3: Don't change the subject

His nonchalance was all the more attractive, because—he just didn't realize, did he? That something as basic as making space in a dresser without being asked, without flaunting it, without needing the pat on the back for simply choosing to prioritize me meant more than I could word.

To feel desired. In more than a physical sense. Without denial.

Ophelia: Tell me what you want
Frankie <3: You
Frankie <3: Here
Frankie <3: Now
Ophelia: I was thinking more visually
Frankie <3: Something to hold me over until I ruin you tomorrow

My body stirred awake like a loud knock on the door in the middle of the night. Warmth blossomed down my spine, between my legs. A train of need passing through me fruitlessly without Frankie there to bring me some type of release.

I crawled to his headboard, easing my exposed body against the dark wood. Then, I unhooked my bra and tossed it to the floor.

Ophelia: Does it turn you on to know I'm naked in your bed?

I slid my thong I'd found in his drawer up my legs, adjusting the thin straps high on my hips.

Frankie <3: You know the answer to that. Show me

My fingers shook as I took another photo, vulnerable, yet grossly unabashed. I'd never felt so confident with a man, and it was because I knew Frankie was really *looking* at me. I was trusting him with all of these parts of myself, knowing he wouldn't ever betray them.

Framed in yellow light, the silhouette of every last curve on display, a teasing smile, waves of my hair falling like a curtain around my face as I untied it. There was a woman that lived somewhere idly inside me staring back at the screen, like she knew a secret I was so *close* to uncovering.

That poised, elusive woman, no matter how much I wanted to take her back home with me, belonged to him. No one had ever had that version of me. She was his.

Ophelia: Finally wore them for you

I attached the photo.

Frankie <3: Fuck me, you're so lucky I can't drive right now
Ophelia: I wouldn't call that luck

A minute passed as I watched him type with my thumb between my teeth.

Frankie <3: I'm going to give you everything you want when I get home, Ophelia. Bet on that

The sentiment was physical, but I pretended for a feeble moment that it was more. A man promising me the world, and me wanting nothing more than to take it from him.

The pressure of my teeth sinking into my lip mixed the perfect amount of pain with the stomach sinking feeling of arousal. I was coiled like a spring. Even the small grazing of my knuckles down my body gave me chills.

Ophelia: Distracted?

The soft murmurs of our friends from down the hallway prompted me to stand and reluctantly dress myself again, recentering without any relief. Frankie's clock on the nightstand read half past nine, it was almost Christmas Eve, and I was another day closer to the end of a trip that I wished more than anything had a pause button.

My phone lit up again.

Frankie <3: You are the most distracting thing that's ever happened to me.

"GOOD TALK WITH YOUR mom?" Nat drew a line of pearls with icing across a graham cracker and stuck it with so much force to the rooftop of her gingerbread house the entire foundation shifted.

Mateo was attempting to construct a walkway of mini candy canes with amusing focus, a furrowed brow and his tongue poking out of the corner of his mouth. I plopped down in the dining room chair across from them and stared at my untouched cardboard platform.

"It's been snowing there for a week," I said. "That's all you guys are missing here, white Christmas."

"I could do without," Mateo replied, sliding the box of crackers across the table to me. His attention darted to my neckline and he smirked. "How's Pike holding up?"

I shrugged, blasé. "What makes you think I've talked to him?"

He pointed the end of a candy cane directly at my chest. "Your shirt is on inside out and fucking backward, babe."

I pulled my scoop neckline away to find the tag dangling. Every ounce of dignity left inside me crumbled as I unceremoniously ripped the fucker clear off and took a sliver of fabric with it.

"Chic," Mateo added. "People pay money for that look."

Nat giggled. "I'm surprised he didn't come home tonight."

"He's drunk." I reclined in my chair with a sigh, crossing my legs on the cushion underneath me. "His mom's boyfriend must have been at dinner."

"Shit."

"*Shit*," Nat agreed.

Mateo groaned. "Frankie needs to catch a break."

"You all keep saying that." My curiosity, while already at an all-time high, peaked. "What happened, exactly?"

Whatever it was, they either didn't know how I'd respond, or felt like the explanation belonged to Frankie and an invisible boundary was about to be crossed. They stared at each other until Nat nudged her boyfriend and he rapped his knuckles on the table. "The only reason I'm telling you this and not leaving it to him is because I love my best friend but he'd never say a bad word about his ex."

A muscle in my jaw stiffened and I sucked in an anticipatory breath. "Did she cheat?"

"Cheat?" He scoffed. "Cheating is hiding a couple cards under the table. Stealing the catcher's signs. Vanessa was fixing the whole fucking game."

I frowned. "While you were deployed?"

"He found out after she fucked off that it started way before the crash."

I sat up straighter. "What crash?"

Nat looked between the two of us silently and despondently. Mateo heaved a hard sigh and shifted in his chair, pushing his edible house out of the way to make room for all the eccentric hand movements that accompanied his storytelling.

"They met in North Carolina right before he got picked up for Delta. Only had a few months together before they sent his unit out to the Pacific," Mateo explained. "But he'd already made up his mind. It's not easy to be in a relationship in the military. Most guys aren't doing it for love—if anything it's benefits, security, boredom." He shrugged. "Frankie doesn't do shit out of boredom, Ophelia. He's a calculated son of a bitch. He wants it, he takes it, and he does it better than anyone else."

The tightness in my chest lessened to appreciate that with a sad smile. "She didn't feel the same?"

"Maybe for the first few years. We were gone *a lot*. A fuck ton of sacrifice is made when that's the life you choose. I don't know how men with families do it, I really don't. It's lonely, it's hard work, it's dangerous. Days pass without taking a shower, months without seeing anyone you love. And they're just back home, going to the grocery store, seeing a movie, meeting their friends out for dinner. The whole time, he was counting the days to get back to *her*."

I swallowed a mixture of pity and jealousy that felt like nails scraping down the dry column of my throat.

"He had to have written her a hundred letters," Mateo said. "I'm not kidding, every one of us single guys would be out wherever we were stationed, having our plates worth of ass—" Nat pinched him under the arm. "Ow, fuck. I'm telling a story, sweetheart, it's all part of it." He lifted her hand and kissed it.

"Let's leave the 'plates worth of ass' at the table," she remarked.

Mateo regarded me again. "As I was saying, plates worth of ass—and Pike wanted nothing to do with it. He's loyal to a certifiable degree. She got everything he could give without abandoning the promises he made to himself for his family, and for his country. Vanessa was only ever worried about being taken care of. She was a fucking user."

I *hated* her. I didn't know the woman save for a photo and a story and I fucking hated her. For how she treated Frankie, and for how selfish she was to ever let him go. To be friends with him was wonderful. To be loved by him...would be incredible. I kept that to myself.

I wanted to say a million things in that moment, and all of them led a trail back to the attachment I shouldn't have, and the feelings I needed to collar.

"How did he find out?" I asked.

"The details are his to tell." Mateo's knee bounced under the table and Nat soothed it with her hand. "Pike was medically discharged from Delta right before our contracts were up. It was supposed to be a cut-and-dried op, we were outside the wire, he was in the chopper, shit went sideways, evac was a fucking mess and...he crashed. *We* crashed."

"Oh, shit." My pulse hammered against my neck.

"Recovery took longer than Pike thought it would, but he didn't help himself either. He didn't think he deserved it. He blamed everything bad that happened on himself, and never took the people he *saved* that day into consideration." I had an innate feeling that this was a conversation the two of them had had many times before. "It was ugly, O, that's no doubt his biggest regret."

"Vanessa didn't stick around when he needed her to," Nat said.

"Surgeries, recovery, physical therapy, all of it. He needed her and she didn't step up to the plate. When the going got tough, she got going down to fucking Fayetteville to find someone to dangle shiny things in front of her again. Spoiled bitch."

Normally I'd be averse to name calling but...*spoiled fucking bitch.*

"They were two complete opposite sides of a coin." Mateo continued. "Pike saw her through rose-colored glasses, and he still does. He still faults himself for her leaving and stepping out on him. He thinks if he was home more, if he had asked her to marry him before we deployed, if he'd pulled himself out of the depressive episode after the accident, that would have fixed everything. But he doesn't see what we do."

I pulled my knees to my chest, wrapping my arms around myself in what felt like the closest thing to a hug. My understanding of Frankie waxed and waned with every passing hour. I was on a boat that was sinking, without a raft, and the worst part was that I was the one letting the water in. I was becoming obsessed with knowing him, learning him, being a part of his life, getting too *involved.* Finding out about his ex only made me want him more. Because he was so deserving of everything he ever dreamed of having in life that it overwhelmed my own self-preservation.

It made me think about Colorado. How good we could be for each other if we ever had the chance to make something *real* out of this. How much of each other we still had to discover.

Mateo's explanation of what had happened with Vanessa only added several pieces to an already intricate and still unsolved puzzle. I was saving those bits of curved, edged information instead of trying to shove them into place, confident patience would prosper and every missing jigsaw was something I had yet to experience. Perfectly incomplete.

As if his ears were ringing, we all looked down at my phone buzzing to life on the table with Frankie's name etched across the screen. **Tell Cap he's not out of the woods for keeping secrets for my mom.**

I laughed quietly, a brazen smile taking over the moroseness.

"He says you're in trouble," I relayed across the table.

Mateo chuckled, pulling Nat into his side and rubbing away an invisible chill down her arm. "That's my favorite place to be."

The Christmas tree sparkled wistfully behind them in the living room, raindrops of light sprinkling down onto the gifts waiting to be opened underneath. The reflection of the three of us sitting there played off the uncovered windows where night blackened the world outside and turned us kaleidoscopic.

Ophelia: This isn't very friends with benefits of me, but I kind of miss you

As eagerly as it was sent, another message returned.

Frankie <3: This isn't very friends with benefits of me either, but I told my mom about you, too

27

Ophelia

CHRISTMAS EVES GROWING UP were spent in quiet solitude or utter chaos. My dad was somewhat estranged from his family from the moment he married my mom, and the grandparents I had on my mother's side moved south when I was old enough to start school. I saw them in the summer on a trip to Arizona every year, but when the holidays came around we remained a family of three.

As a teenager, every other Christmas I got one parent or the other, and then one set of siblings or the other, and the least magical morning you could ever imagine, spent holding an industrial-sized garbage bag open for all the younger siblings' torn bits of sparkly wrapping paper.

In adulthood I was the "*can you grab an extra bag of ice*" or "*I forgot to pick up cookies to leave out for Santa*" daughter, and the twenty-fourth of December made me feel like the stretched-thin elf of your worst nightmare.

A far and insignificant memory compared to being guided through a restaurant by a possessive palm on the small of my back. Wrapped like a present with a bow cinching me together at the waist of my velvet green mini dress, complete with high heels, black sheer stockings, golden bangles, tiered hoop earrings, and lips red like pomegranate.

The air tasted expensive, an aroma of charred meats and spices carrying us through the dimly lit and festive dining room. Dark, wooden booths were decorated tastefully in fir branches and brambles. Pinecones and needles weaved in and out of floor-to-ceiling pillars, and the chandeliers hung low enough their light just brushed the tables.

Mateo and Natalia sat and I felt a tug on my waist, Frankie's fingers digging into the soft skin above my hip enough to have me falling back against his chest. His chin dipped to rest on my shoulder briefly, lips grazing the shell of my ear.

"You look unreal, you know that?"

I released too shaky a breath to play off, and his smile widened against my skin. Every touch had been charged since our fleeting hello as Natalia and I had filed into the backseat of Mateo's car when they picked us up. While we drove, he reached an arm back to clasp his warm fingers around my ankle.

I felt a massive, anticipatory weight on my body—but instead of hurting me, it amplified everything to an acute degree. Every emotion felt unapologetic, graceful touches became godless, an innocent look ignited something *hotter*, like wick to flame. Something had changed in the two days since I'd last seen Frankie. Whether that be the way we viewed our arrangement, or the way he viewed his future after visiting his family—the urgency between us was heralding.

My stomach felt empty, yet entirely occupied throughout dinner. Wings flapped in the cavity of my body so incessantly the pasta in front of me had nowhere to go. I had never been so anxious around a man in my life. It was first-date-level imbalance. The type of nuclear nervousness that would accompany sitting down across from a handsome stranger for the first time knowing nothing about them but the surface.

I *knew* Frankie.

He'd literally had his fingers inside me. I'd taken the man down the back of my throat like it was an Olympic sport in broad daylight on the coastal highway. Aside from those intimate instances, we'd confided in each other things that made us much more than strangers, but it was as if the last two weeks were a blur.

"Eat," Frankie murmured, leaning over and filling my empty glass with a crimson blend of wine.

He looked straight out of a magazine. I was convinced dress pants had never fit a pair of legs and the curve of a man's ass so perfectly, and positive I'd never looked so hard before. His consistently casual T-shirt and shorts, while attractive in their own right, were nothing in comparison to him in Oxfords and a blazer.

I quickly brought the wine to my mouth and took a generous sip of sweet, woodsy liquid, leaving a faint ring of color on the polished glass. The dry sting of cabernet danced on my tongue as I poked it out to traverse my bottom lip—only pausing when I realized eager brown eyes followed every chaste movement.

Heat colored my already flushed cheeks. Frankie was regarding me like I was his next meal—urging me to eat, watching me indulge. Such a primordial instinct, and so innocent in the quiet room. He and I knew it wasn't, though. There was tension buzzing between us.

"How was the drive home, Frankie?" Nat asked across the table. I was finally distracted enough to focus on the carbonara in front of me and picked aimlessly at a clump of green peas.

The men had cleared their steaks and draped their arms lazily over our chairs while we continued at a more savoring pace. Frankie's fingertips grazed across my shoulder, and then blatantly gathered the hair at the side of my neck I'd let fall like a curtain in front of my face and tucked it behind my ear.

The part of me that was very desperate, and embarrassingly wet, clenched.

A piece of chicken suspended on a fork between Natalia's mouth and her plate dropped back into the risotto as her expression turned from intrigued to utterly disbelieving. Watching in real time as the line blurred somewhere vital in Frankie and I's arrangement. He was a very hands-on friend.

"You know when you're kind of in a fog while driving," Frankie said, "and you start daydreaming, and all of a sudden you can't even hear what's playing on the radio anymore? It's like a mindless autopilot because your brain is just somewhere else entirely? One second you're in the car, and the next you're home and you don't even remember how you got there?"

My nerves lit up like fireworks, a surge of energy pilling the skin hiding beneath my dress in goosebumps. I slid my hand from my lap to rest secretly just above Frankie's knee, his quad flexing on impact and then relaxing under my palm.

"Maria's boyfriend was that bad, huh?" Mateo laughed.

I felt his eyes on my profile, but remained purposely aloof.

"Funny," Frankie answered, "I didn't think about that once."

My NYLON-COVERED TOES DUG into the carpet in the living room, finally free from the much too ambitious and half a size too small pair of stilettos I'd thieved out of Natalia's closet. I had never been the best at sensible fashion, and the fanciest restaurant in

Pine Ridge was the Applebee's on Main, so there's to say the red bottoms didn't exist in any universe of mine.

Embers crackled to life across the room as Frankie, bent over on his knees, fiddled with the mechanics at the base of their fireplace. His jacket was tossed over the armchair, the top button of his dress shirt flicked open, and then the second...*and another under that one.* A flirty display of his chest tickled my already reprimandable adoration.

I only realized I'd been staring when my eyes unfocused and the room turned into a watercolor painting of blue-black darkness. Muffled voices from the kitchen rose over the telling sound of cabinets closing and glasses clinking, the Christmas tree buzzed faintly, the lights burning for two weeks and remaining twinkling against all fire safety and hazard warnings.

Back in Colorado my parents would just be sitting down for dinner, Dad and Amy having brought the kids to church an hour before, Mom and Josh standing over the stove together cooking. The already unending energy of my siblings at dangerous levels, as if the day itself was a drug and the Santa tracker on the iPad in the corner was a new high every hour.

I did a perfunctory web search on my phone out of curiosity as Frankie plunked down beside me, pinning me unwittingly into the corner of the couch.

"Santa Claus is in Iceland," I informed him.

"We better get to bed soon then," he joked, the amber reflection of the fireplace turning his brown eyes caramel, melting me just the same.

I thoughtlessly lifted my fingers to brush the wild hair off his temples and run my nails softly across his scalp. He wrapped an arm around my shoulder, pulling my thigh to rest on his lap, connecting us eagerly and intentionally.

My mind raced with the things Mateo had told me the night before. I hadn't had a moment alone with Frankie yet, and while our bodies sparred for things we'd yet to address, I wanted to be more to him than a warm bed. "Are you really okay?" I asked. "Yesterday..."

"I'm perfect right now," he insisted casually. "Magic's back."

"Magic's back," I agreed. Silver bells faintly chimed beneath the brandish of the holiday. I felt relaxed for the first time since I was a child, safe, in someone's embrace. Sure of myself and the future I wanted, the type of person worth building it with, the hopeless romantic in me that grew up watching Hallmark movies sighing on the sidelines as the credits rolled.

Myself. I was me.

Not *their* Ophelia. Not a biennial statue, or forgotten plate setting, the extra folding chair on the end of the table, or the last few gifts under the tree in the morning. If someone had told me a month ago the answer was in leaving it all behind, that what I didn't know I was looking for meant individuality, freedom, independence, confidence, *bravery*—I wouldn't have believed it. Because I liked who I was before I became this fuller version. Now I liked her more, and I loved the person I was with *him*.

"Not too bad for a third date." Frankie's thumb traced ovals into my knee. "Fancier, more serious, romantic."

The corner of my lip curled. "You're very impressive. I just have one qualm."

He hummed, a singular eyebrow arching patiently.

"Too much company."

On cue our friends glided into the room with an extra glass of sparkling wine in each hand. A sharp laugh croaked out of me at Mateo, garnished head to toe in his infamous Santa suit once again.

"No, please—I'm still having nightmares from the last time I saw this outfit," I said.

"Ho, ho, ho." Mateo bent down to hand Frankie his champagne, which instead slipped through his white-gloved hands and doused his roommate's dress shirt.

"Matty, for fuck's sake," Nat groaned.

"Jesus Christ." Frankie jolted, untangling from me quickly.

Mateo grimaced, running his sleeve uselessly down the buttons of Frankie's shirt. "My bad. But hey, this is perfect because it's showtime anyway, big guy."

Nat joined me, snuggling into my shoulder, tucking her bare feet under her legs while I rested my head on top of hers.

"All right," Mateo clapped. Frankie reluctantly stood beside him, wet and towing a thread-thin line between aggravation and anxiousness. "Let me set the mood."

A stream of music started playing out of the tiny speaker on Mateo's phone, the cacophony of *bu-booms* followed in turn with the low horn rhythm and unmistakable sound of Eartha Kitt's voice singing "Santa Baby".

"No, Cap, you're on your own—" Frankie shook his head, the apples of his cheeks deepening a shade.

"Tradition is tradition, Pike. The ladies deserve to know." Mateo swayed back and forth with the melody, training his eyes on his girlfriend lovingly and crooking a finger toward her to join him. "We strip."

"What?" I gasped.

"You ever seen *Jarhead*, Ophelia?" Mateo asked.

I shook my head, staring back and forth between him and Frankie.

"Jake Gyllenhaal, look it up."

"You idiots were in the Army." Natalia laughed as Mateo pulled her off the couch and spun her in a circle. The long tips of her hair shined with every twirl past the fireplace.

"Delta is made up of all kinds of salty motherfuckers, my love. MARSOC, Air Force Pararescue, Army Rangers. I'll give you a pass because you're goddamn beautiful and I'm taking you directly to bed after this."

Mateo peeled his fluffy red suit jacket down provocatively, rounding his hips in sensual circles and singing along to the rich notes of festive jazz. I hooted from the couch, cupping my hands over my mouth to egg the pair of them on. My cheeks burned with laughter, the muscles in my jaw aching.

Natalia picked up and whipped Mateo's jacket around her head like a banner when it hit the floor.

"Fuck it." Frankie gave in. His fingers went to his chest, slipping the clear buttons through their holes in succession until his full, tanned upper half and the outline of his muscular torso were on full display.

My insides contracted, a slow swirl of heat pooling low in my stomach. Every sinewed vein on that man was working double time apparently, because my eyes found and registered each and every root from his hips to his shoulders.

"Take it off!" Natalia roared as Mateo's fingers snuck beneath the stretchy band of his pants and teased them up and down, his green briefs peeking out every few seconds.

"This is so twisted." I giggled, enjoying every sordid second of it.

My attention whistled back to Frankie as he tossed his dress shirt to land in my lap. Unsure as he might have been, we locked gazes and he trailed his perfect hands slowly toward the buckle on his belt. "Eyes over here, Trouble."

"Yes sir," I mumbled suggestively. My legs felt like gelatin, and every inch of me from the waist down buzzed.

He worked himself open, black leather sliding like a greased conveyor through one loop and then two, deft fingers curling around metal and loosening the buckle until it hung near his zipper like an invitation.

My chest rose with an inhale...and it stayed there, the breath caught in a limbo of concentration. The less air that got to me the more incessantly aroused I found myself. I needed to be alone with him. My eyes flitted from his belt to his face and that same echoed expression was there looking back at me, thickening the air in the room to fog.

I lifted the champagne flute to my lips and took one long, slow pull of liquid down my throat, emptying it.

The final lines of "Santa Baby" faded out and Mateo lifted his girlfriend off the ground, wrapping her legs around his waist. His red pants pooled at his feet and he didn't even shimmy out of them, hopping toward the hallway as Nat cackled, holding onto his neck for dear life.

"See you in the morning, Phee!" she squealed over her shoulder.

"Merry Christmas to all, and to all a good night!" Mateo sang back before burying his face in her neck.

I peeled my eyes away from them and back to Frankie. The weight of a few moments before was just as pressing and even heavier despite our distance.

A muscle in his jaw clenched and softened, a timid smile stretching itself across his cheeks. Then, he did the opposite of my expectation and crouched down, sitting alongside the gifts beneath the tree. "I got something for you."

"Me?" I perked up, floating on a cloud across the living room to take a place beside him on the carpet. His bare skin glowed even brighter up close, the flames from the fire rippling gold and yellow against shadow.

Adonis, I thought, embarrassingly. The man was my living, breathing, mythical god.

"Something to commemorate your Christmas in Coconut Creek," he said, pulling a small box from under the tree that had obviously been wrapped by his hands. The crinkled edges and overlapping tape were veritably charming. "It's very lame, now that I think about it."

"It's not," I assured him, twisting the gold foiled box in my fingers. "Should I open it?"

"Go ahead." He nodded.

I tore the paper, unveiling a white box with a bow around it. The top popped off as I tugged the fabric away and that air-less, tight-chested, speech-disabling thing I'd found happening around Frankie more and more often came on with force.

My lips parted, the singular expression of vitality.

"It's a Blue Morpho," he explained as I lifted the gorgeous, crystal-like butterfly by its necklace chain out of the box. Teal wings spilled into black, angular tips. "Like the one that you wanted to take off with at the museum." He chuckled quietly. "I figured it liked you for a reason."

"Frankie..." I didn't know what to say. My fingers quaked nervously, handling the piece as if it were glass. "What the fuck?"

He paled. "I know, I know—what the fuck was I thinking." He moved to take it from me and I yanked the necklace closer to my chest.

"No—what the fuck? I got you *pajamas*," I scoffed. The last thing anyone had ever one-upped me on was *gift giving*. "Plaid pajama bottoms to replace your holier-than-thou ones."

Color returned to Frankie's face, slipping down his neck, re-suscitating the near-dead moment. "My heart just stopped," he huffed. "Don't fuck with me like that, O."

"I'm not fucking with you. We need to go to the mall tomorrow."

"The mall is most definitely closed on Christmas Day," he reminded me.

"The day after."

"The twenty-sixth is the biggest return day of the year."

"I need to fix this."

"Or..." He reached for the hand still pressed to my chest and peeled it away delicately, loosening my fingers from their tight grip around the chain. "You can stop being a crazy person, turn around, and let me put this on you."

My heartbeat began a steady climb, thrumming in time with my movements. First hesitant, pinning Frankie with a wary glare, and then more deliberately as my body twisted away from him and I felt the first touch of warm fingertips across my nape. He brushed my hair off my shoulders in sweet, useless strokes.

"Hold on." I gathered my curls in a ponytail, lifting it to expose the long lines of my throat and every nerve ending across my neck ignited in anticipation. I had always loved being touched there. My skin was sensitive to the attention in a cruel way; it disabled me, loosened my muscles, waking up every last untouched part of my body until it was nothing but craving.

There was silence behind me before two hands passed in front of my face and I got a perfect glimpse of the blue butterfly as it lowered to settle in the dip between my collarbones. The charm was colder than I'd expected and I pulled a quaint breath through my teeth. I was on the edge of a cliff in my mind. Dangling, I wanted to fall—I *wanted to fall*.

Frankie's knuckles brushed against my pulse and my eyes drooped closed. He must have felt the adrenaline coursing through my veins, and I would own the fact that I didn't give a damn anymore. The clasp snapped together at the top of my spine but his hands remained and the quiet lingered, so deafening I could hear the candle whispering across the room.

Neither of us moved a muscle. My stomach hollowed out like a cavern.

Then I felt his *lips* claiming the curve where my neck met my shoulder. I sighed out a sound that could only be described as a whimper as my hair fell back through my fingertips. Somehow one of the most innocent things he'd done to me felt the most sultry.

"I know," Frankie exhaled against my neck.

His forearm came across my middle, pulling me to his chest. His legs opened around my hips and he buried his face in the swell of my throat, warm, wet lips tasting every open inch. My breasts tightened, and as if he could decipher my need like a map key, his hands traveled exactly where I wanted them, squeezing me through the fabric of my dress.

"I've been thinking about this," he said. "Two fucking days this is all I could think about, Ophelia."

I hummed agreeably, using the small window he'd opened to dig my hand into the hair at the side of his head and pull his mouth over mine. Our tongues connected instantly, nothing timid or explorative to be had—it was pure pent-up lust cracking like a sheet of ice. One of his hands palmed my throat, toying with pressure, and the decision to let the night take us somewhere slowly was shot to hell.

I kissed him like he was mine to consume. We battled back and forth, lips crashing, teeth nipping through short gasps. He tasted warm and sweet. A purr rumbled in the back of his throat as my grip tightened in his hair and the heat radiating off his naked chest against my spine increased.

Frankie's fingers pinched my cheeks, popping me off his lips but holding me there with dominant command. "Do you want me to fuck you?"

"Yes," I answered without hesitation.

Then I was on my back, the decorative skirt beneath the Christmas tree in my peripheral, starlight radiating from the branches over my head, nothing but the sound of crackling fire and our terse breathing dancing in the space around us.

"God, you made me wait though, didn't you, sweetheart?" He settled between my legs where I could clearly see him straining against the zipper of his pants. I traced the thick outline with my eyes, my core throbbing more every second for his touch.

Gentle hands grazed up both sides of my thighs, dipping beneath the velvet skirt of my dress and curling around the tight band of my stockings. He was stoking an already raging fire. In any other instance I might have wanted the delicate foreplay, but I was so ready for him that if I didn't feel a trace of satisfaction any sooner I would implode.

"Don't treat me like a flower," I coached. His hands stopped, a sinful smirk playing over his features. "I'll tell you if it's too much."

Not a moment later the flimsy nylon on my hips was torn away from my body, ripping all the way down past my knees. Frankie shed the ruined fabric and tossed it away, then dipped down and bit a mark so intensely into my exposed inner thigh I yelped.

As quickly as the pain came it was soothed away by his tongue. He edged his nose up my leg further, pushing my dress above my hips, leaving me completely exposed save for the thin strip of damp fabric covering my center.

"You are so much dirtier than you let on, O, you can't even hide it." His finger slipped beneath my panties and pulled it away, then let it snap back into place, stinging my clit with pleasure. "Look at this mess."

"*Fuck me.*" My elbows dug into the rug beneath me.

"I'm getting there," he murmured, dipping his fingers back beneath the cotton and yanking it down fully. My hips jarred forward with the motion as his dark eyes settled between my legs.

A chill grazed me, immediately swallowed by the warm cup of his mouth on my intimate, bared skin for the very first time. I arched involuntarily toward the ceiling, my nipples straining against their confines. Heat blossomed so violently in my core I moaned out of sheer reflex.

"My god, you sound as good as you taste," Frankie murmured against me. His tongue traced the bud of nerves at the peak, flicking it in slow circles. Every hair on my body stood on edge, pleasure radiating through my bones like heavy bass. "Spread your legs nice and wide for me, Trouble. Let me go a little crazy."

I parted without question, letting my knees fall open around him. His mouth delved back down, this time tasting every inch on the way to my opening and plunging his thick tongue inside of me.

My fingers flung to his scalp, holding him tightly for support as my arms gave out and my spine hit the floor on a tortured groan. "Yes," I praised. "Yes, yes." I tightened like a spool, every muscle in my lower half suddenly with a mind of its own, contracting and relaxing with every single stroke of his tongue. He sucked and tugged at my clit, pinching it between his lips.

"I like that word." His hand snaked up my body, pulling the neckline of my dress down to reveal the lacey cups of my bra. "Take your fucking tits out for me." His voice was strained, the words muffled behind his teeth. "Christ, O, I can't wait to feel this pussy for real."

What was it about the filth that came out of this man's mouth that dissolved me to liquid magma? I was so turned on I could count down the seconds to my orgasm.

Sweat beaded on my temples as I crisscrossed my arms over my torso and gripped the bundled fabric of my dress, arching my back to pull it directly over my head in one swift movement. My bra followed as I unclipped it eagerly and spread myself bare on the cashmere-colored carpet.

Frankie's movements stalled, the fire in his eyes no longer just a reflection of the glass and flames behind my head. There was desperation so flagrantly on display I felt for a moment like the most powerful woman in the world. I was on my back but he was lying down before me, my satisfaction his only precedence.

He teased a finger inside of me, the familiar feeling of it making every lash of his tongue land tenfold. My hips buzzed and the tightening in my lower belly became unbearable.

"The way your body responds…" Frankie whispered. "It's so fucking hot." He pressed another finger inside me with the first and I gasped out a sharp moan as they curled in slow strokes, petting a spot that rendered me blind. Satisfaction floated from my mouth in a symphony. "Hi, beautiful." He laughed sweetly, the sound branding itself in my core memories on impact. "There she is, there's my girl."

"Frankie, oh…*God*." My thighs squeezed around him.

"Is it good, baby?"

My eyes got lost somewhere in the back of my head. "So…" I mumbled. "So…"

"Show me how good."

His mouth found my clit again and I erupted in pleasure. My insides clamped down so violently I saw nothing but darkness for a moment before my vision returned, the tidal wave of an orgasm sucking every last breath of air from my lungs. My chest rose and fell in a chaotic rhythm as Frankie dragged the final spasms out with his fingers.

"Fuck yes." He brought them to his mouth without missing a beat and tasted the evidence. I was immediately captivated again, humming for another moment like the one I'd just experienced.

I'd not even touched him, yet it was like we were on the same level of euphoria. Frankie's pupils were dilated to eight balls, his hair askew, skin glistening with a thin sheen of sweat. He sat up on his knees and I ran greedy fingertips from the center of his chest to the trail of hair around his navel and didn't stop there.

"I want this," I murmured, tugging him by his open belt buckle.

We'd all but forgotten where we were—in the center of the living room floor in the dark. His calloused hands ran up my body from the tops of my thighs to the curve of my rib cage, skating over my nipples, then to my throat and back down as if he were reading me like braille.

"Take it," he said firmly. Frankie reached into his back pocket and pulled free a condom, placing it in the valley between my breasts. "Take anything you fucking want from me."

I wanted his time, his memories, his adoration, his *future*. I wanted so many things from him, but more than anything in that moment, I wanted him buried inside of me. I wanted to feel him come apart.

I made quick work of his zipper, my hands lingering obsessively on the length straining against my palm. His trembling fingers joined mine, shoving his briefs down as I tugged, as if we couldn't work fast enough. When he sprung free he sighed, as if it hurt him to have been caged for so long, and my mouth watered at the sight of his own desperation beading at the tip of his cock.

Frankie's size was so impressive I spent a minute just exploring it with my hands, stacking my fists on top of one another around him, stroking it from base to head, rubbing his arousal in circles with my thumb. He jerked and huffed as the lower muscles in his abdomen stiffened and loosened, then repeated.

"I love watching you play, Trouble"—his voice was pinched—"but I'm about three good strokes away from painting you white."

God.

I tore through the condom wrapper with my teeth and rolled it eagerly down his shaft. Frankie's large frame came down on top of me as he shucked his pants off, his forearms closing me in on both sides of my head, until the glow of the room was nothing but a silhouette around his shoulders.

We connected like magnets to metal, and in an instant he was inside of me, with one swift plunging thrust that my entire body reacted to. Everything from my toes to the roots of my hair came alight.

Frankie's lips dropped into the crook of my neck, stifling a graceless groan. "Fuck me, O, that is so tight." His fingers fastened on my hips, aggressive energy coursing through him.

His cock throbbed, taking up every last inch of space it could as my walls pulled him deeper, begging for friction that he granted with another roll of his hips.

"You," he growled, thrusting forward again. "Are..." Another hard snap into me. "Unreal."

I closed my thighs around him, ankles crossing on the small of his back as he continued to move in and out of me. I was on the precipice of another rapture, his dick angled perfectly into my core, grinding on that soft, debilitating spot that made my vision cloud around the edges.

I could still taste myself on his tongue and that ignited a secondary lust so unbearable all control was lost.

"You feel so good," I mumbled against his lips. "It's never felt this good."

Our breaths mingled as he tore away to stare down into my eyes. "Say that again. Best you've ever had? Huh?" His pace quickened and I whimpered into his open mouth. His lips claimed the sounds, swallowing them. "Come on, O, I know you're thinking something fucking depraved up there. Tell me."

Frankie's forehead came to rest on mine, our noses bumping intimately. I should have been embarrassed at the sounds my body was making but I felt nothing but security and gratification. Hedonistic fulfillment at its basest level. My fingernails skated down his back and dug in, sealing myself to his body so harshly I could feel each individual muscle in his torso working against me. My touch caught raised skin, thick and scored dash marks above his tailbone. His scars.

"More," I pleaded. "I want to feel you in my throat."

His hand tangled in the hair at the back of my head, lifting me slightly from the carpet to cradle my skull in his palm.

"I knew it would be this way," he muttered. He dragged his mouth down my chin, my throat, licking at the dips in my collarbones, branding me in hot trails of his tongue. His teeth clamped down on one of my nipples and tugged it feverishly. "I knew you'd fuck me up, Ophelia. I knew it."

My core tightened around him, quivering with need, preparing for release once again. Frankie held my hips down with his heavy body and ground himself so deeply inside me I opened my mouth to scream and nothing came out.

Again, again, again. I bit my bottom lip and threw my head back, realizing that his hand was the only thing there to keep me from hurting myself. The way he fucked was bruising and I would wear the evidence of it like a fucking medal. *This* was what I did to him; *this* was the loss of control.

"Hike these knees up so I can get my cock nice and deep, baby." My limbs were putty, but he hooked his arms under my knees and opened me over his lap easily. My thighs met my torso and his weight kept them pinned there. "You want it all, you're gonna take it all, pretty girl. I told you I would ruin you for anyone else."

Already done.

He pulled all the way out, an empty second where I remembered how to breathe, and then buried the full swell of himself inside me, gliding over every pleasure point I never knew I had. The coarse hair at the base of his pelvis brushed against my clit and the room started spinning.

"I'm gonna come," I confessed in a voice that sounded nothing like my own. The pitch was edged, and my throat struggled with the syllables. "Are—are you gonna come?"

"Ophelia." He coughed out a laugh, then lowered his lips to mine in a hard, raw kiss. "You have no idea, do you?"

Whatever that meant, it didn't matter, nor register. My core pulled taut in one instance and then fluttered around him the next. I didn't just tumble off the peak I was standing on—I jumped. Everything around me came crashing down, and Frankie froze to feel every last pulse of it.

"Fu-uck," he swore, dragging out the lone vowel. My nails dug into his back, undoubtedly leaving trails of pink and red passion, and then his spine stiffened beneath my fingertips.

"Please," I whimpered. "Let me hear you."

Frankie's hips slowed and stuttered, and with one last hard shove inside of me, his chest rumbled and he bellowed out a sound so animalistic it shook me. And God, I would remember every last note of it for the rest of my life.

Years of emotion rolled off him in long, deep breaths as we both rode out that high. I let him relax on top of me, still inside of me, our bodies going from stiff and coursing with adrenaline to nearly unmovable. Still his mouth peppered the center of my chest in small kisses.

Our connection was deeper than sex. So much more poignant than fucking. What we'd just done was a cumulation of something bigger than the two of us were ready to address. I bent my head despite it, kissing the crown of his head in the crackling ambiance of fire and Christmas lights. The room reeked of lust and pine needles, a lingering hint of vanilla bean. It was fucking perfect. It was like I was dreaming.

If life was made up of highs and lows, this was a pinnacle. A peak of slowly piling moments leading up to me and Frankie lying naked on the living room floor, enjoying each other unapologetically.

After a minute, he turned his face into the hollow of my neck. "I like you, O," he murmured. "I want to lock you up and keep you here so you can't leave. So no one else can ever have you but me."

My throat purred with laughter, but my heart stuttered so violently I wondered if Frankie could feel it against his cheek.

28

Frankie

IT'D BEEN YEARS, BUT my body never forgot the feeling of a woman wrapped around it. Soft legs, warm skin, flower petal fuzz underneath my wandering fingertips. Not too harsh to wake her up, just enough to keep her blissfully sedated. The metronome of her heart playing against my rib cage, her thigh bent and snug tight over mine.

I was always an early riser. The military further ironed that into me like a cattle brand, making it permanent. And though I'd gotten no more than two hours of sleep between talking to Ophelia and burying myself inside her, rest would remain evasive.

So instead I watched her sleep—as if she could do it for the both of us. Her chest rose and fell, the blue butterfly around her neck the only thing left to be worn on her entire body. For the rest of my life I'd be chasing passion like what I'd experienced with her—I already knew it. But the thought of that with anyone else spun in my stomach like I'd spent the whole night drinking.

This was that attachment I swore I'd never develop coming to collect. Somewhere along this so-called path of self-rediscovery I'd promised to myself, a jumbled bag of feelings got involved. My past got dragged into it, and I was telling this girl I'd known for two weeks shit I didn't even understand about myself. She fell for the confident, charismatic asshole on the plane, but that's the act I liked to play while the real me—the understudy, the guy who'd never made the cut—stood behind the curtain.

I'd taken all the best parts of my military buddies' personalities—Mateo's confidence, Sam's humor, Tyler's prowess—and layered it like clay over myself. I built a mask and only removed it when I was alone, like peeling off a second skin. Until that skin couldn't be peeled away anymore and it just became who I was. Or who I'd tricked myself into believing I was. When you lie enough it starts to sound like the truth.

Ophelia was taking a chisel and a hammer to all of that, uncovering a fossil of a man who didn't even know he was slowly entombing himself until he couldn't move.

I looked down at her, counting the points of her eyelashes against her cheek, tracing the button curve of her nose. Her bottom lip was in a permanent state of poutiness, and my fingers ached to pinch it. I couldn't help myself as a strand of hair fell in front of her face and I swept it away, back into the long mess of it splayed across my shoulder and the pillow.

She stirred and my entire body straightened like a board. If I woke her up I'd feel like a fucking dick, especially after the night we had. We could both use a shower and a few bottles of water, but not until the sun was up first. I was content to lay in it for a while longer. The flowery smell of the perfume she wore to dinner still on my hands, dried sweat like a film across my brow. Not something I wanted washed away.

Greed was a terrible thing but nothing else came close to describing what she did to me. I could be possessive, predatory, addicted, unhinged, but I'd never wanted to *take* like I did with Ophelia. I wanted to bleed whatever endorphin this was dry.

When she settled again I wormed my way out from under her, pulling the dead limb of my arm from beneath her heavy head, wiggling my fingers back to life. The mattress creaked as I stood and I froze for a second time, watching her rib cage expand and contract in that same soft rhythm until I was sure she was still asleep. Before I escaped the room I tugged on a pair of sweatpants and pulled the blanket to her shoulders.

The kitchen was dark and stagnant. I kept the lights off and moved around by the soft glow of morning seeping through the living room windows. Over the half wall the tree remained dimly lit. My eyes scoured where O and I had been rolling on the floor and my cock twitched.

I needed a coffee, some fresh air, and time alone to talk myself out of the fantasy that was waking up every morning the way I just had.

After a one-sided argument with the world's noisiest coffee machine I stepped out onto the patio where the dew wasn't yet dry and the orange sunrise was peeking over the backyard fence. It was too cold to be shirtless, but the breeze had the perfect amount of bite to wake up the parts of my body the coffee couldn't reach fast enough.

That early in the morning, I felt like the only person alive. Or so I thought.

"Merry Christmas, Francesco."

I twitched away from the sound of a voice in the neighbor's backyard as a pair of garden shears lifted just above the fence and snipped the air. "Shit! Mr. Barry, I didn't know you were out here."

Gino's short frame toddled to the edge of the property line and I looked over as he tended to several buckets of plush red tomato plants. The man was fully dressed and put together. Beige slacks and a red button-down tucked into them. Brown belt, brown shoes, the Catholic cross hanging around his neck.

"Merry Christmas," I returned. "Going somewhere?"

"Church."

"Ah, right. My mom will be on her way there soon, too."

Gino assessed me with squinted eyes. Crow's feet stretched at the corners and wrinkles ran like crop lines across his forehead. I hadn't gotten too good a look at myself, but if Gino's expression were a mirror I'd say I looked fucked. Literally, physically.

I instinctually ran my fingers through my hair to tame it and crossed my arms over my bare chest.

"No church for you?" he asked, continuing to spin and pick the ripe fruit, placing them in a yellow speckled bowl.

I looked back at the house. "I have some company."

Gino hummed. "You're in love."

"I wouldn't say love." I quipped.

"What is it then?"

The mug I was holding was scalding my palm, but that was more comfortable than trying to classify my relationship with Ophelia to the prying old man that lived next door.

I'd never had a conversation about relationships with someone outside my buddies. It was easy to talk about sex—locker room shit, the tasteless back and forth I never felt fully comfortable participating in but learned to live with, especially in the Army.

My father passed before I had my first kiss. The one time I got caught with my dick in my hand my mother cried every time she looked at me for three days. When I was fifteen I asked a girl to homecoming and the next day there was a box of Trojans on my nightstand and we never spoke about it again. The familial history I had with intimacy was thereby nonexistent.

"It's just fun." I shrugged complacently. "I'm figuring it out."

"You're too old for just fun, Francesco."

My eyebrows inched together and I perched my arms on the top of the fence. "I'm thirty-five," I stressed. "Why has every time I've talked to someone in the last few weeks felt like watching my life fall through an hourglass?"

"Because you finally found a person that makes it feel like exactly that."

I opened my mouth to argue but my jaw snapped right back shut.

"You *know*." Gino abandoned his tomatoes and pointed a finger at the center of his chest. "You know right here when it's right, because it starts to hurt. Even when you're happy, it hurts. Because it aches to imagine not having that happiness. You worry, you lose sleep, you act out. Anything to keep that feeling from becoming comfortable. When you can bear it, it's lost."

My teeth caught raw flesh on the inside of my cheek as a half-circle of sun peeked over the palm trees, cold air dissipating into a band of warmth. "She doesn't live here," I found myself saying.

"Home is subjective." He waved my words out of the air. "A smell, a place, a feeling, a memory. A *person*."

"Sounds great." My smile didn't reach my eyes. "And easy. Things for me are never that easy."

The world around us yawned, dark blue skies bleeding into cobalt like God turned a dial. Bird song became background music, damp grass dried beneath my feet. The glass door at the back of Gino's house slid open and a sweet face peered out at the two of us.

"I've been married fifty-three years." The old man stuck his shears in a garden tote and tucked the bowl of tomatoes underneath his arm. "Not one day has been easy. But every single one has been worth it. You do good by them, be a good man, a good lover, a faithful partner, a solid wall. So what she doesn't live here—because that would be easy, eh? *Easy* is comfortable."

Gino took a few steps toward his house as his wife came out onto the stone patio and waved to me. She was too far away to hear the last notes of conversation. "Does your chest hurt, Francesco?"

I inhaled, dragging my fingers across the plane of my chest, sticking them like little daggers into the cavity, almost *forcing* myself to feel something.

Pain. Discomfort. A pulse.

The fact that I was begging myself to react at all told a silent secret. The person I was around Ophelia would know the answer to that question right away. He was like an open book, feeling things to extremes, without remorse, without embarrassment. She was like a master key to my psyche.

By the time I stopped trying to decipher pain from placebo, Gino was guiding his wife by the small of her back into their house. I was alone again in the backyard, my coffee was cold, and my head was spinning like a carousel.

I didn't want to imagine a Christmas morning ever again that didn't look like this one. Waking up next to her, soft, sensual sex, coffee on the patio. Then deep inside my mind I imagined something *more* than that. A big, lazy dog hanging out at the foot of our bed, a clan of kids crashing through the bedroom door in their Christmas pjs. *Santa came, Dad. Santa came.*

My throat dried like a fucking tumbleweed. Was that what was missing? My own family to care for the way I did best? A purpose beyond working and providing for the people around me and never myself? The only thing that would ever truly slow me the fuck down.

My perspective had shifted into a completely different realm. I used to be content being stagnant; now I wanted a life I'd thought up so badly it felt like I would never know happiness until I had it.

She was doing this to me. Everything I was learning about myself started and ended with Ophelia—I wasn't so naive to deny it. One day I'd look back and thank the higher powers for sending her into my life, even just passing through, because it was exactly what I needed when I didn't think I needed anything at all.

29

Ophelia

I'D NEVER SEEN A better-looking piece of meat in my entire life. Thick, pink, and round, juices dripping out of every pore onto my careful fingers. I took an innocent look around the room, biting my lip before bringing them to my mouth for a sly taste. Salty tang exploded on my tongue.

God. I groaned as my nostrils flared. *That's fucking delicious.*

I admired it a minute longer—the girth, the weight, the way it *sweated* under the bright lights. I pulled out my phone and took a picture. Even put that shit on portrait mode because what was in front of me was nothing less than a piece of modern art. I captioned it *Ophelia's Meat* braggingly, and sent the image away in a group text.

Then, just like my mother always taught me, in a tragically Shakesperean show—I stabbed the fucker.

Then I stabbed it again with a giddy smile and wooden tooth-pick pierced with a round ring of pineapple and maraschino cherry.

The famous Brody family Christmas ham.

Pride blossomed in my chest at the perfectly roasted, dressed, and tended dinner I'd prepared for our little group of four. I'd never cooked for a holiday; I wasn't even confident I could pull it off by myself with the scarce directions in the string of half-assed text messages from my mother. Autocorrect repelled her on her most focused days, never mind Christmas morning with pre-teens.

Growing up Mom had a very specific way of doing things, and you either followed directions or got swatted out of the kitchen by a wet dish towel. I learned my lesson early on that the latter wasn't worth the former. But as an adult, spending my very first Christmas away from the familiar doily-lined tablecloth, I was testing my ability to extend all these traditions.

"Need some help?" Frankie slid down the island at my side and pressed his cold bottle of beer to the back of my neck.

For the first time in hours my shoulders relaxed and the muscles in my back loosened. "I'm sweating like this pig right now."

"I want to eat you just as badly, too."

Natalia stopped folding cured meat into flower petals on the charcuterie board across from us to tilt her head curiously. A bashful blush crept up my neck. "I could use one of those beers, if you don't mind."

Frankie dragged the head of his bottle up my jaw and to my parted lips, tipping it back, feeding me a refreshing mix of hoppy liquid. Not the most hydrating option by a long shot, but replenishing enough to widen my heavy eyes. His focus zeroed in on my mouth, and as soon as the bottle came back down, he leaned in and replaced it with a kiss.

It was chaste and sweet, and as quickly as it was there it was gone, along with it Frankie, who nonchalantly moved to the refrigerator and returned with a fresh, unopened beer.

"I like you bossy," he remarked, snapping the cap off with a bottle opener and placing it on the counter. "What's next?"

"He just kissed your mouth." Natalia pointed a spoon at Frankie. Fig jam slid off the tip and hit the white marble counter. "You're kissing each other's mouths out in the open now."

Her perception was sharper than a carving knife. I ran my tongue over the top half of my teeth and lodged it into my cheek. "Friends kiss."

"Friends kiss," Frankie agreed, his voice lower. "And...do other things."

I shoved my elbow back into his lower stomach and he grunted. It wasn't like what Frankie and I were doing was a secret, quite the opposite, but my focus was imperative in keeping Christmas dinner from becoming yet another thing I'd only think fondly of in childhood memories.

I ran down my mental checklist and busied my hands to avoid Frankie and Natalia's friendly staredown. The lasagna in the oven, plating roasted peas and carrots, slicing the bread, stirring the sauce in the pot on the stove.

"So This Is Christmas" played from a speaker across the room, cutting into the loaded silence.

"You know what you can do, Frankie?" Nat requested, jutting her thumb toward her boyfriend in the living room. Mateo stood with his hands in his pockets and stared longingly into the golden ornaments hanging off the Christmas tree. He looked hilariously, uncharacteristically lost. "You can tranquilize Mateo. He's been pacing the house for two hours. Something is bugging him."

That morning when Frankie and I had finally emerged from his bedroom, Mateo was lapping the house with a feather duster,

squaring off crooked picture frames and smell-testing each candle for his favorite one. I thought I'd missed a memo and we
were expecting more company, but Frankie assured me Mateo
just wanted to "set the mood" for the holiday.

Apparently the mood was neurotic, and the sound of the season was the sharp clicking of a remote control searching for the
perfect playlist for over an hour.

"Will do." Frankie sighed, tapping his fingers on the countertop.
He snagged another beer and kicked the fridge door closed behind him before joining his friend across the hazy living room.
Frankie's arm sunk around Mateo's shoulder as he whispered
something indecipherable in his ear and they clinked their bottles together.

"If either of them had a pussy we'd be useless." Nat snorted.
"True loves."

"Reminds me of us."

Nat cut into a piece of provolone and popped it into her mouth.
"Fun night?" she asked, her dark eyebrows wiggling perversely.

The oven beeped behind me and I turned away from her in
a hurry, every memory of Frankie and I from the night before
rushing back. The tenderness between my legs hadn't dissipated
at all throughout the day. I felt him every single time I sat down;
it was fucking sadistic.

"You can say that."

Nat rose from the barstool and pulled a placemat out of the
cupboard, throwing it down on the formal dining table to make
room for me to place the lasagna as I pulled it out of the oven.

Fuck, I was good. The edges of the pasta bubbled with ricotta
and the house smelled like we'd just walked into an expensive
Italian restaurant.

"That's it?" Nat badgered me. "You've been edging each other
for weeks and all I get is a 'you can say that'? I have blue balls over

this, Phee. I'm losing sleep at night wondering if my best friend is getting the dick she deserves."

"You're ridiculous." I laughed, just as the patio door across the house slammed closed and Frankie and Mateo disappeared into the backyard. "Okay fine." I dropped my pitiful, demure mouse act and groaned out a dramatic breath. "It was fucking unreal."

"Really?" Her eyes widened salaciously.

"Best I've ever had."

"You're *lying*."

"May Santa come down this chimney right now and mollywop me."

"God *damn*." She clicked her tongue and spun around to the dishwasher, emptying four clean wine glasses. "We need a drink before you tell me more. Was it rough? I always pinned Frankie as a freak. He's got so much pent-up shit that needs an outlet."

My skin warmed, the ghost of his lips all over my body. "No, it was kind of...*passionate*?" I said. "*Detailed*. If that makes sense? I finished every single time."

"You fucked *multiple* times?"

I shrugged, embarrassed again. "Like four times."

Nat walked around the circular table, setting it with sil-ver-lined dishes and cloth napkins as I put all the rest of the food out in the middle. "I'm horny again," she groaned.

"This is the horniest Christmas vacation of my life. I need to be spayed after this," I joked. "The men in Pine Ridge are never going to satisfy me again anyway."

Nat stopped walking around the table and her playfulness sobered. Talking about Pine Ridge was like a puncture wound. Too many mentions of home and I'd bleed out. Colorado was calling and answering the phone was less and less appealing as the days dwindled.

"Tell me if you need me to pull you out of it." Natalia insisted, the meaning behind her offer not lost on me. But admitting I might need her to bring me back to a reality where Frankie and I weren't playing a game anymore was a weakness that I was too proud to show. Sure, I was deeper than I should have been with him, but I didn't need someone to babysit those emotions. I could handle it. I needed to prove to myself that I could handle it.

"No it's perfect," I assured her, stepping back to admire the dinner table in all its delicious, aromatic glory. "It's just what I needed, honestly. Frankie is a *good* man, he's gentle with me, a staggeringly solid listener. I think we're both really great for each other right now, a big part of that is knowing we're on borrowed time. No holding back."

"Okay." She said, rubbing her palms together. "You know you best. But I'm still here."

"I know, and I love you." I held up a knife and a carving fork. "Now let's eat this pig."

FRANKIE BRUSHED HIS FINGERS through my hair as I lay in his lap, rendering me motionless, soft touches coaxing me into a food coma. I could barely keep my eyes open, the house so warm from hours of the oven being on we might as well be in a cocoon.

Full, exhausted, comfortable—the perfect storm of festive ambiance catering our unforgettably peaceful afternoon.

He adjusted himself beneath me and unbuttoned his fly, alleviation sighing out of him. "Sweatpants would have been a better choice."

I snapped the band of my leggings. "Fashionable *and* functional."

"And your ass looks great in them, don't forget that part."

Natalia twirled into the room and plopped down on the opposite end of the sofa.

"Where's Mateo?" Frankie looked over his shoulder toward the hallway.

"On the phone with Sam Swan," Natalia trilled. "Ironing out the details for next week. They're flying out of Salt Lake on Thursday."

"It's been fucking forever since we've seen them." Frankie reached down and twisted the chain of my necklace between his fingers impassively. "Since we all got out."

"You've never met them before?" I asked Nat.

"Nope." She shook her head. "But I feel like I've known them forever between you and Matty." She gestured to Frankie. "Sam is a sweetheart, and Tyler is a brutish, womanizing whore."

"That about covers it." Frankie smiled impishly. "Hope you two are ready to drink your tits off next weekend. We're gonna be celebrating."

"Celebrating what?" I raised my eyebrow just as Mateo marched into the living room and stole our attention away.

"Swan boys' flight lands on the thirtieth at three." He clapped his hands together and rubbed them down his thighs. The neck of his sweater looked to be choking him as he stood in front of us awkwardly instead of sitting on the couch.

The nervous energy from early in the day returned like a smog over the room. Nat and I were perplexed while Frankie remained placid. He nodded subtly to his friend and Mateo took a deep, exaggerated breath.

"Are you okay, babe?" Nat stood and touched his forehead with the back of her hand. "Sick or something? You feel warm."

Frankie sat me upright gently, tugging me into his side. His honey brown eyes glimmered with excitement.

"What is it?" she pressed.

"I think it's about time I did this." Mateo wrapped both his girlfriend's wrists delicately in one hand, reaching around to his back pocket with the other. "Natalia Russo..."

Nat staggered back as Mateo dropped ceremoniously onto one knee in front of her, holding a black velvet box between them and popping it open.

I gasped, clapping my palm over my mouth as realization dawned. Frankie's smirk lengthened beside me.

"I have never loved someone so fully in my entire life. You are my world," Mateo recited. "I want to make you laugh and give you the cutest little meatball babies anyone has ever seen, and shrivel into raisins in our old age together."

Natalia's eyes glistened and she squeezed Mateo's fingers to stop her own from shaking.

"I want you to be my wife, Tally. Will you do me that honor and marry me?"

She nodded feverishly as tears streaked down her face, a little bounce starting to lift her off the carpet. Mateo pulled the ring from the box and it shined like a Swarovski crystal ornament, light glinting off it so brightly it was like catching the sun in a magnifying glass. "A little verbal confirmation would be great, sweetheart," Mateo teased.

"Yes!" she wailed. "Yes! Oh my *god*. YES."

Her happiness was so loud it pierced our eardrums and I realized I was *also* crying. Frankie's thumb swept across my cheek to wipe the emotion away as we both watched Mateo slide the massive diamond onto his new fiancé's finger.

My best friend was getting *married*.

"You knew this whole time." I turned to Frankie, shoving his chest. "You didn't tell me!"

"I was under very strict direction not to ruin the surprise. My balls were on the line."

"I can keep a secret," I pouted.

Frankie tugged my bottom lip with a pinch of his fingers. "I've only known you to have loose lips."

Butterflies fluttered in my stomach and I leaned into his touch, biting the tip of his thumb. "It was more fun to be in the dark anyway."

A hand sprung into the small space between me and Frankie, attached to it the most eye-catching diamond I'd ever seen. Natalia wiggled her fingers, flaunting her impressive engagement ring in front of us.

"It's so perfect," I squealed, stretching her hand out in front of me to take in the whole thing. "It's like he pulled it right off your Pinterest board."

"How strange," Mateo commented, pulling Frankie into his chest for a brotherly embrace.

"I called it, Nat." I laughed. "Frankie and I are now doomed to the most awkward bachelor party planning to ever exist."

Her eyes rolled. "Something tells me you won't mind spending the time together."

"Congratulations you two." Frankie sniffled, his emotions getting the best of him then, too. My heart pulsed like thunder inside my chest, warming like the crackling fire.

"We need to toast," I said, leaning down to the coffee table for what was left of my wine, my friends following suit with their drinks. "To love," I proclaimed. Frankie watched me intently, the corner of his lip lifting into a devilishly handsome smile. "Best friends, happiness, Coconut Creek..." I continued. "And to planning the most kick-ass fucking wedding anyone has ever seen."

30

Frankie

THE GIRLS LAUGHING FROM the living room the minute I stepped through the front door turned my mood from sour to sweet. I spent the morning stretched out on a table playing puppet with a physiotherapist—which was my least favorite fucking thing to come out of my accident.

At first, it was a couple times a week. Cardio, strength training, learning how to sit down on a fucking toilet again without rein-juring myself—that wasn't dehumanizing *at all*. Slow and steady exercises leading to me standing on two feet again, and then moping about the therapy unit with a cane I'd thought about beating myself to death with a hundred times over.

The stronger the fusions got in my back, the less I had to report to the doctors. Until it was only every few months to keep me healthy and progressing. Because I was thinking about going back out in the field I unfortunately needed to swallow my pride and take all medical advice sternly and seriously. Even if it meant crawling out of a warm bed away from a beautiful girl under the false pretenses of "going to work."

Ophelia hadn't asked me about my scars. She touched the long, precise lines on my lower back though, tracing them when she thought I was asleep. The conversation I longed to have about it burned at the tip of my tongue as I lay there, but I couldn't force myself to turn over and address it. I hated the way a person's face warped into pity when they knew the details, and I didn't think I could stomach that look from her. Nor did she need a fucking trauma dump every time we were alone together.

I was supposed to be her *good time*. Her fun, breezy, guiltless pleasure.

If she asked, I would tell her.

"There he is," Mateo called out, sitting in front of a game of cards with O and Tally. "Back from...*work*." The idiot winked, knowing full well we didn't have any security installs until after the new year. "Sorry I couldn't make it into the office today, Pike. I was just telling the ladies that I have no idea how I'll manage shop when you ship up to Colorado. You're the only partner I trust."

"Make sure you lick my balls, too, while you're down there sucking my cock, Cap." I popped open the fridge and took out a tray of leftovers.

"I'm serious!" he rattled on. "I have the business mindset, we know this. But I don't deal well with fucking morons, so you're the negotiator. You look like a puppy, and people love puppies."

Ophelia hopped off her barstool and preheated the oven, stealing the Pyrex of ham out of my hands and taking over.

"Hi," I mumbled through a smile.

"Hi," she answered back bashfully.

We'd been playing house for three days. We woke up, had coffee, ate all our meals together, showered together, played every single board game Ophelia scraped out of the hall closet, scrolled through Netflix for long enough to get bored and let our hands wander—and then we had our merry way with one another until the sun came back up.

I was a spoiled fucking brat by all shreds of the cloth. Generally I'd never let a woman lift a finger for me, that's not the way I was raised. But watching Ophelia prance around the house like she was a permanent staple—leaving her contact case on my nightstand, sifting through my drawers, wearing old T-shirts that ran down her tan thighs all the way to her knees—I'd let her do just about anything she wanted.

If that meant running my laundry through the wash with hers, saving me the largest piece of leftover lasagna, and finding a place for all our clean plates out of the dishwasher in foreign cabinets—who was I to complain?

She was an organized, calculated woman. At any given moment I could tell there was a trapdoor of endless lists and theoretical questions just behind her eyes. As if she didn't keep busy, the perpetual background noise in her ears would come to a complete stop altogether and there would be nothing but a black hole of silence.

The only time that jittery energy evened out was when it was just the two of us. Time stopped in the little space between our bodies, reducing everything to slow motion. Like we were stuck inside a snow globe that someone had just given a shake.

Tally put her hand of cards down on the table and revealed a royal flush.

"Goddamnit!" Cap threw his cards down in frustration, his chair scraping across the kitchen floor as he stood and did a tantrum lap behind it.

"He's right, Frankie." Tally snorted. "Your patience is crucial to the entire operation. Clients will be leaving in droves when they get a hold of this sore loser."

"Bratty isn't on the content schedule today, sweetheart. But if you want to push it..." Cap pressed against his future wife's chair and put his palms on the table on either side of her, showing a very uncomfortable amount of dominance. It quickly felt like Ophelia and I were props on a plaster movie set.

"You're getting ahead of yourselves," I said, squashing the moment. "This is all assuming I'd even be leaving in the first place, and I don't see any job offers on the table. I had *one* interview." I leaned back against the counter and crossed my arms. "I've learned my lesson about getting my hopes up. I'm not going to extend that to this."

Only now the "this" I was referring to felt shamefully double-sided. "This" wasn't just the chance to fly again, or teach, or simply feel like I was fulfilling a purpose beyond existing aimlessly. I was a damn good fucking pilot and that wasn't something I stopped believing in—it was my ability to take care of the people I loved. The "this" that was up in the air at the moment was a coin flip between a new job and an entirely new *life*.

What if I did go to Colorado? Would Ophelia still want me out there? Would she want me to reach out to her for a *real* date or bring her coffee or *be* with me like I'd known for weeks I'd want to be with her?

Or were we still just playing a big old game with one another like we said we would? Practicing how to be better for *other* people, when other people wouldn't hold a fucking candle in a hydrogen room.

"You are daringly pessimistic this morning, brother." Mateo inched over and patted me on the back. "I like to think all the stars in our lives are aligning and everything you've ever dreamed of is about to bite you in your grumpy fucking ass."

I rolled my eyes and watched Ophelia dip down to pull my plate out of the oven. The gentle curve of her hips made me want to sling her over my shoulder and take her down the hallway without another word.

"He's hungry," Ophelia defended me. "And he barely got any sleep last night," she added.

A bee sting of pride stabbed into me and Cap's lips pinched shut like the teeth of a zipper. I followed O to the table like a chaser follows whiskey: good-intentioned and sweet on her heels, pulling out one chair for the two of us and sitting her right on my lap.

"Yeah, these walls ain't as thick as you think," Cap complained, curling his lip in disgust. "Hey, I have an idea. How about you two put some of that, frankly concerning, amount of stamina to work and help take down these Christmas decorations?"

"No!" Ophelia and I protested in unison.

Tally's attention lifted from her sparkly outstretched finger to us.

"You can't take the decorations down until after New Year's." O tapped her finger impatiently on the table. "Everyone knows that."

I didn't know that.

In fact, the only reason I didn't want to take down the decorations was because it felt too much like pressing go on a countdown. In the same way I liked to keep her on me physically, the thought of removing all those material reminders of the last few weeks with Ophelia was like running my fingers through still-wet paint. It wasn't time yet. Give it a chance to dry on its own.

"So let me get this straight..." Mateo squinted, doing a dramatic look around the house. "You show up and convince this man to let you make the place look like the inside of Santa's fucking workshop." I grimaced as a finger was pointed in my direction. "Pick a tree that sheds like a goddamn Labrador—I'll be finding pine needles in my asshole until I'm ninety." Ophelia tugged her bottom lip into her mouth to conceal a laugh. "Staple a pineapple to my garage with industrial grade hardware...and now you expect *me* to be the sorry son of a bitch who cleans it all up?"

"You're talking with your hands like your mother," I pointed out.

"Don't you dare bring my mother into this."

"Phee is right," Tally spoke up, reading something off the screen of her phone. "There's some Pagan, Christian, folklore tradition that says you gotta keep the decorations up until the sixth because that's when the Three Kings arrived at the manger."

"Do I look like a fucking apostle to you, Natalia?" Cap replied humorously, setting his sights on O sitting in my lap again. "This one sure as hell ain't the Virgin Mary."

It took but one completely unexpected jibe to have me choking on a piece of ham. Worried eyes pinned me to the back of my chair as I beat my chest with a fist to dislodge it. So violently, actually, that my eyes started to water until I was crying, not only from the lack of oxygen, but from laughter, sucking in heaping gasps of air between fits.

It was clear that I wasn't in any real danger, and Mateo's joke still played on a loop, setting me off again once I'd caught my breath. A real, honest-to-God, howling laugh that I couldn't restrain.

Ophelia's girlish giggling joined mine. Behind it I could make out the deeper chuckle that was Mateo, stacked on top of Tally's own warm bellow of amusement.

In the grand scheme of things it wasn't even that funny, but sometimes things just tickled you the right way. Laughter indicated more than levity; it was a looking glass to happiness, fulfillment, pleasure.

I was a bubbling mixture of all of those things, finally spilling over.

31

Ophelia

"OKAY." I PRESSED MY fingers to my lips. Hot tub jets sloshed warm water around my torso, and the only thing illuminating Frankie and I save for the full moon was a soft red glow of lights beneath the water. "Worst date you've ever been on?"

He stretched out across from me, hiding a humored smile behind the lip of a beer bottle. "I'm not drunk enough for this."

"Oh, come on," I flicked water at him and his jaw clenched as the splash trickled down his cheek. "Whatever your story is, I bet I could top it."

"What are we betting?" He splayed both arms out on either edge of the tub until he was all broad chest and shoulders above water.

"Anything you want," I offered evocatively.

Frankie's interest piqued, gears shifting in his head before a devious flare darkened his playful expression. "When I was twenty-two I was home on leave and decided to take a girl I met at the bar out for ice cream."

"Very PG." I smirked.

"I let it slip that I speak Spanish, and apparently she'd been trying to teach herself how to speak it for a while, fucking Rosetta Stone or some shit like that."

"God, you are a dinosaur."

"That's enough commentary from the peanut gallery." He splashed the water back in my direction. "Because she was learning, she insisted on communicating in Spanish for the entire date. Literally every sentence. I spent more time correcting her than having an actual conversation with her. It felt like a tutoring session."

I covered my mouth. "You're kidding."

"Halfway through my cone I was faking brain freeze to put an end to it, but that's not even the kicker."

"Don't tell me that."

"When I eventually took her home, we pulled into the driveway at her parents' house and she leaned over expecting a kiss." Frankie snorted to himself, pinching the bridge of his nose. "But doing that, she tipped her entire milkshake over and spilled sixteen ounces of chocolate malt into my fucking lap."

"Nooooo." I grimaced, holding onto a laugh.

"She was profusely apologetic—in Spanish still—very dedicated to the character. All while patting the crotch of my pants with a bundle of paper napkins like her life depended on it. And that is just not the sight a father wants to see when he looks out the window to make sure his daughter made it home safely from a date."

My jaw unhinged, secondhand embarrassment flaming through my body.

"I take back what I said." I cackled. "I don't have anything that'll top that. That's the shit you see in movies."

Frankie rubbed a hand down his face, smoothing down the fine hairs on his cheeks and above his lip. The tips of his shaggy hair were wet with condensation as steam lifted from the water, blanketing us in warm fog.

"I have a lot of stories." His tone dipped into self-reflection as he picked at the label on his bottle. "Some good, *most* bad and ugly."

I tilted my head, demanding Frankie's attention remain connected to mine. He was distancing himself from the deeper conversation we were on the precipice of. I wanted to meet him in the middle, but I didn't want to push him too far.

"Do the jets feel good on your back?" I traversed gingerly.

Frankie's lips twisted, his eyes thinning curiously. A silent understanding passed between us.

I'd seen his scars, he had to know that, and it wouldn't take a professional to ascertain that they were surgical. Even if I played dumb, I could see in the change of his posture across from me that Frankie knew the truth.

His arms folded anxiously over his chest, as if guarding the very heart beating behind it. There was nothing outwardly fragile about him, and Frankie did well to protect that image. We were similar in so many ways, great at shoving our grief into boxes without considering first that the walls are glass. You can watch it fester from afar, taking it on in other ways, or the feeling itself gets so violent the containment shatters.

"Don't be angry with Mateo," I said.

Frankie's eyes fell closed transiently, but reopened with a glimmer of relief. Like I'd pulled out a splinter and he could put pressure on that part of himself again.

"I should have expected it," Frankie said. "Cap's got the biggest mouth, and he also holds the longest grudges."

"Is this why you're so cynical about the job in Colorado? The pressure? You're worried about not meeting their standards?"

"No, Ophelia. I'm worried about not meeting *my* standards." He let out a heavy exhale. "How much did he say?"

"I know you weren't at work this morning," I admitted, picking at my softened cuticles under the water. "You were at PT because you were in some kind of crash in Central America that got you medically discharged from Delta."

Frankie worried his bottom lip between his teeth. "What else?"

I didn't want to say her name, because I didn't want to give credence to it. Mateo's warning that Frankie would never speak maliciously about the woman who broke his heart did something like driving a nail into mine.

But, we were so *close* to everything that had been willingly left unsaid.

Frankie and I were never meant to be more than placeholders to one another, but the time we spent together had changed that. The boundary that had been drawn like a curtain between heedless enjoyment and a deeper connection thinned to a translucent veil.

"Your ex," I muttered.

His disposition softened. "I already told you I would tell you anything you wanted to know."

"I want to know everything," I confessed before I could stop the words from tripping out of me.

Frankie took another long sip of his beer and discarded the empty bottle. "This is your one chance to tap out," he offered lightly. "We can shelf this and just go back to doing what we do best."

"I think I can handle it," I assured him. "But it's up to you."

His body shifted, making me bob in the short wake of waves. "The crash happened on one of our last ops in Costa Rica, right before we were set to ship back home. Great timing," he added sarcastically. "The whole thing was routine. Our unit was going in to clear what was tipped off to us as a link in a chain of illegal arms checkpoints, those of which were funneling into the states. Cap led, Wink..." He paused, then clarified, "Sam Swan, you'll meet him, is a sniper. His brother Tyler, who we call Echo, was the muscle behind the two of them and at least four more guys filing in together. My job was extraction."

A twist of unease whirled in my stomach like windswept leaves.

"Like I said, easy peasy. The boys drop in, hike the distance through the canopy to the house, and make quick work. But when they got there it was apparent the place had been abandoned. Whoever tipped us off, word got back to the dealers we were on the way and they'd taken off into the village at the base of the valley. Turns out it was a complete guerrilla coup there—nothing like we were prepared for. So my order was to land, pull the guys out, and head back to base to regroup."

"You didn't," I guessed.

Frankie's head shook languidly back and forth. "I should have done what I was told, but there were *kids* there. Their mothers were basically throwing them at the chopper when I landed, Ophelia. It's hard to describe how helpless I felt, how *wrong* it felt to look at them and say no. If we left and came back and they were gone, that's blood on my hands. It's a battle I have to have every night with my own conscience."

I pictured my own students home safe right then, naive to how lucky they were. My throat swelled painfully with a spindle of emotion I tried with fervor to unthread while Frankie continued.

"I started taking people on, and Cap followed *my lead* for once." He said deprecatingly. "He'll never make that mistake again. We pulled as many kids as we could onto the helicopter. The whole time I knew in my gut I was pushing the limit too far and putting us in danger. But I fucking did it anyway."

Frankie's knee bounced beneath the water and I reached over to calm it.

"I was halfway to altitude when the first engine went. There was too much weight, but we were too high to drop safely and going back wasn't an option. Military choppers can handle an engine going, but that's only with the right amount of bodies on board. Suddenly, it was like I was playing God.

"The choice wasn't between flying or crashing. It was crashing on the next sliver of flat open land, or taking my chances on the emergency rafts and crashing in the ravine. I figured at least with flat land, no one's going to have to know how to swim."

I was chewing a hole in my cheek so deep I tasted iron on my tongue. Frankie gave me the chance to back away from the details, and I understood why. No part of this could be easy to reflect on again. I was grateful he trusted me enough to drum it back up, and I would make damn sure he didn't regret it.

"I accepted that I made a mistake," he stressed. "It was my burden to bear, and the best chance of the passengers surviving meant I needed to take the brunt of the impact at the nose and pray I'd done enough good in my life to come out of it."

"I'm so glad that you did," I muttered.

"By some saving grace they all survived with minor injuries. Broken bones, a few concussions, nothing fatal. Taken safely into US custody to be reunited with their families. I got tossed around the most, lost almost complete feeling in my back and was pretty sure I was paralyzed, but it was actually the shock that froze me. I truly thought I'd be seeing my dad that day."

The emotion I'd wrangled before stung my eyes and Frankie laced his fingers through mine on his knee, swiping his thumb back and forth.

"So I had to have what's called a posterior lumbar spinal fusion, to correct fractures and herniated discs in my lower back," he explained. "That's what those scars are that you love to touch when you think I'm sleeping."

"I'm a little obsessed with what you look like naked," I admitted quietly. Frankie's dark eyes softened on cue and I was pleased with myself. "You are so much more than you give yourself credit for. It's fucking cliché, I don't care, but you're a *hero*. You know that, right?"

"Not flying away from endangered children isn't heroic, O, it's human. Unfortunately I'm not as robotic as the military expected me to be. Or Cap, or Sam, or Tyler. We paid for it though, I guess."

"To those kids you are. I doubt those mothers go a day of their lives without thinking about you. Would you? If it were your kid?"

Frankie's throat bobbed up and down, the veins in his neck lengthening with the tilt of his neck as he turned toward me. "No," he conceded. "I wouldn't."

"You were meant to be there that day. There's a reason for everything."

"Technically, if I didn't get injured that day I wouldn't be sitting here right now with you, so maybe you're onto something, Trouble."

"What do you mean?"

"Well, I got home and immediately went into recovery, which for me was a fuck ton of time lying on my back in bed, feeling sorry for myself. I needed help doing the most basic things, and even shit I could manage on my own became impossible because my mental health was in the gutters. I was convinced I'd never fly again, and honestly afraid to try. Still afraid to try." Frankie's voice tapered off. "I was a lot to deal with. Not my proudest moments, and Vanessa suffered for that."

A chill crawled up my spine and bit into my skin. "Don't you fucking dare."

Frankie's eyes darted to mine, surprise creasing his forehead. "What?"

"She *cheated* on you."

"It's more complicated than that." He shook his head.

"There's nothing complicated about it," I fired back. "You trusted someone with loving you. That doesn't get a dismissal when things get too *hard*. You needed her and she fucking gave up on it."

"I wasn't there *for her* like she needed me to be. I was useless for a while."

"You were fucking hurt! You don't need to be everyone's wall, Frankie. I know you now. I know you try so hard for everyone around you all the time and never for yourself. You're worried about your mom and sister, you're worried about your friends. You don't want to leave here and chance someone *needing* you. But what about *you*? What happens when Frankie needs something, and everyone else has already gotten what they wanted out of you?"

My chest rose and fell harshly. I'd worked myself up into an embarrassing emotional outbreak and Frankie looked just as perplexed by it. He continued brushing his thumb across the back of my hand softly, tracing my tense body with his eyes. The silence around us roared.

"Are we having our first argument?" he finally replied with a touch of amusement.

I snorted, the thud of my heart relaxing again. "I'll fucking fight you on this any day of the week."

"Come here." He pulled me carefully against him.

"Why?' I pouted disobediently, giving him a lazy amount of resistance.

"Stubborn woman." He pulled harder, until I had no choice but to fall into his lap, resting my thighs on either side of his hips. Despite the sincerity of the conversation, our centers connecting beneath the warm, bubbling water demanded its own attention. "Because it hurts when I can tell that you're mad at me, but it also sadistically turns me on a little bit. So this fixes both of those things."

His charm continued to emotionally castrate me. "How did you find out?" I asked.

Strong forearms tightened at my lower back and rocked me gently. "I'm pretty fucking sure she wanted me to. She left her emails open on the counter one morning and went out for brunch with some friends. I'm not the guy that's gonna snoop but when I see names popping up in her inbox that I know—my chain of command." His lips thinned into a straight line. "Something was off. Vanessa came home and I asked her about it, and she didn't even deny it. She looked *relieved*, honestly, and the worst fucking part? I didn't even ask her to leave. She just did."

I leaned down and left a short peck on the tip of his nose, then whispered against his lips, "She didn't deserve you."

Frankie's hands whispered like silk up my spine and to my shoulders, curling around the sides of my jaw and tucking the sweat-slicked curls of my stray hair behind my ears. "You make me believe that."

"Good," I answered, closing the short distance between our lips and claiming his mouth and tongue instantly.

We'd learned each other so well. He held me against him, asking for more of my attention without words, commanding our movements with the same amount of care as he did passion. I was swollen with his kiss, breathless and eager for as much of himself as he was willing to give.

Our tongues played, and my teeth grazed plush sensitive skin before biting down and an impatient grumble started in his chest. Frankie doubled down, licking a teasing line from my chin to my top lip, flicking his tongue suggestively.

My fingers curled into the hair at the nape of his neck. "You kiss me like this and I forget how to think straight." The physical heat and the one between us mimicked some kind of head high.

"Stop thinking," Frankie returned. "There's nothing you should be thinking about right now but how I feel pressed against you."

"Easy enough." A hum turned into a squeak as I rocked my hips down against him hardening in his swimsuit. My insides clenched, so blatantly ready for his breach with no questions asked.

"Look at me," Frankie groaned, shifting his pelvis and sliding against the nylon material of my bathing suit. "Look at what you do to me, O. It's fucking pathetic isn't it? I could have you taking my cock all day, and with just one bat of those eyes I'm ready for it again."

"Should we be doing this out here?" I asked, but that last shred of my self-preservation floated toward the sky along with the billows of steam as his face came down between my breasts.

"You owe me something," he mumbled into my skin, ignoring my question. His lips traveled through my cleavage to the thin fabric over my nipple, grazing the peak with his nose. Goosebumps flared to life all over my body and my back arched toward his touch. "You made a bet."

"I did." I nodded, hardly listening. His teeth clamped down over the pointed bud and I whimpered, sensation shooting straight to the nerves in my clit. "I know I did."

"You know what I want, Ophelia?" Skillful fingers skated to the middle of my spine and pulled loose the string holding my top together, and the entire thing came tumbling down. My eyelids fell to half-mast, jaw slackening as he took my bare skin back into his mouth this time, swirling his hot tongue over and over again.

"To kill me." I sighed.

Frankie's laughter sent vibrations through my body. "Never."

He stood us, turning me away from him, my back pressed to his front like a blanket, shielding me from the cold air. Then he guided me like I was Bambi tripping across the hot tub to the opposite edge. I caught myself on hard plastic as his hands came around and slammed down next to mine.

Frankie's breathing was stunted, heavy and bowing in and out against me. A tickle of his mustache ghosted over my shoulder, then my neck. The curve of my rib cage settled against the edge as I was carefully bent over, my ass lifting out of the water and notching into the cusp of his hips. He was *everywhere*. Lips at my nape, his chest at my spine, cock rocking in swivels, teasing my core.

"Has anyone ever"—he dragged my bottoms down leisurely, inch by inch until they were rolled into a tight band down by my knees—"touched you here?" Frankie's middle finger dragged from my tailbone down the center of my ass, dipping carefully to circle that intimate, tight ring of muscle.

My breath caught, all my joints tightened to steel, and I was unable to react with anything more than a short gasp. Every hair on my body bristled.

"N-no." My voice shook.

"Of course not. Because you're so fucking perfect for me, aren't you? This ass." A sharp crack of his palm came down on my backside. "This pussy." The same assaulting fingers slid through the seam of my cunt and circled my clit from behind.

"F-fr—fuck…"

"Fr…fr… Say it, sweetheart," he taunted. Two fingers slid into me and my limbs went from stone straight to putty. "Say who makes you this fucking wet." He curled against my favorite little spot, and I could hear my own pleasure around his fingers. "God *damn*, O."

"Frankie," I whined. The possibility of us getting caught shot adrenaline through me. I thought I was invincible in our tiny voyeuristic bubble, and I'd never been so staunchly horny in my life or I would have never suggested what I did after that. "You can." I convinced myself as his fingers stroked in and out of me. "You can fuck me there."

Frankie's movements slowed, petting me instead of thrusting; my clit throbbed for attention. "No." His forehead came down between my shoulder blades and he kissed his way up my back tenderly. "I'd make it fit, but it would fucking hurt and I'm not wasting any time with you doing anything but rolling those pretty eyes into the back of your head."

They did. They did roll directly into the back of my head when he said that.

The telling rustle of his suit snapping away from his body and being wrestled down his thighs behind me made me restless. I wiggled my hips invitingly, finally feeling his hot, hard skin against mine, the tip of his cock getting lost between my legs.

"I don't have a—"

"I don't care." I was nearly shaking with anticipation.

His pause was short before the irrational and frankly irresponsible decision was made for the both of us. He tapped himself against my entrance, nudging the thick beginning of it inside, his fingers digging into my hips as he slid into me in one, savory slow thrust.

My nails dug into my palms. It didn't matter how ready I was, I'd always have to adjust to him. He put pressure on every nerve that garnered a reaction, and my walls softened to accommodate.

"I didn't think it could get fucking better." Frankie's voice was choked. "Look at you, taking me bare. You look so good on my dick, Ophelia. So pretty."

Peeking over my shoulder at him, Frankie's eyes were pinched shut, his jaw slack. Each pump of his hips slapped against me, hitting so deeply that every breath I took had a sound to it. Broken, high-pitched, humming, crying bursts of air. He was truly the best fuck I'd ever had and it wasn't even close. There was no denying the way my body reacted to him.

"Trust me," Frankie breathed. "Just trust me." His thumb slid across my lower back, gathering droplets of warm precipitation, ushering them toward that unexplored part of my ass again. I stiffened when that finger grazed me. "You have to relax, O," he coached. "Say no."

I clamped my mouth shut. I wanted it, wanted to give him that part of me that I hadn't given anyone else. I wanted all these intimate moments to be attached to a man I felt unmistakably connected to. I wasn't going to tell him no.

A low groan rumbled out of him as he continued to fuck me steadily. My clit ached, and I reached down and circled it with my own practiced fingers.

"Say yes."

"Yes," I cried out.

The blunt tip of his thumb breached me and a sting of pleasure followed. How something so intrusive felt so godly was lost on me. My lips shaped into an oval, my eyes closed.

"You okay?" Frankie was huffing harder than me. The still night held the sound of bubbling water, snapping hips, and terse, shallow breathing.

"Good," I managed, pushing my hips toward him. "I can take it."

"I know you can." He pressed his finger in farther and a spark of heat licked up my spine. I dropped my face into my elbow and bit down on my forearm as he filled me in two places at once, dominating me in a way I was more than happy to be.

"So good," Frankie mumbled as he quickened his pace, pounding into me. The pressure was addictive, my core throbbed around him, and my clit tingled readily. I was overtaken with sensation, as if I could feel every last vein and ridge of his cock touching me from within, riding me to a point of no return. My lower belly tightened on cue, the corners of my vision blurring.

Frankie's finger wriggled inside my ass and I saw stars.

"I can tell when you're there, O. Is this about to make you come?"

I moaned a pathetic confirmation, nodding my forehead up and down against my forearm.

"You like being all filled up like this. You love it."

God, he knows everything.

"I plug this tight little hole up, and your pussy starts milking me, Ophelia. You can't hide shit from me when I'm inside you. I know exactly what this cunt wants."

"Fuck," I keened. My legs started shaking and I played rapidly with the swollen nerves at my peak. Frankie's strokes were debilitating. His breath fanned in and out over my back, hoarse grunting complimenting my shriller, weaker whines of ruin.

One of Frankie's hands wrapped around me, putting perfect pressure on the expanse of skin over my middle and I broke, like throwing a rock through a wall of glass.

"*Oh, Godddddd.*" My nostrils flared, vision glitching momentarily as I was shot into a long, hard release.

Before I had time to relax my arms were wedged behind me, wrists bound to my lower back by his strong palm. Frankie continued to fuck me harshly, pulling his thumb from inside me and lifting me so my back met his chest and I was completely at his mercy. My nipples met cool, crisp air and my teeth sunk into my bottom lip.

"You just came on me raw, O. I felt every fucking drop of it," he mumbled against my ear. "Pretty little orgasm. Everything you do is so beautiful it makes me crazy."

He was owning every inch of my body, manipulating my limbs, taking what he needed to reach that delicious, sought-after peak he was on the very edge of. I could sense it in his longer strokes, the air catching in his throat in gusts with his mouth against my hairline. His free forearm came across my chest and bracketed me to his body, taking away my ability to move except for my hips as I bounced them into his lap to encourage that well-earned end.

"I'm gonna come," he warned.

"Please," I begged. "Please, please."

He squeezed me so hard it felt like I very well may be crushed to death with a beautiful and shockingly well-endowed man buried to his fucking nuts inside me. But a second later Frankie unsheathed himself so violently I gasped out of sheer, emptying loss.

Hot ropes of his spend splashed across my ass and lower back, a strained roar rumbling along with them. I let my head fall back and rest against his shoulder as his warm breath fanned across my cheek, evening out just enough for him to tilt my jaw toward his lips and claim my mouth in a satisfied kiss. One that felt gratified, appreciative. Like every time I let him have me, he needed me to know it meant something.

"I can't believe we just did that outside," I said.

Frankie dropped down into the hot tub gracelessly, running a hand over his face as I slunk down next to him. My bikini floated in front of us like a sad sailboat.

"I can't believe you just let me put my thumb in your ass."

32

Ophelia

WE'D LIVED OFF SUGAR cookies and leftover ham sandwiches, pop-ping the corks off wine bottles in our pajamas, since Christmas Eve.

Every few hours Frankie and I emerged from the blanket cocoon we'd turned into an erotic fun house, stood around a shared plate of cold food, and used our hands as utensils in the most barbaric and unsanitary way possible.

I'd never lived with a man before, or shared more than a few nights and very early mornings with the same one. Usually having a steady hook-up for me entailed being very drunk on liquor I could no longer drink in good faith, a bed without a headboard, and my internal clock jolting me out of sheets that I realized much too late I didn't particularly enjoy sleeping in.

I very, *very* much enjoyed Frankie's bed. The coffee he made me with the fancy espresso machine, the closet of endless military-issued sweatpants and sweatshirts that Frankie hadn't fit in for almost two decades at my disposal, and waking up with said man's head buried thoroughly, hungrily, between my legs.

There'd been more testosterone rocking its way through the walls in the prior three days than a Zeppelin concert.

Ghoul Nat returned in full force after the proposal, and Frankie and I took turns guessing whether or not our friends were filming or having genuine, albeit flamboyant sex. Hell, I'd thought about asking Frankie to film *us*, as a souvenir to take with me and reminisce under the covers back home in Colorado. For the first time I understood why someone may sell a theatrical version of themselves getting fucked on a full-queen, because I would damn sure pay to see Frankie nude and gyrating from every single angle imaginable.

It was all that downright illicit energy needing a rest that sent us out of the house and to the beach for the first time in days. Mateo complained about being torn away from the bedroom the entire ride, and if it weren't for us burying him up to his neck in the sand, I was sure he would have been trying to take his new fiancée for a ride in the lifeguard tower.

Frankie patted the ground around Mateo with a tiny plastic shovel. All that remained visible of his best friend was a thick neck and thicker head, sun-washed brown locks peppered with all that naturally shiny grain.

The late December sun was scorching as I flipped from front to back on my towel like a Pop-Tart in a toaster. Every single time I moved, the man next to me perked up a bit, brown eyes tracking me beneath the shade of a pair of sunglasses. There was nothing subtle about it, but I pretended not to notice. Frankie had a way of making me feel like the only person for miles. There were a hundred attractive women on the beach and his attention never strayed.

Every so often Natalia lifted her hand and inspected it like a compact mirror, or pulled her phone out of her bag and took a photo with the foam-rolling waves as a backdrop.

By mid-afternoon I recognized that flashy movement as a conversation starter, and if my best friend weren't basically bursting at the seams to talk nuptials, I was more than happy to iron out details like hors-d'oeuvres, seating charts, party favors, and all the delicious drama that came with stuffing big, opinionated families together for a long weekend.

"What are you thinking venue-wise?" I lifted my shades to the top of my head. "Are we doing a destination? Keeping it close to home? I'm trying to mentally budget the next several months to years of my life."

"Early summer. The Keys. Black tie, long dining tables, white roses, absolute class," Nat rattled off. "I already have an appointment at the bridal boutique because the dress is custom and six months is already pushing it on time, but we should be in the clear."

"June is such a great month for a wedding," I said wistfully, rooting around in my bag next to me for something to scribble down bullet points. "Fuck, I wish I brought a pen."

"That's unlike you," Frankie commented. "You're slacking, Ms. Brody."

"Six months?" Mateo spouted from his hole in the sand, his neck doing all the gesticulating. "What ever happened to enjoying an engagement? There's no rush, sweetheart. Give me some time to pay off that rock first before I'm abusing my wallet again."

If I knew one thing about Natalia, it was that she got what she wanted one way or another and there wasn't a man, woman, authority figure, or governmental body that would be able to sway it. June would be the wedding, it would be in the Florida Keys, there would be white roses, and long dining tables, and everyone would be dressed like they were crossing the red carpet at the Academy Awards. End of.

"My internal clock is ticking, Mateo Duran, and you're not going to be the dad at school orientation that gets mistaken for a grandfather." Nat's slender finger scrolled through an array of aesthetic photos as she tilted her phone toward me. Palm trees, white marble, hanging lights, string quartet. This shit was going to be extravagant *and* expensive.

"That'll be Pike," he joked.

"Watch it." Frankie dumped a shovel full of sand close enough to Mateo's ear for discomfort. "I'm at a lethal advantage here."

I leaned forward and swiped a broken seashell away from a helpless Mateo's ear canal earning a hardly admonishing look of disapproval from Frankie.

"Why wait?" Nat threw her hands up. "I've been preparing for this for years. I knew the first time Mateo brought me coffee at work we'd be walking down the aisle together."

"Weren't you seeing that guy Andy from the mortgage loan department?" I chimed in.

"Andy was the only one who thought I was seeing Andy." Nat batted me away with a flick of her delicate wrist. "We'll have the bridal shower of course." She started counting on fingers. "Bachelorette party, rehearsal dinner, the wedding itself, morning-after brunch."

I was mentally counting how many days the school would approve of me taking off, and how many free airline miles I could mooch off my dad. Bachelorette wouldn't take too much finagling; I could spare a Friday here or a Monday there. Cindy was metaphorically thrown into the fire for me for weeks, so a stray day in the classroom would be a cake walk. Bridal shower was another circus I'd tackle when it came to it, and then of course the wedding. But by June the school year was over, and what better way to celebrate another semester of massaging young minds than absolutely losing mine in the tropics?

"Vegas," Mateo added. "A weekend of our worst behavior."

"I can do that!" I raised my hand. Colorado to Vegas was short and sweet.

"Good luck getting all three of my sisters to Vegas at the same time." Nat snorted contemptuously. "Doctor, lawyer, top-selling real estate agent in all of Collier County. That's why my parents take a vacation every year for the holidays. None of us are ever together at the same time."

"And *that* is why it's not my problem, but that of my best man." Sand cracked and dislodged around Mateo's fingers as he spoke with his hands, even with them buried underground. "That reminds me. Pike, are you gonna stand up there next to me, buddy?"

Frankie sat up, his head tilting thoughtfully. "What about Angelo?"

"My brother wouldn't know responsibility if it uppercut him in the jaw." Mateo did something akin to a shrug, crumbling more sand around his chest. "God loves him, but you're the only one who's never let me down."

"I—" Frankie flashed a look up at me and Nat grinning. He would learn to take a compliment if I had to threaten it. A world of intriguing, silent thought passed over his complexion followed by a tender, bashful smile. "I'd be honored, Captain. You know that."

Mateo wiggled, breaking his two arms free and Frankie flattened himself awkwardly to the sand, wrapping Mateo's head instead in an awkward hug.

"It's going to be amazing," I assured Natalia. Regardless of if it were me or one of her sisters taking on the maid of honor title, nothing would be getting in the way of a perfect wedding.

I would make sure that every last inch of fabric—dress or tablecloth, curtain or gossamer drapery, was ironed and pleated to the very nines. The flowers would smell like someone plucked them fresh that morning, there would be a mimosa in every hand at the twitch of Natalia's perfectly manicured fingers, and there wouldn't be a goddamn cell phone poking out of the crowd during the ceremony or I would remove the wrist that held it myself.

I was born for this responsibility. Lists and schedules were my thing. Checking boxes next to my swirly, decorative, honestly obnoxious ballpoint penmanship was like a shot of serotonin straight to my veins. I craved structure, loved deadlines, and there was a very specific and probably certifiable definition for the pinball machine in my brain that only all of the above did anything to sooth.

I'd only ever found one thing interesting enough to slow down time, and he was ephemeral.

Storm clouds rolled toward us, rumbling down the beach. Pink lightning struck through the newly gray sky. It amazed me how minutes prior there wasn't a hint of rain in the forecast, and if you looked a few miles up the beach, it still glowed with the blue promise of a sunny day. The lifeguards stood on their white cedar stands, waving their arms at the people caught out in the thickening surf and whistled everyone to pack up and head off the beach.

"It'll pass in a minute," Nat complained. "I don't understand why we can't just wait it out. It's not even four p.m." Another crackle of lightning cascaded down to argue.

"Not all of us are blessed with a natural bronze," I said, packing my high-powered SPF away as the wind picked up and tendrils of hair escaped from my ponytail. "My sunburned ass is more than ready for a shower."

"Agreed," Mateo grunted, busting his way through several layers of sand and coming out of it looking like a freshly dusted sugar cookie. He shook his entire body like a dog and covered all three of us in the runoff.

"You're hosing off before you get in my car," Nat said pointedly.

Frankie reached over as the first cold drop of rain fell onto my shoulder, handing me my bundled bathing suit cover-up, and pulling me to my feet. Our fingers tightened reflexively around one another.

"I'm ready to get you home," Frankie said, mumbling between only us. His heavy gaze drifted down my body, cataloging it. We were very clearly about to have another one of those long, sleepless nights like the previous three. My body had already adapted something of a Pavlovian response to his attention. Tender nipples, blushing cunt, heat rising in all the secret, intimate places it knew he'd soon be taking care of like his own.

"Shit," Nat groaned, reluctantly gathering her beach bags and folding her chair underneath her arm. Her colorful bangles rattled as she picked herself up from the beach, pouting and stalking in the direction of the street access, leaving Mateo half-dressed and scrambling behind.

More rain pelted down as Frankie and I rushed to shake out our towels and slip back into clothes and shoes. Our slow walk to the parking lot turned into a lazy jog through the sand and my shins were screaming as we reached the pavement and the sky opened up, drenching us.

Mother Nature was a temperamental bitch. Thunder boomed and every crack of lightning turned the gray clouds cotton candy pink.

"Let's go!" Mateo yelled over his shoulder as he caught up to Nat and pulled her along in her dangerously wet sandals. Eventually he stopped and bent into a half-squat so she could jump onto his back and continue.

I turned to request the same from Frankie just as his phone rang, muffled and trilling through the pounding of rain on the pavement. He fished it out of his bathing suit pocket as we fell further and further behind the other two. Frankie stopped walking completely, holding a finger to one ear and his phone to the other beneath the torrential rain.

Nat and Mateo sprinted and I remained in a limbo between the two.

The flimsy cover-up I threw on was glued to my body like silk tulle and my hair was soaked to my scalp. I thought about complaining, but that emotion came out in a sprinkle of laughter instead. I tilted my head toward the sky, spread my arms like wings at my sides, and let the full rush of the storm envelope my senses. The salty brine of the ocean sweeping under my nose, howling wind at my neck, goosebumps sharpening on my body as cold rain met warm skin. With my eyes closed I was *submerged*; the world outside those receptive walls didn't exist.

I couldn't remember the last time I stopped like that, to let myself become overwhelmed. When I was a kid, maybe. In the snow on the mountain, like I'd told Frankie. Wispy flakes of fresh powder dancing onto my nose. Snow angels in the moonlight, dark skies, Ursa Major, Orion, the Little Dipper. The crunch of cold, packed earth beneath my head, the frozen lick of melted snow dripping down my neck. Pink, tingling fingertips, icicle eyelashes, the puff of hot breath gone into the air as quickly as I breathed it.

Life flashed like reels in an old film between the two, molding the feeling of each core memory into one grounding, starkly human experience. Standing in the rain, lying in the snow, letting myself be elementally taken over for a brief, pretty moment.

I'd been standing there for several minutes when two strong hands braced against my biceps and pulled me into a solid, soaking wall of muscle. "Hey, you." Frankie smiled down at me. Raindrops dripped from the bill of his hat and landed on my cheeks.

"All good?" I looked him up and down, searching. "Everything okay?"

Frankie's grin extended up his cheeks, those fine lines of age crinkling the corners of his eyes, and his grip on me tightened as if full of energy he needed a place to exude. "That was the base in Colorado."

"Oh?" I herded my response like wild animals into a pen as my stomach tightened into a nervous knot.

"Yeah," he breathed. His cotton T-shirt was drenched straight through and I curled my fingers into it right at his chest.

"And?"

The real possibility of Frankie moving to Colorado was exhilarating—and terrifying. It seeded a hope inside me that I could *have* him, all the time. I wouldn't have to waste my time looking for a person to replace what he was to me, in whatever unsatisfying way they would attempt to, because I didn't see it possible. We could continue on this unusual and magnificent friendship, see it bud into something more relationship-shaped. Water the soil.

What was terrifying was doing all of those things, hoping for something beautiful and being crushed if it didn't come to fruition. The more my heart was willing to take that chance for him, the more my head pushed back rationally. Still, optimism took precedence.

"They want me back at the end of January for another interview."

We couldn't see two feet in either direction through the rain. It dripped down my lips, and wet my teeth as my mouth bowed into an animated smile. My heart lurched against my chest as I squeezed him harder. "That's good?" I nodded. "That's fantastic, right? This is amazing."

Frankie's arms cradled my lower back briefly and then dropped to my thighs, scooping me off the ground and bringing us face-to-face. My fingers wound through the wet hair at the nape of his neck.

The answer was in his eyes, tracing me in a pointed triangle. Pupil to pupil to parted, waiting lips. The gesture felt like a promise—a cross your heart, or mark the spot, or write your name in blood dramatically promise.

Frankie nudged my nose to the side, angling our mouths, and then he kissed me.

We spun in a slow circle, rain pouring down, expressing every emotion in a hard, sensual, never-ending clash. Frankie's tongue swept through my mouth, playing with mine, the tip of his nose digging into my cheek as we both tried to feel one another *deeper*. Dull fingernails caressed my ass, holding me tightly against his stable body.

His hat cascaded to the blacktop, the thunder a glorious and fitting backdrop as I nipped and licked at his plush lips. Satisfaction rumbled out of him through every short, shared breath we took.

We were a spinning, doting, devouring spectacle and I would have drowned with him like that. Or let the tide rise up and kick our already unsteady feet out from underneath us and carry me and Frankie into the brutal surf. Swept away was the perfect metaphor.

But like taking a fork to an outlet, a horn chirped several times, and headlights shone toward us through the rain. It was too late to feel embarrassed; we'd been caught hilariously and ostentatiously red-handed.

"You can touch each other in the back seat!" a familiar grating voice called out of the driver's side window as Mateo rolled it down a smidge. Frankie bowed his forehead into mine and exhaled as he lowered me to my feet. "And you're lucky these seats are leather!"

33

Frankie

I AM INHERENTLY A decision maker.

Or I'd taken on that title as an unfortunate circumstance of the life I was both given and then the one I chose out of primordial obligation.

I didn't love being faced with options. I liked having *one*, and that option being the right one, and then everything else just effortlessly falling into place behind it. If you gave me a conflict, I would likely spend no more than five minutes finding a solution, ingesting the red or blue pill, and then following the expected map of events until I was faced with another crossroads of metaphorical medication.

My father died and I swallowed the responsibility pill. That looked like early mornings, paper routes, teaching myself how to use a pair of pliers, how to tie my own tie, blood trickling down my neck as I stared in the mirror with a dull, forgotten razor I'd found in the medicine cabinet in my hand. It was shoes that didn't fit right, answering the door to strangers, suspending belief in things like the Easter Bunny, and the Tooth Fairy, and Santa Claus so that Adriana didn't have to.

It was cutting my finger open with the utility knife and needing stitches, but wrapping it up in paper towels and electrical tape and shoving it into the pocket of my one, too-small sweatshirt because that was a medical bill we had no business paying.

I knew all my teachers, and all my sister's teachers, and the mailman, and the Culligan man, and the FedEx driver. The neighbors, their kids, their grandkids. I befriended the ladies at the grocery store checkout, and the pharmacy, and the church on Sunday. Accepted every hand-on-head prayer when I knew full well if there was a God, he was a dickhead at best, and my obligation to be there for my mother's sake was perfunctory and performative if not already obvious.

I approached decision-making like a blueprint rolled out on a table. Do this thing...and then this one. Here are all the pieces: follow the directions, study the key, take your time, build the foundation first, take a step back, reassess.

And I did that, until it came time to ship out for the Army. That was swallowing a completely different, muskier tasting, settled in your stomach like a ship hitting the bottom of the ocean supplement. That one meant I had made a decision, and now I would forget what it felt like to ever have to make a decision again. There were only orders.

The Army dictated, and that's what I wanted. The most submissive I'd ever been in my life was signing my name across that contract. Giving a piece of paper the power to disarm me.

Still, a decision nonetheless. One I made just as easily as I did the first, and one that I was proud of and had not once regretted in almost twenty years. Not even now. Not after flight school, or the Middle East, or South America. Not after my accident, or Vanessa, or the last few years of learning how to literally and figuratively stand on two feet again.

That trip out to the base in Colorado was a small blip in the canvas, an ink stain on the floor plan. Half of me treated it like a joke—not the actual interview of course—but the set-up with Tyler, letting Mateo find me a suit, the fucking Hook(Up) dating in Colorado Springs as if I could return to the early-twenties era of my life and play the field like a kid that finally got to go away to college. If I didn't get the job, or if I realized I didn't want it in the first place, there was no permanent harm done. I just...continued on.

But then I got on that plane...and somehow ended up with the most beautiful woman in the world attached to my side like the piece of a warped puzzle I expected would never have a perfect match again. Her curves marrying my lack of, her fingers stitching perfectly into the gaps in mine.

Ophelia—soft, warm, full of untainted innocence and that bright, unbreakable outlook on life I had no business believing I deserved. But as we lay in my bed, her nails running in figure eights up and down my bare, shuddering torso, kissing my ribs every few minutes, letting me know she was still awake, I did believe it. I knew that parts of me needed parts of her, and I didn't want to let her go back to whatever life she lived before we met. I didn't want her to see me as a lesson, or practice, or a fun time when our lives inevitably crossed paths again. I didn't want her giving herself to a man that wasn't me. Holding a hand that wasn't mine. Having someone else elicit that throaty, sweet laugh, sharing moments yet to come in her life that should belong to me.

That wasn't supposed to happen.

But, decisions, right? I didn't have a red or blue pill this time. I had a rainbow assortment with a laundry list of side effects next to each.

One looked like the present moment. We could die in my bed together. It was dramatic, and it would take a while, and Ophelia might decide to be the captain of her own destiny and leave me to wilt into the sheets alone. Though, that option looked a lot like another, which was remaining in Coconut Creek, denying the secondary interview, continuing to work for TechOps, and living with my friend and his wife, and eventually their litter of kids. That was actually less appealing than becoming one with my mattress the longer I imagined it.

I could go to Colorado, take the second interview at the end of January, see Ophelia and fly back home again, play the never-ending waiting game. Sit in a room half stacked with boxes, hoping on one hand to get a call that I *didn't* get the job, while the other hand searched for apartments in Pine Ridge just in case.

Then there was Mom. Addy. I'd spent so much of my life away from them already, and I was finally in a place where we could all be together like we used to, relying on one another for the love we needed and the family we lacked. I had become so accustomed to long periods of time away from them that I never prioritized it when I finally came back home. Shit got in the way, life, jobs. I was busy, Addy was busy. Excuses I shouldn't have been making as the man in the house. Nevertheless, I was sacrificing a sure thing for something that might not work out over time, letting my heart do that stupid fucking thing Mateo warned me it would and putting blind hope in futile emotion.

The fact of the matter was, none of my options gave me everything I wanted: a job I loved, my best friends, my family—and the full, satisfied, rumbling happiness that felt like that first spring sunshine after a winter of gray personified.

Ophelia. All the time, every second of the day. I wanted her like a tattoo. I wanted her in my veins, ink scabbed over, healed inside of me, part of me, on display, branded.

I lifted her thick brown hair off my arm, rubbing it between my fingers idly. She was so quiet as we lay there, tired from the day. It was the first time since I met her that we actually sat in silence. The only other moments she was sedentary or voiceless were asleep or underneath me, when we needed nothing but tongues and touch to voice our thoughts. Even dog-tired, breathless, hungover, intoxicated, we found something to say to one another, a joke to be told, a memory to cajole, a small, unimposing fact that could use an audience.

In fact, I didn't like the reserve one bit, or that this might be one of the last times I had her all to myself for quite some time. The house would be loud with the Swan boys come tomorrow, and the party would remain on through New Year's, celebrating engagements and job interviews, drinking, laughing, avoiding the obvious, which was her leaving in less than three days.

When we'd had sex earlier it was different. Not without the normal, syrupy passion that didn't take any effort from either of us, not different in that it didn't feel *right*. Different like we were both entirely on the same page and somehow also dusting over the epilogue. Our bodies were there, *fuck* they were there. But both of our thoughts were not.

She kissed my side again and I trailed my fingers down her scalp like a slide, drawing circles with the pads of my fingers on her shoulder, dropping them down her naked spine, squeezing her closer to me. *Closer* to me.

When I finally spoke my voice was rough from the unuse. "What time does your flight leave on Sunday?"

She stiffened beneath my touch. Soft, slow puffs of breath coming more rapidly against my skin, her fingernails halted at the center of my chest. I put my fingers overtop them, flattening her palm to my hot skin. The steady beat of my pulse thrummed through her hand and knocked on mine.

"I don't know," she replied faintly.

I didn't believe that. Ophelia was a planner—she knew dates and times, she remembered birthdays and star signs, and the name of the nail polish color on her toes so she could get it again the next time. She carried a notepad around with her in case of emergency, and that afternoon was the first time I'd actually seen her unprepared for the spontaneous use of the fucking thing.

I didn't know it for sure, but I would have put money down on a girly little calendar with the flight numbers and departure schedules highlighted somewhere in red and green marker. It was a lie or a tell that she was actively unaware, but the latter made more sense the deeper I let it sink in.

Because just like me, the haze of sex and fun and carelessness was dissipating like condensation on a mirror for her too. Now we were reflecting, and considering, and watching reality materialize in the glass in front of us, and that reality looked the same in her mirror as it did in mine.

"We fucked up, didn't we?" I put words to it for the first time.

A subtle nod of her head came in return. My eyelids pinched together, emotion swirling deep inside me that had been lying dormant, seemingly waiting for it to be voiced like a whistle into action. A knot tightened beneath her palm and mine, making it hard to speak without a jolt of pain.

"It hurts," I murmured against her forehead, putting more pressure at the center of my chest with her hand to show her. "It hurts right here."

She sighed, both anguished and relieved. "I know exactly what you mean."

34

Ophelia

A HOUSE FULL OF large, loud, animated, and spectacularly attractive men was quite similar to standing outside the glass at an exhibit at the Cheyenne Mountain Zoo.

Nat and I were basically furniture in the presence of the four former operators, observing them silently from across the room with our glasses of wine and the scraps of a charcuterie board. They were like boys again together. Burly laughs hitting the low ceilings like an echo chamber; teasing, taunting conversation; slaphappy palms on jean-clad asses. They wrestled as a way of affection, headlocks and hair tugs, brute force establishing some benign form of a pecking order when it was aggressively obvious they were all different suits of the same deck.

Frankie and Mateo put on a show alone, but introducing another pair added kerosene to the chaos.

The Swan brothers were tall as trees, fair-skinned, square-jawed. They looked every bit alike and at the same time nothing at all. Sam was softer, more athletically built, his hazel eyes an almond shape and his nose a dash more rounded at the point. His hair was short and ashen brown, faded from a full mop at his crown down to the skin at the nape of his neck. Clean shaven with full lips and a perfect line of teeth. Like his brother, Tyler, their brows were thick and slightly hooded, eyelashes so long it would make any woman jealous. They had the same smile, and the same laugh, the same hand-on-hip way of standing casually and brushing their fingers down their chin when listening thoughtfully.

Tyler's chin, however, was thick with a coarse beard, the hair on his head clipped down to a dirty blond buzzcut. He had eyes so sterling blue they could halt traffic, and if his height wasn't disarming enough, the mass of very well-earned muscle tightening the sleeves of a cotton tee to his tattooed biceps did the job. He was like Thor, with less fanfare but equally natural charm and seduction. His voice started and remained at a husk so artlessly baritone it was like listening to ASMR. Your eyes just naturally softened in his presence.

"He is so hot in person." Nat leaned over and murmured from behind the shade of her wine glass. "I'm married. I can say that."

"You are *not* married," I corrected her. My gaze shot back and forth between the four men, Tyler's arm slung over Frankie's shoulder, Mateo clinking the head of his beer against Sam's. "Which one are you talking about?"

"Exactly," she gloated. "Pictures are one thing, but it's crazy to see them together. I'm glad they made the effort to get everyone under the same roof again."

"They're going to be seeing a lot of each other for the wedding festivities, I'm sure." I sized up the bigger brother again as he curled Frankie into his side and whispered something that earned a playful punch in the ribs. "Tyler is the one who got Frankie the interview in Colorado?"

Nat laughed. "He's apparently *very* close with one of the staff sergeants. I think anything Tyler wants he gets one way or another, but Frankie didn't need the help at all. Sure, having a contact is always good, but his job history does all the work for him."

"He told me..." I started casually. "About everything that happened."

Natalia's attention drew away from the men across the room for the first time. "Seriously?"

"Yep." I slipped a cube of cheddar cheese between my lips. "I felt like he was holding back a little bit, but it was probably more for my sake than his."

"That's *huge*, Phee. Frankie doesn't talk about that to anyone. Mateo tries all the time, but he just ices him out. The fact that you got through is amazing." She paused. "You two are so good with each other, it's kind of heartbreaking."

"Heartbreaking?" I forced out a laugh, twirling the stem of my wine glass between my fingers. "I think we both just knew we could confide in one another because we're practically strangers. Free therapy." What a blatant lie. A stranger was the person sitting next to you at a crowded bar, not the man that stayed awake all night playing Connect the Dots with the beauty marks on your back. Not the one you could pick out by the sound of his voice in utter darkness, or the one you knew to choose flowers that attract butterflies for a Christmas gift for their mom.

"Don't fucking lie to me. I'm your best friend." Nat reached over and tugged the chain of my butterfly necklace intentionally. "Strangers? You're trying so hard right now to pretend that leaving in a few days isn't killing both of you. We're past the point of no return. I see it, Mateo sees it."

I rolled my eyes, letting them land directly on Frankie on the recoil and catching his already-there stare. My short smile was returned with a comforting wink that sent a warm flutter to my belly. "So feelings got involved," I admitted.

"You think?" she said.

"It doesn't matter. This is typical of two people with a long history of loneliness. One ounce of healthy affection does *not* mean we're completely compatible. Lust and love are easy to mix up, especially when it's been so long for both of us. This was spontaneous, and irresponsible. The entire trip feels like I'm having an affair with my own life."

"Shut up," Nat teased. "You're allowed to be bummed out. And there doesn't have to be a textbook answer to everything, Ms. Teacher. Sometimes shit just stinks and you light a"—she sat forward and twisted the candle on the table toward us—"vanilla bean latte candle and pretend it doesn't."

"I hate everything about that sentence."

"Well you just hate everything about the truth, then."

"Can we put the angst on the back burner for now?" I asked. "I'm leaving on Sunday and I'd rather not spend the duration of it being tiptoed around like my dog just died and making sad champagne toasts."

Nat conceded with a dramatic sigh. "Feed me more cheese, that'll shut me up."

I swiped a cube of cheddar off the platter on the table and stuffed it into my best friend's mouth.

The ruckus of voices across the kitchen dispersed as the boys crossed the room to join us on the couches. There was a creak of leather and bow of the cushion behind me before I felt a secret, cheeky pinch on the side of my ass. As quickly as it was there it was gone as I turned toward the culprit with a playful look of warning.

After our conversation the night before I'd been trying not to give Frankie so much of my attention.

Less of a conversation, more of a realization.

It was one thing to be pseudo-dumped by a guy I wasn't even truly in a relationship with—I'd done it before and I could do it again—but there was another layer to it this time, because we'd both found something that felt wrong to let go of. I'd wanted the rollercoaster ride, the adrenaline, the free fall, something to wake up the dormant, excitable woman inside of me. Something to distract from spending the holidays away from my family for the first time ever, despite feeling like I hadn't truly spent Christmas with them since I was a kid.

I wanted to *use* Frankie, and that was okay, because he wanted to use me, too. We swore on it. We *kissed* on it.

But what I'd found was the type of man that melted ice, thawed me to my core where I never imagined a flame being brought to life again, and then somehow lit it.

I needed to pull back, start to let reality leak its way back in again. I would see Frankie a few times over the next six months preparing for a wedding, and then the slate was blank with possibilities. He would either come to Colorado or he wouldn't, but the worst thing I could do was put hope into a decision that wasn't mine to make. I knew how he valued family, the ways relationships had burned him in the past. I couldn't imagine the fear of getting back into a helicopter again after three years and the traumatic last ride he took.

Backing away slowly, preserving what was left of my emotions so that I might still have something to give to someone else—*that* was the right thing to do.

"So, Ophelia." A velvet voice called out to me, and in my peripheral I could sense the deep, brown gaze of Frankie's worry searing into my cheek. "You're a teacher?" Sam asked.

"Yes." I cleared my throat. "Fourth graders are some of the brightest and most animalistic humans I've ever had the pleasure of teaching American geography to."

"I still can't point out Utah on the map, and I turned out just fine," Tyler commented beside his brother, his broad wingspan taking up nearly the entire back end of the couch.

"That probably has something to do with how many times you got your head knocked in," Mateo added. "I swear to God they designed our helmets with Echo's track record in mind."

"You know, a door can be breached in with a boot, or a shoulder..." Frankie pointed out.

"I've never gotten a critique until now, so I think you two should stop licking each other's asses so often and be thankful that I was the one doing all the heavy lifting."

"All right, all right." Sam shook his head. "The girls are here. Let's be gentlemen, right?"

Mateo snorted. "You should hear the two of them talk. Seductresses. Feeding off us like leeches for the last two weeks."

The Swans both raised an eyebrow, the left corner of their mouths turning up in interest, looking every bit the pair of brothers with mirrored expressions.

The tips of my ears reddened as I realized the attention was on me and Frankie entirely. Of course Nat and her future husband would be boning—but the girl from Colorado and their old friend who was in a forest fire of a relationship last they knew of was unexpected.

Frankie clasped his palm over the back of my neck, squeezing the tense points of pressure affectionately. I immediately dropped my shoulders from where they'd ended up at by my ears.

Tyler ran his icy eyes from the tips of my socks to the crown of my head, surveying me like an elevator making a stop on each floor on his way to the top. It was no wonder women apparently fell at his feet; the assessment was scorching and deliberate. Not in a flirtatious way, but something more calculated. More so reading me like a book.

I squirmed free of Frankie's touch, his fingers lingering down my back briefly. "So, what is it you guys do?" I addressed both brothers.

Pleased with the runaround, as if it told its own little secret in and of itself, Tyler perked up.

"I own a bar," he announced proudly. "Best spot in Salt Lake."

"Have you ever met a bar owner that also *bartends* at their own place?" Sam said.

"That must be fun," Nat commented. "It's very hands-on. I'm sure your staff loves it."

"I like to know what goes on," Tyler agreed. "Get to know the clientele, show my face, make sure there's no funny business."

Someone would have to be out of their mind to start a fight with Tyler Swan. He was scary as all sin and I couldn't imagine a bouncer alive that was as intimidating as this man.

"What he means is," Sam interjected, "he likes to know what women are coming in and out of his bar every night and make sure they get the *very best* customer service experience possible."

"Is that wrong of me?" Tyler looked to everyone but his brother, outstretched palms like landing pads. "I'm very passionate about those Yelp reviews."

"Echo is a full-service man," Mateo testified. "Always has been."

"I'll cheers to that." Tyler stretched his long body across the coffee table and tapped his beer to Mateo's. His shirt sleeves bunched up his arm revealing twists and curves of a serpent and a sword inked into his skin.

"What about you?" I reinvested in Sam with glowing curiosity. His friendly copper gaze reminded me of a puppy. "If he's the bartender you must be the...sous-chef?"

Frankie cackled beside me. "Wink once put his instant mac in the microwave without the fucking water. Almost burned the entire barracks to the ground in three-and-a-half minutes."

"Like you never sat post all night and did some dumb shit when you got back in." Sam laughed. "Actually now that I think about it, Pike, weren't you the sorry son of a bitch that fell asleep and missed call time not once, or twice, but on three separate occasions? We got *fucked* for that."

"Cicadas put me to sleep." Frankie shrugged. "Not like you could fly anywhere without a pilot. I needed to be alert."

"So *not* a sous-chef," I surmised, giving Frankie's thigh a teasing squeeze.

"You're a saint for dealing with him, Ophelia." Sam said. "I work for a nonprofit called War Paws. We pair animals with veterans who need support after returning home from areas of conflict."

"I *love* that." Nat brought her palm to her heart. "Rescues?"

"Always," Sam promised.

"I'd have a new dog every week. I couldn't stand the cuteness."

"I did adopt my first week," Sam confessed with a short laugh. "Big guy spoke to me. I have a soft spot for the labs."

"I want one." Nat turned to Mateo, wrapping her arms around his neck. "We should go to the shelter next week, babe."

Mateo's steely stare zeroed in on Sam across the room. "We'll see, honey." He caressed her back and turned a middle finger toward his friend that everyone but Nat could see.

"Do you want dogs?" Frankie asked me.

Again, all eyes in the room trained on the two of us. Such a mundane question, yet so loaded given the circumstance.

"Yeah." I nodded, feeling perplexed. "Yeah, I want dogs."

"Not for nothing, Ophelia. If you'd have said no I would probably have to kick you out." Mateo shrugged. "I don't make the rules." Then, a second later, he amended, "Wait, yes I do."

"No one's kicking anybody out," Frankie argued.

Nat stood from the couch, clearing the plate of cheese and crackers and the empty bottle of wine off the table. "I am," she declared. "I'm kicking us out for the night. You boys try not to get into too much trouble before tomorrow. Coming, Phee?"

"What do you mean?" Mateo followed her tail. "We're just getting started."

"*You* are just getting started." She turned and tapped his nose. "Enjoy your night with your friends, and remember being hungover is absolutely no fun when you have to drive the next day so tread carefully."

I tried to stand from the sofa and strong, possessive hands threaded together over my middle and tugged me back down.

"I don't remember agreeing to this," Frankie objected. His lips grazed the shell of my ear and a whole string of explicit words and images shuffled through my mind.

"You'll survive," I assured him, doing everything in my power to inch off his lap, when all I wanted to do was stay glued to it.

I meandered into the kitchen, clearing empty beers and dented metal caps off the island, sweeping a dust of chip crumbs into the pull-out disposal, then turning to help Nat load the dishwasher with oily plates from the pizza. Nat was right—the men deserved at least a little bit of time to themselves after a few years apart.

It was a great idea actually, forcing Frankie and I to separate after several days being attached at the...well, being attached in several places. We needed to get used to sleeping alone again, to not having a person to share body heat, or waking up in the middle of the night with wandering touches. I needed that, because I was having an admittedly hard time coming to terms with giving all those aspects of this arrangement up in three days.

Cold sheets? Faulty staffroom Keurig coffee instead of that beautiful hot cup sitting on the bedside table for me when I woke up? God, it was horrible, and the bandage had to be ripped off.

"Stop cleaning my kitchen. You know I hate it." Frankie pulled a pint glass out of my hand and placed it back down, then caged me into the counter. "Can we talk about this?"

His doe-brown eyes and pouty lip nearly had me, but the more plausible, sensible side of my brain knew that letting him have his way would only prolong the inevitable and that wasn't good for either of us. I ducked my head and escaped underneath his outstretched arm, backing out of the kitchen and toward the front of the house.

"See you guys tomorrow!" I shouted to the Swans. It was returned with a grumble of goodbyes I couldn't decipher as one or the other.

"Ophelia," Frankie complained, following me. He reached out and tugged the back of my shirt, keeping me from walking away. My back met a hard chest and then the wall as I was spun into the shade of the foyer away from everyone's eyes but his. "I don't want you to leave."

The light from the moon shone through the windows and illuminated half of his face, inches from mine. "I'll see you in twelve hours."

"Too many." He shook his head.

"You're ridiculous." My palm connected with his chest and was met with solid resistance.

"Do I have to get on my knees? Is that what'll do it for you?"

"I do love you on your knees," I placated him, running my fingers from his chest to his jaw, entwining them into his hair. "But no."

"If I don't get to fuck you tonight, I'll lose my mind."

"You won't, I promise."

"I've been thinking about it all damn day, O. Please, baby, put me out of my misery."

His begging was playful, but the words hit in a way that was anything but. "Stop it."

Our breathing mingled, the sweet bitterness of his beer dancing across my senses. My tongue ached to slip out and taste it. We were basically there—my top lip feathered across his, our noses brushed. A familiar heat stirred to life between my legs and as if he could sense it, Frankie flattened me to the wall with his entire body, his thigh slipping into the gap I'd left in mine.

"Don't do this," I murmured lazily. All the while my grip in his hair tightened and a slow circle of my hips began on its own accord.

"Do what?" I heard his smile.

"Try to get me all riled up when you *know* I'm leaving."

Our mouths swept against one another again, this time slower, leaving the sensitive flesh tingling for more. Frankie's hand came down on the bone of my hip, riding it like a wave, guiding me back and forth more intentionally against him.

"You're doing everything all on your own, Trouble."

I opened my mouth to challenge him as plush lips sank down and claimed mine, rendering me speechless in one searing, hungry kiss that felt like a day's worth of contention let out like a pinhole in a balloon.

My eyelids drooped closed for a moment, but then snapped open resiliently. I wasn't so easy to persuade, no matter how gorgeous and doting the man doing the persuasion was. But, fuck, I sucked at this. One off-guard moment nearly had me skipping down the hallway to his bed.

I put all my strength into my closed fists and pushed him away, catching Frankie in an instance of weakness himself. He reared back, surprise coloring his face as I weaseled my way to the open front door before he could gain his bearings and find a way to pull me right back in.

"*Goodnight*, Frankie," I simpered, passing Mateo on the walkway toward a waiting Nat in the car.

35

Frankie

ONE THING ABOUT BEING in the trenches with a group of men for as long as I had been is that they learn to see right through you. You don't spend a decade of your life beside people you consider your brothers without also forming a bond that makes it hard to hide exactly what the fuck you're thinking and feeling at all times.

We sat on the dimly lit patio, crickets chirping, the low hum of the hot tub sending a wave of vibration under our feet. I had been nursing the same piss warm beer for an hour and picking at the label with the raw side of my thumb, willing my phone to ping with a message.

My focus waxed and waned alongside every conversation. I was too in my own head about Ophelia and the way she left, and I knew that feeling was only going to get worse and more permanent until I forgot what it was ever like to *not* miss her.

Which wasn't an option, because I refused to be the down-on-my-ass friend again. The one that everyone worried about from afar and talked about privately. When I sat with it though, life was moving forward for everyone but me. Sam had his nonprofit, Tyler owned a business, my best friend in the whole fucking world was getting married, undoubtedly starting a family close behind. But I was at a crossroads.

What I wanted and what I was ready to commit to were two opposing forces, and I wished like hell that someone or something could just *show me* the right path to choose. It didn't have to be the easy one, or the obvious one. No matter what I did at this point, I was giving up something that I cared about anyway. In Colorado I didn't have my family, in Florida I didn't have my job. I was losing my grip on Ophelia whether I liked it or not. Not spending one of the last nights we had together was forcing me to face the reality I'd been avoiding.

"Who shit in your Cheerios, Pike?" Echo kicked the leg of my chair. "We boring you?"

"He's sad it's just him and his hand tonight," Cap said.

I flicked my bottle cap off the armrest in his direction. "Fuck off."

Sam sat up. "You're getting soft on us."

"This one's gonna buy his fiancé a puppy tomorrow because she gave him a look, and I'm soft?"

"The difference is that I own my shit." Mateo pointed at himself. "I know that I'm whipped and I'm happy to be here."

"What happens when she flies home?" Tyler asked me. "Are you going to get over it?"

"There's nothing to get over," I lied. The warm beer marinating between my sweaty palms tasted like spit as I tossed it back to avoid the third degree. "It was sex."

"You bought her a necklace," Cap reminded me.

"It was Christmas." Fuck, the beer tasted like shit.

"Oh, shit." Sam sighed dramatically.

Cap and Tyler shared a wordless glance that made me oddly defensive. As if gifts during the holidays were some foreign concept, and having no-strings sex with someone was so out of the ordinary for any of them either. Maybe what really fucking bothered me was that they were hitting the nail on the head, and I wore every sorry emotion on my sleeve despite my attempts against it.

Ophelia and I knew we were more involved than we ever intended to be, and things had been tense all day because of it. She kept me at an obvious arm's length after breakfast, and I respected the unspoken distance she put between us because I knew how I felt, so I knew how she must have too. I, on the other hand, was on the opposite edge, wanting nothing but to savor it all while we still had it, and rip the stitches out when the time came.

The corresponding emotions were an elixir of self-doubt, anticipatory grief, and tragically an unwavering boost in libido even after she'd closed the door and drove away.

"There's so much shit going through my head right now, I don't have the patience for pity. So you three say what you want to say and be fucking real about it or get off my ass."

A low whistle pitched from between Tyler's lips. "Are you going to Colorado?"

"I don't fucking know," I answered honestly. "I'll go for the second interview, but the only thing I've ever known outside of the service is home. Home is here. It's not that easy to uproot and start over. And my mom's getting older, too."

"Nobody's pressuring you, brother," Tyler said. "We just know you. We don't want you down here feeling stuck when there's a world of opportunities somewhere else." He smiled that broad, toothy smile that got him just about anything from tips to tail. "And you have no idea the kinky shit I had to do to get you that interview."

"Ignore my brother," Sam cut in. "You're a fucking ace of a pilot. You earned every last one of your medals—we were all there. There's not a base in the country that wouldn't want you teaching in the ranks."

"That's a whole other thing." I exhaled, swiping my hat off my head. "I haven't flown since Costa Rica. I'm rusty as fuck, performance anxiety or whatever."

"It's like riding a bike." Cap shrugged. "You don't forget how to fly."

"You also don't forget what it feels like to crash."

Silence breezed over us, Wink's eyes, more copper in the light, downcast into his lap, while Echo stared at me straight. They didn't expect me to bring the crash up so bluntly, because I hadn't before. I'd never wanted to talk about it. Mateo would still try every now and then but I brushed him off. What was there to say? The past was the past and there was no use flipping the fucking dirt over and tilling old ground.

"Well, I don't know much about flying," Sam said. "But I do know that lying down for dead isn't much your style, Pike, and neither is choosing the easy way out of things. If that day did anything, it was solidify what everyone already knows—that you're the best of the best. Not a single fucking casualty."

"He's right." Mateo nodded. "I'll accept it if you don't go because of your mom and Addy. I'm still making you move out," he acknowledged lightheartedly, "but don't pass on this opportunity because you're afraid to fail."

"That just makes you a pussy," Echo added bluntly.

A terse laugh shot out of me. "I'll take it all into consideration."

"Take the girl into consideration too, while you're at it," Sam suggested. "Sweetens the deal doesn't it? Something to come home to."

The thought of walking through the door every day to a waiting and willing Ophelia made the center of my chest do that aching, uncomfortable thing again like coiling barbed wire around an organ.

"We're friends," I forced myself to say. "She's a good girl, and a good friend. I needed to get myself out there again after Vanessa."

"Vanessa?" Tyler's eyebrows shot to his hairline. "You haven't gotten fucked since Vanessa?"

"Give him a break," Cap urged.

"You may screw a new chick every weekend but none of us have a date for the wedding in June," I pointed out.

"Doesn't Natalia have, like, three sisters?" Tyler asked, flicking his own bottle cap at me. "I'd be a fucking fool not to show up hungry to a buffet."

"Not happening." Mateo put a foot down. "My sister-in-laws are off-limits. It's nonnegotiable."

Tyler smiled. "We'll see."

I tipped back in my chair, taking in the full curve of a waxing moon. The stars were all out, blinking rhythmically. Brisk air burned the shallow wells of my nostrils and the corners of my mouth tipped up. "I missed you guys."

36

Ophelia

My previous New Year's Eve looked a lot different than this one. I was snowed in by myself as Pine Ridge endured a record accumulation for the last day of December. There wasn't a car on the road that wasn't a plow, and if you could even see out your windows past six o'clock, there was nothing but a blanket of powdery white reflecting the moon and turning the outside one muted shade of gray.

I had curled up on the couch in the baggiest pair of sweats I owned, a monochromatic green number that made me look like a peapod, shoved my face full of cheese puffs because there wasn't a Postmates in the state delivering, and indulged in the trashiest reality dating show I could find.

I laughed, I cried, I ironically screamed at the women on my television for not recognizing a man's blatantly obvious red flags.

By the time I remembered to check the clock it was after midnight and I'd entirely missed the ball drop to ring in the new year. In lieu of champagne I did a shot of tequila and sent myself to bed.

Miami Beach was so far removed from Pine Ridge they might as well be on opposite poles. Spending the night in a swanky downtown hotel and pregaming with bottles of Veuve Clicquot was even more out of my element. Despite the promising night ahead, I was still painfully aware of the dwindling hours I had left in Florida.

We split into two cars for the drive south, Sam and the soon-to-be Durans in one car and Frankie and I with the company of Tyler in another. Echo was a talker, filling every spare second of quiet with a story or a joke. I got an earful about Frankie in Delta, his aversion to the bugs in the jungle, creative ways he found to make freeze-dried meals more palatable, the little battery-powered sound machine he kept in his sleeping bag that was the butt of many jokes.

Tyler's booming laugh was so infectious that by the time we arrived in the Magic City the muscles in my cheeks were tired and aching. He slung not only his bag but mine and Frankie's over his shoulder like a bundle of groceries and smooth-talked us all into a luxury suite at the top of the tower.

"That upgrade will go straight to his head," Frankie said.

"He's got what they call *je ne sais quoi*." I shrugged.

"Or a venereal disease that sounds close to it."

I elbowed Frankie between the ribs, digging the sharp bone in as deep as I could to get a rise out of him. He only pulled me closer, hooking his arm around my shoulders until my nose was level with his armpit and I got a full musky inhale of sandalwood and sweat. I'd grown so fond of the way he smelled: fresh out of the shower, after sex, in the middle of the day as I shoved my face into his shirt.

The lobby was massive with golden vaulted ceilings, chandeliers hanging like spiderwebs, avant-garde indoor fountains, and lush potted Zanzibar. Music echoed against the walls from somewhere deeper in the hotel, and the sound of Natalia's heels striking tile stood out against the hum of a hundred conversations.

Frankie's lips connected with the top of my head and he twirled a strand of my hair around his finger. He was so naturally and physically affectionate, something I realized was never notable with other men I dated, and I was going to crave that type of intimacy when it was gone.

"I missed you last night," I said. We fell behind our group, watching the bob of Tyler's close-cropped head weave in and out of the busy main level. "Nat isn't much of a big spoon."

"You could have texted me," Frankie acknowledged. "I would have, but I didn't want to pressure you too much. Things are weird right now."

Weird was putting it in a more quirky, less honest, and painful way. Fortunately there was nothing a good few drinks couldn't dull the sharp stab of. Even so, ignoring something so blatantly apparent was immature and burdensome and it was much better to be in agreement.

"It'll be hard enough to say goodbye," I told him honestly.

"I know." His mouth twisted. "I know what you're doing and I get it. I'm glad you're setting that boundary, because I'm not physically strong enough to deny myself any part of you, especially the soft, tight little nooks I squeeze so nicely into."

A delightful pang of heat melted through me as his hand slid down to rest on my hip as we walked. "Let's just have fun tonight, okay? We're both on the same page. That's what matters."

"Right," he agreed. "So let me eat you out before we leave later."

"No!" I elbowed him again, his grip tightening as I tried to wiggle away. Frankie's full lips curved up on one side, that flirty, mischievous smirk giving me just enough pause to consider how my body reacted so sweetly to his advances. "Maybe."

"As friends," he added, patting my ass.

I was never as strong as I pretended to be.

I SAT IN BETWEEN Natalia's legs on the floor, staring at my reflection in the wall mirror as she dropped my hair in thick, ringlet curls down my back. My blood pressure spiked every time she laid the burning hot iron on the white down comforter on the bed beside her.

Our hotel suite was magnificent. Floor-to-ceiling windows in the shared living room looked out across the city, bright and neon lights like pinholes in a dark tapestry, traffic twisting and winding on the streets below. We could make out the tiny dots of people in parallel windows moving about, TV screens, and Christmas trees still lit up inside residential complexes.

Everyone separated into their own spaces to get ready for the night out and Nat and I called dibs on the biggest room with the deep cradle bathtub and double vanity, as if we'd be spending any time in it beyond getting dressed and sleeping. Frankie clearly expected that he and I would bunk together and stood in the open doorway with his arms crossed expectantly while Nat and I discussed our outfit choices. Until he gave up and sulked away.

I stretched my legs out in front of me, assessing the red polish on my toenails that had begun to chip away since our trip to the spa a few weeks ago. So strange to think how different things were. Frankie and I barely knew each other then; I was certain I had him figured out and I couldn't have been more wrong. I never would have guessed I'd be mourning the loss of the man I met on that plane, especially not while he was still very much available to me. But there I was getting emotional about needing a new pedicure.

"I can't believe tomorrow is my last full day," I said. Nat's eyebrows were scrunched in concentration as she twirled a brown strand of hair around the silver barrel.

"Don't remind me." She frowned. "Let's never go that long without seeing each other again."

"Never," I swore. "I'm going back to Colorado with a list of dates to take off for the wedding and I already switched on the price alerts for flights to Florida."

"I'm proud of you." She stopped curling and we regarded each other in the mirror. "For stepping out of your comfort zone to come down here and spend the holidays with us. I know it wasn't easy putting yourself before your family. If you're half as great a sister as you are a friend I know they're missing you profusely right now."

"My dad called this morning and insisted on picking me up from the airport, and that man insists upon nothing, so that was all I needed to know," I told her. "I miss them, too. But I'm not ready to go yet."

She sighed. "I know. As much as I wish it were me you're sad to leave, I can take a back seat to Frankie because he made this whole thing worth your while. I just wish he'd take his head out of his ass and make a decision about the job already."

"I *am* sad about leaving you." My eyes rolled. "And I will miss Frankie, but I'll also miss Mateo, and fuck, I'll probably miss the other two if I'm being honest. I'm just going to miss the feeling of *togetherness* as a whole. That's what I've been lacking for so long."

"You're the queen of deflection." She paused. "If playing him down is your lame way of cushioning the fact that you're leaving the only guy you've ever had feelings like this for—just say that."

I squinted at her scrutinizing reflection, my left eye twitching faintly. "Don't make me."

"If he knew there was a chance, Phee..."

"He does! He does know that," I explained. "But it's selfish of me to hope he might leave his family here and follow me to Colorado when we've only known each other for three weeks. This is the honeymoon phase of a relationship where everything is new and all we want to do is have sex and get fat together. What if I realize eventually that I hate the way he folds towels or he goes bald and I can't stop imagining myself sleeping with Howie Mandel? What the fuck then, Nat?"

"Have you seen that man?" She raised an eyebrow. "He's never going bald."

"The towels are still a problem."

"You're reaching so far you could hook the moon."

"The point is that I can't get my hopes up. I've been let down too many times by too many people, so I'm going to make the most of these last two days and *try* to detach myself. Even if that means lying to my own face in the mirror. We are practicing self-preservation in the new year."

"Well that doesn't start for another six hours." Nat rolled off the bed and bounced on the balls of her feet into the bathroom, calling out through the open door, "So forget the damn resolutions and wear those pants I told you to wear!"

37

Ophelia

WHEN I THOUGHT ABOUT it in my normal, very deep, and entirely too metaphorical for the average person sense, Florida was coming together like two sturdy bookends. My Coconut Creek Christmas started and ended with pregame alcohol, an outfit that squeezed every breath of air out of me, strobe lights, sticky bar floors, and bass thudding so violently through my bones that speaking to the person next to me was like doing so underwater. The longer the night went on the more the crowd built, until we were a sea of bobbing heads and flailing bodies, and everything not directly in front of me started to blur.

Natalia pulled me in and out of the swell for all her favorite songs, which were most of them, until we were misted in a sheen of sweat, and our calves were aching from hours of exertion. The difference between then and that first night out was the company. It was hard not to feel invincible with four former special operators close by, following our every move. Mateo and Frankie like watch dogs, sporadically joining in and keeping us hydrated, and even when we thought we'd lost Tyler or Sam for good, they'd show up with their hands full of shot glasses to pass around.

The music changed and I felt a chest at my back and fingers lacing through the loops of my waistband. My hips went one way and Frankie's shortly followed, the familiar strength of his arms guiding me to roll against him. My head dropped to his shoulder and his lips lowered to the juncture where my jaw met my neck. The second I closed my eyes and the room started spinning I realized exactly how drunk I was.

"Let me get you some water," he offered, kissing the skin. His lips were cold and I lifted up on my toes to follow them as he pulled away. "Sam got us a table."

I jiggled my empty glass of vodka and juice and let him steer me by my hips to the edge of the crowd where the sound flattened like popping your ears at altitude. Tyler Swan was deep in conversation at the edge of the bar, tracing his fingers down the spaghetti strap of a blonde's tank top. She stepped closer to him, standing between his legs.

"He's good," I said out loud. "Whatever he's saying, she's into him."

We lingered between the table and the bar for a moment. Frankie's fingers tightened on my waist. "You think you'd be?" he asked, motioning toward Tyler. "I've never seen someone turn him down."

"Before we met." I laughed, my vision swimming as I looked from Tyler to Frankie. His lips thinned into a flat line. "He's very hot, and I'm very shallow."

"I forgot that little detail about you," he said sarcastically. "Must have gotten lost somewhere in all those private conversations."

"You're the only one that gets that side of me." I nudged him, inching onto my toes to get closer to his face. Frankie's eyes dropped to my lips and then leveled with me. "The next guy will be a poor, underappreciated bastard after you."

His mouth opened to say something, thick brown eyebrows pulled together like curtains creasing his forehead. We were cutting the air between us into pieces with silence and I swear his pupils dilated into black holes. Then his jaw snapped shut, the haze dispersing as he backed me toward the half-circle booth where Sam was sitting alone.

"Stay here," he instructed me. Then he pointed at his friend. "Make sure this one doesn't get herself into any trouble. She's very good at that."

Sam lifted his right hand in salute. "Copy that."

I plopped down beside him on the leather cushions, feeling all that adrenaline from the dance floor simmer to nothing but a dull throb in the heels of my feet. Frankie stalked away, toward where Tyler was standing against the bar.

"Not much of a dancer?" I asked.

"It's more fun to watch." His gentle cadence somehow rose over the music. "Observing people being weird and human is a favorite pastime of mine."

"Really?" I snorted, plucking his drink out of his hand and taking a generous swig of bitter brown liquor. Then regretting it instantly. It tasted like motor oil and burnt citrus, and the cherry at the bottom did nothing but sour my taste buds after I shoved it into my mouth. My teeth slid across my tongue trying to scrape the flavor away.

"Like that." His lips tugged up at the corner. "You just went through the seven stages of grief over an Old Fashioned. I got to see a little slice of life happening in this head." He tapped his pointer finger between my eyes.

"So you're sitting here, watching people have fun, and that's *your* definition of fun?"

"Look over there." Sam pointed through the crowd to a couple standing in the corner. I scooted closer to his side, squinting at them. Sam Swan smelled like mint and that same citrus I was still trying to forget the taste of. "She is so not interested in him. It's painful at this point," he said. "My guess is this is a first date gone wrong, or catfish situation. He probably said he was six-one when the guy is pushing five-nine in those clunky fucking dress shoes. He's been drinking Long Island Iced Teas, which is a disaster waiting to happen, and she's had her nose stuck to her phone screen for twenty minutes. Probably coming up with an excuse and an alibi before midnight so she doesn't get stuck smooching Mr. Wrong."

"Or maybe," I suggested, "they've actually been together for years but they got in a fight on the car ride over. Something about her taking too long in the bathroom, or him leaving all the lights on and forgetting to feed the cat. Really lame reasons but both are too stubborn to be the one to apologize first. So being resentful, he decided to start slamming Long Islands to take the edge off, because they're delicious and guaranteed to get you fucked up, while she's on the phone begging her friends to get here faster."

Sam's light eyes twinkled in amusement. "Right, well, you don't seem like you're having fun at all, Ophelia."

"It's a little fun," I admitted.

"What about these guys?" Sam put a friendly arm around my shoulder and veered my attention toward two men sitting by themselves in a large booth. Both were wearing black, save for the flashy silver jewelry that turned fiery under the lights every time they strobed past. On the table in front of them sat a few unopened bottles sweating on ice and neither of them were speaking or remotely interested in the other's company, which was obvious as they kept their heads on a swivel.

"A bunch of assholes," I jeered. "Waiting for women to come to them because they're wearing flashy, tasteless watches and have a couple bottles of Dom Pérignon on the table. The reason they have to do that is because no one would be interested in them in the daylight. I can guarantee that one or both of them have a podcast or trade Bitcoin and they think they are so *much better* than everyone else here because of it, but come later tonight they'll be totally alone in their barren apartments writing a manifesto on the fall of femininity."

Sam leaned back a tad, taking a sip of his drink and giving all those words that spilled out of my mouth the space they needed. His arm around my shoulders loosened, but remained across the booth behind me. "Tell me how you really feel." His bright smirk was just as ravishing as the wink that accompanied it.

"Too much?" I laughed. "I don't hate all men, I swear. I am a man lover. Men are amazing. I'm a big fan."

"I'm convinced." He assessed me. "I spend a lot of time reading people. Believe it or not I've had you pinned since yesterday, and you passed the test."

"What was the test?" I turned fully toward him, and Sam's eyes flitted behind me briefly, something catching his attention just enough to amuse him.

"If you're good enough for my pilot," he said bluntly.

I shifted uncomfortably, finding a loose seam in my jeans to pick at. "Frankie and I are just—"

"Friends," Sam finished, placing a hand on my arm to keep me from turning away from him. "Yeah, he said that. And you're both full of shit."

"Really—" I swore, stiffening as Sam's thumb began grazing back and forth across my arm.

He leaned closer. "You want to know how I know that there's nothing platonic about what's going on with you two?"

Did I? My throat had gone bone dry and the feeling of another man's fingers on me, even as innocently as that, sent a chill of discomfort across my entire body.

"Because for the last few minutes I've been talking to you, but I've really been watching Pike over there by the bar white knuckling that glass of water he's holding. He put you here because he knows you're safe, and he trusts that I'm not interested—and I'm not," he said. "But I know my friend and, don't take this the wrong way, sometimes he needs someone to play with his toys to remind him he doesn't share well with others."

My spine tingled, as if I could *feel* Frankie's eyes burning into me. I attempted to turn again, but Sam hooked a finger under my jaw and kept me from doing it.

"He says you're just friends, but he *hates* that I made you laugh. That really pissed him off. He hates that I held your attention, that we found something entertaining to talk about when he wasn't here, that you can even fathom a connection with someone who isn't him. And he's holding his breath right now because I'm touching you and he wants to fucking kill me, but he knows he has no right to feel like that. Because you're just friends, right?"

"Right," I squeaked.

"And what about you?" Sam's head tilted slightly. "Every ounce of your blood went cold the second I laid a finger on you. I'd be offended if I didn't know it has nothing to do with me, and everything to do with Frankie and the emotions he wears so blatantly on his sleeve. Always has."

I cleared my throat, rolling my neck on my shoulders. There was really no use playing clueless anymore. Sam had a way of stripping the protective layer away from me *and* Frankie, apparently. Maybe it had something to do with the affinity for observation. Maybe we were just shit at hiding it and no one was as brash as Sam forcing me to face it.

"And what exactly are his emotions saying right now?" I bravely inquired.

"He's losing his mind over you." Sam's chin lifted, gesturing behind me. "Turn around and see for yourself."

I finally slipped through his gentle grasp, cool air washing over the small spots his fingers had been. Anticipation gave me pause, unsure of what might be going through Frankie's mind at that moment or if I was ready to answer to it.

For all the same reasons, I said fuck it, and twisted back in the direction of the bar. Only to be met with the slap of ardent displeasure, so hot it could brand me, and the most daunting glare I'd ever seen on a man before.

38

Frankie

ENVY WAS A NASTY, ugly thing—and I was full of it.

Sam was not the brother I was supposed to be worried about
making eyes at Ophelia, and from where I stood that was exactly
the wrong assumption. Sure, I could have just been hyper-aware
of her body language, and the way she leaned into him so easily
was probably my mind making things out to be worse than they
actually were. But I was already walking a tight rope between
keeping her and losing her. Seeing how easy it seemed for another man to slide into my seat, steal her attention, make her
laugh—*make her fucking laugh*—did something rogue and hateful
that snapped the thin string still holding my veil of courtesy
together.

I could almost hear them, talking about life out West, how
similar their upbringings were, all the mountains in Utah that
the Swans spent their winters skiing and snowboarding, just like

Ophelia mentioned she used to do with her family. He could take her to that cabin and lie in the snow, looking at the sky and catching happy fucking snowflakes on their tongues together. There would be dozens of Sams throwing themselves at her in Colorado once she got home.

The glass of water in my hand was sweating so much it was in danger of slipping through my fingers. For a very short, depressing moment I thought about letting it do just that, to see if Ophelia would even turn around or notice. What made my pity party worse was that I knew Sam would never pursue her. Any conversation they were having had nothing to do with his interest in taking her, but his insistence in keeping me from making a mistake I couldn't easily come back from.

No part of me actually believed it was so easy for her to move on, and I wouldn't have, if I wasn't drinking, or feeling sorry for myself, and letting those sadistic, intrusive, rampaging hypotheticals have their way with me. What if the bubble we were living in popped the second she flew out of state? What if this younger, peppier, life lesson of a woman was just that? And we were hindering one another by not letting lust be lust? I forgot what it felt like to have a woman clenched around me, underneath me, praising how good I felt in my ear. It was like a high, and everything else was painted gold no matter if it was pink, blue, purple, or glaringly fucking red.

I convinced myself that *that* was what I didn't want to lose. Just like I convinced myself that Sam's arm around her shoulder and his fingers on her chin were clear signs that she was ending this whole thing between us before midnight even came knocking. I couldn't blame her, but it did nothing but choke my ego and make me sick to my stomach with jealousy.

When she finally whipped around, brown curls of hair falling off her shoulder and halfway down her back, and my favorite soft blue eyes, hooded with happiness latching onto mine, it reminded me exactly why I couldn't let her leave me worse than she found me. I couldn't let losing Ophelia send me to another rock bottom that I'd need to drag myself out of, because this one was a long way down.

Tyler saddled up against the bar top, flanked by two women, and slid another amber-colored beer in my direction, the foamy head sloshing over the glass onto the wood grain. I traded Ophelia's water for it and sat back on my heels, digging my lower back into the counter until it started to pinch a nerve.

"What's wrong?" Tyler asked. "And don't say nothing. You keep your face like that any longer the scowl will become permanent."

"You sound like your dad," I replied gruffly.

Tyler turned to face the floor, catching what I'd spent the last five minutes staring at. Sam and Ophelia were still chatting, but she'd scooted a good foot away after catching a glimpse of me and I couldn't tell if that was out of pity or guilt.

"Sometimes I forget that you have real feelings in here." He poked at the center of my chest. "Sam isn't trying to steal your girl, Pike."

"I know." I sighed, lifting the beer to my lips. "But it doesn't really look like he has to."

"You're reading into it because you're worried."

"Maybe." I shrugged. Ophelia glimpsed over her shoulder at Echo and I again—then to our left at the two women still lingering next to him. A muscle in my jaw ticked. "Who are your friends?"

Tyler blinked slowly, culpable passiveness sending his tongue into the side of his cheek. My friend might have been a dog but he was loyal like one too, and much like his brother, he could read intention on my face like it was written out in permanent marker. "Do you actually care?"

"It's a bit rude of you not to introduce them," I said. "Wouldn't want to give that impression."

He shook his head. "You're not dragging me into this."

With a huff of annoyance I pushed him back against the bar, extending my hand out toward the girls standing there. "I'm Frankie," I said to the raven-haired one, then her blonde friend, who quickly traded places with Tyler and ended up beside me with her own little palm extended.

"Elle," she squeaked.

Perfect. Trade one letter for another. Elle was a good foot shorter than me in heels, and had full, red cheeks like cherries and pinched little lips. There was a perfectly round beauty mark right under her nose and I spent a second too long looking at it because I couldn't tell if it was real or drawn on.

She was best friend's little sister cute, veritably bubbly, and entirely too young for me to even be entertaining a conversation with. Like, first year out of college young. Which was more concerning to me than anything. I knew I couldn't be mistaken for twenty-something, and neither could Tyler.

Despite it, and because my internal intentions were clear, I noticed her razor-pointed nails were curled around a nearly empty drink, and I offered to buy her a new one.

"Were you in the Army like your friend?" she asked.

"Yes," I answered.

"Do you live around here?"

"I don't."

"Work around here?"

My head shook back and forth.

"Just visiting?"

"Just visiting," I confirmed distractedly, peering out of the corner of my eye toward the booth where I'd left Ophelia.

"You're not much of a talker," Elle acknowledged.

I chewed on the end of my tongue. I didn't know what the fuck I was doing except being petty and retaliatory. I had no interest in wooing another woman into bed with me. This was partially to prove to myself that I could if I wanted to, but at the end of the day, I really, really didn't. "Can I be honest with you, Elle?"

She shifted on her heels, pressing further into my side, her breasts skimming the thin material of my dress shirt. I disliked it so much that a log of unease lodged itself at the base of my throat and every muscle in my face struggled to stay neutral.

"Of course," she replied.

"I don't go out to bars and pick up women, especially not ones that are as young as you, and I don't intend to start doing it tonight." She twirled two little black straws around in her drink, right where her cleavage was spilling out of her dress. "You're very pretty, and there's a fuck ton of guys here your age that would lose their minds if you gave them even a second of your attention."

"But you're the one that bought me a drink," she pointed out. "Very contradictory, Frankie."

I grinned softly. "Because yours was empty."

Again, my attention flitted toward the booths where I caught Ophelia, this time looking directly at me. Returning some of that fiery contention I'd felt inside myself minutes earlier. Her brows pinched together, lips pursed. I would bet she was leaving little semi-circles of frustration on the skin inside her closed palms. The look of possession she wore, the warning of something volatile brewing beneath an otherwise beautifully collected woman—that excited me. I wanted to stoke that ember until it ignited into something more.

"I only date older men," Elle said matter-of-factly. "The ones my age are boring, quick on the trigger, and can never get me off."

She slid one of those pointy nails down the outside of my arm and I bristled like a fucking porcupine warding off a predator.

"Your confidence in me is flattering, and misplaced. And a tiny bit concerning, Elle," I said gently, peeling her fingers off my arm and closing them into my other hand like a Venus fly trap. "It's not going to happen with me."

She flipped my left hand over. "No ring."

"I'm not married."

"Gay?"

I rolled my eyes and shook my wrist out of her hold.

"Oh, I see." She took a step backward, seemingly reading me with a scan of her darkly lined eyes. "You're hung up over someone. Either she broke your heart, you messed up, right person, wrong time, or the one that got away," she guessed. "I'm not here looking for commitment, Frankie. You can take all that middle-aged, sad, military man frustration out on me as a token for your service."

If that weren't already a pathetic enough bargain, she saluted me eagerly, sending a splash of vodka soda onto the floor between our feet.

"I have a bad track record," I mumbled.

Tyler scuttled away with Elle's friend, and Mateo was somewhere in the masses of dancing bodies in front of the DJ with Tally. Sam was the last person I wanted to wave a flag to for rescue, but it didn't matter anyway, because the table where he and Ophelia were sitting was vacant. My blood cooled instantly as I whipped around looking for them, dying to be wrong about my assumptions and worried about the person I was about to become if I wasn't.

I loosened the tie around my neck until it hung at my chest, shucking the buttons open with forceful pinches. A sweat had begun to bead at my nape and I wasn't certain if it was the crowded club or my body responding to my woman falling like sand through my grasp.

A cool, wet glass graced the back of my neck and I turned once again, assuming I'd have to ward off Elle for a final time, but was met instead with an amused, albeit cold Ophelia where the girl was standing seconds before.

She raised an eyebrow, waving in the direction of the crowd. "If you're looking for the blonde, she just got picked up by her parents."

"Where did you go?" My tone was immediately aggressive and I couldn't take it back.

She breathed out a sigh of disbelief, jingling the glass of water and its half-melted ice cubes in front of my face. "Coming to get the drink you got too distracted to bring back to me."

"You seemed pretty occupied yourself, O. Didn't want to interrupt."

"Oh, you can't be serious right now." The strobe lights painted us both in blues and greens as loud music vibrated the floor.

"I can't be serious? I have two eyes just like you do."

"Maybe you need to get them checked. Sam is your *friend*, Frankie. You were the one who brought me over there in the first place. I didn't tell you to get caught up at the bar with Blondie, but you were quick to do that."

A bitter laugh ripped out of me. This girl was nothing short of a constant challenge. "We both knew how this was going to end, Ophelia. That was fine, but I thought you might at least wait until the plane fucking boarded first to find a replacement."

"He was being friendly." Her eyes zeroed into dark pinpoints.

"Friendly?" I stepped close enough to feel her little puffs of aggravated breath on my throat. "When I touch you like this, am I just being friendly?" My finger hooked through the belt loop on her jeans and I tugged her toward me, flush against my chest, then pinched her chin between my thumb and forefinger as Sam had. "Tell me, honestly."

"Honestly?" Ophelia's hands sunk into my shirt and she shoved me away. "This is you being a jealous dick." She whipped around, swaying toward the exit doors that opened onto a dark side street, and I bounded after her immediately.

"Have I ever told you how much I love chasing your pouty ass through bars?" I shouted as I caught up to her, just as she pushed through the heavy black door and outside. "I told you the first time we met, Ophelia. I don't share."

The sounds inside the club were snipped in half by the exit closing behind us. Only a dull thudding bass and the telltale sound of raucous chatter filtered through. My ears popped and my eyes adjusted to the darker alley we were standing in. Cigarette butts were scattered around the concrete at our feet.

"Sam wasn't fucking hitting on me," she growled, finally turning around.

"Only because he knows you're mine."

That visibly knocked the wind from her sails. Her clenched fists softened at her sides, while the crease between her eyes flattened to a silent acquisition. I watched her full, plum red lips part and my body recognized that change in her like an invitation.

I tried to wrap my fingers around the pulse at her neck and drag her to me, but she batted my hand away with little force instead.

"Now I *belong* to you?"

"You're goddamn right you do, Ophelia." I stepped forward, crowding her back into the brick wall, hiding in the shadows where the moon couldn't dip through the buildings and touch us. "We let this happen, we fucking did this to each other, O. And now we have to deal with it like adults. I have to find a way to *bleed you* from my veins, but that doesn't mean I'm not going to treat you like what you are while you're still here, and that is fucking *mine*."

This time when I reached for her she let me. I dug my fingertips into the tangled hair behind her ear, let my palm take on the pounding beat of her heart as it rested against her neck. She was fuming mad, pupils dilated into pools as dark as tourmaline, and our breath mingled in harsh, tandem huffs.

"You can't say things like that," she murmured, shaking her head.

"I don't care."

"This wasn't supposed to happen," she stressed, tugging on my loosened tie until it was wound around her little wrist. She was so close I could taste the hint of fruity alcohol she'd been sipping all night on her breath.

"Well it did."

A wave of loud cheering erupted from within the building, and the music hushed to rhythmic ticking, like a countdown on a clock. We both looked toward the door, neither moving, listening to the descent of muffled numbers as they dropped from thirty to twenty and then heightened to an unmistakable chorus as they began from ten.

Our friends were probably looking for us. I could read the same thought crossing Ophelia's mind, and yet there wasn't a fucking hurricane that could sweep through the city at that moment that would have pulled the two of us away.

"I want my New Year's kiss." I traced my thumb over her lips, pulling down the trembling bottom one to reveal little white caps of clenched teeth.

A muscle in her jaw tightened.

"Bite hard if you're going to."

The counting rattled down. *Three*. I nudged her firmly into the wall, wedging the cap of my knee between her thighs. *Two*. My grip on her jaw tightened and I tipped her head back, brushing the tip of my nose down the ridge of hers.

One.

Ophelia jerked me forward by my tie and molded her mouth over mine with a hard gasp like she had been holding her breath. I answered, sliding my tongue across the sharp edges of her canines, dipping it deeper to massage along her own. Kissing her was always tender, warm foreplay, but this was something more charged and desperate. She tugged on my lips with her teeth, biting me, licking me, directing us with her fingernails wedged into the long hair on the back of my head.

I ran my shaking, hungry fingers down her chest feeling her nipples bud against her soft velvet top. I squeezed her tits in my palms, pinching and tugging, rubbing quick circles, as she whimpered into my mouth. I would rip her fucking clothes off in the shadow of this alley without another thought, but it was a risk and this wasn't something either of us wanted interrupted.

She ground herself down onto my knee, catching the seam of her jeans exactly where she wanted to and sighing out a fuck-all sexy sound of pleasure. My dick ached like I'd never quite felt before, bulging against my belt. Half of my mind was already back in the hotel room, giving her every last deserved inch of it.

As if she could sense it, Ophelia reached down and fumbled with my buckle, pulling blindly with our lips still attached. She skated her nails up and down the length of me and I stifled a downright growl into the gentle curve where her neck met her shoulder. I wouldn't last another minute of it.

"We're leaving," I told her. "Now."

39

Frankie

WE FUMBLED LIKE NEWBORN deer learning how to use our legs for the first time through the door to the hotel room. My key card glared an angry, denying red twice before the lock finally gave in and we crashed forcefully into the first wall we could find, at last shut into a private, secure place where I could touch her without the threat of someone else's eyes on the girl that was mine.

She'd gone from pure, saturating anger, seconds away from throttling me in that alley to a predatory feline, targeting all my weaknesses while she knew there was nothing I could do but grin and bear it. By the time we fell out of the car and into the elevator I was one good tug or hot mouth around my dick away from losing it.

That ended the second the door closed behind us. Her control was admonished, the pedestal kicked out from beneath her high-heeled feet. Shoving her to the wall with my hand around her neck, I kissed her with such a bruising force that our teeth clattered together and she cried out in pleasant shock.

"I hope you enjoyed that ride back where you thought you had the control here." I leaned in close to her ear, making sure every last word touched her skin. "You got my cock so hard, baby. Now, you're gonna take care of it."

She instinctively wrapped her legs around my waist as I picked her up, carrying us the short distance to the bedroom Mateo and I were supposed to share. *What a fucking joke that was.*

"I'm so fucking mad at you," she spoke though gritted teeth, kissing me nonetheless. My tongue got lost in her mouth, swirling around all that misplaced malice and attitude, fucking her with it, shoving it down her throat. Her legs tightened around my waist, little fingers cinching together at the back of my neck, still fighting the inevitable way I was going to undo every last inkling of her conviction.

"Good, stay fucking mad at me. Fight me. Hit me. Give me your worst, Ophelia. Give me every last thing like a punishment, because I'm going to be thorough, and I'm going to remind you why there will never be someone else."

She lurched forward and bit my jaw so hard her teeth left jagged marks and all it did was turn me on more than I knew possible. I laughed through the short-lived pain, and then that laugh turned into a sound that started in my gut and rolled like thunder through my chest and onto her heaving body, vibrating against her.

"Fuck yes." My eyes rolled closed briefly, like flipping a docile switch, giving me that last green light I needed to keep all my promises.

I unwound her fingers and pinned her wrists above her head in one quick, harsh movement. My hands enveloped her bones. She couldn't break free if she used every ounce of her strength to do it.

"Bastard," she murmured, sticking her chin up, watching me through the thin slits of her eyes. Her tongue dipped out and wet the pad of her bottom lip.

"Bastard," I agreed. Her hips rolled against mine. "You want me to fuck you so badly you're grinding your pussy on me like a little cat, Ophelia." I crossed her wrists over one another, pressing them to the mattress with one of my hands and freeing up the other to slide down and cup right between her legs. "I'm going to pull your panties down and they're gonna be all wet and ruined. Aren't they?"

She tugged her lip into her mouth and ignored me as I traced the seam on her jeans from the top of her pussy to her ass.

"Because you like this so much," I taunted. "You like being dominated. You like being owned, and played with, and fought over. You like that I'm jealous enough to pin you to this bed and shove my cock down your throat until you admit that you're mine with pretty fucking tears streaking down your face. Right?"

"God, you talk a lot," she quipped, still avoiding looking at me. Her face was flush and dewy, a thin sheen of sweat breaking out against her temples and in that small hollow of her throat.

"I'm done talking," I decided. Her top was cinched together at the front with cheap, pliant clasps and I dug my fingers into the hem and ripped it open, corset tearing beneath my fingertips like pulling out stitches from skin. The second her taut, dark nipples were exposed to me I latched onto them, twisting and teething while her back arched beneath me.

Her dark jeans were painted on, so tight and firm against her flesh they drove me crazy all night and drove me even fucking crazier trying to get them down her legs. The button nipped my skin, the zipper fought me tooth to nail. I tugged and tugged, lifting her ass off the sheets and even giving it a frustrated, aggressive slap as she wriggled out of the denim attempting to help me.

I was sweating through my shirt by the time I wrung the damn things off her ankles and whipped them onto the floor, wasting no time wrenching her legs back open and shoving my face right into the damp, warm cotton covering her. I licked her over it, tasting the tang and salt and sweat, her perfect natural smell winding around my senses like vines. I loved the taste of cunt. There was nothing flowery to it, but I fucking loved Ophelia's pussy like I loved crackling fire, apple pie, and the first sip of a cold one after a long day. She was a staple fucking sensory experience for me. The kind you find yourself nostalgic over on a random Tuesday afternoon.

My thumb hooked through her thong, pulling it aside so I could see that throbbing pink mess she'd made, and my fingers slid dutifully inside her like dipping them straight into candle wax. Her walls constricted like a pulse around them. "So wet and perfect. You're too good to me, O."

She sounded strangled, chewing on a string of moans as I fucked her with my hand and opened her up. I couldn't help myself—I licked her alongside the glide of my fingers, twirling her swollen clit around my tongue, sucking on it until she started to whine and the desperation in her voice made my cock feel like it was caged.

I rubbed something ridged and shallow inside her and her whole body pulled taut.

"Right there?"

"Yes." She gasped out a confirmation that turned my grin wolfish.

Ruin her. Ruin her, so no one else can even come close.

"Remind me who makes you fucking come," I said sternly, lifting my head just enough to watch her answer me between jagged breaths.

"You do."

"No one else."

Her head rocked lazily back and forth against the bed. "No."

"Why is that, Ophelia?" My skin was on fire. I was ready to tear out of my clothes. Still I circled her clit with my thumb languidly, focusing every point of pressure into the stroke of my fingers inside of her.

She muttered out something unintelligible, still defiant and bratty and fighting me relentlessly so I reached up and pinched the peak of her nipple hard, sending a jolt of something painfully sensual through her. Ophelia's eyes snapped open and her jaw relaxed, her mouth curving into a soft circle.

"Speak up, I need to hear it."

"Because I'm yours."

I turned my head and sunk my teeth into the inside of her thigh, purposefully sucking a dark mark to the surface that was framed like art by the indent of my canines when I finally let her go. "That's my good fucking girl."

Ophelia struggled against my fingers and my mouth, battling equal parts pain and rapture until I shoved my tongue back between her legs and she melted like ice.

"Fuck, I'm going to come," she managed to cry out. Seconds later her thighs started shaking around my head, closing in on me like ear muffs as I lapped her from her twitching opening to the bead of her clit. "Pike...I'm..."

Pike.

I moaned against her pussy. My lips latched on and I devoured what felt like every last nerve in her body as it liquified onto my tongue. She came like an angel, writhing, whimpering, holding onto me like a solid anchor until she uncoiled from the high and deflated, satiated and sedative.

Unfortunately for her, I was quite the opposite, strung like a spool so tightly the wire was about to snap. "Sit up," I instructed her. My belt jingled as I slid leather through it, completely loosening and opening the waist of my slacks. It was so quiet between us I could hear the teeth of my zipper falling apart. "Come over here now, and wrap those defiant fucking lips around my cock and suck it."

I expected some amount of pushback, but she surprised me, folding underneath herself and onto all fours, dragging my pants down my hips eagerly, and watching me spring free right in front of her face. The release of that pressure felt good by itself, but then her tongue teased a hot, wet stripe up my entire shaft and I choked on the noise that came out of me.

I undressed fully as I grappled with the feeling of her entire mouth taking me to the base. That perfect tongue circling me, the back of her throat contracting on the head of my dick every time she swallowed.

"Choke on it for me."

I fisted her hair into a ponytail, rocking her head back and forth to take more and more until my balls drew tight and I couldn't waste another second not buried inside her.

Even as I dragged her up my body by her hair, reveling in the way she stopped and kissed every inch of my torso, leaving a trail of her mouth in her wake, igniting more than lust between us, it was pure fucking passion and affection. Despite me being rough, regardless of the wall of pain we were ignoring—or the reason we were even naked and sparring one another in the first place—there was so much respect tangled into this mess.

Ophelia kissed her way up my throat, to my chin, and I wretched her against my mouth in another hard lock of our lips that lasted heartbeats longer than I intended it to. Our bodies melded into one; I could feel her every breath like it echoed in my bones.

"I love kissing you," I whispered against her lips, "but I really love fucking you, and I need it right now. I need to feel you from the inside, baby. Okay?"

"Okay," she said.

"Are you still mad at me?"

"Furious."

"Good." I pinched her nipple and tugged on it. "Lay on your belly and hang your legs off the edge of the bed."

She hesitated, still dangling on her last thread of resistance. My fingers relaxed into gentle strokes and I turned her body, flattening my palm into the space between her shoulder blades, bending her toward the ruffled sheets. I stood on the floor behind her and dragged her by her ankles all the way to the end, where her ass was the perfect height for my waist and then tugged that final obtrusive layer of her panties down to her feet.

"You tell me you want it and then you fight me." I lined myself up between her legs and let my cock rest at her entrance, sliding it back and forth tauntingly. Half the friction was for me; I was dripping precum, and my dick was so full it was nearly red. I curled myself over her back until my chest was flush to her spine and my lips grazed her shoulders and neck. "It's fucking hot."

"You're obsessed with me," she mumbled with her cheek squished against the bed. All her hair was in disarray around her face, hanging in her eyes and over her lips. I bent her arms and pinned her wrists right at her tailbone.

"And you're a tease." The tip of my cock breached her, dipping in a mere inch, just enough to wet me and alleviate some of that pressure. She wiggled her hips, swallowing more of my length before I was ready for it and my whole lower half turned into one beating pulse that rang like a gong.

Fuck gentle, fuck passionate, fuck calculated. She needed it just as badly as I did, and if we were going to use one another one last time, it was going to feel like seeing God and living to imbue it.

I grabbed onto her waist, her skin melting between my fingers, and thrust into her all the way to that deep, sensitive wall that had her screaming my name. Ophelia's pliant cunt wrapped around me with every hard punch of my hips inside of her. The deeper I pushed myself the more impossible it became to have a sense of surrounding. Just me and her, the euphoria that was being connected, every nerve ending vibrating, stimulated, heating to an explosive, catastrophic climax.

I made sure she felt every last hard inch of me all the way in and out with nothing to do but take it and babble every colorful swear word she knew into the fluffy white hotel duvet.

"I am obsessed." I sunk my teeth into her shoulder as our bodies moved together. A damp film of sweat was starting to curl the short pieces of hair at her neck. "I'm obsessed with this pussy. I'm gonna fuck it so full you never forget how empty it feels without me."

"Frankie," she whined. My thrusts hit faster and her hips lifted off the bed. "Please—please."

The grip around my cock tightened, warm walls contracting in warning. "Oh, you're gonna come on me, aren't you?" Her nod was so faint and lazy, I tugged her back by her hair and forced her face off the bed. "I don't want your little whimpers. I want to know who you belong to, and whose cock you're gonna come all over like a good, submissive, grateful fucking girl."

"Yours," she ground out. "All yours, it's all yours."

"So give it to me," I grunted, reaching beneath her hips and rubbing my fingers over her clit. Ophelia wilted like flower petals, curling in on herself. Her muscles tightened around me, her pussy fluttered like the wings of a butterfly, one big swooping movement followed by a hundred smaller spasming ones.

My eyes rolled somewhere into the back of my head.

I miraculously managed to pull out of her before I went over the edge too, flipping her tiny, exhausted body onto her back and then shoving my cock right back inside of her. I cried out from the pleasure. Her groan was a hot mix of shock and overstimulation. Sharp fingernails dug into my back, right below the curve of my shoulder blades, and *my god* it would have been a miracle if she hadn't drawn blood.

"Mark me, baby. Leave me with something. Make me think about you every single time I fucking breathe." I didn't want to shower without the sting of water on tender flesh, or lie down without feeling her hands on my back. I wanted her long after the night poured into the morning and I had to pretend I didn't. "It feels so good. I don't want it to end."

Ophelia's lips twitched, knowing that confession transcended the sex. The pads of her fingers crawled up my neck and cupped my face, dragging my mouth down onto hers.

"I don't want it to, either."

My hips stuttered, and everything from my head to my heels hummed together in glorious unison as my cock flared inside of her, emptying in long, numbing pulls. All the while Ophelia held me the way I needed her to, clutching and digging, sinking into my skin where we both knew I'd never fully be able to heal the scars.

40

Ophelia

IT FELT LIKE YESTERDAY I was filing out of baggage claim with blind hope about a snarky pilot I'd met on the flight. Now I was attempting to shove three weeks of self-discovery and a pseudo-relationship into the bottom of my rolling luggage for the return to Colorado in a day.

For once I wasn't homesick for mountains and snow. I didn't care to return to the fresh scent of wind-swept pine needles. I didn't miss the cold air or the bite of frost every morning on the walk to my car. I wasn't worried about my siblings, or my students, the lesson plans I didn't write or the emails I left unanswered.

What I was dying to sweep like sand into a little glass bottle to keep was the smell of espresso leaking out of the coffee machine. The feel of my skin wrapped in flannel and cotton, warm fingertips tracing tan lines beneath the shade of covers. Secret kisses, butterfly wings, waves of brown hair tangled in between my fingers. I wanted to liquify the sound of his sleepy voice the first thing in the morning. Shove all of the moons we looked up at, and all the grass we walked on, and all the flowers we stopped to admire into a jar and keep them forever.

Big, annoying feelings for the woman who spent so much time thinking emotion like that could never exist.

"Your carry-on looks like you robbed a toy drive," Nat said.

The gifts I'd wrapped to take home were stacked inside a tote bag and garnished with silver bows. I couldn't shove them in the suitcase without crushing everything, and Nat already had to sit on it while I wrestled the fickle zipper shut.

Her guest room was empty and hollow, all the drawers clear of clothes, the closet back to Natalia's own wardrobe overflow. Ironically we'd spent more nights across town at the house than we had the quaint little apartment.

"Remind me why you still live here again?"

"Independence." She shrugged. "But really because I told Mateo I'd never live with a man without a ring on my finger and now look at me. Full commitment in less than a year."

"Evil genius." I cackled. "Is that the secret? Be obtusely unavailable? Play them at their own game?"

Nat collapsed on the bed on her stomach and kicked her feet up behind her. "Men are so simple. You make everything an ultimatum with you on one end and whatever bullshit misogynistic thing they learned from their mother on the other. At the end of the day Mommy isn't the one on her knees."

My nose wrinkled. "I hate when you make good points the bad way and send me farther and farther away from grace."

"Grace doesn't come back from Miami covered in *bite marks*, babe."

My hand shot to the side of my neck. "He made me a whore."

"You always were, deep down. You just needed the right key to unlock it."

I put my hands on my hips and did a cursory glance around the room. "What if...there's only one key? And all the other keys are too jagged or small or just try to shove themselves in and break off inside the keyhole?"

"Well..." Nat tilted her head. "If there's only one key, and then you lose it, you can always...go get a replacement that does the job just the same. It might just take some time."

"I'm very attached to my key."

"It's a good key."

"Very sturdy," I added.

"That's an important quality," she agreed.

"Versatile."

"Mine's been known to open an Amazon package or two."

"Well endowed."

Nat grimaced. "I can't keep playing this game."

"Fuck." I blew out an overwhelmed breath. Which turned into a staring contest with the ceiling where my eyes welled with tears and I tried and failed to will them away with my tongue in my cheek.

"Oh God, Phee. I'm sorry." Natalia hopped up from the bed and embraced me, tucking her shorter frame under my arms and laying a cheek on my chest.

"It's my fault." I sniffled. "You warned me."

"I also totally condoned it, and up until a few days ago had no regrets because you guys *needed* each other. I guess I just didn't realize how much."

Natalia thought we needed each other like someone might need a vitamin. For enhancement, a push, strength, better overall well-being. No, Frankie and I needed each other like an IV.

"I'm as shocked as you are," I admitted. "I feel like I met someone who really sees me. He dug up all these habits I thought were rooted and made me reflect on them instead of water them."

"He also made you a fucking poet apparently."

I laughed, the motion releasing a solo tear down my face that I wiped away. "What the fuck? This vacation was supposed to be relaxing and quiet and now I'm crying in your guest bedroom over a man I didn't even know a month ago."

"This isn't the end," she said. "He's in Mateo's life like you're in mine. You'll see him at a million more functions. And who knows? Maybe in a few months he'll be out in Colorado too."

In a few months we could also both be completely different people if this entire experience had taught me anything.

The bell chimed at the front door and we pulled away from one another gently.

"Dinner's here," Nat chirped. "Come out when you're ready."

She disappeared through the open door and a few seconds later the chatter of voices sifted down the hallway, reaching me in whispers. Instead of joining them, I curled in on myself, checked the bathroom for the hundredth time, opened and closed every last drawer, pretended any of my dresses might have gotten mixed in with Natalia's. Then I organized my outfit for the plane, folded it like I would at a department store, made a physical note in my phone not to forget the charger plugged into the wall behind the nightstand, and got down on my hands and knees to stick my head under the bed and check I hadn't lost a stray sock.

It was only then that a shadow eclipsed me from the doorway, followed by the gruff clearing of said shadow's throat.

"You could knock," I quipped, retreating from under the frame. Too quickly though, and I smacked the back of my head on the low-hanging metal. "Son of a bitch."

"I didn't want to scare you." Frankie's voice came closer. "And I was enjoying the view." Two big palms hooked under my arms and lifted me off the floor and onto the bed. "You okay?"

"I'll survive," I muttered, rubbing the crown of my head.

"Did you find what you were looking for?"

A trap door, a safe room, a little hole to crawl into if it meant avoiding that final dinner with my friends before I had to go back to Colorado.

The longer I prolonged it the farther away it got, right?

"Not exactly." I sighed.

Frankie sat next to me with his hands clasped between his knees. His blue jeans were tight around his thighs, the flannel shirt he wore rolled perfectly up his forearms. I started mapping the veins as they overlapped one another.

"You forgot a few things at the house," he said. "I didn't know if they were important." He emptied the contents of his pocket into his palm.

"Bobby pins?" I snorted.

"I'm assuming *not* important, then."

I shook my head, letting him dump the straight clips into my hand.

"Then there's this." Again, diving into the pocket at the seat of his pants, Frankie pulled my red thong out and dangled it in front of me. "Not really my color. Or size. Not for lack of trying."

"I'd have to make that judgment for myself."

"You don't want to ruin your perfect image of me right before you leave." He nudged the panties in my direction again but I pushed them back at him.

"They're all yours," I said. "A souvenir for all your hard work."

"I already kept your body wash," Frankie admitted. "My skin feels like a fucking baby seal."

"It's amazing what graduating from bar soap can do for you."

"You were into me before you knew what was in my shower." He winked, folding my underwear back into his pocket without another question.

"Well I'm keeping this." I gestured to the oversized Army sweater I was wearing. Then curled my fingers into the sleeves and wrapped my arms around my body.

"You look better in it than I ever did." Frankie reached over and tugged on the neckline, uncovering the necklace beneath it and rubbed the little blue butterfly between his fingers.

I dropped back onto the mattress, staring up at the ceiling while Frankie leaned over me. His warm palm skated across my belly and snuck under my shirt, tracing little circles into the hollow of my rib cage.

"This bed is so uncomfortable," he whispered.

"Thank God some guy let me crash in his."

"His bed must be really cold and lonely, because you are a sweaty little space heater and now there's just an Ophelia-shaped divot in the mattress."

"That feels like it should offend me."

Frankie dipped down and lifted the sweater just enough to kiss the sliver of my exposed stomach. "You are so perfect I'm not entirely sure I'm not dreaming."

My eyes fluttered closed. "That's better."

Because we woke up naked and hungover in a hotel room and had to opt for a late checkout to make sure there was enough time to drag Tyler Swan and his *guests* out of bed, I hadn't eaten all day. My stomach started making whale noises as a result.

"There's a burger with your name on it out there." Frankie sat up, bringing me with him by my limp arms.

"Bacon?" I mumbled.

"And extra crispy fries."

"With—"

"A cup of ranch on the side. I even opened up the box so it didn't get soggy while you hid in here under the bed."

My gut did this hollow thing that felt like it was swallowing itself and emotion like heartburn delved deeply into the cave of my chest. "Be mean to me." I gripped the collar of his shirt. "Do something really fucked up and cringy so this is easier for fuck's sake."

"No." He chuckled. "No, I can't. I'm being selfish, but if it's hard for me it's gonna be hard for you, too. You can hate me for that."

"That's what she said."

Frankie blinked hard, shaking his head. "Get out." He brought me to my feet and nudged me toward the door. "The most incredible thing is that I'm not even surprised in the least."

41

Ophelia

SMALL TALK IS TEDIOUS and awkward, even more so when everyone is walking on eggshells around you. No one brought up Colorado, or flights, or asked if I was all packed up to go. We mostly ate in silence with the radio filtering in the background and an occasional comment about the night before.

I was grateful I didn't have to pretend I was looking forward to returning home when I was clearly dreading it. Instead, Frankie ate with one arm tucked behind my chair, our knees bumping beneath the table. He stole my fries, I helped myself to his beer. Natalia complained about the quiet after a while and filled the void with wedding chatter, ring choices, honeymoons, guest favors.

Then Mateo offered to do the dishes for the sheer excuse of *not* talking about wedding details. Frankie saddled up next to him and the two of them did the slowest washing of dinner plates and silverware I'd ever clocked while Natalia and I collapsed onto the couch with the Swans. Both of whom were still exhausted and hungover from the night before and would have much rather been back at the house in bed recovering.

Eventually the two arms that had begun to feel like home slid around me from behind, warm lips found the soft, tender side of my neck, and I knew without words it was the beginning of a goodbye we'd been avoiding for more time than was borrowed.

Nat squeezed my knee.

"I think it's about time we head out of here," Mateo said gently. He stood at the edge of the living room, rubbing his hands together. Tyler and Sam groaned as they peeled themselves off the couch and my heartbeat picked up inside my chest.

"Girls," Tyler said, shuffling over to Natalia and I and pulling us each into a bear hug. "It's been a pleasure-filled few days. We'll see what kind of trouble we can get into next time."

Sam nudged his brother out of the way, giving us each a friendly kiss on the cheek. "We'll see you in a few months. Safe flight, O. And if you ever need something, Salt Lake is a quick trip away." He winked at a hardly amused Frankie as he let himself out.

"Mateo." I grinned, outstretching my arms toward him. "Thank you for all the kind hospitality." He hugged me hard, squeezing my shoulders, rocking us off-balance back and forth. "You're welcome for all the beautiful Christmas decorations."

"They're so beautiful I'll probably just keep them up until next year."

"I'm sorry I almost burned down your house making cookies. And for stapling a pineapple to your siding." I winced. "And for walking in on you having Santa sex with Natalia."

"Let's forget about that," Frankie chimed in.

"No one forgets these tits," Nat acknowledged.

Frankie rubbed a palm down his face. "Then let's make a conscious effort to keep this little secret between the four of us, yeah?"

"I'm good with that." I raised a hand.

Nat shrugged. "That's fair."

"And thank you," I added, "for letting me be here for one of the most important moments of my best friend's life. She picked a good one."

Mateo pulled me in for another more emotional embrace. "You're family," he said. "Wouldn't have had it any other way."

Frankie and I found each other across the room and the air fell silent. That little muscle in his jaw was jumping on an otherwise indifferent face. I couldn't school myself like he could. My lip quivered despite worrying into it with my teeth, and emotion scrunched my nose.

"We'll give you guys a minute," Nat said, backing toward the front door.

No words felt significant enough to eclipse what the past three weeks had meant to me. The more I tried to string it together the harder it was to articulate, until I was just shaking my head with fragile little tears clouding my eyes.

"Baby." Frankie enveloped me, closing me into the cave of his arms with my head pressed into the center of his chest. "Please, don't."

"I think I'm about to get my period or something." I shrugged, hiding my red nose in his cotton T-shirt.

He let me have the excuse, instead running his fingers through the tangled waves of my hair, caressing my spine, swaying us gently on an invisible gust of wind.

"We don't really have to say bye, you know," he murmured. "I'll be there before you know it, the end of the month. I'll call you, and you can let me take you somewhere fancy for dinner."

His heartbeat rang in my ears. "And then what?" I asked vulnerably. "A couple weeks? A few more months?" Frankie's hold on me tightened, his fingers halting in place. "Am I waiting for something to be real between us, or am I just prolonging the end?"

"This is real, Ophelia." He lifted my chin and I couldn't hide the emotion streaking across my face. "Don't ever fucking minimize what this is. Your name is right here." As he lifted his hand to point at the center of his chest, his fingers were shaking. "It's under my skin."

I leaned forward and pressed my lips to the place his fingers were.

"I'm trying," Frankie confessed, sentiment scratching his throat.

I knew how nuanced that was. He was trying to be more emotionally available, trying not to fall into old habits, trying to separate his old life from a new one, forgive himself for things he couldn't have controlled, believe he could be the person I knew he was.

"So, no," he tacked on. "I'm going to save my goodbye. I know that goes against all these rules we had, but we fucked all those to hell anyway."

"Okay," I stammered out in a breath of amusement. "I'll save mine, too."

"Good."

Frankie dragged me closer. His lips met my forehead, then slid down the curve of my nose and connected there, finally falling right on top of my own and opening me gently to the familiar caress of his tongue. We kissed for a long time, training our memories with it, filling our cups. I would dream about his mouth on me forever.

"This was the best Christmas I've had in longer than I can remember," Frankie vowed once we'd broken apart.

"By far," I agreed.

We could have stood there all night "not saying goodbye", finding more things to blissfully agree on, stealing one more deeper kiss. I was the one to rip the bandage off and start the slow, silent trek to the front door.

"I'll see you in a few weeks, Trouble." Frankie tucked a strand of loose hair behind my ear. "Don't be getting in too much of it."

"As long as you promise not to lose my number the second you walk outside again."

A flicker of color returned to his dark eyes. "Who else would I have to sext at one in the morning?"

"The ladies at the retirement home, probably."

He scoffed alongside a smile, running his tongue across his top teeth. "Do me a favor?" Frankie asked as he cracked open the front door and stepped a foot outside. "Delete that fucking dating app off your phone."

I was pulled across the threshold into one final claiming kiss, and before the cold had fully swept out with the closed door behind him, I was emptying an entire folder on my cell into a trash bin.

42

Frankie

I WOKE UP BEFORE the birds. Earlier than my usual. The house was still dark, and a tiny sliver of moonlight cut through the windows into the living room. I stared at the coffee machine for a while before deciding to skip it, then opened the fridge and contemplated a beer before slamming it shut.

Routinely there'd be about an hour of time I spent alone in the house before Mateo rolled reluctantly out of bed. I'd have already showered, done some kind of cardio or weights with the rusting barbells in the garage. I'd have read the news, eaten some cereal, walked down to the mailbox and back and waved at the neighbors leaving for work like the good guy I was.

That regimen had been steamrolled by a western wind that made me never want to get out of bed in the morning again. Unless bringing her some breakfast or to brush my teeth and end up right back between her legs where I was supposed to be.

Instead sleep evaded me entirely and I found myself in the backyard with the indigo backdrop of still burning stars to keep me company. That lasted for about a half hour—before sitting in silence turned into sparring with my own thoughts. The best way I could imagine to curb that was by turning on the lawn mower and cutting three weeks of neglected grass down to a golfing green at five o'clock in the morning.

By six I was looking for gardening shears for the bushes, which turned into reorganizing the entire shed with a flashlight clenched between my teeth. When it was done, the sun was up and dogs had started barking around the block. I was covered in a sheet of dirt, sweating through my tee, and no less pathetically irritated with myself over Ophelia.

So I went to the fridge and took that beer.

I didn't even look up from the spot I'd zoned out staring at on the patio when the back door closed behind me.

"Tally just sent me two pictures and asked which color I liked better—Meet Me at Midnight, or Grease Lightning," Cap trilled. "Maybe I'm colorblind but I'm looking at the same fucking black suit."

"Just assume you're always wrong," I said.

Mateo sat at my side. "It's five o'clock somewhere." I felt his judgmental stare before he dusted a finger down my arm. "Where'd you bury the body?"

"Shed was a disaster."

"Yeah, well you missed a spot on the lawn, too."

I sat up. "Like fucking hell I did."

"I'm pretty sure there has to be laws against cutting your grass before the ass crack of dawn."

My lips pursed as I shot a look over the fence at Gino's house with a smidge of regret. "Can I be honest about something?"

"About time," Cap replied.

I fidgeted, tapping the armrest of the chair. "I don't know what the fuck I'm doing."

"You're drinking a beer in the backyard at eight in the morning. You're covered in dirt, you're practically jobless, soon to be homeless, and the best thing that's happened to you in years is getting on a plane right now while you sulk about it to the only person who isn't gonna give it to you covered in lube."

I buried my tongue in my cheek. "Can't you pretend?"

"Then I wouldn't be your best friend."

As much as I hated it, I needed to hear it. Cap had been with me through some of the most physically and emotionally challenging times in my life. He'd pulled me out of the dark, gave me a purpose when I thought I had none, and recemented years of confidence that had weathered away. He wasn't pushing me out of spite, he was pushing me out of love.

"I'm not about to sit here and watch another Vanessa happen to you, brother," he continued. "This is not that. This is someone kind and good. She cares about you like I want you to be cared about. You know me, I put my faith in no one but my fucking family, and it's my job to make sure you're okay. I wouldn't be doing this if I thought you weren't."

"This is nothing like Vanessa." I scoffed at that comparison. Her image was like taking off your glasses—blurred edges, foggy details. Ophelia was clarity. "I'm not even sure I was ever actually in love with Vanessa after the last three weeks."

Mateo turned toward me in his chair, the corners of his mouth widening into deep dimples. "Do you hear what you just said, man?"

"What?"

"You're in love with her."

My skin prickled. Was I? Was real, romantic love something I'd never known, so I couldn't explain it with Ophelia? Maybe subliminally I thought I didn't deserve to feel it, so I hadn't even let myself try.

These were the reflections I never would have spent time harping on before.

"What do I do?"

"You go," Cap pressed. "Get your shit together, stop feeling sorry for yourself in the backyard, and do something about it."

"Go?" I laughed. "Go where? To Colorado? I don't even have a job there. I don't have a house. I know one person, who, as you so graciously pointed out, is hopping on a plane right now to return to her family, her job, her *life*—all these things that make sense for her to do."

"You're being a bitch again." Cap stood, his body blocking the low-hanging sun in front of me. "If the interviews go well, which they will, then you'll be moving out there soon anyway, Pike. Why wait?"

"What if they don't?" I battled. "I go out there with nothing, I don't get the job, I'm out of my element, I leave my mom and my sister and *you*. I need some guarantees here."

"You have one," he reminded me. "And so fucking what if that happens? You'll figure it out like you always do. Your mom and your sister are fine, they told you themselves. Maria is in good hands; she has someone who loves her, Addy close by. You can visit whenever you get the chance, or she can fly out to see you. There is nothing holding you back right now but *fear*, man. Fear cannot control you forever."

I ground my teeth together enough to make my jaw hurt. The worst part about being stubborn and self-effacing was the cement-in-your-stomach feeling when someone else was right. I could live in my ditch of safety, or I could decide to finally do something for myself that was frightening as much as it was thrilling. I was one decision away.

One thing I couldn't argue was that I wanted her morning, afternoon, and night. I wanted snowstorms in the mountains, and summers by the lake. I wanted all the rest of my firsts to be hers—first homes, first children, first face I saw every day when I woke up. I wanted to meet her parents and her siblings. I wanted to be there to fill all of her worries with hope and doubts with promises.

I wanted Ophelia.

Across the lawn a fleck of blue caught my eye, swooping in circles, idling on the edge of the bushes. All doubt got stuck in my throat as a Monarch landed, basking on the flowery branches like a bright little omen.

I thought of my mother looking for my dad in the butterflies. The way I adopted that strange, hopeful superstition into my life. There was a necklace hanging from Ophelia's neck to prove it. And it was too perfect to be a coincidence.

"Did Tally drop her off at the airport yet?" I asked, bounding to my feet.

Mateo followed me into the house, cell phone to his ear. "Calling her right now."

43

Ophelia

SOMEHOW BEING DROPPED OFF at the airport in sunny Florida was worse than being left in the shitty snow at the terminal in Colorado. I would take negative temperatures and a blizzard any day over being forced to hastily hug Natalia goodbye with a symphony of car horns rushing us along.

"I can't believe this is it." She frowned, throwing her arms around me as I dragged my suitcase out of the backseat of the car. It landed with a thump that sounded exactly like how I felt. "We can't wait this long to see each other ever again."

"We won't." I squeezed her tightly. "We have a wedding to plan anyway. I'll see you in a couple months, tops."

"Let's hope Matty doesn't kill me first. I'm pretty sure he's organized all my emails into spam." Nat rolled her eyes. "Men."

The car's hazard lights flickered, a stench of exhaust filling the tunnel we were idling in. I bent down and extended my suitcase handle. "Thank you for everything. I needed it. This was the best holiday I could have ever asked for."

"Let's do it again...next Christmas?" she offered.

Coconut Creek becoming a tradition was a somewhat terrifying prospect, one that required a level of self-reflection that I'd only just reached thanks to the last three weeks. Regardless, it tugged on a sentimental heartstring and gave me the bleakest taste of hope. "Definitely."

A mist clouded over Natalia's eyes, and like a yawn it was contagious to me. I pulled her into another hug and we wiggled back and forth. "It's gonna be fine," I assured her. "I'm going to get so drunk right now that I go full Kristen Wiig in *Bridesmaids* on the flight and hopefully pass out for the entire thing."

"Maybe not *full*," she suggested. "I can't imagine something worse than having the spins at thirty thousand feet."

"It's happening." I shrugged, backing away. "I need distraction. Mind-numbing forgetfulness."

"*God*, he was really that good?"

"There are at least four mimosas speaking in my ears right now." I pitched my voice higher, getting closer and closer to the terminal door. "*Ophelia, drink us... Drink us!*"

"I'm seeing a lot of regret and fancy airline paper bags in your future," Nat groaned. Her phone started ringing and she slipped it out of her pocket. "It's Mateo," she announced as I retreated with a sinister smile. "At least eat a bagel or something first!"

"Tell him I said bye!" I shouted. "I love you!"

"Love you, text me when you land!"

I filed inside, finding first the dreaded check-in, then the mile-long security line. My back ached as I kicked my carry-on of perfectly organized gifts along the slow-moving queue, only to have every present removed and inspected as if it were filled with gunpowder.

I should have expected that.

I fucking hated airports.

When that was through, I had enough anxiety over losing one of my sibling's gifts to TSA that I slipped through the metal detector without taking my phone out of my pocket, becoming enemy number one of every other person in the terminal standing on the floor in their socks. I got a very friendly pat down by a very unfriendly agent, and then ditched my phone entirely into the bottom of my bag out of spite.

Dad was picking me up; he'd already let me know he was tracking the flight by the minute, so it wasn't like I needed it. At the beginning of December the screen would have been the distraction, but now it was a reminder of what I was leaving behind. Frankie promised me, though, it wasn't the end. Simply a pause in the track. Life could continue on around us, but we would remain in place for at least a little while longer. Until the end of the month. That was one thing keeping me from coming apart completely. But not enough that I wasn't tingling with a need to drink away some of that apprehension.

I made up for it with an hour of mimosas while I waited, chasing a couple with tequila against my better judgment and then swayed onto the bridge to the plane like a drunken pirate walking the plank.

To top off every emotion and depressant combining into their own mixed drink of sorts inside of me—it turned out I also had a middle seat.

Not only a middle seat, but one with a very large, excitable rowmate filling the aisle seat beside it. And he was dressed for Colorado. Sweater on top of sweater, fur-lined boots, a red beanie with the fuzzy pom-pom on top. The man was the live-action version of Yukon Cornelius. I pulled a deep breath through my nose as I stumbled forward, realizing I reeked of booze, and lifted onto my tiptoes to shove my carry-on into the overhead.

The compartment popped open and a giant, heavy boot came careening down and connected with the center of my forehead.

"What the—" I complained, rubbing the knot that formed immediately.

"Oh boy, that'll be a nice egg," the man commented. He stood, ushering me into my seat as he picked up the boot and put it back, then shoved my bag of gifts into the overhead for me, resorting to punching it repeatedly until the hatch closed.

I was past protesting. I'd tried to fight the airport and lost. Miserably.

"S'not bleeding," my mountain man seatmate told me as he plopped back down. My seatbelt got lost somewhere underneath him and I whimpered quietly.

"Ma'am." A flight attendant stood over us with a little plastic bag full of ice. "For your head."

I noticed then that every single pair of eyes on the flight was turned in my direction and my skin flushed with heat.

"I won't cause any more trouble," I joked as I took the ice and squashed it to my wound. I actually didn't feel a thing; the benefits of alcohol always outweigh the detriments.

"Let us know if you're feeling dizzy, any nausea, double vision, ringing in your ears," she requested. "Seeing things."

"Got it." I nodded.

"Taking off in just a few minutes," she replied kindly.

My eyes fluttered closed as she disappeared and the attention on me subsided. Which only reminded me how wickedly tipsy I was when my entire equilibrium shifted and the shuttle started spinning. God damn Natalia for being right, and fuck me for thinking I could house a couple hours' worth of drinks in a couple minutes on an empty stomach. That airplane paper bag was whispering to me.

I slid the ice down my face to rest on my neck and keep from overheating and through half-lidded eyes a familiar mop of brown hair and a faded black hat waved into focus down the aisle.

I sat up, too fast. "Frankie?"

Maybe I hit my head harder than I thought.

"No, my name's Karl," the man sitting beside me said. "You sure you're okay?"

I blinked hard, sobering miraculously fast, the pulse in my neck picking up in my ears.

"I'm fucking seeing things, Karl." My fingers clamped around the metal armrests and my gut twisted the closer he came. Until it was undeniable that Frankie was stalking toward us, head shifting side to side scanning the already filled seats. "Frankie!" I shouted louder.

He looked up, nostrils flaring and gaze hooking onto mine. I could tell he was out of breath from running. He lifted his hat, passing a shaky hand through his hair and replacing it with renewed determination.

"What are you doing here?" My mind raced. "Why are you—"

"I don't want to wait until the end of the month to see you."

Every single humming conversation came to a deafening halt around us.

My lips parted, astonished. "What?"

"He said he doesn't want to wait until the end of the month to see you," Karl reiterated from between us.

"I—thank you, Karl. I think I got this." I actually couldn't believe what I was seeing, that he was standing in front of me. The plane was about to take off to Colorado, which meant...

He *came for me.*

"I don't understand," I told him. "I thought..."

"It's simple," he started, fingers fidgeting at his sides. He took a deep, centering breath. "I don't want to be away from you. I don't want to *wait* to have you again. I don't want to waste another day of this weird, insane, intense fucking thing that we've made together."

Karl nodded intently, nudging me with an elbow.

"I don't want you to go back to Colorado and eventually date other men, because I don't want to stay in Coconut Creek and date other women. Okay? I—" His brow deepened and he took a step closer. "What the fuck happened to your head?"

"Oh." My hand instinctively shot to the blossoming bruise on my forehead, shielding it from scrutiny. "Is it bad?"

"Got her good with my boot," Karl informed him.

Frankie massaged the bridge of his nose with one hand as he dug into his pocket with the other, pulling a crumpled airline ticket from his pants and handing it to the man beside me. "Can we do a trade? I have a *great* seat a few rows back."

Karl unwound the ticket and shrugged at it.

"What about now?" Frankie dug back into his pocket for a wallet and cash.

Karl finally stood and swiped the small fold of bills out of Frankie's hand.

"You're insane." I huffed a sigh of disbelief as he dropped down next to me. "What are you going to do? The job, your mom—"

"I don't care. I don't care about anything right now but this, O. I care about you, and being with you, and figuring it out one day at a time. But what I don't need to figure out anymore is—" He cupped my face gingerly, battling with his next thought. I got lost somewhere in his eyes waiting for it. "Fuck it—I'm in love with you."

An atom bomb must've exploded inside my body. The waves of that confession ricocheted from the top of my head to the tips of my toes. I lit up like a firework. "You're..."

"I love you," he repeated. "I love you, Ophelia. I said I wouldn't get attached. I said I wasn't ready for anything serious. I lied, okay? I lied about every last bit of it. Because I knew the second I met you I was fucked forever." Frankie's thumb swiped gently down my jaw over and over again. "Forever."

My throat was so dry it took several seconds of swallowing around the lump stuck there to whisper out those three profound and necessary words. "I love you."

"Yeah?" he breathed, as if worried I wouldn't feel the same. Stress evaporated from his face and his fingers slid into the hair at the nape of my neck. Something was shaking—his hands, maybe.

"Yes," I confirmed eagerly, brushing his nose with mine. "What the fuck, Frankie. Yes."

All that love poured out of the two of us in a desperate kiss. I wound my arms around him, pulling him closer, my hip digging into the armrest. My head still throbbed, but every single thing was right in the world despite it. I was in love. And I knew that before Frankie ever said it. I was in love with a man who chose me over everything else—his fears, his family, his past—and he was in love with me, too.

A crescendo of applause broke out and all eyes were on us around the cabin, peeking over seats, hiding behind cell phones. The flight attendants waited enamored, but impatiently, for the show to be over. I laughed into the crook of Frankie's neck and the bill of his hat hid us away as he curled over me, picking up the forgotten bag of ice and running it over my head tenderly.

"Can't leave you alone for five minutes, Trouble."

"I agree." I said. "You should never, ever leave me alone again."

"I'm glad you said that, because I am in *dire* need of a place to stay."

"I'm sure we can figure something out." I shrugged casually. "You did share your bed with me in my time of need."

Frankie leaned down and kissed me softly again. "You think they'd notice if we snuck off to the bathroom?"

Heat flecked my cheeks and I bit back a grin. "You never quit."

"Never," he said. And that was a promise.

Epilogue

The deafening beat of helicopter wings whirling above the cockpit stuck my already terrified body to the copilot's seat like glue. I couldn't hear myself think, let alone Frankie shouting at me from across the landing pad as he hopped into the humming aircraft with a round green helmet and placed it snugly over my head.

"How's it fit?" he asked.

I tugged the buckles down on both sides, fumbling with the snaps while my ever so helpful and impatient boyfriend batted my hands away and secured the heavy helmet effortlessly. "Are you sure this is a good idea?" I shouted back. Frankie patted my head and knelt down between my knees so we were level. "Does your boss know you're doing this?"

"Calm down, co-pilot. We're in the clear." He tightened a harness around my chest. "Do you trust me?"

I relaxed as he ran his palms up and down my thighs. "Of course."

"It's gonna be great." He beamed, leaning forward to place a reassuring kiss on my lips. "And remember, what goes up must come down."

"Fuck off," I groaned.

Frankie buckled himself in beside me and started flipping switches. It'd been months since he started flying again. Training at the base had begun almost immediately after he was hired at the end of January. I watched his first flight from the sidelines with a rock in my stomach and he nailed every single spec like we all knew he would.

It was amazing to see that shine of confidence back in his eyes, his reinvigorated love for his career and the talent that had been shrouded in shadow rise to the surface again. I was so proud of him and the progress we were making, both apart and together. Still learning new things about ourselves and our relationship every single day.

Bringing home a complete stranger after a few weeks away was an...adjustment for my family, to say the least. Dad was skeptical picking us up from the airport. It was a long, interesting ride, but he softened easily to Frankie's mature station and infectious personality. They got along like best friends in no time, my brothers clung to him like a hero, and my sisters batted their lashes and had him in the palm of their hands.

My mom knew right away that Frankie was my person. She told me she could see it in the way we found one another in every crowded room. He put me first, and continued to, and we fell further and further into the deep cushion of life mixed with love until they became the same word. There wasn't one without the other. There wasn't me without him.

"You ready, baby?" Frankie's voice crackled to life in my ears through the helmet.

"Shouldn't you close the doors?" I looked to my side at the wide-open edge of the helicopter.

His modulated laughter rang out as the first tip and lift of the chopper took us off the ground slowly. "Frankie." We rose rapidly, leaving a plume of dust below us, the wind swirling the branches and leaves in the trees off the tarmac. "Francesco."

"Don't threaten me with my government name like that. You know how it turns me on."

He took us over the city and circled the mountains. The sun setting and kissing the peaks so perfectly all the snow reflected into kaleidoscope-like bursts. A sea of purple sky and the seam of night collided at our altitude. It was the single most amazing thing I'd ever seen.

I'd lived in Colorado all my life and never experienced it like this. Like we were sitting on the pinnacle of heaven and earth.

"Holy shit," I gasped. "This is beautiful."

Frankie's lips curved into a pleased, radiant smile. "Pretty incredible, right?"

"You bring all your girlfriends up here?"

"I'd never bring a girlfriend up here," he said. "This is wife territory."

My gut panged and my neck snapped toward him. If not for being strapped to a chair my knees would have probably gone soft underneath me as well. "Wife, huh?"

Those tantalizing muscles in his jaw twitched and he nodded toward a zippered compartment in front of me. "Mind opening that?"

I looked from the bag and back to him frantically. "Are you proposing to me right now, Frankie Casado?"

"Just open it, Trouble. Let me have this. C'mon."

"I can't." My heart was in my throat, adrenaline buzzing through me.

"Then I guess I'll just have to take my hands off this control and go digging myself."

"Don't you fucking dare." I shot forward, fumbling with the zipper and opening the bag to reveal a little black velvet box sitting inside. My stomach knotted into a ball, and tears sprang freely into my eyes.

"Because you asked." Frankie looked over. "Yes, Ophelia. I am asking you, the love of my life, the turbulence to my calm, the brightest fucking sun I've ever had the pleasure of seeing in all my time in the sky—will you drive me crazy forever, baby? Will you marry me?"

My life was a series of downward slopes, plateaus, tiny upticks of brightness in a mostly underwhelming gray. Then I met *him*. He wrapped me in gold and pulled me to the highest peak he could find, and I would be damned if I ever spent another day denying myself what it felt like to truly touch the sky.

"Yes."

THE END.

Acknowledgments

I imagined that writing my first book was going to be the scariest experience of my publishing journey. Well, that came and went and it was incredible at times and terrible at others. I laughed a lot, I cried more, I made a community of friends and writers and artists and bloggers and book lovers that have made writing and publishing this second novel beautiful and rewarding—but at the same time even *more* terrifying than the first. Because now, I have people rooting for me and expecting something that will not only live up to that first one, but exceed the expectations brought on by it.

When I started writing Christmas in Coconut Creek I wasn't even officially an "author" yet. It was a quirky book baby in my Google docs that I was posting chapter by chapter for free, and then episode by episode on Vella, until I realized the book baby needed a bigger stage and the characters were becoming more three dimensional every time I sat down to write about them.

Frankie and Ophelia were hard to ignore chirping in my ear, but then Natalia and Mateo started butting in as well, and Sam needed a place for all his charm, and Tyler was such an attention whore he basically kicked in the window and demanded I find a place for him as well. Thus, the Dirty Delta series was born.

I'd run out of paper trying to acknowledge every person who has been there on the sidelines for me during this process, but as always, my husband, Joe. Who has not only allowed the abuse of our limited funds for things like commissioning nude character artwork and fancy wrapping paper for book boxes, but encouraged it. He is my very first and biggest supporter, my most fiercely opinionated beta reader, and the very best book boyfriend inspiration I could ever ask for. Frankie is Frankie because you are you. I love you more than words on paper.

My kids. My kids that I promise will need for nothing and always be free to create.

Mom, Dad, Tommy, Nan, Granda, Hannah, Kim, Dan — the extended lot of family who didn't blink when I told you I was writing books and you probably shouldn't read them. It's been an adjustment and a delight to share these milestones and special moments with everyone important in my life. Making you proud has always been my number one priority. No stopping now.

Kelli Mazanec, you know how vital you are to my sanity and my process, not only with writing but in life. You are one of the most open ears for listening, and solid backboards for advice. I couldn't imagine not having you around to share our many passions. Thanking you endlessly!

Charnie, for listening, for advising, for your ideas, your friendship, your inspiration and your impeccable hospitality. You next!

Ren & Rachel, for always being there and sharing your amazing talents with me.

Tara, who watched me pull my hair out from the other side of the coffee shop table twice a week for months during this writing process. For being my oldest, dearest friend and someone who has watched this journey happen for me for far longer than I even knew it was happening.

The ladies of The Last Wyrd for all their brilliance, humor, talent, advice, and friendship. I'm so glad to have been let in on your little world of words and stories. Thank you, thank you, thank you.

My beta readers! Marlee, Anna, Haley, Rachel, your time and suggestions to bring this book to life mean the world.

Makenna Albert, my amazingly meticulous and encouraging editor. Let's do this again, a bunch more times, please.

Sam Palencia, Ink + Laurel Design Studio for the most perfect cover imaginable.

You, my reader, who decided to take a chance on me or are returning for more. Thank you.

About the Author

#1 Amazon bestselling author Karissa Kinword writes sexy, contemporary, and out of this world (literally) love stories. She accredits any and all inspiration to an early love for literature, fanatically obsessive personality, and innate fascination with the human condition. She writes and lives in the Hudson Valley of New York with her husband and toddlers.

Connect with Karissa on social media!
Tiktok @karissakinwordwrites
Instagram @karissakinwordwrites
Twitter @karissakinword

Made in the USA
Columbia, SC
01 December 2024